DAN KENNER

Awakened

The Lightbearer Chronicles: Book 1

First published by KDP Kindle Direct Publishing 2020

First edition

Editing by Rachel Harris (www.metaedits.com)

This book was professionally typeset on Reedsy.
Find out more at reedsy.com

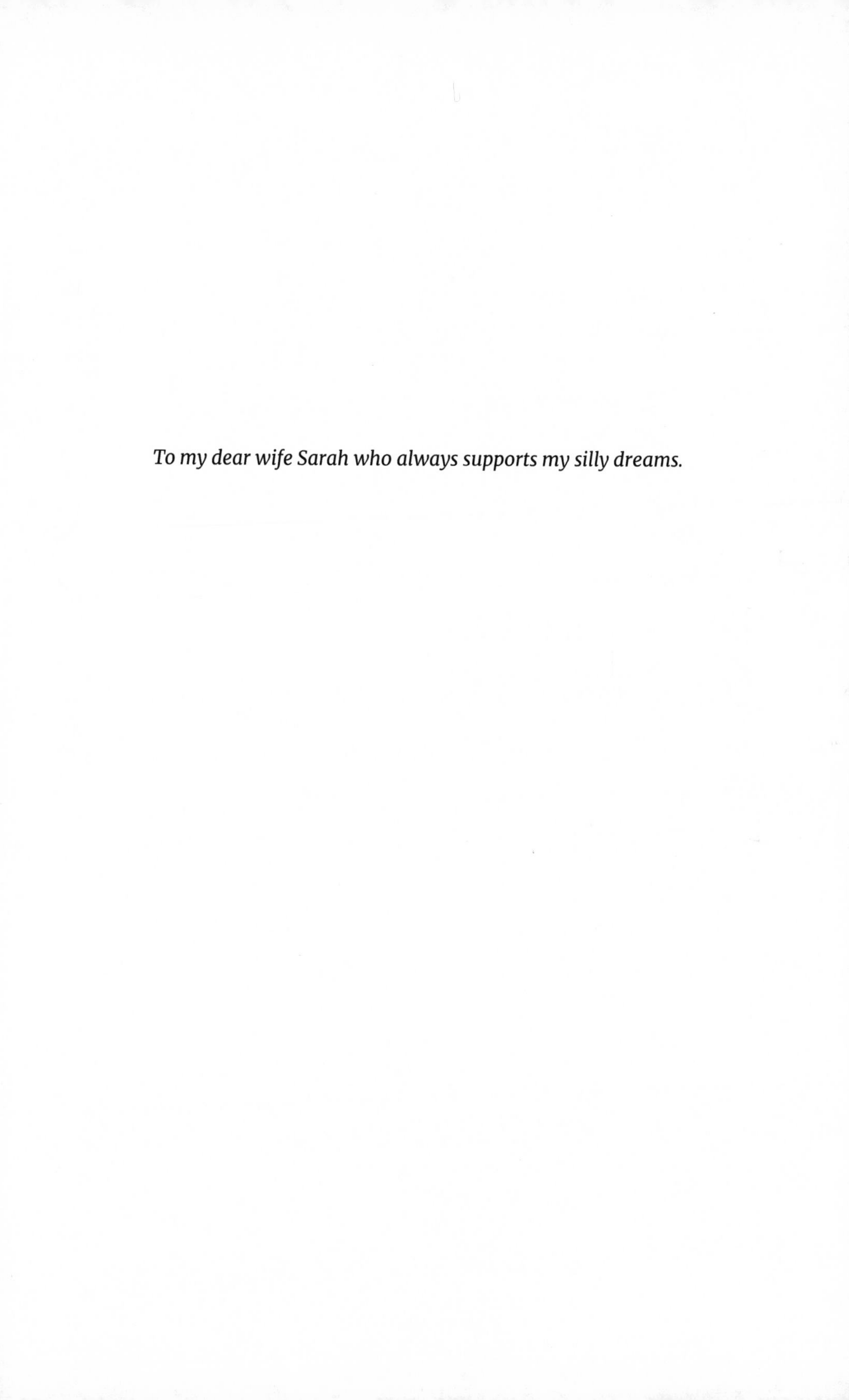

To my dear wife Sarah who always supports my silly dreams.

Contents

Acknowledgement

I am thrilled that *Awakened* is published, and I owe it all to a few amazing people. First, I'd love to thank my wonderful wife, Sarah, for supporting my lifelong dream of writing a book. When I doubted myself and if this was a venture worth spending money on, Sarah was there to support my dream. The amount of time she spent reading, proofing, and discussing this book will always be appreciated.

I must thank my editor, Rachel Harris, for the immense dedication she gave to making *Awakened* the best that it could be. The pace in which we moved was incredible and a bit unexpected, but she ran with it the whole way and did an incredible job the entire time.

Lastly, I'd like to thank my friend, Angie, for finally getting me to actually start writing. For years, I wished and imagined a time when I would write a book, but it wasn't until she challenged me to begin writing that I actually did so. Her faith in me and tough love was exactly what I needed, and I'm not sure I would have had the courage to start without her pushing me.

This book wouldn't be what it is without my support system of friends and family, so thank you all, truly.

Map of Lindrad

N
W
E
S
STILTEN
TERRIS GREEN
WATCHLIGHT COMPOUND
PLAINS OF ERISDELL
PORT LINDLE
T'ARREN VALE
WURREN
ARIVAN
LINDRAD

Prologue

Janis had been waiting far longer than she normally liked. She hated the fog, especially on the days when she'd overslept. This time she had almost missed her window of preparation for her meeting with Luden—at least, for the time that they were *supposed* to meet. Missing the chance to arrive early and check her surroundings would have proven costly. She had to ensure that there were no surprises set up by Luden's goons. Fortunately for her, whoever was coming was very late.

Janis put her hands to her temple and massaged her aching head, the street lamps seeming to make it pound more.

I really ought to give up the drink, she thought. *It only causes more trouble than it's worth.*

From her position just above the street atop the local bakery, the fog seemed even more imposing; filling the streets with thickness, permeating every nook and cranny in sight. It was less thick from her position above, making the fog below seem suffocating even though breathing through it was quite possible.

Perched on the rim of the roof, Janis had the advantage of viewing both corners leading to the bakery, though the fog made it tricky to see details. She'd learned from her past encounters with Luden that being able to see movement was sufficient preparation, since he had about as much finesse as a blind and deaf dog and tended to hire lackeys with his same stealth level.

Standing just taller than the average woman, Janis's lithe figure was lean and strong. She kept her jet-black hair cropped shoulder length, as it was now. Normally when she was on a job, it was pulled back by her likewise jet-black tie, but now she let it flow free. The more she looked like a woman, the more likely Luden and his men would underestimate her abilities. That had come in handy on numerous occasions. Her encounters with Luden had proven unsatisfactory, to say the least. On her first job for him, he had attempted to dupe her by having one of his oafs attack her from behind. She had easily taken care of him with a jab to the eye—poor man didn't even see it coming.

Good thing you really only need one eye to see, she thought as a sly smile spread across her face.

Since then, Luden and his men had been more cautious in their dealings with Janis. However, that also meant that they were a lot more wary of working with her. His cronies had always been difficult to work with; only giving her the worst of jobs, and attempting to pay her unfairly. Unfortunately for her, Luden and his men were not quite scared enough to treat her with respect.

She'd have to work on that.

Movement in the corner of her eye made her tense. She squinted through the fog to see how many were approaching. Two men appeared around the corner and made their way toward the bakery. They didn't seem to be in any hurry, but that wasn't a surprise. Luden had never cared to listen to her demands for efficiency when they dealt with each other. She'd never seen these two before. The taller of the two was built like a beast: broad shoulders, thick arms, and a chest that puffed out of his thin shirt. In contrast, the other was short, thin, and wore baggy clothing as if attempting to hide behind the folds.

"I don't see why we have to meet with the wench—don't we got better things to do tonight?" said the small one, sounding annoyed.

"Luden said that he needed someone he could trust to bring this job to the Shrew. I reckon that be more of a compliment than anythin', given our past history of job-doin'," offered the tall man. His voice was oddly high for someone so large.

"I'm pretty sure he doesn't see it that way . . . likely he expects us to kick the bucket after this meeting. I ain't heard nuttin' good 'bout this wench and I ain't expectin' that it'll be good for us here."

"I might not be callin' her a wench if I were you. She is an assassin, after all."

"No matta, she ain't here anyway. It gives me the crawlies bein' out here in the fog—yeh never know what might be lurkin' in the thick of it, eh? Where is this killer, anyway? This is the right place, ain't it?"

They kept on like this for a few minutes while Janis observed the situation. They each had a simple rapier on their left hip, but didn't appear to have other weaponry.

These clearly aren't Luden's normal mercenaries, she considered. *But that doesn't mean they don't have something else up their sleeves.*

She imagined they each had to have some daggers or other hidden modes of killing, otherwise Luden really was as inept as she thought he was. Janis glanced around once more. Then, when all seemed well, she leapt from the roof of the bakery and landed smoothly on the cobblestone street a mere three feet from the men.

The smaller of the two sputtered and reached for his sword, nearly dropping the linen sack that he held in his left hand just as the larger of the two ripped his sword free from the scabbard at his side. Before the small man could slide his weapon free, Janis had one of her black daggers at his throat and was holding him from behind.

"Surprise," she said with a grin. She felt annoyed that she had even bothered to leave her hair untied since she had decided to surprise them in the end, but so far, based on their reactions, it was worth it.

"Unhand him, else I cut you through. I'm much faster than ye might s'pose . . . miss," claimed the big man. He added the last part with uncertainty, likely feeling he ought to have manners in the presence of a lady. This made Janis chuckle.

Perhaps it was worth it to let my hair flow this time.

"Now, now. Let's not be hasty. You know I could take care of this runt and be away before you could finish your thrust." she teased. "Nevertheless, let's be civilized, hmmm?"

She let the man go and shoved him slightly away from her body. After taking a few steps back, she continued, "Luden's got a job for me then?"

The small man, face beet-red from the scuffle, fixed his cap and nodded, not sure what to say next. He glared at her angrily.

"That's right, it's a big 'un for you," said the large man. "Go on, Trigger, hand it over."

Once again, he just glared at her. She thought about the little one's nickname and figured he must have some talent with the crossbow, else he wouldn't have such a name.

Note the likely presence of a hidden crossbow on him. Janis thought, taking inventory.

"It ain't proper and right to threaten those that are offerin' you a job, eh? You're lucky I didn't have my bow on me, else you'd be on the ground cryin' instead of smirkin'," he growled, standing a bit taller at the mention of his skill.

Scratch that, she thought. *Note that Luden is as dumb as I thought for sending unprepared men to meet me.*

"You aren't dead, are you?" she noted. "Let's move on before I kill you from boredom."

"Fine." The small man tossed the bag to Janis with a slight grunt. She caught it with ease and noted the weight of the sack.

"What's this then?" she asked.

"That's the job. Open 'er up and you'll see the mark."

"This is not Luden's normal mode of giving the target—why the change?" she inquired with skepticism.

"Luden let us know that this ain't your usual mark. Look here, yous got what yeh need. Yeh have two days t' handle the job, then you'll get yer payment."

Janis felt the sack, and after some consideration, decided that the contents of the sack clearly weren't a trap. She pulled open the sack and peered in.

Thwack!

The small man's chest sprouted a bolt head and he let out an agonized gurgle. Blood splattered the cobblestones and sprayed into Janis. Panicked, she leapt backwards under the eaves of the bakery and dove behind some crates piled there.

Blast it! she thought, *How could I let my guard down?!*

The large man spun around and lifted his sword, expecting something else. She clutched the sack to her chest and scanned the roofs of the shops across the street. Her pitch black dagger was held up like a ward just as a second bolt slammed into the stomach of the larger man. A groan escaped his lips and he fell with a thud.

The street was silent, except for the large man's groans as his life drained onto the stones. For several minutes, Janis kept as silent as she could and waited for something else to happen. When nothing did, she considered her options.

Perhaps they didn't see where I landed, she thought with little confidence. *Whoever shot those arrows clearly has considerable skill. They'd need a keen eye to land those right where they did.*

Before she could think of what to do next, a dark figure dropped from the roof two shops down from the building just across the bakery. It was hooded and wore a deep blue cloak that was so dark, it seemed black. It appeared to be a man, as she could see his chest muscles bulging through his thin shirt just through the cloak. He stalked slowly down the street with confidence. His left hand held the large crossbow from which the bolts had flown. As he moved forward slowly, Janis noted that the back of his right hand bore a strange tattoo. She squinted in the moonlight and saw it was an eye shrouded in a beam of light, almost like the sun bursting through clouds.

The man continued forward until he stood over the corpses, as the larger man had died not too long before. The stranger looked down with what appeared to be pity on his face. As she looked more closely, it seemed his cheeks were deeply pockmarked. Her gut twisted when she realized that it wasn't pockmarks, but scars from his nose to his ears.

"There's no point in hiding behind those boxes." he suddenly said.

Janis tensed in anticipation, knowing that the fight was about to begin. The man had been skilled with the bow, but he looked too large to be quick on his feet like she was. She rocked back on her feet, readying herself to spring up from the boxes and attack head-on.

"Be still, Janis."

She froze. That was unexpected.

"Yes, I know who you are. I also know your reputation. Likely you are crouched behind the crates preparing to attack me at full speed. I'm not here to fight you, however, which *is* such a shame. Regardless, I just want to discuss the very job that you were about to take on."

She stood slowly, hand still clutching her dagger expectantly.

"Based on the way you handled these two, forgive me for not believing that you want to *talk*. Give me one reason why I shouldn't slit your throat and be on my way."

He turned slowly and glanced at her.

"Fifty gold fronds," he said smugly.

She started slightly. That was *also* unexpected.

Fifty gold fronds! That's ten times what Luden normally pays for one of his jobs!

"I see that as expected, my reason is quite a good one for you." The man tossed a small pouch filled with coins to the ground before Janis. She didn't dare reach down to grab the pouch, but based on the jingle from inside, the contents were indeed quite a large sum of money.

"You just received a mark as a target for elimination. Our request is simple. Rather than kill him, we need you to *protect* him instead."

Silence. It dragged on for what seemed like an eternity. But she didn't know what to say. Protect someone? That did not align with her idea of a 'clean' job, nor one that she wanted to engage in. Especially with this shady figure.

The tall man began to pace slowly a few steps this way, a few steps that way. He didn't seem at all nervous to be conversing with a skilled assassin.

A fool's mistake. Underestimating their opponent.

"I'm an assassin," she said, "what makes you think I would be able to protect someone?"

The man scoffed at the comment, obviously amused.

"The skills of an assassin do not differ much from that of a protector. You fight, you kill, you get paid. The only difference is you kill the ones that threaten the ward, rather than drop him yourself."

"But I'm *not* a guardian. You said it yourself, I'm an assassin."

"For fifty gold fronds, couldn't you become one?" he teased. "Be a little flexible, hmm?"

"If you know me at all, you know that flexibility is not the way I work. Flexibility can get a girl killed."

He sighed as if he was bored of the conversation.

"I don't have time for such banter with someone like you. Take the job, protect the mark . . . or die."

She chuckled at that.

"You don't scare me. I've been threatened by far worse than you."

"Oh, it wasn't a threat. It was a promise. This isn't how I wanted to spend my evening, so don't waste my time. You must be wise enough of an assassin to know that I didn't come here alone."

Fear blossomed in her breast as she felt a knife blade touch the small of her back. *Blast! How could I have been so sloppy?*

"As you can see, we've made the decision much easier for you."

It was true. She didn't have much choice, and it didn't appear that she had much time either, given the blade was just moments away from cutting her spine.

"Fine," Janis spat. "I'll do what you ask."

He stopped pacing and faced her directly.

"That's a good girl. Take your money and find the mark. Protect him at all costs. Should you fail in your duties, I think I can assume that you know your fate."

He nodded to the figure behind her and she felt the knife disappear from her back.

"What's the deal with the mark, anyway? Why go to the trouble to protect him?"

"WE AREN'T PAYING YOU TO ASK QUESTIONS!" the man shouted.

Janis dropped slightly, twisting sideways while whipping her dagger to the side. His shouts had put her on defense. However, he didn't attack, nor did anyone from behind. Instead, he closed his eyes and breathed slowly for a few beats.

"Protect him, that is all you need to know," he said through gritted teeth.

This man has quite the temper, doesn't he?

He turned and stalked towards the corner away from Janis. When he had gone a few paces, he paused and said, "And Janis. We'll be watching. Whatever you do, and wherever you go, Watchlight will be watching."

Watchlight? What in the blazes is that? she thought.

The man continued walking until he was out of sight. Janis took the time to turn her head to where the person had been holding the knife behind her, but found no one. After analyzing her surroundings, she found it safe to move again.

Bending over, she snatched the pouch and noted the contents. Indeed, fifty golden fronds were there. Pulling the sack from under her arm, she opened it with hesitancy. Inside was a simple brown tunic and a small bit of parchment. Likely the tunic was there for a hound to catch a scent for easy location.

Won't be needing that. I'm a fine tracker myself.

She pulled out the parchment and read the name of her target—now turned ward. On it was scribbled the name of a man that she had never heard of.

Marric Norst

Chapter 1

Marric sat on a fence staring out at the fields just outside of town. The breeze was lightly blowing the wheat, which was lazily moving in waves. At the edge of the fields lay the treeline of a forest that had always been forbidden to him and his friends since they were young. Not that it had mattered anyway, Marric and his best friend Jord had spent plenty of their free time roaming through it.

He sighed and shook that thought out of his mind as quickly as possible. *Those were simpler times,* Marric thought.

Marric's muddy blond hair blew along with the fields as he watched. His father always thought he was silly to keep it long, but he liked the feel of it as the wind blew through it on stormy days or as he ran through the town. He kept it just hanging over his ears and just above his eyes. His eyes were piercingly blue—an odd color for those of this town. Most of the town of Wurren had dark eyes: brown or black. He assumed his abnormal ones had come from his mother as his father had dark brown eyes himself. At sixteen years of age, he stood slightly smaller than other boys who tended to grow rapidly in these years.

Life was largely monotonous in his town. Wurren was small in size, a small town in Lindrad at least, but it was reputable in nature. It had always been an industrious town due to the many skills that its inhabitants boasted. Everything from the best blacksmiths to the most skilled bakers lived here. The most exciting thing about Wurren was the high amount of traffic in and out, although its actual residents were few.

Marric's father was the town fletcher. As a child, Marric had thought that his father's job was the most exciting, it being related to hunting and war in a direct fashion. He had grown to be disappointed in his father, whose skill was only in fletching and not actual marksmanship. When he had turned ten, he eagerly asked his father when he would take him out for his first bow lessons, only to find that his father was terrified of even touching a bow. It was then and there that he realized his fate as a fletcher was not a good one.

Fortunately for him and his best friend Jord, Marric had secured a bow soon thereafter, and the adventuring began. The first time they ventured into the forest was a few days after he had gotten the bow. He skimmed a few finished arrows off of his father's load the day before and stole with Jord into the forest just as the sun was beginning to rise. Oh, the thrill and the thrum of his heart as they crossed the line of trees into the forest. It was a different world.

Marric smiled at the thought. He was convinced that living in the forest would be much better for him than this small town.

"Marric! What're yeh doin'?! Come 'ere an' fetch me the bucket o' feathers from this mornin'!" said a voice from behind.

He sighed again, then flipped around on the fence and slid to the ground. As he started toward the sound of the voice, he heard the shrill yell once more.

"Git yer tail in here, yeh lazy git! We ain't got time fer yeh to sit on the fence dayreamin' yer days away!"

"Alright, alright, Tins. I'm coming!" he said back. He trotted to the back door of the fletcher's shop, snatched the bucket of feathers he had collected earlier, and stepped in.

Standing at the edge of the table was Tins. She was a portly woman with severe cheekbones and almond eyes. Her dark brown hair was always braided and reached halfway down her back. She wore her normal brown dress and apron as she commanded the other apprentice, Crents. Unfortunately for him, Tins had been given the role of assistant fletcher, likely because of her innate skill of commanding and controlling everything around her.

"Git in here, yeh worthless gripe of a son."

Worst of all, Tins was his stepmother. He had always wondered why his stepmother bothered to marry his father since she had told him straight out that she hated children. Perhaps she thought that it wouldn't be too much trouble since it was just Marric.

"Here's the feathers you needed, Tins," he replied reluctantly.

"Don' yeh give me grief. Yeh knows that I don' need em. Put em 'ere on the table and git to it!" she yelled at him.

He crossed the room and dumped the feathers onto the table, where he and Crents began preparing them for the arrows. Once Tins saw that they had started to work, she nodded satisfactorily and went through the door to their kitchen. It was both convenient and frustrating that their house was connected to the fletching shop. With work and home life being so close in proximity, Marric felt that he would never get a break.

"She's not on a good day terday, eh, Mar?" Crents said lightly.

"Hmm?" he replied. "Oh, definitely not. But then again, when is Tins *ever* on a good day?"

"Yeh know, yeh might consider callin' her ma or such like. She is yer mother, after all."

"You know that I don't think of her much like a mother, let alone a ma. Tins is a slave driver to me—she's the one to boss me around at work."

"Aye, I guess so. At least yeh got a ma. And yer pa is a right good man at that," he said sadly. Crents was practically an orphan since his mother passed away when he was eight or so, and his father was always wasting their funds away on the drink. Marric had only spoken once to Crents's father, but the encounter made working with Tins a delight.

"You're definitely getting a lot faster at that, Crents. I think Tins will be very happy with your work when the day's done." Marric said in an effort to steer their thoughts away from Crents's family.

Crents looked up with a thankful look in his eyes and kept working. He was a wisp of a boy; at a whole head shorter than Marric and half his weight, Crents looked like one caught in the years between childhood and manhood. Of course, he was only fourteen after all, but he was definitely the smallest of his age. His light brown hair was always matted and cropped uneven due to cutting his own hair.

"Thank yeh, Mar. I been practicin' at me home as much as I can. I want to be a good fletcher meself one day so tha' I can provide for me family more than me ol' man. Tho' I'll need to leave town with the likes of yous bein' here as the town fletcher. Yeh are much better than me at this whole thing."

"Crents, you know that I don't want to be in this town as the fletcher no more than you want to grow up like your father. I didn't go to school for nothing."

"Yeh are right lucky to have learned to read an' write. I tried it once, learnin' from Harxby, but she says I ain't got no talent for it."

"There's no need for you to have that type of talent since you definitely got what it takes to be a right good fletcher, eh?"

Crents's eyes flashed with pride and tears welled up in the corners at Marric's comments. He looked down and sniffed, trying to hide his emotions.

"Hey, if we gits the job done today, we could head down to Myrtle's place an' play some twiddle, if yeh likes," Crents said hopefully.

"I'm not sure we'll be getting it done much too early, but if it be the case, I've got some other business to take care of," Marric replied.

"What're yeh off ta do tonight, eh? Sneakin' off with the mayor's daughter ta do some snoggin', eh?"

"Oh if only you knew, Crents. She doesn't have any real interest in any old fletcher's son. She's much too busy sewing her dresses and primping to care much for someone simple like me. Nah, I've just got some business to take care of, like I said earlier."

"Yah, okay, Mar. I'll be keepin' yer secret," he said with a wink.

They did finish early, to their mutual surprise. Not too much early, but early enough that Marric had the time to head out for the business he had been preparing to do. Tins had seen the work they did, and after some more yelling and cursing, decided that she was 'too tired to deal with them any longer', and let them have the rest of the afternoon off.

Marric headed to his upstairs room to gather what he needed. His room was rather simple, but much more austere than the normal resident in

Wurren. The simple square room boasted a raised bed frame with a straw-filled mattress, a small writing desk and stool, and a fine rocking chair that his mother had used for him as a baby. From his window, Marric had a view straight down the street, the fletcher's shop being right at the end of Roddle street. As he stared out the window for a brief moment, he saw Crents meet with a few other young boys at the well in the center of town and disappear around the left corner.

Crents is much more lucky than he can imagine, he thought as he watched them go. Marric had not had much luck with making friends for the past couple of years. Not since the incident with Jord two years ago.

He blinked the tears away and shook his head to clear his thoughts. *No need to get my mind all foggy before the task this evening,* he thought quickly.

Turning to his bed, he lifted the mattress just slightly to find the length of rope, a dark cloak, whittling knife, and parchment he had left there. He added a small pouch full of feathers, which he had pilfered from the bucket he retrieved earlier, and nodded to himself. Now that everything was in place, all he needed to do was wait until the sun began to go down. He replaced the mattress and stood up just as a small rap sounded at his door.

"Who is it?" he called.

"Who d'yeh think it is, eh? Lanser himself com' a knockin' at yer door?"

Marric smiled. "Come in, Pa." he replied.

The door opened just a crack and he saw a hand poke through with the warding sign of the church, thumb to palm, with the four fingers slightly curved in a claw-like fashion.

"I don' wanna be seein' nuttin' I ain't s'posed ta, eh? Yeh better be decent, yeh hear me?" his father teased.

His father always joked with him this way. He rolled his eyes and said with a chuckle, "Pa! Just get yourself in here!"

Narim pushed the door open and strode in casually. His hair was in its normal style, cropped close to his scalp. It had lost all color from his youth and instead showed deep gray speckled with pure white. His dark brown eyes were stark in contrast to his age-lightened hair, but were framed with deep crows feet from years of laughing and smiling. He was similar to

Marric in build, and many people had mistaken them from behind when either was wearing a hat.

"What's me boy up to this fine afternoon, eh?"

"Nothing, really. I'm just trying to relax with my extra time off from Tins."

"She been workin' yeh hard, then? That's me girl. I always knew she'd be a darned good assistant. She's dun proved to be an even better wife!"

Marric winced slightly at that. "I still don't understand what you see in the likes of her," he noted.

"Now, now. I knows she and yous don't see eye-to-eye a lot, but she certainly loves yeh bunches. Tins has always wanted to have a boy such as yous."

"That can't be true, Pa! She says all the time that little whelps such as me don't deserve to live in a place like this with her. I mean, she's even told you right to your face that she doesn't like me one lick!"

"Oh, nonsense, that's just Tins when she's had a bad day. She's just ruffled tha' yer not trained up as a fletcher yet since yer sixteen an' all tha'. I told yeh afore, Marric, I let yeh focus on learning t'speak right so tha' yeh can git outta 'ere someday."

Marric nodded at the comment, remembering the days he had spent studying with the local teacher while his peers all learned their family trades.

"Let's be stoppin' this discussion about yer stepmother. I didn' come up here ta talk about her. I wanted t' talk t' yeh about . . . yeh know . . . how yer feelin' today."

Marric instantly turned cold on the inside. He was doing his best to forget what today was, then his father had to bring it up.

"It's still hard, Pa. It wasn't so bad when I was workin' with Crents in the shop, or when I was dreamin' out on the fence, but if I stop to think too much, it all comes back to me quick, like . . . like a horrible dream."

As he said it, he was instantly back in his room two years ago.

* * *

Marric and Jord sat on the floor of his room laughing as they looked at the small pile of coins between them. The job they'd run that evening had gone smoothly, until they were seen by a little girl on the street as they jumped from roof to roof back to the fletcher's shop and his window. They'd never been seen like this, and on the brink of panic, Jord had done something unimaginable. He had turned his back to her, and dropped his pants, exposing his backside. The effect had been immediate on the little girl as she screamed in horror and ran away quickly. They had been wearing their cloaks, so their identities were secure, but there was no story in the following days of two cloaked boys jumping roofs near dark. They had figured that the girl wouldn't dare claim to have seen a boy in such a state.

They had laughed for what seemed like hours and when they had finally begun to gain control, the money had been divided between the two.

Jord and Marric were both smaller, which actually is what made them grow so close to one another. They had always said that the small should band together against the tyranny of the large boys. As was typical of Wurren looks, Jord had brown hair, cropped close to his head, and dark brown eyes. He and Marric were identical in stature—that is to say, small, wiry, and perhaps a bit younger looking than their actual age of fourteen.

"This righ' be the best job we done 'ere! We gots ourselves eight coppers an' three silvers!" Jord exclaimed with delight.

"Here, you take the extra silver. After what yous did, yeh deserve a little somethin' extra." Marric replied, holding back another chuckle.

"Ah, Mar. Yer too kind. If I'd known tha' I could git extra from a pull, I'da dropped me knickers long ago, no doubt!"

They burst out laughing again.

Containing himself once again, Jord finally said, "Aright, me ma and pa be waitin' fer me back at the house. I best be goin'."

As Jord began to stand up, he got a strained look on his face. Suddenly, he doubled over as if in pain and groaned loudly. He dropped to his knees as his eyes rolled back in his head. Just as Marric rushed toward his friend, he felt himself get yanked backwards toward the open window. He landed hard on his back, pain lancing up his spine and into his skull. The candle on his desk snuffed out and the room plunged into darkness. With a grunt of effort, Marric sat up quickly and called for his friend in the darkness. He fumbled for a time with the flint and steel to light his candle once more, and felt movement all around him, seemingly toward the open window. At last, the sparks flew and the candle burst to life. Swinging around, Marric saw a man, all in black, with the hood of his cloak folded down. Twin scars ran from his nose to his ears, thick and purple. The man grinned, dashed toward him, and then all went black.

Marric woke to his father shaking him awake. He felt hot wetness on his face, and realized after a few moments that it was blood flowing from his nose. In a panic, he shouted for Jord. His father only looked at him with confusion.

"Jord ain't here, Marric. What happened?! Why're yeh bleedin'?!"

He had never answered. All he could remember was that wicked scarred face, and that Jord was gone.

* * *

"Marric, come back to me." He felt his father shake him slightly until his eyes refocused.

"I'm sorry, Pa. I—"

"Yeh went back, din' yeh?" Narim said. "Look, yeh din' do nuttin' wrong, it's not yer fault."

"I know. I just don't understand. It all happened so fast. I was so confused and scared and I wanted to help, but—"

"Be still," his father interrupted. "We must do what we can to move forward, not be stuck in the past. How's about we head down the kitchen and make somethin' nice fer an early dinner and then go git some ale?"

"Thanks, Pa." Marric replied. It really was a nice offer. "I think I'll just sit here a while longer, if that's alright. Besides, you know how much Tins likes to be the one in the kitchen."

He chuckled at that, but said, "I understand, son. But if yeh change yer mind, I'll be waitin'."

Narim stood and paused for just a moment. Marric felt his father squeeze his shoulder reassuringly and then head for the door. As he heard the door close, he stood and wiped the tears from his eyes. He had a job to do, and it was the best way that he could think to honor Jord and their friendship on this day.

* * *

Marric stood on the edge of the roof four houses down from his own, swathed in his black cloak. He watched as a woman carrying her clothes in a large basket passed through into the house across the street. After waiting for a few moments, Marric tied one end of his rope to the chimney, and strode back to the edge of the roof. Pausing once more to make sure all was still, he tossed the end over the edge, letting it fall freely to the ground.

Testing the rope with a firm tug, he determined that the rope would hold. After a brief pause, for Marric still was a bit uneasy with height, he began walking backwards, easing himself off the roof slowly until he was rappelling with the rope just off the roof. The baker's house, from which he was currently hanging, had three stories and was the tallest house in the town by far. As he lowered himself from the roof, he noted the distance to the ground and had to pause briefly to control his vertigo. After a few moments, he continued until he was level with the second story window. The room was dim and appeared to be empty. Just to be sure, he peered closely into the window. Satisfied, he secured his feet on either side of the outside sill and pulled out his small knife.

Slipping the knife into the crevice between window and frame, he began shifting the knife upwards slowly until he felt it catch on the window latch. With some effort, he pulled up firmly until he heard it slide out of place. A little further, and the window swung open slightly, permitting him entrance to the room. He had practiced the maneuver many times and was grateful for having done so. Grabbing the rope again, he supported his weight with one arm and used his other to open the window wide. After switching his hands, he swung nimbly and let go, landing just inside the window with a soft thud.

Marric had to stand there for a moment to allow his eyes to adjust to the dim light from the setting sun. They always used to do their jobs as the sun was going down since the town folk retreated long before sundown into their homes. No one wanted to be caught out in the dark with their wares and unarmed. That was asking for Ugglyn, the unlucky anti-god, to prey on you and your goods. Also, they couldn't work with candles, as it would defeat the purpose of their stealth. So they used the waning light as the prime time to benefit from both the darkness and the light. The former for hiding, the latter for seeing.

Eyes adjusted, he crept forward toward the desk of the baker. As expected, the baker hadn't yet counted his profit for the day and had only recently descended to help prepare dinner for his family. Marric felt the thrill of adventure and risk as he padded softly to the desk and noted the amount of money laying there. They never took it all. No, that would be too risky. Instead he counted ten coppers and a silver from the load, and tucked them in his breast pocket. He began the silent trip back to the window, when he heard steps approaching the door to the study. Heart pounding, he ran to the window with purpose as the door creaked open. Panicked, he leapt onto the sill and spun to see the oldest son of the baker looking curiously in his direction, candle held high to see better. Acting quickly, he reached to his pouch of feathers and threw a handful directly at the face of the poor boy.

The tight ball of feathers burst on impact, and the boy shouted in surprise. Marric took the moment to leap out the window and grab hold of the rope. Shimmying up the rope as quickly as possible, he cleared the roof edge and yanked the rope upwards with haste until he had it all. Holding his breath once more, he backed away to the chimney and waited. He heard the boy shouting below, something about a crazed bird attack and a figure at the window. Heart racing, he began to chuckle quietly to himself.

Well that *turned out to be far more fun than I expected. If only Jord had been here with me . . . .*

A pang of sadness ripped through his chest at the thought, causing his chest to tighten suddenly. Now that the mirth had passed, there was no reason to revel in the moment any longer.

After catching his breath, he turned, gathered his rope, and ran along the roof to jump on the rooftops towards home. He remembered his first time leaping over the spaces between roofs and how his heart thumped heavily in his chest each time. Now it was second nature to him. Gaining speed, he leapt the several-foot-gap to the next house and continued at the same clip.

I don't really understand why this was so difficult for me for so long, he thought, *I imagine it's the closest thing we can get to feeling like flying.*

Up came the second gap, he cleared it with no trouble. Continuing along the roof, he noticed a disturbance down below and glanced at the street. He saw a couple of drunk men— though who, he couldn't quite make out—throwing fists at each other sluggishly. Watching the scuffle as he ran, he mis-judged the distance to the next gap and was forced to jump hastily to avoid falling off the roof. Without the strength from the launch, he landed with only his toes on the lip of the neighboring roof. His heart skipped as his foot slipped into the empty air and he began to fall.

Suddenly, a force tugged at the front of his shirt heavily, pulling him up fully until he landed on the roof, coming back to reality. Marric felt numb, fear still gripping his entire being as an imagined scene of the stone road speedily approached his view, pain and possible death following. He felt nauseous, his fear of heights overcoming him finally. Realizing what just happened, Marric's head cleared and he shot upright to begin looking around for whoever had yanked him before he fell to his death. To his surprise, there was no one in sight.

Who on earth was on the roof at this time of night? Of the numerous times he had been out running jobs like this, never had he seen a soul sharing the rooftops with him at this hour. Not only was this person also on the roof at this odd time of day, but his reflexes had to have been superhuman to make that save as quickly as it had happened.

Deciding that there was no likelihood he'd find this strange savior, he stood up and breathed deeply through his nose, trying to regain his composure. When he felt that he'd done just that, he more carefully than ever made his way back to his room.

No sooner had he slid through his window when he heard his stepmother hollering up to him from the kitchen below.

"Dinner be ready, Marric! If yous don't come now, yeh can say farewell to any chance of eatin'!"

Shaking his head in annoyance, he shed his cloak and stashed it along with his other adventuring items under his mattress. Eyeing the pouch with the money he'd just taken, he shoved it in his trousers and headed down to dinner.

* * *

After finishing up his dinner, he let his father and stepmother know that he was feeling quite tired and headed up to his room. Setting the lit candle on his desk, he fished out the bit of parchment from under his mattress and sat down at the desk. He'd been grateful to learn not only how to read, but to write quite nicely. Using the quill and ink, he scratched a short note onto a small bit of the parchment and tore the section free from the rest.

"For the Barstands. May Lanser watch over you and your family."

Satisfied with the note, he took the parchment and the pouch of money from the baker's office, donned his cloak once more, and headed out the window. Getting to the roof unnoticed was very easy—his room being on the second floor of their home—however getting to the street was more tricky. Standing on the sill of his window, he took a deep breath, then leapt sideways to the sill of the window of his father's own study. Balancing himself there, he held the inside pane of the window's side, and leaned outward until he could reach the vines running up just next to the window.

The vines were not always reliable, which is why it made the journey downward so difficult, but it was the quickest way he knew. Choosing one, he tugged down firmly to check its hold, then leaned onto it with his weight until it held him. Hand-over-hand, Marric descended until he was three armspans off the ground. Right then, the vine gave and he fell the last length, cursing quietly to himself. After regaining his footing, he slinked down the street in the shadows, passing lit windows and the occasional man on his way home. He reached the end of his street, then turned left down Mollis Road.

This was always the best part of the jobs. It was never about the money, only about the thrill of adventure. Not to mention he liked developing his stealth and knife skills. If anything, it would likely lend him aid should he ever find himself in a bad situation. No, the best part of the job was giving the money to someone that could benefit from the funds more than he. He knew just where to take this lot. Reaching the crossing of Mollis Road and Turnt Street, he paused at the house on the corner.

The house was in need of some important repairs, but it was clear that the residents did not spend time on those things. The door was crooked on its hinges, windows were missing shutters, the roof had dozens of haphazard patches that were themselves also breaking down. There was a flicker of a light through one of the windows to the left, but otherwise, the house was still and dark. Bending over, he dropped the pouch of money with a plop.

Removing the bit of parchment with the note, he laid it carefully on the pouch, then rapped on the door softly. Pausing, he listened for approaching footsteps, and when he heard none, knocked a bit harder on the door. That got someone's attention. There were a series of loud thumps that grew louder, then he heard a timid voice say, "Pa, yeh sit back down an' rest, eh? There be no need fer yeh to visit with no one, 'specially at this hour."

Marric slunk around the side of the house and pressed up against the wall there in the shadows. He heard the door scratch against its frame as it was pushed open. Marric peeked around the corner and saw the young boy peering out. Crents looked around, confused at the absence of anyone at the door. Finally looking down, he started at the pouch and bit of parchment. Bending over carefully, he picked up the small pouch and looked at the note. Crents didn't know how to read, of course, but perhaps his father in a sober state could interpret the words for the boy. He looked thoughtful as he warily pulled open the top of the pouch and looked inside. A slight gasp escaped his throat and he began to cry softly.

Crents looked upwards at the sky and spoke quietly, "Oh Lanser, thank yeh! Thank yeh fer this gift. It means a righ' bunch to me an' me pa. Bless whoever dun gave this to us!"

At that, he pulled the door closed with a soft thud and retreated back into his house.

Leaning back against the wall of the house, Marric breathed in deeply through his nose with satisfaction. The cool night air was refreshing after the hot day. The sun had been down for a couple of hours now, and it was dark as could be with no moon out for light. He tilted his head back, looking up through the narrow space between the houses that made up this alley and looked at the stars shining brightly. He always liked being out at night. It felt calm. The darkness made him feel safer, which was ironic, considering the superstition that he grew up being taught. Most slunk away from the darkness, fearing the unknown, unseen, or some imagined monster. Marric loved it. It was a protection, a safe haven for him.

A breeze picked up and funneled through the alley where he stood. That normally meant that the fog would be blowing in within a few hours. Letting his head fall back and rest on the wall, he tried to enjoy his last moments of clear fresh air. Taking one last deep breath, he turned back to the street to return to his house. Before he could even make it to the street, he froze at the sound of heavy hooves on the cobblestone. Peering around the corner to the left, he saw three men on horseback coming around the bend.

I've never seen such large horses, let alone three at once! Marric thought as he watched them approach. Horses were extremely rare in Wurren. He'd only known of two in Wurren and they looked small and sickly by comparison. One had died when he was about ten, the other looked to die any moment. Regardless, these creatures were magnificent. Atop the horses were three men of high rank, or at least they appeared to be, based on their clothing. Each wore travel cloaks made from soft material of a deep maroon which were held together by expensive-looking silver clasps. The men trailing behind wore thick chain mail shirts and had thick leather armor over their trousers. They wore their hoods up so that Marric could not make out their features. Unlike the others, the man in front had no armor to be seen, but wore a vest over his tunic and trousers of fine material. The man in front had long light brown hair that ran just past his shoulders. His eyes were almond shaped and his nose was sharp and pointed. Clean shaven, he appeared a boy in features, but a man in body.

Marric was so preoccupied in the sight of these creatures that he almost didn't notice that the men were talking as the horses approached.

"We'll need to find a place to stay, possibly for an extended period. I'm not sure how long it might take to find the boy," the man leading said back to the others.

"We could always scare 'em into tellin' us," one of the men—Marric didn't know which—replied.

"Harmel, *that* is exactly the reason our past expeditions haven't always been successful. If they don't trust us, they won't give up the boy's location easily. If we need to build a little trust before they hand him over, then we'll do it. Likely it will be quicker," long-hair said back.

"S'ren, I see an inn up ahead, near the end of the street," the third voice said.

S'ren? Why on earth would they address that man in this way? thought Marric. That title was reserved for those of power. Not *political* power, which is what this man appeared to have, but *literal* power. Marric had only ever heard it used in prayer to Lanser, the prime deity.

The horses paused a moment while they deliberated further. Marric had to creep toward them in the shadows to make out what they said next as they had moved past him and out of earshot.

" . . . mustn't let the lad know too much, lest he get spooked and run. We'll hole up for the night, then tomorrow we'll begin the search," the man, addressed as S'ren, whispered.

"Tha's right," the larger of the hooded men added. "The las' time we went ta collect one of these *Tar'n,* we lost 'er to Watchlight. She almos' ran into their clutches when she saw us."

"That's right. We mustn't let the locals get the wrong idea about why we want him. Build trust, then take him back with us when the time is right."

Marric was lost without the context. *What is a* Tar'n? He was only remotely familiar with the word; it sounded like a glyph of some sort. *And who is this Watchlight?*

"S'ren, what'd the Seer says 'is name was?" a hooded man asked quietly.

"Marric. He wasn't able to discern a surname, but I suspect there aren't that many Marrics in a small town such as this."

Marric suddenly felt cold. His vision blurred and the world seemed to sway slightly as he lost focus.

Could the men be here for him? Why in Lanser's name would they be here for him?!

A face flashed in his mind. A face with a cruel smile, scarred from nose to ears. He shuddered and his throat closed up in fear. He missed whatever else the men said as he leaned against the wall, losing strength momentarily.

He couldn't panic, he certainly wasn't the only Marric in the town of Wurren. Was he?

He scoffed at that last thought. He knew every person in Wurren; he was the only one and he knew it. But he felt that it was a desperate attempt of his mind to protect him.

The horses had turned and continued on to the inn.

Marric turned away from them as quickly as possible and took the back way, the long way, home. He needed to hide, and he needed to do it well.

Perhaps if he hid well enough, they'd give up and leave.

Something told him that they wouldn't fall for that. Despair descended upon him darkly at the thought.

Chapter 2

The sun rose silently over the horizon, pouring light through the window. A beam shone directly onto Marric's sleeping face and he winced, scowling at the sudden brightness. Rolling over, he wiped the sleepiness from his eyes. Normally he didn't hate waking up like this, in fact, he enjoyed the fresh coolness of the morning, but the events of last night had left him awake far longer than he had intended.

After overhearing the conversation of the mysterious men last night, Marric had rushed home and spent at least an hour pacing his room quietly, mind racing. Finally, he had sat on his bed and let his head fall between his legs. He had thought interminably about what he was going to do the following day. He'd gone through all the options he could think of, from running away to trying to attack the men in their sleep. The former was not a good option, because even with his bow, he'd likely die from his lack of survival skills. The latter was just ludicrous. Marric's stomach twisted at the thought of killing someone. Not only that, but these men had swords and likely combat experience that Marric lacked entirely. In the end, he'd decided on convincing his father and Tins to call him by his middle name, Lorn, from now on.

Head pounding slightly, Marric groaned as he forced himself to sit up in his bed. On occasion he would stay up late . . . sometimes later than last night, but never did he feel this way when waking in the morning. The stressful events from the night before had taken their toll on him. Pulling his knees to his chest, he considered how he was going to deliver the news to his father. Should he tell him of the mysterious men that were looking for him? No, that didn't seem wise. His father didn't even know that he went out late at night in the first place, and he certainly wouldn't believe the story if Marric told it as it was. Perhaps he could convince him that the name change was just him wanting to try something new.

He sighed. That wouldn't work. His father would know that something was up as soon as he tried to tell him that.

Footsteps just outside his door snapped him out of his thoughts. A heavy hand pounded on his door a few times. His heart skipped a beat as he realized he was still wearing his dark cloak and clothes. In his exhaustion, he had fallen to sleep in the same garb from the job the night before. He hurriedly threw the covers from his bed over his body and pulled them to his neck, feigning sleep.

"What are yeh doin' boy? Come down 'ere an' git yer breakfast afore it wastes from yer draggin!"

That insufferable woman. One of these days I'll . . . .

The pounding resumed, loud and annoying.

"Oi! Are yeh still a-sleepin' in there?! Git out here afore I come in there an' git yeh myself!" she shouted when he didn't answer.

He gritted his teeth, stopping the angry retort he'd been saving up for her, and instead said, "Yes, Tins. I'm dressing now."

"'Bout time yeh spoke. I'da thought yous was kidnapped or dead with yeh bein' all quiet like. Sure'd be a right good mornin' should tha' be th'case."

He heard her say something else, but he'd stopped listening because her voice faded while she spoke. Her heavy footfalls rang quieter and quieter as she descended the staircase down to the kitchen and shop below.

Taking a few deep breaths, partially in relief, partially to prepare himself to tackle the day, Marric stood and dressed quickly. Coming down the spiral staircase, he spotted Narim at the table finishing up his breakfast. Looked like eggs this morning. A slight smile spread across Marric's face as he saw this. That meant he would be spared from Tins's slop they usually ate for breakfast. He crossed the room to the table and sat in the chair exactly opposite of Narim, who didn't seem to notice due to the large book that he was studying intensely. His father had a tendency to get lost in reading.

Marric always forgot that his father was a skilled reader, probably even more skilled than himself, despite his lack of education in youth. Narim never bothered to speak in any sophisticated way, and when others asked why he still maintained the Wurren uneducated accent, he simply replied "I ain't tryna fool no one. I'm from 'ere, I'll die 'ere, an' I can speak from 'ere." He was nothing if not loyal to his hometown. Marric was different. The fact that he'd excelled at reading and could stifle his accent lit the rebellious fire in him that kept him going. It was a fire that drove his desire to someday leave Wurren, even though it would be so painful to his father.

Stabbing a couple eggs on the plate in the middle of the table and moving them to his own, he began to eat quietly and considered what to say to his father. He had time, since Narim was clearly lost in what he was reading and wouldn't notice him for at least five minutes. Taking his time, he cut intentionally small pieces of egg and chewed slowly. He would stall as long as he could to give himself time to prepare.

After a few minutes of consideration and planning, he finished his bite and said, "Good morning, Pa."

Narim jumped slightly in surprise and looked up from his book.

"By jove, Mar. Yeh startled me righ' good. How long have yeh been there a-watchin' me eat n' read?"

"Sorry, Pa, but you looked really into this one and I didn't want to disturb you one bit."

"Tosh waddles, I can read later. How was yer night, eh? Yeh went to bed right early.

Marric squirmed inside. He hated keeping things from his father.

"Unfortunately, not so good," Marric replied, scooping up a third egg and getting to work on it.

"Really? Nightmares about Jord again?"

Shaking his head, Marric said, "Not this time. It's just, well . . . I was considering how I might change things around here. Day to day seems a little slow and predictable. I was wondering if you'd help me change my name just a bit. I was thinking—"

The front door to the house burst open and Crents dashed in with an excited look on his face.

"Marric, Pa Narim! You'll never believe what happened!" His eyes were wide as he strode to the table and plopped a small red pouch on the table, clearly filled with coins. "Las nigh', I was tendin' to me father and I heard a tap on the door. A'course, I was nervous t' be answerin' the door at such an hour. I opened the door an' found that there righ' at me feet. It's *ten copper* and a *silver*. Who coulda done this? I thanked Lanser for hours after seein' the likes of this."

Marric feigned surprise, Narim showing real surprise of his own.

"Well lad, that's mighty nice of that fella'. I reckon' they'll be blest ten bits fer this deed."

"He sure does deserve such a thing," Marric added, pleased with the outcome of his efforts. When Jord and he had first run a job, they worried the person they took from would report to the sheriff quickly. They were pleased to learn that the money swiping occurred before it had been counted. Though accidental, it helped them learn that timing is key. Knowing the baker's routine, Marric was confident that the money hadn't yet been numbered by the rotund man.

"Not jus' that!" Crents spoke again quickly. "There be some rich bein' men 'ere with horses. *Real* horses. On me way to work this mornin', I saw three horses tied at the inn. Took a few moments to speak to Levin, the innkeeper, an' he said they done paid him a fair silver to git the best rooms he's got!"

Marric had to hide the pang of fear he felt at the mention of these men, and instead he feigned excitement at the news.

"Rich men, eh?" Narim questioned, "What're men such as tha' doin' in a place such as this?

"Levin said they be here to collect a little somethin', though he din' say right much." Crents said, sputtering slightly.

"Meh, I better git over their quick-like, else I miss an opportunity to sell me wares at a premium price. Men like these outta have a good reason t' go huntin' if not fer sport."

"Oh, they ain't there now," Crents said. "They left righ' early, says Levin.

I guess they be needin' t' find what they need, quick-like."

Narim plopped back down into his seat with a disappointed look. "Well I'll be catchin' them another time, then."

"What do yeh think they be lookin' for, Pa Narim? I'm hopin' that they'll be lookin' fer someone to take back with'em. Maybe lookin' fer an apprentice of sort."

Crents seemed even more a child now as he dreamed up the possibility of becoming a stout warrior for an army somewhere far off. Marric smiled at that. The boy did have a way of keeping dreams alive.

"Don' know 'bout that, but they sure ain't leavin' without some wares from good 'ol Narim," Marric's father said with determination.

The conversations continued on while Marric lost focus of what they were discussing. He knew what—or who— they were looking for, and he didn't think that it was for any apprenticeship. Though, when Crents had mentioned that possibility, a small glimmer of hope sprouted in Marric's thoughts that they were seeking something as innocent as that. But the way the men whispered so secretively, and how the leader of the pack was called *S'ren* made his stomach twist, knowing there was something far bigger at play here.

"Mar, you arigh'?"

Marric re-focused on the two and realized they were both staring at him inquisitively. Looking back and forth a few times, he nodded, but didn't say anything else.

"Yeh don' look good t'day. Ain't yeh interested in why the rich'n men are here?"

Not sure how to respond, he ended up saying, "A bit, I'm just tired, is all."

Narim's brows knit at the comment. He clearly saw that something was up, but didn't want to pry with Crents here in the room.

"Well, nuff 'bout the men, I reckon we oughta git goin' on the work t'day, eh?" Crents said with finality.

Marric nodded, then started to get up.

"Actually, Mar. Might yeh go into the market an' git me some things I be needin'? I think that perhaps gettin' some fresh'n air might be right good fer yeh this mornin." Narim offered.

Glancing at his father, a look of understanding showed on the man's face. He didn't know what was on Marric's mind, or what he was feeling, but he knew a break from the monotonous work and the chittering of Crents would be greatly appreciated.

"Sure thing, Pa," Marric said gratefully, "What things are those?"

"Meh, I'll write 'em down on some parchment fer yeh. Go on, git yerself ready t'go an' I'll have a list ready fer yeh."

Nodding to his father, Marric climbed the stairs to his room. As he climbed, he could hear Crents and his father continue their conversation about the men. Entering his room, he sat on his bed and pulled on his shoes. While he secured them in place, he thought more about the men and their hushed conversation last night that he was sure he was not meant to overhear. He thought of the terms they used: Tar'n, S'ren, Watchlight . . . what could these mean? What were they hoping to gain from this person they were looking for?

Marric stood and began toward the door when he paused and considered the knife hiding under the mattress. After holding for a beat, he turned back to the bed, retrieved his dagger, and secured it with the loop he'd added to the inside of his leather vest. He hoped that he wouldn't need to use it, but felt more comfortable knowing that he had some way to defend himself should he get into trouble.

Reaching the bottom of the stairs, he saw his father alone at the table with a parchment and a small pouch of coins.

"Yeh doin' alright, Marric? I'da thought yous were sick with fear th'way yeh reacted ta the news of the men."

Wincing at the mention of his reaction, he replied, "Just tired, is all. I had a hard time sleepin' last night. That's it, Pa."

Narim narrowed his eyes, but didn't challenge the explanation. Internally, Marric berated himself for his pronunciation slip. His father knew that he was lying when he let his accent in.

"Sleeping, I mean," he corrected.

Narim narrowed his eyes but didn't press the issue further.

"Well, if yeh say so. I'll trust yeh. But yeh know that if there's somethin' that yous want ta talk ter me about, yeh can indeed."

"Yes, Pa. I know that," he assured his father. "Is this the list of what you need?" Marric held up a parchment piece that had been laying on the table where he usually sat.

"Oh, yes. Here yeh go. Just a few things we'll be needin' fer dinner tonight an' a few other odds and ends. Take yer time. I know that yous could use a break from the stuffy ol' shop, eh?"

"Thanks, Pa. But I'll be there and back right quick. I know that Tins doesn't like me out during working hours, no matter how short a time."

"Oh, tosh, don' yeh be worryin' about Tins. I'll take care of the likes o' her. Jus' go and enjoy the air a bit. Crents an' I can do the work."

"But Pa, I was hoping to talk to you about something—"

"*Go*, Marric. Git on!" Narim nudged him toward the door with a smile.

Giving his father a grateful smile, and shriveling inside at not having been able to address the change, Marric strode through the door and onto the street outside. The cobblestone road was mostly quiet, as it often was during the day. Most of the town's activity would be around the market, which is where he would need to go for the food and gear he needed. He made his way on a straight course from his house toward the public well, one of the four they had in town. As he walked, he nodded to a few of his neighbors that were just outside their homes working. Reaching the well, he paused a moment to look back at his house. Being the house that closed off the end of the street, he had a clear view into the front windows when the shutters were open. He would have to thank his father profusely for taking the brunt of Tins's anger when she found him not hard at work in the back.

Turning back to the well, he continued straight onto Slynd Road. Passing five or six well-built and smart-looking two stories, he took the next right onto Myrk Street. Right as he made the turn, he could see the tents just up the road and the bustle of the marketplace. He had always liked this place. White canvas tents high on wooden poles connected to create quite a large market space with stands and tables of fruits, meats, vegetables, and other kinds of foods.

He'd need to speak with Tarind, the butcher, to get a good cut of beef for their stew this evening, and he considered stopping by the baker's booth for some fresh bread before remembering that he'd just stolen from him. He imagined that Storldin, the baker, wouldn't be in a good mood after the events of the previous night. Noting that, he reached the edge of the market tents and inserted himself into the throng. The large gathering of people didn't bother him; he somehow felt safer with all the men, women, and children bumping into each other, making it easier to hide in the crowd. Reaching the butcher's booth, he got the meat he needed and moved on.

He knew the booth layout so well that gathering everything his father needed was easy. Very soon he had secured the meat, potatoes, eggs, short whittling knife, and length of cowskin for a new apron. Realizing that he had habitually rushed through the process, Marric decided to peruse the other tables and booths for a time to prolong his freedom from Tins's shouting voice.

He soon arrived at the far end of the market where artisans crafted beautiful works out of many mediums. He saw necklaces, jeweled weaponry, shawls, new cloaks, tapestries, and other things of this sort. Marric stopped at a beautiful tapestry of the night sky. The second moon of three, called Mallan, shone brightly on the cloth, with all the constellations that he was familiar with, glittering as if it was the real sky. While examining the tapestry, he caught sight of a woman just past the hanging art. Tearing his eyes from the work, he noticed that she was looking in his direction. As he thought about it more, he realized that she was looking directly at him. They locked eyes for what seemed like forever, before her brows knit together and she looked away, continuing with her work.

Marric examined her a little further as she gathered the wool from the ground and piled it on the table. Her hair was dark black, dark as night. It was tied tightly to the back of her head as she worked. She was taller than most women he'd seen, and she appeared old. Not *old* as in of the older generation, but old enough to be married and have at least a few children. However, she worked alone with the sheepherder's wife and her hand showed no signs of a marriage band. The dress she wore was blue and simple, but strangely in good shape, as if it were new. That was also the case with the white apron she wore over the clean dress. More strikingly, he realized she was quite beautiful.

Why was she looking at me so intently? Marric wondered. He'd never seen her here before. This was an industrious town, of course, and new people and faces traveled here regularly, but those were buyers. She appeared to be selling alongside the sheepherder's wife.

Perhaps she's their niece, Marric thought.

Watching her work for a few more moments, he noted that she looked particularly awkward working with the wool, and even more out of place wearing the simple dress. She looked almost annoyed at the whole situation, as if she would rather be doing something else.

Not realizing it, Marric's head started to tilt slightly as he continued to watch the woman work. A tap on the shoulder snapped him out of his thoughts and he spun to find a familiar man staring right at him. Feeling his body stiffen, he felt the instinct to run as fast as he could. A lump formed in his throat, almost causing him to choke in fear.

The long-haired man from the previous night stood before him with a warm smile on his face.

"Hey, lad. Do you know where we might get a bit of bread? We are in need of some provisions lest we need to leave quickly on a journey," he said warmly.

Marric just stared.

Furrowing his brow, the long-haired man thought for a moment and said, "Lad, are you quite alright?"

Blinking for a few moments, Marric realized that the man hadn't seen him the night before nor did he know who was. Shaking his head slightly, he replied shortly, "Yessir, right over there," pointing in the direction of the baker's table.

"Thank you." he said, still looking worried. "Are you quite alright? You look like you've seen your worst nightmare."

"Oh . . . no sir," Marric stammered. " 'S just tha' I never seen a sword like tha'un afore now."

He intentionally laid his Wurren accent on thick, for some reason feeling that it would disguise him, even though the man had no idea who he was.

The man smiled again and nodded slightly, understanding his shock.

"You needn't worry. This sword is merely for protection against bandits and wild animals while my companions and I are out on journey. My friends and I do a lot of traveling and we need to be sure that we are safe as we go."

Not knowing how to reply to that, Marric merely nodded vigorously and kept staring at the man.

"Say, lad. What's your name? You look like you're about, what, sixteen now?"

Marric felt fear starting to grip his chest again as he struggled to know what to say to the man. Realizing that a long pause might sound suspicious, he started to say the first name that came to mind.

"M'name's Cr—

"—Might ye be interested in some fine wool to keep yeh warm during the night, sir?" said a woman's voice suddenly.

The man was taken aback as the woman in blue forced herself between him and Marric. Taking a step back, the man put his hands up and shook his head politely.

"No thank you, ma'am. I am quite alright. We brought sufficient supplies to help us stay comfortable during our travels. Now, if you don't mind, I was just about to learn more about this young—"

"But sir, yeh don' think tha' you'd be able to sleep as fine without some wool such as this, eh? I be thinkin' that yer travels be much much more happy if'n yeh buy one a these," the woman said forcefully.

As she spoke, her foot came out from under her dress and nudged Marric softly. Stunned, Marric looked from the woman to the man, and back again. Her foot came out again and shoved him, harder this time.

"Madam, I assure you, we have what we need—"

"Oh, yeh don' know wha' yeh need until yeh *try* it. Here, try it around yer shoulders fer just a bit."

She rounded the man, threw the wool over his shoulders, and slightly turned him about. As she did, she gave a very pointed look to Marric that said *get out of here before I make you.* Understanding the look, but not why this woman was bothering to give it to him, he turned quickly and hurried off with the wares for his father. As he ran, he could hear the objections of the man as he tried to make the strange woman go away.

Marric ran until he started to run out of breath, then he started walking. He felt that he was reasonably far enough away that he didn't need to hurry as he had before now. Finally gaining his breath again, he began to think of what had just happened. From what he gathered, the strange yet beautiful woman had distracted the foreign man in order to help him escape.

Why in Lanser's name did she bother to do such a thing? he thought as he rounded another corner. He couldn't fathom why she would take the time to do that. *Perhaps I'm just overthinking the situation. She likely just saw a man with apparent wealth and saw a fit opportunity to make a handsome profit.* This must be the reason she took the time to insert herself between the two of them. *But those shoes. . . .*

Marric couldn't help but notice the strange nature of the woman's shoes. Boots. The woman was wearing almost pitch black, tight laced boots under her seemingly perfect dress and apron. He'd never seen a lady like her donning such a masculine form of footwear. He wondered even more who this strange woman was and why she had chosen such an impractical pair of boots for her status. He thought that maybe this was one reason she wasn't married with children yet. Most men often thought such things were off-putting and unattractive.

As he approached his house, Marric realized that he was away from the workshop for a mere fraction of the time that Narim had instructed him to be away. Stopping just short of his home, he considered what he could do to leverage the time away from Tins and his menial tasks. Pausing for a few minutes, he decided to head toward the side of his house and sneak the wares into the kitchen. As he made his way to the door, he heard shouting from inside the workshop at the back.

Darn, the blasted woman is in the back with Crents. Poor boy.

With Tins in the back, he would be unable to sneak his way to the kitchen and leave the things on the table without her seeing him and snatching him back up into her clutches. As he stood there wondering what to do, the door opened unexpectedly and his father almost walked right into him. Stopping abruptly, Narim's eyes focused on his son standing there, guiltily, holding the bags of things he had ordered. Standing there quietly, Marric could tell Narim was noting how early Marric had returned and was deciding what to do about it.

"Narim! Do yeh know where tha' blasted boy of yers is?! I'll be killin' 'im if he don' git back 'ere soon!"

Marric tensed, waiting for his father to let Tins know that he was back.

Without hesitation, Narim yelled back, "Tins, I sent th'boy with quite a long list, eh? Give 'im some time. I wan' to be sure tha' he don' ferget what I told 'im t'get."

"But Narim, tha's *my* job, not a boy's. Next time yeh let me do the shoppin', eh?"

"Oh yes, yes, Tins." Narim replied, raising his finger to his lips to quiet Marric. "I'll be goin' out meself fer a bit. I'll be back afore yeh know it."

"But Narim, I—"

The rest of her statement was muffled as Narim pulled the door closed behind him.

Taking the bags from his son, Narim gave Marric a nod that dismissed him, indicating to Marric that he should head away for a while longer. With a grateful smile, Marric turned on his heels and returned to the front of his house. Reaching the front, he headed to where the vines grew up the wall and climbed the now seemingly short distance to his window on the second floor.

Now might be a good time to practice my shot a bit more with the bow, he decided.

Entering his window slowly, he softly stepped into his room and padded to his bed. Lifting the mattress just a bit, he retrieved his finely made bow. He crouched down to his knees, reached under the bed to the far corner, and grabbed his quiver of arrows. Swinging the quiver over his shoulder, he headed back to the window to make the descent to the road.

He hadn't found the time to practice with his bow in what seemed like forever. It had been so long that he probably couldn't hit an apple from a mere five feet away. Marric felt a bit depressed at the thought of that. As a kid, he'd always wanted to be an amazing hunter and make a living selling furs and traveling around the world.

There's no chance of that anymore what with Tins terrorizing me daily, Marric thought to himself. *If she had it her way, she'd work me to death while I'm still young.*

He jumped the fence to the field behind his house and began heading toward the line of trees a few hundred feet away. The sheepherder must have just let his sheep out, as there were a few dozen grazing throughout the field. Marric loved that his house was on the edge of the town. It made for an easy escape into the wilderness when he needed a break from the monotony of life.

He sighed. That had been the way it was a few years ago before his father had met and married Tins; back when life was simpler. Nowadays she kept a keen eye on him and didn't even like him setting foot past the fence. It was almost as if she thought he might run away and leave her alone with his father. Lanser forbid she had to spend too much alone time with the man she 'loved'.

Considering this oddity, Marric made his way through the sheep to the treeline. Weaving through the dense group of animals, he let his hand graze the backs of the beasts that he passed, enjoying their soft coats.

"I don't right think yer s'posed to go in them trees. They be dangerous without trained soldiers or hunters," a voice said close by.

Marric stopped suddenly, a bit startled by the comment. He hadn't realized that there was someone among the sheep a short distance to his left.

Drat, he thought, *It's a bad habit getting lost in my thoughts. Could become an issue if I'm not careful.*

Glancing over, he was baffled to see the same woman in blue from the market.

What is she doing here? I thought she was manning the booth for the sheep herder?

"D'yeh make a habit of ignoring those talking to yeh?" she said, smirking at him.

Marric blinked, not sure how to respond. "Uh . . . sorry." was all that he could manage. "Wasn't expecting anyone out here right now."

"I see," she replied curtly. "Well, yeh best not go out there without a proper guide or hunter. Yous look like free food t'me. I'da bet the likes of you'd be eaten within the hour should yous go out there."

Marric puffed up his chest a bit. "I am a *lot* better with this bow than you might s'pose. Been shooting since I was small in those very woods. I'm not dead yet, am I?"

A sideways smile slowly crept up her face, as if she thought this was a silly idea.

"Well if yeh say so, lad. Don' expect me to come a'runnin' if I hear a beastie chasin' yeh for an early dinner."

The woman quickly turned and made her way back to the fence behind the shop just next to his father's.

"Wait— " Marric said without thinking. *Blast, what in Lanser's name am I doing?*

She paused, then turned sideways, head reaching back to look at him.

"Uh . . . thanks for helping me back there at the market. I'm not sure why you did it, but I sure am thankful."

She cocked her head to the side, face showing a confused expression.

"Hmm? Oi ain't done nuttin' ta help yeh. Oi've never seen yeh afore now. Not sure what yeh might be talkin' bout."

"The men." Marric explained. "You distracted them so that I could . . . well, I'm not sure exactly what you thought I might do."

"Ahhhh, yes," she said, finally catching on. "Lad, that weren't for yous. I know a rich man when I see one. I was just try'n to make a good bit of money there and yous were in the way. But I'm glad it worked out for yeh."

She shook her head slowly as she turned and stalked back to the fence.

Marric watched her for a few beats, then turned toward the forest and continued the trek.

"Oi, lad!"

He stopped and turned to look. The woman had stopped but did not turn herself. She stayed facing the town.

"Don' go git yerself killed out there."

With that, she hurried to the fence and leapt over it. It was so fluid, that Marric hardly believed it, and probably couldn't have managed it himself. She had used only one hand and the rest of her body glided far over the top with ease. Another pang of curiosity sprang through his mind as he considered all the oddities he'd seen from her.

What a peculiar woman, Marric thought as she rounded the corner of the building and disappeared from his sight. Turning, he completed the trek to the edge of the forest and passed through the treeline into the foliage.

* * *

Janis came around the corner, then quickly hunched down low behind the building, intending to use her position to watch where the boy would enter the forest.

Staying low, she leaned slightly out from the edge of the wall and spied the boy, Marric, entering the forest right where she'd left him just moments before. Satisfied that she would be able to track him from that spot, she stood and pressed her back against the wall, taking the time to think about her position. She could trail him directly behind. She was definitely stealthy enough to stay within twenty feet of him and not be heard or seen, but that wouldn't let her see what may be ahead of him. Getting ahead of the boy would likely be the better choice.

Janis hated the way she was speaking. She found small-town accents quite annoying. However, she had to blend in. Fortunately, accents were part of her training from Macks.

Hearing footsteps approaching on the road behind her, Janis leaned sideways on the wall and began inspecting her hands, looking casual. A balding man, slightly shorter than Janis and a lot plumper, stopped as he noticed her in the alley between the two house-shops.

"Oh, hullo Alain," he said, inspecting her with what seemed to be a pleased expression.

"Hullo there, Torlin! Done sellin' fer the day?" she replied brightly, trying to play the part she'd created for the past week since she'd arrived in Wurren.

"Not quite. I jus' fergot a few bit of things at me ol' house. What are ya doin' back 'ere at the house? I thought ya might have gone sum'ere with that fella yous met at the market," his expression darkened a bit at this.

Janis felt amused at his comment. The poor man had developed quite a fondness for this *Alain* character she had created. After getting within the town limits just under a week before, Janis had tracked down the home of Marric Norst within a few hours. It wasn't hard in such a town like this. She had selected a home just a few houses down from his to set up as a vantage point. Knocking on the door, she decided to play an innocent daughter of an abusive father. It wasn't hard to fool them, though it helped that they were so generous.

"Nah. I was jus' try'n t'get him to buy lots of wool fer a coat. No luck. Righ' stingy man he was. Not the type fer me."

Torlin's face brightened a touch at this comment. "Well, we appreciate yer fine sellin' skills this week. Sellin's been a bit slow in the recent weeks. Care to join me on the stroll back? I'll only be a moment in the house."

"No, no. I got a bit of thinkin' to do, meself. Thanks fer the offer, my good man."

"Well, if yous be changing yer mind, I'll be there a few moments."

With that, he looked her up and down with a pleasing smile and stalked back down the road.

Cursing, Janis spun and leapt the fence once more, sprinting to the forest. She had lost a lot of time chatting with the old sheepherder and thought that she may have lost the chance to get ahead.

Janis made to follow Marric, until she realized she wouldn't get far in the forest in her current attire.

This blasted dress is slowing me down. I can't track the boy properly if I'm restricted by this annoying fabric.

Reaching the same entry point Marric had used, she grabbed the skirt of her dress and pulled it over her head, tossing it to the side. Beneath it, she had her usual black trousers, black knee-boots and black shirt.

That's more like it, she thought, pleased at having her ability to move returned.

Entering the forest, she began tracking Marric's path.

* * *

Normally, he'd only go about two hundred or so paces into the forest, but with Tins's shouts and the three mysterious men seemingly after him, Marric felt like getting as far from the town as possible. Plus, he'd never had the chance to explore the forest. That was silly, considering he'd lived here his whole life. There was a sudden emptiness within him knowing that he'd never been beyond the fifty-foot depth he'd been to at least a hundred times.

Stepping over the familiar jutted root that marked his own personal set boundary, Marric felt elated to finally feel some excitement in life. His chest constricted with anticipation as he made his way through the thick foliage. The ground seemed to slope downwards slightly as he walked, making him feel like he was going down into the belly of a beast. As he walked, the canopy above thickened, blocking most of the sunlight. It felt strange to him that it could be so dark during the day. The brush also thickened, making it tricky for Marric to walk quickly. He had to push through the leaves and branches of the forest and could feel his hands and face getting scratched by the plants. It felt as if he were in a crowd of people, all trying to grab at his limbs and clothes, hands desperately clawing at him for help.

Marric pressed forward until he saw a shimmer of light ahead.

Could this be the other side of the forest? That couldn't be. This forest had been called endless by traders and merchants that traveled to Wurren from afar. The road ran north from the town, but Marric headed east into the forest from his house, so descriptions he'd heard of the forest's size might not apply from this direction.

His foot caught a thick root, causing him to pitch forward through some branches. Stumbling, he found himself blinded by the sudden sunlight. He blinked a few times, letting his eyes adjust before he was able to see his surroundings. Once his vision cleared, he saw that he was in a clearing about a few dozen feet across. The ground was covered in soft and spongy moss, but was otherwise clear of vegetation. Up above, the sun shone through a break in the canopy of trees and lit up the clearing as if it were a shining diamond in the dark recesses of the forest.

Marric suddenly felt comfortable and at ease with the place. It seemed like a safe location for him to do a little practicing with his bow. He decided that he should start with some closer targets and fewer obstacles to work on accuracy before going straight to the complicated targets. He had a tendency to jump to something difficult and new rather than working on the basics. It was often why he struggled with the work he had to do in the fletcher's shop.

Stretching his arms, he puffed out his chest confidently before smoothly snatching an arrow from his quiver and attaching it to the string in one fluid motion. At least he still had *that* motion down. Looking at the trees not quite directly across the clearing, but slightly to the left, he chose his target and focused on it intently. There was a knot in this tree, just below eye level, where he aimed his arrow. Breathing evenly, he focused on the knot and released the string. The arrow flew straight and true, making a thunking noise as it slammed into the tree just left of the knot.

Letting out a brief sigh, Marric nodded to himself, satisfied that he hadn't completely lost his touch after all this time. Most of this was muscle memory after all, and he depended on that as he nocked and shot the rest of the arrows at trees adjacent to the first. Most of the arrows landed, though there were a few that missed the mark entirely and went flying into the treeline.

After emptying his quiver completely, he trotted over to the other side and began gathering his arrows to start over again. He ventured into the forest to find those that went astray, but settled for the couple that he was able to find easily so as to not go too deep into the brush. In the dark forest, tracking them all would take far too long. He could just make more if he lost too many here. Marric was glad he had learned that skill on his own, though the nature of his father's profession aided him as well.

Getting into a rhythm with his practicing, Marric was lost in thoughts of recent events. He found that thinking deeply was how he preferred to practice anyway. Who were the men that were looking for him? What could they possibly want with the son of a fletcher? They looked far too important to have any connection with a simple boy like himself. Despite that, the three visitors appeared to be looking for him.

Did they mean him harm? They did have sharp swords on their belts at all times. Isn't that why they needed to 'gain the trust' of the town for a few days? But when Marric had met the long-haired man, he had been so kind.

This thought made Marric uncomfortable. In his mind's eye, he saw the three men sitting at his father's table, sharing mugs of ale and laughing with his father. Even Tins appeared to admire these men, hoping that they might rid her of the nuisance that was Marric himself. The leading man knocked back another swig of ale and made another joke, causing the whole table to burst into laughter once more.

Shuddering, he shook the images out of his mind and continued firing his arrows. After a few more shots, another alarming thought came to him.

Were these the same men that came for Jord? Could they be related at all?

That couldn't be. None of the three sported the eerie scars that the man I saw two years ago had, Marric reasoned.

No one really knew why Jord was taken, or what the motive was behind his capture. Jord's family was not rich by any means, nor were he or his father notable figures in society. His father was a woodsman, one of the dozens that Wurren had. He chopped down and collected wood, nothing more. What did these men see in Jord that made them snatch him away to some unknown fate? Even more perplexing was the method by which they came. No one met, saw, or heard any of those that took Jord. The only evidence of them being there was Marric's word at seeing them and the destroyed carts just outside of Marric's home. For some reason, the men had obliterated a few tables and merchant carts that were parked in front of his home and those of his neighbors. Nothing was stolen, the carts were just in pieces.

No, these new men *couldn't* be associated with the men that had taken Jord. These men had introduced themselves to people in town. They were taking the time to be seen and to build trust. Plus, they hadn't destroyed anything in town yet. However, they still made Marric uncomfortable. They seemed imposing in their own way, carrying swords and seeming gruff.

Snap!

Marric came back to reality at the sound of a branch breaking. Whipping around, he scanned the treeline to his right, where the sound originated. On instinct, he stooped low and strung an arrow in preparation. Heart racing, breathing speeding up, he felt the fear-thrill of adrenaline rushing through his body. After a few moments, nothing happened. Suddenly, a burst of grey fur launched out of the forest toward where he stood. On instinct, he released the arrow toward the beast, hearing it collide with a small thud. The beast cried out and landed a few feet short of him. Backing up quickly, Marric fumbled for another arrow to nock in his bow.

Fear was crawling into his limbs, slowing them down. He kept himself facing the beast, knowing that turning his back would be death. Locking eyes with it, he realized it was an enormous wolf, the ones he'd heard of from travelers. Its head was in line with Marric's own, indicating that it was larger than Marric imagined from the stories. He'd struck this one in the shoulder, but it appeared to annoy the beast more than anything. It growled and leaned back on its haunches, preparing to launch itself at Marric. He had finally been able to get ahold of an arrow and was nocking it when the wolf jumped at him. Panicked, Marric tripped backwards, arms flying into the air as the wolf landed on top of him.

Flinging his hands in desperation, he pushed the wolf with all his might and was able to get the beast off slightly to his left, allowing him to quickly squirm out. Rolling to his right, he gracefully got to his feet with unexpected speed and faced the threat again. With a rush of energy, he pulled the arrow string taut and was about to release, when he realized the beast had stopped moving. With a quick inspection, he noted a black-handled dagger protruding from the neck of the wolf.

What in Lanser's name?

The wolf was dead.

Marric panted, feeling his legs weaken under him. Once he realized that the immediate danger was eliminated, his adrenaline rush left him and he fell to the ground, head feeling light. He sat there for a moment, breathing hard. After a few moments, he got to his feet and moved to examine the wolf carcass.

It had been killed by what looked to be a hunting knife. Marric scanned the trees where the knife had to have come from, only to find empty, quiet forest. Standing up, he walked a bit closer to the trees, hoping to find his savior to provide a proper thank you. Unfortunately, all he saw was the dense, dark green foliage and a few small animals skittering up the sides of some of the trees. Once he decided that there was no one, his attention returned to the large wolf carcass.

Creeping forward slowly, he inspected the knife handle. It wasn't a throwing knife, for the handle was quite large, but this one appeared to have been thrown at the beast while it was in motion. Judging from the location of entry, this one had been thrown deliberately for immediate death of the creature. As he reached the corpse, he began to relax. He muttered a quick prayer of thanks to Lanser that the large wolves didn't run in packs like normal wolf breeds.

Marric grabbed hold of the knife handle, and with a grunt, pulled the knife free. It was a simple knife, black handle wrapped in cloth for a better grip with an inch-wide blade slightly curved from handle to tip. It was long for a blade, being at least the length of his forearm, perhaps a bit longer, making this almost a small sword. Seeing the size of the knife made Marric wonder at what skill was required to throw such a blade with that accuracy. Even Grond, the town's most skilled hunter, couldn't throw a knife this size with such accuracy. It made him a bit nervous knowing there was a man out there with such skill. Why did this man bother to help, then disappear?

Looking to the clear sky through the break in the leaves above, Marric was alarmed at how dark it was getting already. He hadn't realized how much time had passed since he'd entered the forest. Without a view of the sun, he wasn't sure exactly how late it had gotten, but judging by how dark it was getting here, it was going to become increasingly dangerous in this forest now that he would hardly be able to see just feet in front of him. His stomach growled, and his dry mouth made him realize he'd somehow been here most of the day without anything to eat. He had brought a waterskin, but that had been emptied long ago. Marric's gut wrenched at the idea that he'd been gone from home for that many hours and he dreaded Tins's reaction. Even his father couldn't protect him from what was likely to come.

Marric dropped the knife-sword and began hurriedly gathering the arrows from his last round. To his disappointment, he wasn't able to locate too many of the arrows due to the darkness that had crept up on him so quickly. Grumbling at his lack of attention to the time and how much it would cost him in arrows, he snatched the large knife and carefully slid it into place within his quiver. Finally, sliding his bow into place over his right shoulder, he turned toward the treeline to begin the journey back to his house and Tins's inevitable shouting.

He froze. Which way had he entered the clearing? He felt his stomach drop as if he had just swallowed a large stone. The gravity of the situation hit him and he began to tremble, fear growing in his chest as he slowly scanned the trees around him.

How could I be so careless?! He thought in exasperation. *Why didn't I mark my path of entry before I got distracted?!*

Marric's heart began to beat faster as his fear reached a peak. His senses heightened and it was as if he could see, hear, and smell everything around him so acutely. A snap rang out behind him in the trees and he whipped around expecting another wolf to leap out at him. A flash of movement to his left made him spin in that direction. Reaching back, he grasped not his bow, but the handle of the knife, ready to yank it free in a moment. He spotted a hole in the brush and broken branches. Something had broken through the foliage here, and it was big.

Marric stopped, and a realization hit him. *He* had fallen through the trees earlier that afternoon. Relief flooded his body from head to toe as if a wave of cold water rushed around him.

Heaving a huge sigh, he relaxed his hand and pulled his arm away from his quiver and the deadly weapon there. Stalking to the disturbed plants, he peered into the dark. Even though he really couldn't see well, this somehow felt right and familiar. Smiling to himself and remembering his almost breakdown just moments before, he stepped into the almost black to feel his way home.

Fortunately, the trek back seemed shorter than the journey into the forest. As he walked, he swore to himself that he'd never go that far again. The encounter with the wolf had been far too much excitement for him today, possibly for the next month. Marric saw a bit of light—firelight, poking through the trees in front of him and he sped up his pace. If it hadn't been for that man, probably a hunter with immense skill, he'd have died at the claws of that monstrous wolf.

May Lanser bless that man.

As he reached the edge of the darkened forest, his feet hit something odd. It felt like . . . cloth. Reaching down, he grabbed what indeed was cloth. Holding the cloth up to the waning sunlight, he saw blue; a blue dress and white apron, perfectly clean except for a bit of dirt from sitting on the ground.

Lanser's beard! Could it be?!

Marric remembered the strange woman's choice of footwear below her simple dress and marveled. Now she was wandering around the forest doing who knows what without her dress on. That, combined with the strange flying knife that had saved him was enough to make him want to leave the forest as quickly as possible.

What sort of woman is this?

Shaking his head, he rushed through the field to the fence on the far side. He hadn't come directly through the forest in line with his home, but rather a few houses down. He hopped the fence easily and walked behind the houses to his own. Only moments before entering did Marric realize that he couldn't enter his home with a woman's dress in his hands.

Blushing furiously, he scanned his surroundings and finally shoved the dress and apron into a crate of potatoes by their neighbor's home.

By mar, could she be walking around . . . naked? He blushed a deeper red at that thought. To get his mind off of the idea, he walked quickly to the door and pushed it open a bit. The sound he heard locked his joints and brought a more horrible fear than what he'd experienced in the forest.

His father was laughing as he entertained apparent guests in their home. The sound of entertaining and laughing wasn't what gave him pause. It was a voice that Marric recognized, but only because the sound had been burned into his ears by fear.

It was the long-haired man and his two companions.

Chapter 3

The laughter was loud and raucous, shoving its way into Marric's face as he peered through the crack in the door. He could see his father sitting at the table, a mug of ale in his right hand, talking loudly and gesturing in a grand manner, obviously telling some story. He also could see another man sitting just to the right of his father. This one had short, dark brown hair and dark brown eyes that were almost black. He wore a beard, though it was also cropped close to his face. His chin jutted out in an unusual fashion and seemed a bit larger than normal.

Marric was sure that he'd never seen this man's face before, but he somehow knew who it was. This was one of the hooded men from the night before. Perhaps the one that addressed the leader as S'ren. One might have thought that Marric was overreacting and that he couldn't be sure that all three men were in his home waiting for him. If it weren't for that voice.

He heard him. The long-haired man called S'ren. He couldn't forget the voice that struck fear in his chest the previous night. The man who journeyed seemingly far just to retrieve a boy—to retrieve *him*, for some unknown reason. Before he could stop himself, an image came to his mind of this man chasing Marric with a sword. Marric imagined being tied by the hands and trailing behind this man's horse, a captive for the rest of his life. Had this happened to Jord as well?

He stared for what seemed like an eternity before realizing that they hadn't seen him peeking through the cracked door. As slowly as possible, he eased the door closed and backed away from the house. His mind was spinning as he thought about what he had to do. There was really only one thing that he could do: run. He had to run. The way that these men had gained favor in his father's eyes, and undoubtedly Tins's eyes as well, meant that these men were far more crafty and intelligent than he had already assumed.

Perhaps he could hide somewhere, like at Crents's house. Or at the Constable's office. No, those would be the first places his father would check. What about across town at a stranger's home? That just seemed silly. The town was small enough anyway that hiding there wouldn't buy him much time at all.

He wasn't sure where or how, but running seemed his only option. Marric was alarmed at how logical it seemed and how at ease he felt with the decision. The only question that remained was where. Where could he run? The next town was ages away—so far, that he wouldn't make it on foot before running out of food and supplies. He could steal a horse and increase his chances of making it out, though.

Yes. Stealing a horse would make this possible. Marric hated stealing for this purpose, but it seemed to him that he could justify it in light of his situation. The town's only poor creature was mostly skin and bones, but still strong enough to carry one man and some supplies. Feeling comfortable with this plan, he started toward the front of his home and the thick vines granting access to his bedroom. As he rounded the corner, he heard the side door open where he'd just been standing.

"I only need to relieve myself!" the man shouted. "I'll be back before you know it!"

Marric shivered knowing that he'd missed this man by only seconds. Holding still for signs of trouble, he listened as the man finished his business, then went back into the house to the laughter inside. Marric waited for a few moments then, feeling the cool evening breeze blow down the street and into his face and hair. Fortunately, it was the warm season, so the air was fresh and cool. That would make his journey more comfortable at least. Marric hugged the wall of his house to the ivy and picked a thick bunch to climb. He noted the possibility of the vines breaking, as it had the tendency to do, and was more deliberate in his selection as he made his way to his second-story bedroom window.

Slipping into the room, he crossed quickly to the mattress and retrieved the hidden knife, rope, and even the parchment. Marric wasn't sure if that would come in handy, but since he'd never left home in this way, he thought any provision would be helpful, no matter how insignificant it seemed. Sliding across his room quietly, he grabbed his quill and reached for his inkwell. In his haste, he nudged the side of the inkwell and knocked it from his desk. Scrambling to catch it, he flung himself on the desk, grasping for it as it fell to the ground with a loud thunk. The laughter downstairs halted, and Marric's heart pounded in his ears.

"Marric?! Is that yous up'n there?" Narim called from the room downstairs.

Marric held his breath, hoping in vain that this might make them unhear the dropping of the inkwell. Footsteps sounded on the stairs and he knew that he'd been caught. Time seemed to stand still as he thought of what would happen when they found him in his room. He'd blown it, there was no escaping now. How could he be so stupid?! He shouldn't have been so rushed!

The steps grew closer as he turned toward the door, just waiting for it to open and his father to step through to confront him. He was preparing what he'd say when strong hands grabbed his shoulders and hauled him *toward* the door in a flash. Letting out a yelp, Marric was shoved into the wall just to the side of the door and a hand pressed to his lips.

"Shh! If we're going to get out of this, you need to not make the *slightest* sound."

It was a woman's voice, one that he vaguely recognized.

The mysterious woman from the market! He thought. *The woman in blue. Who was this woman?! How did she get into my room?*

He remembered her dress stuffed in the potato crate and a lump filled his throat. What was she *wearing*? He felt his face warm and he flushed intensely at the thought of this woman, body pressed up against his tightly on the wall wearing who knows what.

His door opened in front of them and candlelight flashed into the room, brightening it just so that he could see his companion's face. He was relieved to see that she was indeed dressed in something decent. Oddly, though, she was dressed in men's clothing. All he could see at the moment was a long-sleeved black top. She narrowed her eyes at him, and he got the message clearly. *Don't move or make a sound.*

"Marric?" his father spoke into the dark room. "Marric, are yeh in here?"

The woman held perfectly still against him. Narim stayed in the doorway while the two of them were blocked from his view behind the door. It felt odd to be hiding from his own father, but what choice did he have? Especially now with a strange woman pressed against him.

"Well I'll be a spinehog's dinner," he said after glancing around. "Ain't nobody here."

Pausing for a moment longer, Narim backed into the hallway and pulled the door closed. They waited until they heard the man's heavy steps reach the lower floor before relaxing. The woman nimbly stepped away from Marric and said, "What else do you need before we go?"

We?! Marric thought in surprise. *Why does she think she is coming along?*

The woman huffed in annoyance and said desperately, "Boy! We only have moments to leave before your parents get worried and come looking for you. Get to it!"

"They aren't both my parents. It's just my Pa," was all he could say as he bent to snatch the inkwell. After securing it with the rest of his supplies, he turned to see her standing by the window, moonlight on her face. She looked amused at his comment.

"Well?" she said, gesturing to the open window. "Show a girl how it's done?"

Her comment confused him. Based on how he'd seen her hop the fence earlier, she was not some 'girl' needing help. Regardless, he narrowed his eyes and made his way to the window.

Pausing just next to the sill, he finally asked, "Why are you helping me?"

"Let's just say I'm personally invested in your safety."

"So the men are dangerous, then?"

"It's hard to say, but I don't know them and the swords they carry don't inspire confidence that they are looking for you for diplomatic reasons."

This conclusion seemed reasonable to him, despite this woman's strange nature. A part of him irked at the knowledge that he did not know this woman or what her intentions were, but she'd already saved him twice. Satisfied, he turned and climbed out the window. Climbing down seemed easier for some reason, as if he had found a new purpose in his escape. He plopped to the dirt road and turned up to see the woman in blue repelling the house effortlessly. She touched down with so little sound, it seemed impossible.

He took a moment to look at her more closely. Her pitch black hair was tied back in a tight ponytail. Her almond-shaped eyes were grey. She was alarmingly attractive considering how manly she seemed in her black pants and shirt.

Noticing Marric's scrutinous gaze, she furrowed her brow and began walking along the side of his home.

"Wait," he said softly.

She stopped, keeping her back to him.

"If I'm going to trust you to help me, at least tell me your name." Marric explained. "I mean, you know mine already."

She didn't speak immediately, but after a beat said quietly, "Oh good, you don't always sound like an uneducated buffoon like everyone else." She spun around to face him after that and said, "The name's Janis, kid." With that, she turned and stalked around the side of the house.

At least I got a name from her. Something tells me that I'm lucky to have even gotten that, he thought grimly.

Marric followed her around the side of the house. The second moon, Mallan, shone bright above. He could see the alley between the houses clearly with the crates piled on the left. Just as he passed the side door to his home, it burst open toward him, almost knocking him over. A cry of surprise startled Marric again and he turned to find himself a few feet away from the long-haired leader of the visiting pack of men.

The man had crouched slightly into a ready position with his right hand extended to the side as if waiting to catch something. After realizing that there wasn't a threat, he relaxed and stood up, studying Marric closely.

"Oh, you must be Marric. How do you do, my boy?" he said with a slight smile, extending his hand.

A force gripped Marric by the left arm and dragged him to the field quickly. Dazed, he let it pull him away, running along with it. It took a moment, as he was tugged over the fence and into the field, for Marric to realize it was the woman, Janis, pulling him along. Snapping to, he began working his feet, charging to the field. He heard the man shout something, but it was lost in the rustle of the grass and branches of the trees.

Running in the field was challenging with its uneven ground, but the night made it so much harder even with Stellan's light. He stumbled at least a dozen times before they reached the treeline.

Out of breath, Marric huffed out, "T's too dark. I can't see in there!"

It took a considerable amount of time for him to gasp the words out, but Janis seemed to not care a bit. She grabbed his shirt and pulled him into the dark.

How can she be so confident?! She didn't seem the least bit worried about the animals and creatures in the forest, not to mention the fact that it was pitch black.

"You still have my dagger don't you?" she said gruffly.

"Well yeah, it's right here in my—"

"Good. That's one of my favorites and I wouldn't be happy if you had left it."

"—hang on. *You* are the one that killed the wolf?! How did you do that?! I mean, it was in the air and you—"

"Shh!"

He lowered his voice, but kept on while they walked in the dark.

"Where did you learn to do that? And how can you see here in the dark?"

Janis sighed. "Are you always this chatty? Because that would make me reconsider taking this job."

This job? He thought, perplexed. *What does she mean by that?!*

"Look . . . ma'am. I just don't understand what's happening. I almost died out here before and here we are without hunters or soldiers—"

"We don't need them. I'm all we need."

She stopped in front of him, making him bump into her softly. "The dagger, now."

Marric snapped to it, alarmed at her tone and the fact that she stopped so suddenly. Fumbling for his quiver, he felt through the arrows until he touched the cloth-wrapped handle. After sliding it free, he held it out as Janis yanked it free.

"Look, boy. I'm an assassin, and I guarantee I'm scarier than anything out here. I was paid a nice chunk of money to keep you safe, and I fog well will."

At that, she grabbed his arm once again and continued leading him deeper into the forest. Marric could hear her dagger snapping in the air every once in a while as Janis chopped a branch here or a bush there. He thought it was silly that they were supposed to be quiet and she was making all this ruckus. Their progress was slow, probably because of him, and as they moved forward, the air seemed to get cooler and more humid. Despite the circumstances of their situation, Marric quite enjoyed the smell of the clean earth and fresh air. He closed his eyes—he couldn't see anything anyway—and took in the smell of wet earth calmly.

A breath caught in Janis's throat and Marric opened his eyes to see what had happened. He could see her face outlined by the trees behind her. Her eyebrows knit in stress as she scanned the area behind them. It took a few moments for Marric to realize that he could *see* her at all. Spinning around himself, he saw a bright light shining through the trees. It was like nothing he'd ever seen before. It was the brightest candle he'd ever seen. But the odd part was that it wasn't flickering—it was constant and unchanging, as if the candle was frozen and unmoving. It was also blue, a shade he'd never seen in light before now.

What the— he thought as he stared at the light in the distance.

"Come on!" Janis said forcefully. She tugged harder on his arm and they pushed into the forest. It was a bit easier now that Marric could see from the light behind him. As they moved, the trees in front of them appeared to brighten with a bluish hue. Whoever was behind them was moving in very quickly. They had the advantage of light, after all.

"Lanser's beard, they are gaining on us!" Janis gasped in frustration, likely at how slow their pace was because of Marric's clumsiness.

Janis stopped suddenly and forced Marric into a bush to her left.

"Down, boy. Don't make the slightest sound. I'll take care of this as quickly as possible."

"But Janis—"

"Quiet! I'll only be a few minutes."

And she was gone. She seemed to melt into the darkness quickly with her black clothes. Marric stared at the place she had entered the trees, wondering how she managed to move so quickly and quietly on the uneven ground.

"Marric!" a voice shouted in the dark.

He crouched lower in the brush, heart pounding in his chest like a drum during their hot season celebration.

"Marric! Son, we're not here to hurt you!" the voice said, growing louder.

Fleeing from the sound, Marric slid backward into the brush until his back hit a tree. The light and the voice were to his right as he pressed against the tree, praying to Lanser that they wouldn't find him there. As the man, voice deep and foreboding, came closer, the trees grew bright, casting eerie sideways shadows on the foliage in front of him. During the day, the forest had been eerie enough, but in this constant blue light, it seemed even more threatening and ominous.

Light burst into Marrics eyes suddenly, causing him to squint as he heard a loud clang from the direction of the strange blue Light. His head ached at the sudden bright flash in the darkness. Consecutive clangs were followed by curses from the man as someone engaged him in combat. The trees in front of Marric flashed as the blue Light danced on them, seemingly in rhythm with the clangs from the clashing weapons. He chanced looking to the right toward the flashing blue light. He wasn't prepared for what he saw.

It was what looked like a rod of light, roughly the length of his arm, perhaps a bit longer, but it was so bright that it took a few moments for

Marric's eyes to adjust. There it was, floating in the air in an inexplicable manner. Looking closely, he could see that the man was *holding* the Light in his hand. It flicked quickly and Marric heard another clang ring in the air. Focusing his gaze more closely, he realized that it was in the shape of a sword, though he wasn't sure exactly what kind.

"Wait! I'm not here to hurt you!" the man growled at Janis.

The sword of Light flew again in the air and another loud clang followed. In an instant, the Light disappeared, plunging the trees and Marric into darkness. It was blacker than before, leaving him with the burning outline of the sword in his vision.

Two beats later, the Light blazed again and there was a thwacking sound of metal hitting flesh and the thud of something hitting the ground. Marric heard Janis growl in frustration and he looked around the Light to see her facing the man, weaponless, but unwilling to back down.

"Peace, woman! I don't want to hurt you or the boy! We're here to protect him!" he shouted at her. Marric flipped his eyes to the man and saw that it was the leader of the three, the one with the long hair referred to as S'ren the night before.

"*Protect* him?!" Janis spat at the man, "Yet you bring this . . . *craft* here and try to kill me?!"

"Blast it, woman! Need I remind you that *you* attacked *me*?! I just needed a bit of light to find you in this blasted darkness because some of us can't see like cats in the dark! Can't a man defend himself?"

"I don't understand what strange wizardry this is, but you *will not* lay a hand on this boy without killing me first."

"Look, I know what this might look like, but there is an explanation. I do not intend on killing anyone. However, your threat will not stop me from my objective of getting Marric to safety."

"We've been over this, *I*—"

"Wait!" Marric called out loudly.

Janis and the man stopped and turned to look at Marric, who had crept out of the bushes to face them both. He wasn't sure what came over him—Janis was surely seething at the fact that he'd just blown his cover, but something the man said made him less nervous about the whole situation. He was also mesmerized by the glowing sword in the man's hand.

As his eyes fixed on the unusual weapon, he spoke up.

"What do you mean you're here to protect me? I think it's a bit odd that only in the matter of an hour, two people, both seemingly threatening, have mentioned protecting me. I'm just a teenager from a small town in the middle of nowhere. Can someone *please* tell me what is going on?"

The two protectors both started speaking at once, then stopped to glare at each other a moment. After a silent exchange between the two, the man gave a knowing look of defeat before Janis continued with her side of the story.

"I was paid a good sum of money to make sure that no harm came to you, Marric. And I make good on all the jobs that I take," she said candidly. "I may not know this man, but I tend to not trust mysterious men that carry swords and travel in packs."

The man scowled at this comment, obviously bothered by Janis's lack of common respect for strangers.

"But *why* . . . " Marric paused, not sure how to address her. ". . . Miss, would I need protection?"

Keeping her eyes on the man, Janis said slowly, "I don't know, but I know that very dangerous and influential people care enough to spend a pretty frond for you to stay alive."

The man seemed surprisingly relaxed, considering there was an assassin facing him, crouched and ready to pounce.

"Fortunately, I have an answer to that," the man said cooly. "But, to be honest, I'd rather have this discussion *not* in a dark forest with a raging madwoman threatening to kill me at any moment."

Janis actually smiled wickedly at this, as if she appreciated the description of herself.

What an odd character, Marric thought to himself.

"Whoever you are, woman, I say that we call it a draw at this moment and make our way back to Marric's home to talk like civilized people."

Janis sniffed at this. She kept herself poised to attack, refusing to relax despite the strange man pleading innocence. Marric watched as Janis glanced quickly to the side where her dagger fell. In an instant, she dashed to the dagger and snatched it. Spinning to the side, she flung the dagger quickly at the man who didn't see it coming as quickly as he should. He shifted sideways but was pierced in his left arm just above the elbow. He gasped in surprise and pain, but kept his ground, turning to face Janis again.

It happened so fast that Marric didn't see how the man hadn't been skewered through the middle. He bore up and prepared to engage the assassin again, this time a more determined look on his face.

"Stop!" Marric shouted. "I need to know what is going on! If you kill him, I won't find out what is happening!"

He didn't realize it, but he was starting to tear up, overwhelmed by what was happening. The stress from the situation left him with a slight headache and he was breathing hard, anxiety starting to take over. Marric looked toward the man and started to get a bit dizzy seeing the blood pouring down his left arm where the large dagger protruded.

"He's right! If you kill me, Marric will not be safe! Even *you*, albeit being so skilled at fighting, can't stop what's coming for this boy. This is beyond you, woman. You can't fight what's coming, no matter how fast or skilled you may be."

Janis looked at Marric, then back at the man.

"Why should I trust you to not harm him?" Janis said, teeth bared. "There is more at stake here than even you realize, fog it. If this boy dies, I'll likely be hunted by some cult group with a psychopath man leading them."

"What's this? A cult group?" the man asked, still gasping from the pain and holding his Light blade at the ready.

"*Watchlight* is all the man said. He had a band of people hidden all over. Admittedly, this is the first time I feel stressed about someone possibly overcoming my skills. It doesn't feel good."

The man gave a curious expression at that comment. Despite the sword sticking out of his upper arm, he stood up out of his crouch and lowered his mystical weapon tip to the ground.

"You were paid by Watchlight to protect this boy? Blast it, they already know about him," the man looked at Marric. "If I put my weapon away, will you at least refrain from killing me now?" he said while looking away from Janis, which seemed bold to Marric. He turned to look at the assassin after that. "At least until we can talk about this? If it doesn't pan out, you can kill me, woman."

"Her name is Janis." Marric said suddenly. The man turned in surprise at Marric's tone and timing. He stared at him for a moment. Marric wasn't sure why he felt like speaking for her. Something about how she saved his life in the forest made him feel strangely loyal to her.

"Janis, then. Don't be alarmed, I'll put my sword away, but we still need light to make our way back to the house."

Marric stared at the man's bright sword as it shrank into nothingness—returning the group and the forest around them, into the darkness. A moment later, a smaller light, the ball he had seen before, blossomed to life in the same hand, bathing them in a softer blue light. It resembled a marble, small in size, but the Light was steady and blue, much like the color of the sky in the hot months with the sun high in the sky. He didn't have to squint at the man anymore, which he appreciated, but the nature of the Light made Marric uneasy—it seemed so strange, so unnatural. It was like experiencing a déjà vu, the situation seemingly familiar, but at the same time, new.

No one said anything for quite some time, the tension from the fight leaving them all unsure how to react. The man was the first to move, lifting his left arm to examine the blade piercing his arm, blood trickling off and onto the ground. He seemed remarkably calm for having a knife through his upper arm. Lowering his hand, Marric was startled to see the small sphere of Light remain in the air as if it was being held up. This further deepened the unsettling feeling in Marric's chest. Setting his face in a determined way, the man gripped the knife with his right hand and yanked the blade free, grimacing in pain and sucking in a sharp breath. Pausing for a moment to breath out the pain, the man tossed the blade to Janis, who caught it deftly. Her face showed surprise at the man willingly forfeiting the weapon that had nearly caused his death just moments before.

"If you don't mind, I'd better get this taken care of."

He placed his right hand over the wound, blood slipping through his fingers and dripping continuously to the ground. Marric lost the adrenaline rush from moments before and felt his head getting light at the sight of the blood. Closing his eyes, the man appeared to be concentrating, as if in meditation. For a moment, nothing happened. Then a blue Light, the same color as the sphere and sword just before it, leaked out from beneath his hand. The Light was soft, softer than the sphere, and persisted for just a few heartbeats before retreating below his hand. The man let out a sigh of relief and moved his hand away. Where the cut had been was clean skin, no sign of the wound. It had been gushing blood just moments before, causing Marric to marvel further at this man's strange power.

The man looked up from his work and nodded approvingly to his left arm. Looking up at Marric, he got a somewhat amused look on his face as he saw the reaction from the young boy.

"I know that this is strange—perhaps unsettling, but I am not here to harm you or Janis, Marric." the man explained.

Marric continued to stare, sifting through his emotions and not knowing how to handle it all. He'd gone from terror, to surprise, to relief and now curiosity so quickly that he thought his mind might crack. His headache had increased from crying just moments before, and his nausea from seeing the wound and blood had not yet fled his stomach. But he couldn't help but stare and marvel at the strange occurrences of the night.

Not knowing how to reach Marric in this state, the man adopted another approach.

"It's a very handy gift, I have to say. It has saved not only my life, but other's lives on numerous occasions," he said, as if testing the waters.

This man's attempt for a positive reaction failed on Marric, as he was not in much of a stable state at the moment. The man looked frustrated and put his right arm to his forehead, his face adopting a thoughtful look. Janis, looking equally as perplexed as Marric, but not nearly as affected, stalked to him and put her hand on his shoulder. She shook him softly, hoping to bring him back to reality.

"Marric, you're in shock. As much as I hate it, the man's right, we ought to take you home where you can calm down a bit," she said firmly. When he didn't move, Janis grabbed both of his shoulders and gave him a hard shake. This rocked him enough to cause him to gasp and focus back on the situation.

He slurred the words 'sorry, I'm okay', and shook his head to clear his mind. His sickness didn't leave, nor the uneasy feeling from the strangeness of the man's show of power, but he at least was aware again.

"Good. Perhaps let's start with the easy bit. I'm Avryn. I came from Terris Green, a land ten days ride north of here. I've come for you, Marric, because I'm here to talk to you about your true nature and potential. I have a great deal to explain to you, and I think it's best that we do so within the comfort and privacy of your home."

Chapter 4

Janis sat on a stool in the corner of the small dining room. The room contained a table and chairs that looked a little on the fancier side for a lowly fletcher. The only other furniture were three beat up bar stools and a table with a vase of dead flowers by the front door.

I didn't realize fletchers made much profit off of their work, but perhaps I don't know the value of trade skills, thought Janis to herself. *Either that, or the man is good at duping those to trade their work for his.*

It had taken almost an hour for the three of them to make it back to Marric's house, despite the glowing light. Marric had to pause a few times to get his bearings. He was left very affected by the fight that broke out. Janis remembered her first time witnessing combat fighting and the sick feeling she got watching people getting injured or dying. She thought that Marric was being a bit dramatic, though. She had been only twelve the first time she encountered a similar situation, but then again, her childhood was far from orthodox.

Janis wasn't sure what to think about the man Avryn, or the strange display of power he'd given, but she was not ready to trust him as quickly as Marric was. For this reason, she had intentionally positioned herself away from the group on the stools at the side of the room.

That could really get him killed someday, Janis thought, *Trust should never be so easily bought.*

Then again, who *did* she trust? So far, there was no one. The few people that got close to gaining her trust lost it far too quickly. She wouldn't make that mistake again. As an assassin, trust in someone was a risk that was never worth taking. Money was the only thing that was reliable in this profession, and even that wasn't foolproof.

When they had arrived, one of Avryn's companions, Harmel, had somehow known that something had happened in the forest. He immediately began asking questions about the fight and if Avryn needed him to 'bash heads' in. Perhaps it was that Avryn looked a bit worn from the events, but nothing seemed obvious to alert him to the previous events.

Harmel was a beast of man. He was a bit shorter with bulging muscles that matched his stocky figure, and a squarish face. His dark brown hair was shaved close to his head and his beard and mustache were kept closely cut in the same way. In fact, it almost looked like the hair from his head was continuous all the way down the sides of his face, framing his mouth. The front door opened and Avryn's other companion walked in with a bucket of water. This one, called Shrell, was a handspan taller than Harmel, and was slender, almost lanky. His hair was also dark brown, wavy, and long in length, but seemed short as it clung to his scalp closely. Janis didn't know what to think of this man. His green eyes were unsettling to her.

"'Ere's the bucket for you, Avryn." Shrell said. "It'd be best if you drank up right well. Seem's a good scuffle you had with this one, eh?"

Avryn chuckled a bit at that. "A good scuffle is not how I'd describe that, Shrell. Janis is more than capable with the blade. I feel lucky to still have all my limbs."

He looked at her with his blue eyes, a smile on his face and smile lines spreading out from the sides of his eyes. It was clear that he intended the comment as a compliment and a way to disarm Janis's cold stare, but she didn't oblige. Janis merely stared flatly at him as if his comment meant nothing to her.

Avryn stared at her for just a moment longer before clearing his throat, clearly uncomfortable with how ineffective his comment was, and looked at Marric instead. Shrell took the opportunity to take the fourth seat at the table and Marric's father settled onto one of the other stools in the room. They all looked at Avryn, waiting for the explanation that he had promised them before they had left the dark forest. As they stared at him, he shifted in his chair, a thoughtful look on his face as he tried to select the best words for an explanation.

"I suppose a proper introduction is in order. As I mentioned earlier, my name is Avryn Stoll. These two here are Harmel and Shrell Lindst. Even though their appearances don't show it, they are indeed brothers. They accompanied me here, as they are both fine swordsmen. This increased the likelihood of me getting through the forest to Wurren safely. We all hail from Terris Green, a sanctuary southeast of Stilten, a city quite a bit larger than Wurren that is ten or so days north of here, traveling by horseback, of course."

He said that as if everyone in the room knew what that distance meant, even though they really didn't. Janis had never liked riding horses. When she had first learned, it hadn't gone well. The horse had been apparently terrified of her for whatever reason, and had ended up launching itself in a mad run to knock her off its back. Her reaction, of course, was to protect herself the way that she always did, by shoving her dagger deep into its neck to kill the creature. The horse trainer was livid with her solution and she was forced to pay a fine for the horse's death. After that, Janis just tried to be fit enough to travel everywhere she went by foot. However, she recognized the need for travel by horse and had mastered the skill anyway.

Janis looked at Marric and then at his father, gauging their reactions to the man's comments. They both looked expectantly at Avryn, waiting for more useful information. Neither appeared to care much about what the man had said so far.

Avryn continued when no further questions were asked. "I will say what I'm about to with as much discretion as possible, because it will perhaps sound a bit daft. Also, I want you to understand the seriousness of it all."

He paused, taking a moment to think a bit more before he continued. "Marric, the three of us traveled from Terris Green because we believe that there are unsavory people after you. They come from a cult group that call themselves Watchlight. They are very dangerous and their intentions are not just. We hoped to reach you before they did and get you to a safe place where you can fulfill your potential."

Janis glared at the man after hearing this. There was no doubt that what he said about Watchlight was right; they were bad people, especially given the way that they had cornered her into doing what they asked. It wasn't like she had any type of loyalty towards the group, but the way that he referred to them so casually and in such a forward way made her uncomfortable. They had cornered her so easily and could have killed her so quickly that underestimating this group was not the right thing to do. She hoped that's not something Avryn was doing in this instance.

Avryn paused and let out a sigh. "I think that the best thing to do here is level with you, lad. This world isn't as simple as it may seem to you in this small town. There is a conflict going on between good and evil. Around two hundred years ago, a strange thing began happening to people throughout the land. People began displaying powers that no one could describe. At first, it seemed like a miracle because the one thing that all the powers had in common was Light. This one could heal, that one could create objects from light, another could see into the future, eyes glowing. After a time, these people became very popular, profiting off their gifts in one way or another. Then, when some of those with the powers couldn't learn to harness it effectively, others began to be frightened. The ungifted forced those with the powers out of their towns, threatening to kill them if they didn't leave willingly.

"Those with the power of Light had to go into hiding, lest they be killed by the frightened people of the world. People decided to stop talking about the strange powers and purged all records of the incidents. Soon it became a mere myth, and they shut out the truth of those with the power of Light. Nowadays, it isn't spoken of at all. I'm positive, and you can confirm this, that no one here has heard of such a thing, am I right?"

Marric shook his head, choosing not to speak at all. Janis narrowed her eyes at the man. She didn't believe any of the nonsense that he'd just said. He was clearly spinning a web of lies to draw them in, to gain their trust through his fake knowledge. Whatever had happened in the forest was some dark magic. Her skin crawled at the memory of the strange powers.

When no one protested, Avryn drew his lips tightly together in a thin line, preparing himself for the next words.

"Marric, we have reason to believe that you are one of those with the powers of Light, or what we like to call a *Lightbearer*."

Marric started at the comment, his face showing confusion and disbelief. Narim, seeing the look on his son's face, stood up and walked over to where his son was sitting and put his hand on his shoulder. He faced Avryn with a determined look on his face.

"M'boy is nuttin' of the sort. He's jus' the boy of a fletcher that happens t'be quite educated. But he ain't none of these . . . what's it? Light people."

"Mister Norst, this isn't an accusation. It's a statement of fact. He—"

"A statement of *fact*?" Janis said accusingly, standing suddenly. "You sound like a lunatic here to make ridiculous claims for who knows what reason."

Her quick motion and tone caused Avryn's companions to stand as well, hands moving toward their swords.

"Now, hold on!" Avryn said loudly. "Harmel, Shrell, she doesn't mean any trouble. She's merely frustrated at the strangeness of what I've said. Please, sit."

The two men slowly pulled their hands from the swords and the thicker one, Harmel, settled back in his seat. Shrell, however, remained standing. Both sets of eyes remained trained on Janis, prepared for any signs of trouble. Janis smirked at them.

"Good doggies," she teased.

This caused them to glare even more at her as she continued to stand, seeming to loom over those at the table.

Avryn sighed, rubbing his forehead with his thumb and fingers. "Despite what you do or don't believe, you are one of these Lightbearers, Marric. As am I. What you saw in the forest was the display of these powers. And because of these, you need to understand that you must come with us, for your own safety."

Marric just sat there, a look of confusion and frustration on his face, staring at the table top. Janis actually felt bad for the boy. She knew the feeling herself. Just seeing him caused her chest to tighten, remembering times when she had felt the same way. Her mind flashed to a version of herself, small and weak, bones showing through her thin, starving figure. She sat with her back against the wall, staring at the two bodies on the floor. She rocked slightly, feeling sick, not knowing what to do. The horror of the scene and events from the night branded in her vision like spots left after a bright light bursts into your vision. It was a combination of feelings that left a child's mind in a thoughtless, lost state. First, the horror of seeing violence so closely, yet making it through without harm. Second, the realization that she was completely alone and that her survival was dependent on only herself. Third, a loss of the sense of reality. Such realizations had left her in that stupor for days. Janis marveled that she hadn't starved without eating for as long as she had.

Lost in thought for what seemed like forever, but was probably only moments, her eyes refocused on Marric. There was a palpable awkwardness in the air as the whole group stared at the subject of all the conversation. She felt a bit like a spectator in a gallery, watching a statue and hoping that it would behave or act in an unexpected way. Talking to it would result in nothing, but just staring at it for a long time felt unnatural and strange, as if something might happen out of the ordinary.

Just as the silence in the room seemed to reach its maximum, the door opened and a woman walked in. Janis felt a small flame of anger replace the sorrow in her chest as she recognized Marric's stepmother. She didn't know much about the woman—probably not an ideal position to be in as the protector of this woman's stepson—but she felt that she didn't need to know her. The first day she'd arrived and located Marric, she witnessed the woman verbally abuse the boy and threaten to physically abuse him. She knew the type. This woman was power hungry and she liked her position of lording over others. Oh yes, there was a special place in Ugglyn's house for a person like that. Janis had to stop herself multiple times from knifing the woman in her sleep and ridding Marric of the insufferable woman once and for all. The only thing that had stopped her from doing just that was the chaos such an event would cause not only in their home, but in the whole town. It was small and significant enough that a crime such as that would be the buzz of conversation for months, possibly even years.

The woman, Tins was her name, stopped as she came through the door and stared at the man with long hair sitting across from Marric. Her eyes flashed to her husband, then scanned the rest of the guests as if she was sizing up who she should confront first. Her eyes finally landed on Janis, and there was a moment of confusion which flashed to slightly wide-eyed surprise. After a moment, she narrowed them at Janis, as if she suspected something of the woman. Janis returned the narrowed-eyed gaze obligingly, putting a little bit of 'I dare you to challenge me' into the look as well. In the end, Tins looked away. Janis felt quite triumphant after the exchange and a smirk settled on her face.

Tins looked worse for wear this evening as if she had gotten handled by a few ruffians on the streets. Or, knowing the nature of the woman, perhaps *she* roughed up the ruffians herself, leaving her a bit disheveled. She wasn't overly sloppy, but it was obvious that she had done something pretty physical, leaving her a bit dirty, apron a bit crooked, hair unkempt, some strands falling out of the tight bun at the back of her head. She held a couple loaves of bread in her left hand, and a satchel of what looked like assorted vegetables in the other. After her surveillance of the crowd, she looked back at Narim, eyebrows suddenly high in what was clearly forced innocence, from Janis's perspective.

"Why Narim, yeh din' tell me tha' we'd be havin' guests this'n evenin'. I ain't dun cooked nuttin' fer supper t'night. If I'd known they'd be 'ere, I'd fer sure have—"

"Dear Tins, it ain't no trouble at all, eh? We been enjoyin' ourselves quite nicely t'night with the ale we got," Narim assured her. Then, looking a bit sheepish, he added, "But now tha' yer 'ere, we'd sure fancy a bit of tha' loaf yeh gots there, eh?"

The woman stared at her husband for a moment, not sure how to handle the request, then let a cheerful smile spread across her face. She didn't say anything, but just nodded and made her way past the guests at the table and went into the kitchen to prepare the food. Likely no one else noticed, but slight movements never went unnoticed by Janis. She knew clearly how much Tins loathed her husband's request and how angry the woman felt about not being told about the guests beforehand. It was how she squinted her eyes narrow during the smile. They were too thin to have been part of a genuine smile. She had also clenched her jaw quite tightly when the request from Narim first came. Janis could see her jaw muscles tighten and bulge slightly as she held back what likely was an unladylike response to the request. Moments later, she came back carrying a small tray with the bread.

"'Ere yeh go, Narim. Would yeh like me t'get s'more ale fer yous?" she said, in a tone almost sickeningly sweet.

Janis cringed at the thickness in her response. It was practically dripping with sarcasm, but it was delivered so subtly that she was sure she was the only one that picked up on the hidden meaning behind it all.

Narim looked pleased at her response and only nodded to her in confirmation. Tins kept smiling as she nodded to the other men at the table and moved to retrieve their mugs to refresh them. Harmel and Shrell both politely shook their heads as she reached for theirs, but Avryn happily surrendered his mug to the woman. She last went for Narim's mug, and in one sweeping motion, scooped up his cup and threw her stepson a cold glare before turning and heading into the kitchen area.

It took a moment for Janis to remember where they had left off, and based on the postures and facial expressions of the rest of the group, she suspected that this was the case with the rest of them as well. During the silence, Tins returned with the two full mugs of ale. As Janis watched, she realized how smooth the plump woman was with all of her movements. For some reason, this made Janis uncomfortable. It wasn't necessarily unusual for a woman to be fluid and controlled in her motions, but based on her profession, and not to mention her physique, it seemed unnatural and out of place.

"How can you be sure that I'm one of these . . . people that you say? I have never done anything out of the ordinary. I mean, other than speaking normally and learning to shoot a bow." Marric said, still staring at the table.

The last comment made his father look at him in confusion. This clearly wasn't common knowledge in the family. Janis felt a bit impressed with the boy. He definitely wasn't half bad with the bow, based on what she'd seen in the forest earlier that day. He had to have practiced quite a bit over the years to be somewhat capable with the weapon, yet his father had no idea of his skill at all.

Perhaps there is hope for the boy yet. Keeping a secret like that for so long means he has more promise than I thought, Janis thought to herself.

"Marric, you haven't experienced any of these yet because you haven't—oh, how's the best way to say it?" Avryn knit his eyebrows together, clearly thinking hard. "You haven't come into your powers yet. It's called *intar'nst* in the old language. The closest word in our current language would be something like *awakening*. It's the event of a Lightbearer coming into their powers fully. Normally, this happens when the person is twelve or thirteen, but in your case, it's a bit late."

Janis was so focused on what Avryn was saying that she didn't realize Tins had stayed in the room with them after delivering the bread and ale to the table. The woman was standing near her husband, but had her eyes trained on Avryn. The fact that the man had just told her stepson he was some supernatural person and would become a creature of power didn't seem to phase her. She just seemed . . . angry. Like she was mad that these men had come and disturbed her perfectly normal life. She appeared to be poised to attack the man at any moment, her posture straight, but forward.

Avryn and his companions shared a look with each other as if they were having a conversation of their own, weighing their options and where to take the conversation next. The concern on Avryn's face made Janis wonder what additional implications there were to this 'awakening' he had referenced. He was undoubtedly hiding something and didn't want to alarm anyone in the room more. The conversation seemed to be like a fire dying with its last flickers in the night as the cold ultimately overtook it.

In an attempt to both distract Marric from whatever plagued his mind at the moment and to rekindle the conversation, Janis spoke out loudly.

"Then why by Lanser's beard did Watchlight employ me to protect Marric? If he really is some 'all powerful' Light person, then why not retrieve the boy themselves and take him away?"

Obviously, no one had intended on her adding much to the conversation, as they all turned with surprise to look at her.

"I can't say for sure," Avryn answered, "but the fact that you are here on their will indicates that they also were aware of Marric and his potential."

For the first time since they'd arrived, one of Avrn's companions spoke out. It was Shrell, the tall and lanky one. When he spoke, his voice was much more gravelly than Janis would have expected. It was low, very low for even a man, and sounded like the surface of a metal shovel being dragged along small rocks.

"S'ren, perhaps they were unwilling to risk their lives based on his age—"

"Now's not the time to speculate why they didn't come themselves," Avryn cut in, seeming suddenly impatient. "We can only thank Lanser for their untimeliness and consider it a win for the good side."

Janis stood again and this time pointed her finger directly at Avryn to emphasize her point.

"What does that even mean, the 'good side'? We don't know who you are or your intentions. I know that you are hiding something from us about this *awakening*." She said the word as if it was a disease to emphasize her point. "What are you holding back? If you fully intend on me allowing you to continue speaking with Marric, you better fog well give me a good reason."

The man's face turned red in a combination of embarrassment and anger at being called out like this, and he clenched his teeth as if holding back the emotion. Her comment had the intended effect, and she felt elated inside knowing that her intimidation worked so well. It had taken her a few years to learn the skill of being intimidating. When she'd first been on her own, she was too 'girlish', which amounted to nothing more than being doted upon or mistreated by pigs claiming to be men.

"I'm not trying to be elusive to trick you into trusting us. I was hoping to learn more about Marric and help him see that we are here to help before bringing in the more complicated pieces of the situation. This may not be the place or the time for the boy to hear the more . . . difficult parts—"

"Stop talking about me like I'm not even here!" Marric shouted suddenly, "I may be only sixteen, but I can handle whatever you say."

He looked Avryn right in the face.

"Tell me *everything.*"

The man nodded slightly to him, gaining resolve before opening his mouth. Even though he was respecting the boy's wishes, there was a sort of pain in his eyes as he began to explain.

"There are a lot of things in motion right now, but I will explain what I can with what time we have. I must reiterate the gravity of the situation and tell you that we don't have much time. I can only assume that Watchlight has representatives here in Wurren already prepared to snatch you at any moment. I mean, besides Janis."

He threw a worried glance at Janis as if she was a card that he hadn't expected to enter play in this game. She had found herself in situations like this on numerous occasions. Being in the profession of assassinations pretty much made you the wild card in every game of life. Now, she was an assassin taken completely out of her element. She felt forced into a role that she had never experienced while being in a situation far more complicated than she liked. Assassins learn quickly to stay out of big problems and to prioritize anonymity. You only needed to know information regarding your mark and not anything bigger. Assassins that failed at this tended to get themselves killed. Janis feared she was making that fatal mistake right now. But . . . there was something drawing her to the truth. She hoped that it wasn't a protective attachment to the boy—that would be even more foolish.

"What you need to know is this: the powers of the Lightbearers are being abused in some situations. At first, all Lightbearers banded together to create a protected society for themselves. We all agreed that this society should be carefully built to be self sufficient and a place where we could thrive, not only in life, but in our powers. It was supposed to be a place unknown to all where only Lightbearers could live and learn. After some time, there was a group of Lightbearers that fell to pride, claiming that they shouldn't fear normal people, but rule them. They believed that Lightbearers should use their powers to fight back and take control of the common man. There was a division, and a number of Lightbearers left the society to create their own, stating that they would destroy any that stood in their way for dominance. This is Watchlight. They are actively finding and recruiting Lightbearers, both those with their powers and those who have yet to come into their powers. I can say with diffinity that they are the 'bad side'. They kill mercilessly. Not only men, women, and children without powers, but also Lightbearers that will not join their cause."

Avryn stared at Marric with smoldering eyes. He was very passionate about this, and Janis could tell that he cared deeply about the boy. She didn't understand how, but you could tell by the way he spoke to him, treated him, even looked at him. A pang of jealousy rang in her chest as she observed the exchange. She scolded herself for the feeling, knowing that in her profession, such emotions were the difference between a successful assassin and a dead one.

Blast! How did I let myself get into this situation?! I should not *have let the money convince me to stray from the usual*, she thought in frustration.

"And the part about the awakening?" Janis said frankly. She was trying to distract herself from her thoughts.

Avryn sat back in his chair and let out a small sigh.

"Let me remind you that I did not intend on sharing this with you until after we set out for Terris Green, but if you insist, I will tell you." He paused again, but only for a moment.

"Marric, the awakening is not a—*comfortable* experience. When a Lightbearer comes into their powers, there is a certain effect not only on them, but on the world around them. We don't have time for the specifics right now, but there are some things you must know. The awakening is much like a sudden sickness. You will feel some pain, some fatigue, some nausea; in all honesty, it is difficult to describe, but at the same time, the world around you will change momentarily, and this can be dangerous, not only for you, but for those around you. We have found that the older a person is for the awakening, the more dangerous it is for them and their surroundings. In some cases . . . it can be fatal."

The air seemed to grow cold as it was pierced with intense silence. It felt like a jab with a sharp dagger right in the chest. Janis looked at Marric, gauging his reaction to the news. His brows were furrowed a bit as if he didn't quite understand what Avryn had just said. Anger flashed on Narim's face as he digested the news himself. He stood up and pointed his bony, wrinkly finger at Avryn.

"Yeh won't come in 'ere threatenin' m'boy such like. He won't be one of yous light people if'n yous think he'll be killed."

"Narim, it's not like that—"

"Of course it's like that! I come and let yous in 'ere with trust and yous—"

"How often?" Janis interjected.

The two men stopped and peered at Janis. She stood tall next to her stool, appearing to loom over the two men. It wasn't so much her actual height that made her appear taller than them, but the way that she stood. Her seriousness and stark black clothes made her seem more authoritative, like a cat stopping two dogs in their tracks with a single look. Janis looked Avryn right in his clear, sky blue eyes, hardening her expression to make the point that she didn't want him to soften the truth.

"How often do they DIE?" she said, forcing a bit of anger into her tone.

The intended result occurred. He paused uncomfortably for a beat, then shifted in his chair. She was surprised, however, that he maintained eye contact the entire time before answering her question.

"That, unfortunately, is the bit of it, the *real* reason that we need Marric to come with us. The survival rate of those that awaken at sixteen years of age has proven to be alarmingly low," he turned his eyes to Marric. "We are hoping that with the resources we have, we can help you through this and make sure that you not only survive, but thrive thereafter."

"And . . . " Marric spoke slowly. " . . . what does *alarmingly low* mean?"

Avryn looked pained to hear the question. He clearly didn't want to elaborate further, but it was clear that he wouldn't withhold the real information, regardless of how painful it might be.

"In the history of awakenings, at least, the ones that we have been aware of . . . there has only been . . . *one* instance of surviving an awakening at the age of sixteen."

Time seemed to freeze for everyone in the room. Tins audibly gasped and put her hand to her chest, though it felt a bit of a ruse to Janis. The light in Narim's eyes seemed to disappear, leaving empty holes in their place as they lost focus into the nothingness. Janis shifted her focus to Marric to gauge his reaction again to the news, but he appeared deep in thought. He had his brows furrowed as he worked through the man's words. As he thought further, the realization appeared to hit him suddenly and his mouth dropped open slightly and fear entered his eyes. Another pang of sadness twanged through Janis's chest as she saw the fear. He seemed so young, so innocent, and Avryn had just told the boy that he was likely to die from some mysterious power.

"Marric," Avryn jumped in quickly. "We feel confident that we can save you. We aren't sure exactly what causes the people to die during the awakening, but we have the means to keep you alive. Just not here. You *need* to come with us to Terris Green. If not for yourself, then for your family. Your awakening may prove very dangerous for them as well. I understand that you don't know us or trust us, but you must understand that you don't have a choice at this time. It could happen at any moment."

Marric, looking as if was about to cry, instead sniffed loudly. The sound was scratchy and he choked a bit on the intake of breath. With teary eyes, he sat up straight in his chair, squaring his shoulders. Janis felt a bit of admiration for the youth. He had clearly lived a pretty sheltered life, with the exception of his slightly rebellious behavior. It was obvious that he was losing himself to anxiety and grief, but he didn't want to show that.

"I'll go," was all that he could say as he held in his emotion.

"Wait, now. How do yeh know about all this, eh? Yous don' know the future, do yeh? What makes yeh so righ' darn sure 'bout this?" Narim cut in.

"I am more than happy to discuss the specifics when we have more time, but we must leave as soon as possible. *Tonight,* actually. I can assure you, Narim, that we are quite sure of his true nature, and that his safety depends on our making it to Terris Green quickly."

A slight movement in Janis's peripheral vision made her shift her gaze. The woman, Tins, had swiftly moved her hands behind her back in a curious manner. Janis narrowed her eyes at the woman, feeling in her gut that something was off with her. As she watched her, Marric stood firmly from his chair and nodded to the man.

"Then let us be off, now. I cannot be the reason for anyone in this town getting hurt, especially my father." The boy's lip trembled a bit and he shook it off, trying to mask his fear.

"Mar, hold on just a bit. Yeh can' just git up and leave jus' like that! It's dark out righ' now and there be lots of danger out. Waitin' until mornin' must be a better plan."

"I'm afraid Marric is right. We must leave now, Narim." Avryn said assuringly, "Harmel and Shrell are quite experienced in these woods. They can navigate well in a dark forest and protect the group just the same. I understand this is hard, but we must be off."

Narim looked at his son, pain filling his eyes at the thought of his son leaving, seemingly never to return. The moonlight shone through the window at the front of the house-shop, probably Stellan, the first moon. However, it was turning from the reddish hue to the blue of Mallan. If Mallan was already starting to shine, then it was starting to get late, indeed. Janis herself didn't like venturing into the night too close before Isllan, the third moon. Strange things happened during Isllan's light, and regardless of the men's skill, she doubted they were well equipped to handle a night in the forest during Isllan.

"I'll go. What must I bring on the journey?" Marric said, seeming a bit more confident this time.

"You'll need only clothes and whatever personal items you feel you would like to bring. Our caravan is equipped with materials for you and the journey to Terris Green. Gather what you need, but please be prompt."

Shrell nudged Avryn firmly in the arm, awarding him with a pleading glance. Avryn looked like an annoyed mother hen. There was a brief and unspoken exchange between the two men, then Avryn relaxed and let out an apparent sigh of concession.

"Please, Marric. Take the time to say goodbye to your parents and your home. I understand that this is a hard thing for you and possibly even harder for them."

Without another word, Marric turned sharply and rushed up the stairs. He did it quickly, but deliberately, eyes to the floor. Janis couldn't see his face, but he was clearly hiding emotion there and hoped that in the haste, no one would notice. She could relate to that once again. She had learned young that emotions betrayed you all too often, and that to make it in the real world, emotion could not overtake a person nor be apparent to those you worked with. The room fell silent after he left. The only sound was Avryn taking swigs of his ale and a rustling sound from Tins's dress as her hands fiddled behind her back. The woman was very fidgety at the moment, but she maintained her poised decorum and appeared on her toes as if ready to make a mad dash.

It wasn't long until they all heard a door close at the top of the stairs and the plodding thunks of booted feet descending the stairs. Marric had donned the black-hooded cape that he had worn earlier, since he had taken his things off when they got back to the house. He also had his quiver strapped over his shoulder once again. As he reached the last stair, he walked just before Tins, eyes on the men sitting opposite the stairs, clearly deep in thought. In a flash, Tins's hand flew out towards Marric with uncanny speed. Without a second thought, Janis snatched a dagger from her left sleeve and flung it toward the woman. Slicing the air, the four-inch-long blade of the dagger swished through the space between the two. Unbelievably, Tins adjusted her stabbing motion and rocked back on her feet, allowing Janis's dagger to thunk into the wall just inches above her arm.

Marric jumped at the sound, turning to hear what had made such a noise. Tins was making the move towards the boy again, but Janis was already there, slapping the woman's hand away. Tins held tight to her knife and jumped backwards along the wall, dodging the blow from the assassin's long dagger. She was far quicker than Janis had anticipated, but that didn't make her nervous. Many people thought fighting was always about speed or brute force, but it wasn't either. It was foresight. A slight motion in Tins's right arm told Janis exactly where she was headed. She lifted her left arm to block the blow aimed at her head and sliced the woman under the right armpit with her dagger. The woman cried out in surprise and pain, but twisted out of Janis's reach and danced backwards again towards the kitchen. Her teeth were bared like a feral dog losing itself to madness.

They stared each other down for a moment before the woman shifted forward. Janis watched her micro movements and easily anticipated her stance and blows, daggers clinging together as they engaged for a moment. Tins backed away once more, frustration on her face. Marric's stepmother was fast and quite accurate, but Janis was watching her every move.

"This is no concern of yours, *wench*! Leave us be!"

"You may be late to this party, you wretched woman, but you now know that I will not let any harm befall this boy."

Janis had been so caught up in the action that she hadn't realized the two 'protectors' had pulled their swords and taken up positions on either side of her, blocking the way to Marric.

"*Assassin*, your job is done here. We have failed and now must cut our losses." Tins lifted the sleeve of her right arm, revealing a tattoo of an eye veiled in beams of light.

In a moment of conflict, Janis stared at the tattoo, recognizing it to be the same as the mysterious and dangerous man from the rooftop in Arrivan. Tins was from Watchlight. How could that be?! She had been here for *years*!

"Your job is now to kill the boy, assassin. If you take care of these other men, then I can guarantee you thrice the payment."

Janis was ashamed at the thought, but money had proven all too persuasive for her in the past. Her mind wrestled with her feelings as she considered carrying out the request from this awful woman. But that was it, the woman was awful, and she couldn't let her harm Marric.

Blast, I hope that I don't regret this, she thought, gritting her teeth.

"Let's end this, woman." Janis said definitively.

Tins let out a growl of frustration and spit on the floor before Janis. Her eyes flashed to Marric and with uncanny speed, she let her dagger fly.

Gasping, Janis lifted her arm to attempt to block the blade. It flew just over her outstretched arm and spiraled towards Marric's chest. By some stroke of luck, the boy's father had already made his way to the boy in the commotion and pulled his son away from the flying knife. The man was not quick enough and the dagger slid cleanly into Marric's left shoulder. Eyes wide, the boy collapsed to the ground in surprise. Without hesitation, Janis, realizing that she missed the block, leapt forward towards the woman, swinging her dagger and plunging the long blade into Tins's side. The woman's grimace grew deeper as the knife sunk in and she grasped desperately at the handle. To ensure that there would be no comeback, Janis yanked the dagger free and rammed it once more into the lower part of the woman's side.

Crippled with pain, Tins fell to the ground in a heap, holding her side, blood pouring through her fingers, but the flow was too quick for her to stop. It was like trying to staunch the flow of a river with a few sticks. Looking up at Janis, she held the assassin's eyes with her own, anger showing on her face.

"Watchlight will kill you for your betrayal, woman! We have eyes everywhere and we *will* kill you for this!"

Janis let out a humph at the dying woman's words, seemingly unaffected by the threat. Her heart pounded in her chest, feeling a rush from the fight, the part that she loved about the profession. Full-on fights didn't usually happen as her stealth and training did most of the work on her jobs, but on the off-chance someone fought back, she enjoyed the challenge. Moving closer, she scanned for signs of life in the woman.

Janis then flipped around to see the two swordsmen standing at the ready still, as if waiting for the dying woman to get a burst of strength and attack them head-on at any moment. Smirking, Janis approached the two men and put both of her hands on the sides of their sword blades and pushed softly to the side.

"No need for you anymore, boys. The work here is done. You needn't stand all stiff-like, it doesn't allow for much speed, anyway."

"Not *every* solution has to be straight to killing," the taller man, Shrell, said. "We might have actually gotten more useful information from her had she not been skewered in such a fashion."

Pursing her lips, she replied, "I've found that diplomacy fails on those who themselves resort to starting with a knife rather than words. But don't trust me, I've *rarely* been in situations like these."

Sarcasm dripped in the comment so thick that the man scowled back at her, clearly not as amused as she was. For a moment, she was caught up in the feeling and her own wit before she remembered the knife piercing Marric. Snapping to motion, she shoved through the two men to find a Light glowing beneath Avryn's hand on Marric's shoulder. The glow was intense and blue, exactly what they'd seen in the forest, and with a slight pulse, it snuffed out.

Marric sighed heavily and put his hand to his shoulder, eyes wide in wonder. His father stared in disbelief at his son, then shifted his gaze to Avryn, shock showing on his face. Avryn's response was merely a warm smile. The man sat back on his feet to get his bearings.

"By mars, tha's wonderful, ain't it? How in Lanser's beard is tha' possible?" Narim spoke out weakly.

"I can't even feel the pain anymore, Pa. It was there, then it was gone, as if I'd only dreamed it."

Marric shot to his feet quickly, looking serious.

"Is this something that I'll gain as well when—when I—*awaken*?"

"Unfortunately, we can't be sure. There are different varieties of Lightbearers, and it depends on your class what powers you'll exhibit. But I can assure you, Marric, that you will likely be unique in your powers, which is why you are highly sought after from both us and Watchlight. But there isn't time, we *must* leave now. Watchlight will know all too soon that we've eliminated their operative and more will come. Narim—"

Avryn paused as he noted the old man slumped against the wall, grief on his face and in his posture as he stared at the limp corpse of his wife. Tins had died moments after focus had shifted to Marric and his injury. With the exception of the blood covering the floor, she looked quite peaceful, body still. Though Janis couldn't understand how such a nice man could love or live with a woman such as that, she couldn't help but feel sorry for Narim. For him, this wasn't just the loss of his second wife, but it also revealed the lie he'd been unknowingly living in for the previous years.

She sensed that Avryn had similar thoughts as he crouched next to the man and squeezed his shoulder affectionately. Tears welled up in the man's eyes and he began to sob softly, covering his face with his hands and saying something that sounded like "I'm sorry, Marric." For a while, he cried, and the group let him, no one speaking, not even to each other. Janis crossed to Marric and positioned herself behind the boy as he watched his own father cry at the loss of his stepmother.

Leaning forward, she whispered in Marric's ear.

"I must agree with Avryn. Watchlight must not be meddled with. We must leave, immediately."

"My father should come with us. He cannot stay here alone, not with them after me. They'll kill him now!" Marric said desperately.

"Your father may come," the other man, Harmel, replied. For an inexplicable reason, he was bearing his teeth, as if he was gritting through some pain of his own. "The journey'll be tough, bu' we'll make sure he be fine."

"No." Narim said aloud.

"But father—"

"No," he said again. "I'm too old to make such a trek. I will stay behind and leave Lanser's blessing upon you and those with you, my son."

"Father, you *can't* stay! Didn't you hear?! People will come for me, and when they find me gone, they will kill you too!"

"It's a risk I must take, m'boy. I can' be runnin' like all yous youngin' ones."

"I must agree with your father here, Marric." Avryn added. "I do not think that Watchlight will harm him now. They want your powers, so would gain nothing by threatening your father."

Tears welled in Marric's eyes as he realized that he wasn't going to win this argument. Teeth gritted, he ran at his father on the floor and fell, throwing himself into his father's arms, crying loudly.

Janis felt awkward watching. She may have felt sentiment for the boy's confusion earlier, but such outward displays took her far outside of her element, considering her jobs were taken with a complete lack of emotional consideration.

For what seemed like an eternity to Janis, the boy and his father sat on the ground in each other's arms, sobbing and muttering assurances to the other. During the time, Avryn only whispered a few words to his companions, who went to work in a hurry to make preparations for the journey. The two men had to wrangle the corpse of the fallen Watchlight operative through the side door and dispose of the evidence. After doing so, they exchanged a few more words with Avryn before rushing through the front door, which thumped closed loudly behind them.

Janis thought that moving the body was pointless, considering the inordinate amount of blood covering the floor from the five or ten minutes of the corpse laying there. She hadn't intended on making a mess here, but how she completed her work wasn't known for its cleanliness. It *was* possible, if the employer required such a thing, but in this case, she hadn't even bothered to keep things clean.

Curiously, Avryn crossed to the floor where the blood had pooled, the edges seeming to have dried a bit, changing from the brighter red to a dull brown color. He put his hand to his chin, thinking through something for a moment. Then he knelt down and, for some odd reason, placed his fingers on the floor, touching the edge of the pooled blood. He closed his eyes and appeared to be concentrating for a moment. Janis watched as the Light appeared again, still blue, but a bit softer this time. It ringed his fingers on the floor, lighting the area there before spreading slowly at first, then more quickly until it enveloped the whole area stained with blood. After the area was fully illuminated, it pulsed with the blue Light before the Light vanished suddenly. What was left behind made Janis move closer to investigate. The floor, wooden, looking to be oak, had been perfectly cleaned. Not only that, but it looked as if the fresh lumber had been lain only hours before, perfected. However, it was only in the areas previously covered in blood. There was a distinct line of darkness where the edge of the blood ended and the older, worn and darkened floor began.

"Ugglyn's nose, that didn't work as I had intended," Avryn cursed.

"What did you do?" Janis inquired. "It looks like a perfectly new floor, but only just there." She pointed at the floor.

"I wasn't sure if it was actually possible, as Fixing powers inexplicably apply to only certain situations, but it seems to have worked, if only a bit *too* well."

"I'm sure that I have no idea what you are talking about, wizard man. But I can sure tell you that it doesn't look like a natural floor, at least not anymore."

"Indeed. I may have to ask Harmel and Shrell to manually wear down this area to make it seem as closely worn as the other parts of the floor.

"There you go, they might be able to actually make themselves useful in that. Lanser knows that they were useless earlier in the scuffle with Tins. Put those sharp swords to use." Janis grinned, mostly to herself, satisfied with her jibe.

"I assure you, Janis, that those two are far more accomplished with the sword than you may think. They are just more considerate and deliberate with how they use them, which is clearly not your method. Yours is a kill now, talk later type of method."

She shrugged, but didn't contest the comment. Janis was aware that her methods weren't always the most diplomatic, but diplomacy was never really what her employers were looking for when they paid her for her services.

"By mars, that's incredible," a voice said behind them.

They both turned to see Marric, tear-filled eyes wide as he stared at the spot on the floor.

"I can't imagine what that ability must be like."

Avryn smiled at the juvenile's comment.

"As I said earlier, it's definitely possible that you too can gain such powers, my young friend. We won't know until you fully awaken into a Lightbearer. For now, we must start our journey. During which, I will help you understand the possibilities and be prepared."

Spotting Narim, head still down and sitting against the wall behind Marric, Avryn cleared his throat.

"Were you able to—um, say appropriate goodbyes here?"

Marric only nodded, opting to not say anything for fear of emotion overtaking him. Narim continued to sit, seeming to not notice that they were looking at him or even talking about him. Janis wondered if the man had been broken. Pain from betrayal was almost so real that it was physical, like an actual dagger piercing your chest, or like your lungs failing on you, causing you to suffocate to near extinction. The feeling was all too familiar to Janis, which is why she worked the way that she did. There was nothing more horrible than learning to open up and trust someone, then have them take it all back or go against their word, proving that they weren't what they claimed to be. Living and working alone was the only logical option.

"What do you plan on doing then, Janis?" Avryn said to her. "It seems like your job is over. We'll make sure that he's safe from here."

He furrowed his brow at that, then, scratching his head said, "I guess that doesn't matter anyway, does it? You were protecting him for Watchlight, and you kind of went against them by killing Tins, so. . . . "

"I'm aware of my own predicament here, I don't need you to go over my problems for me."

She really was in a hard place. Technically, the pay she'd received bound her to Watchlight until the job was done, but then, they hadn't really specified the completion criteria, had they? Avryn was right, though he didn't say anything new to her; she knew when she'd stabbed the woman that she had pretty much flashed a rude sign at the organization themselves, regardless of the payment she'd been given. Undoubtedly, they would realize what had happened here, find out that the boy had been taken by—whoever in Lindrad these people were, and be out to kill her by whatever means necessary. So her options were to let them take Marric, forcing her into hiding for who knows how long until she could find a way to make peace with Watchlight, or to join them wherever they were going, and figure out a better solution with at least a couple other swords watching her back, albeit temporarily.

"So what *will* you do?"

She turned toward Marric, the one asking of her. He looked concerned. She doubted that he fully understood the full picture or just how dangerous her predicament was, but regardless, he knew something was up. Had he really grown that attached to her so quickly? They barely even knew each other.

I guess having your life saved would draw you to someone, regardless of how much you knew about them, she thought. *Well, perhaps not* me. *But he's so young, after all.*

"I think that I'll join you," she said to Marric, but posed the next question to Avryn without looking in his direction. "That is, if you don't mind having an assassin accompany you to your lair."

"We'll accept it, although I'll keep my eye on you. Honestly, it might be nice to have another person that is well adept with a weapon. Especially with Watchlight on high alert now that we have Marric joining us. They'll be more vigilant than ever now. Though, we like to refer to our location as a *sanctuary*." Avryn then turned to Marric. "Is there anything else that you might need, son? Or are you prepared to leave?"

Marric shook his head at Avryn, then went to his father again. He leaned to the man and said something that Janis couldn't quite hear. Well, it wasn't so much that she *couldn't* hear, she just chose to tune out the words for fear that they would be laced with too much emotion for her to handle.

Whatever he said, it got Narim to respond by looking up at his son, tears in his eyes. They clasped hands and squeezed them together before he pulled him into a hug once more.

"Janis, is there anything else that you must pack before we are to leave?" Avryn inquired.

"They aren't so much things that I need, but rather things that I would prefer to have prepared. Give me two minutes. I'll gather them and be back by then."

He nodded, and Janis took the opportunity to head to the front door. Glancing once more at the boy and his father hugging tightly, she pulled the door open swiftly and entered the night.

Chapter 5

The night air was crisp and chilly, despite being in the middle of spring in Wurren. As it rushed down the darkened street, the smell of fresh trees and newly blooming flowers filled the noses of the small band of people making their way down the street. Mallan, the second moon, shone brightly almost directly above, lighting the streets. Shadows from the houses and carts were short, as if the midday sun had been covered with a shade itself, darkening the light to a bluish hue. It was still and quiet now, as it often was at this time of night. During the first two hours of Mallan, there was often at least a little bit of life in the small town, a woman closing up her shop here, two more drunk men there, toddling home as if they were learning to walk again in their first years, but normally by the third hour of Mallan, the final hour, the town was dead still. That was exactly how it was tonight. No one dared risk being about during Isllan, the third moon of the night. Strange things often waited until that time to occur. In fact, it's when the fog often rolled out, blanketing the world in thickness. It wasn't clear exactly what caused the unsettling events during Isllan, but some speculated that it was the fog that really opened up the world to the strange.

Janis found the fog annoying at the moment. It didn't particularly make her nervous like it did most people, but rather in a sense-suppression way. She relied heavily on all her senses to not only succeed in her profession, but to stay alive. The fog dampened her eyesight, and even her hearing. Most people likely either didn't notice the effect, or didn't realize that it was the reason they felt uncomfortable in the thickness. Fortunately, she'd handled more than one job during the fog and she knew how to work through it. There were subtle shifts in the grey-white vapor that announced something moving just beyond. It wasn't the actual moving of the fog itself, as it was constantly swirling and twisting as if it was alive. Rather, if it was moving on its normal course and moved unnaturally, often in a completely different direction, then it was being disturbed, by some animal or being of the night. Janis didn't believe in the supernatural traditions of the people in Lindrad, only in the thief, drunk, or assassin that found their way through that time of night.

It had taken Harmel and Shrell far longer than Avryn expected to dispose of the corpse left from the events of the night, much to his chagrin. He had anticipated leaving much sooner than they had and was clearly agitated at the fact; rubbing his hands together, eyes shifting left and right quickly as if seeing movement on the sides of the street. Janis thought it was odd how nervous the man seemed, considering his strange powers and skill with a blade. This impressed Janis for some reason, likely because she hadn't expected the man to be skilled enough of a swordsman to last long in a fight. Instead, he showed quick reflexes and a keen awareness of his surroundings.

After leaving Marric's home, the five of them had made their way to the inn where the three men had been staying to retrieve their bags and horses. It had only taken moments there and before they knew it, they were making their way down the street north to the edge of the town and the forest beyond.

"We should sneak on the outskirts of town, despite how late it is. It would not be wise to take the main way." Janis said before they had made it far.

"It is quite late," Avryn replied. "But I doubt that Tins had a moment to alert any other Watchlight operatives."

Janis didn't agree, but it was clear she was outnumbered in her view by the nods of Avryn's companions. Knowing it was unwise, Janis felt at her sides for her daggers, shifting them slightly to ensure they would be easy to snatch.

Avryn rode on his horse at the head of the group, leading the way down the patchy cobblestone road. It had carried so much foot traffic from merchants both locally and abroad that it was worn down quite a bit, leaving holes and ditches in unconventional places. Just behind him, Shrell rode his horse with Marric sitting behind him, arms wrapped tightly around the man, face white with fear. It was clear that it had been a long time since Marric had ridden on such a beast based on how stiffly he rode, back straight, head pressed against the man's back. He was sure to get saddle sore much more quickly without relaxing and moving with the horse. Shrell was also not pleased with his situation. His jaw was set firmly and he stared forward, obvious discomfort on his face and in his posture at having the boy clutching so tightly to him.

Janis chuckled to herself. She could at least relate with the man, affection and physical touch also being something that made her quite uncomfortable, but seeing the man in such a state amused her. She thought it was quite amusing when men so strong, lean, and skilled with weapons were brought down into such misery by something so simple as non-combatant touch.

She looked over her shoulder to see Harmel atop his mount, taking up the rear just behind her. She was of course on foot at the moment, keeping watch of the surroundings and being prepared for anything. When they'd left, Avryn offered either his or Harmel's mount to her, suggesting that she ride alone while they rode together. She had declined, not only because of her own discomfort while riding a horse, but because their first goal was stealth, not speed. Janis had assured them that she would be more stealthy on foot, and when speed became priority over stealth, she would gladly ride.

Though the town of Wurren wasn't overly small, it was taking a considerably long time for them to make their way through the streets to the front of the town. They had left, unfortunately, right at the beginning of Mallan's second half of light, rendering the town lifeless and exposing the unusualness of their traveling at this time. With the streets empty and the shutters closed, sounds of hoofbeats or talking would alert any Watchlight operatives of their position and likely their intent, especially given the likelihood that the cult group already knew or would know soon of the death of Tins. When they had first set out, they agreed that no talking should occur until they were a safe distance into the forest and out of ready earshot.

Janis didn't mind it this way, she preferred to quietly observe. Talking could be distracting. Plus, being quiet allowed her to pretend that she was alone, completing a job that no one else knew about and being only accountable for herself.

The odd collection of people seemed more amusing to Janis than she would admit to Avryn. He would likely be offended at her assessment, but she could only imagine someone seeing three men atop horses, clearly warriors of a type, a young boy, grasping the upper body of one of the men, and a black-clad woman on foot, stalking quietly through the town to the forest. Perhaps they would think the boy was a prisoner, or that the woman was an insane person who forgot her place. She knows what she'd think. *That group is up to something, and it's worth me following them as far as I can to find out what they're up to.*

They turned the last corner onto the main street leading to the exit of the town. It was surprisingly narrow, considering it was the thoroughfare for the merchants and all the trading that was done here. She could only imagine the hundreds of people, animals, carts, and regular townspeople that moved through this pass. It wasn't much like an alley, but it was only about three armspans wide from one side to the building on the opposite side.

Janis felt uneasy as the group turned and made their way to the entrance. This was the perfect location for an ambush. Two-story buildings to either side; perfect vantage points for marksmen. Doors were constant on both sides, allowing quick access to warriors or assassins lying in wait there. There was even an alley here and there as they moved where shadows loomed, creating perfect hiding places.

She instinctively crouched a bit lower, hands held to the side, ready to snatch any of her hidden blades throughout her bodice. Shifting her eyes quickly and regularly, she started taking inventory of the street and all possible outcomes if an attack were to come suddenly. As she turned and observed her surroundings, she caught sight of Harmel riding behind her. He raised an eyebrow at her, curious at her sudden change of composure. He almost looked amused.

These blasted men, she thought. *What good are they if they aren't even on guard in the most obvious times of risk?*

They made their way slowly down the street and they could see where the road met the forest line about a hundred yards outside of the town. All was still quiet and there didn't appear to be any sign of trouble, but even if there had been, Janis wondered if Avryn and his men would even detect it before they had a sword through their chests. She had to give them some credit, though. If they had traveled here on their own, they couldn't be completely useless.

As they approached the last few houses, Janis turned to look down an alley on the right and froze, staring straight into the eyes of an old man. He was standing at a community well, gathering water. His white eyebrows raised with surprise as he looked at the group. He looked guilty, as if he was doing something he shouldn't be. He was stooped forward, causing him to look like he had a large hump on his back, and his hair was pure white and messy as if he never bothered to touch it for any reason. Crows feet deep set on the edges of his cheeks deepened as he narrowed his eyes at them.

For a moment, the two stared at each other, not moving. The first two horses of the caravan kept moving, but Harmel stopped his mount just behind Janis, noticing her sudden stop. Then, after the pause, the old man flashed a brief smile, then turned toward a door to the house just behind him. As he turned, he began whistling a merry tune that pierced the silent night. A chill ran up Janis's spine and she seized a small dagger from a pouch hidden just below her left armpit.

"Run! Now!" she shouted loudly, shocking Harmel and making him jump in his saddle.

Avryn and Shrell turned curiously, just realizing that Janis and Harmel had paused twenty feet behind where they now were.

"Woman!" Harmel whispered harshly. "What are yeh doin'?! We agreed tha' *no sound* was—"

A loud thump announced the arrival of an arrow as it sprouted from the wall of the building to the right of Shrell and Marric. Harmel let out a curse, but Janis was already moving to protect them. Avryn shouted in surprise as one more arrow thudded into the wall, while a second caught Shrell's mount in the flank, causing it to scream in pain and buck the two riders off its back. The two men tumbled painfully to the ground, Shrell on top of Marric, who looked terrified.

Without hesitation, Janis shoved Shrell off of Marric before the man launched himself up. Shrell's quick response proved to be lifesaving, as he pulled his sword free in time to block a man's blade who had appeared from the alley to their left. Yanking Marric to his feet, Janis tugged on his arm and forced them both into a flat sprint toward the forest. She wasn't acutely aware of what was happening behind her, all she knew was that Marric would be dead without her. A hooded figure leapt in front of them from the house just at the edge of the town and Janis spun and flicked her right hand, launching the small dagger directly into his throat. His eyes grew wide and he fell to his knees, clutching the wound in a panic as the two rushed by.

A feeling in her gut made Janis stop and throw her left shoulder sharply into Marric, pushing him to the ground. In that moment, an arrow lodged its way into her back, just above the shoulder blade. Gasping sharply, she again pulled Marric to his feet and forced them into a run. Pain flared through her shoulder and she could feel her left arm starting to weaken from the blow. She heard another arrow clatter to the right of them as they reached the treeline and plunged themselves into the foliage and the darkness there. With one last shove, she pushed Marric into a bush.

"Don't move! Stay low, stay quiet," Janis hissed.

She turned and ran back into the clearing between the woods and the town, just to be blinded by a flash of Light and the loud sound of splintering wood and a man screaming in pain. Despite being blinded, she continued to run towards the entrance, yanking her large dagger from her left sheath and dashing into the battle. A second flash hit her vision again, followed by more exploding wood and another scream. When she arrived at the scene, spots swimming in her vision, a man lay dead in front of Shrell, blood on his sword. Harmel pulled his horse up to the two and he jumped off. Wood lay broken on the road next to the building before Janis, as well as a building twenty feet before that. Mingled with the wood were the corpses of two archers that must have been atop the structures. She glanced up, seeing in the blue moonlight that the buildings before the corpses had gaping holes at the top in the front face as well as in the roof.

"Blast, man!" Shrell said to Avryn. "That'd be the quickest way t'let every foggin' person know that we're here!"

"There was no time, Shrell. We would be dead if I hadn't simply eliminated the problem!"

Doors began opening from the surrounding houses and they each took that as the signal to leave quickly, ending the argument. Shrell's horse was beyond saving, and would likely bleed out soon. He had clearly come to the same conclusion, as he sliced the straps holding the packs to the horse and yanked them free. Harmel was already riding up on his horse with a hand extended for Shrell, who grabbed it and smoothly swung into the saddle behind him. Avryn had a cool look on his face, almost emotionless, as he extended a hand to Janis. She grudgingly took it and felt his strong arm pull her up. She lithely shifted her weight and slid onto the back of the saddle behind him, but held onto the back of the saddle rather than put her arms around him for stability.

Spurring his horse into motion, the two of them galloped out of the town and crossed into the treeline. The thick forest surrounded the road on all sides from here on, providing good cover for their escape. Shouts had begun from behind as the townsfolk saw the dead bodies and identified the three strangers among the perpetrators escaping on horseback. Janis doubted that any of the townspeople would even attempt to follow them since they didn't have the means, but she had a feeling that they wouldn't greet strangers like this coming into the town again without proper reasons or merchant licenses.

"Stop here," Janis said loudly over the horse hooves.

Avryn pulled the reins to stop the horse and she swung off before it had stopped fully. They hadn't left the road, so they were still a bit exposed in the moonlight. She crept into the trees around where she had shoved Marric.

"Marric," she said out loud. "It's Janis and Avryn. We need to move."

Snapping branches announced Marric as he stumbled in the darkness. She heard the noise roughly to her left in the darkness and saw the form of the boy, a mere blob of color, in the shade of the trees. Without too many words, she snatched his hand and led him to the road and Avryn's horse standing there. Sounds from behind made Janis turn to find a handful of men with various tools shouting and running from the town toward them.

Well, they are more gutsy than I would have guessed, she thought. *They don't pose any real threat. They're just disgruntled quiet town folk.*

"It isn't ideal, but we need to move quickly," she said up to Avryn. "Can your horse handle the three of us for a short time to gain us distance? Marric and I are slight enough that we can probably fit for a time. Isllan should be here soon. With any luck, we'll have the fog to hide us."

"You are indeed a strange woman," he said, wonder in his eyes. "I don't often hear anyone use luck and fog in the same sentence. Yes, she'll do fine for a bit. She's not a war horse, but she's strong."

He patted the horse's neck with fondness and rubbed her mane a bit. Whatever history he had with the horse had obviously bonded him to the creature. She'd never understand why men grew so attached to such things. It only amounted to more feelings when eventually the creatures died, for they always did.

Helping Marric up turned more into forcing him up as he had entered another one of his shock trances again. Grunting, the two were finally able to get him settled and she easily pulled herself onto the horse's back in time for Avryn to kick the horse into a run. The men had come within ten feet before they were off, but the horse could easily outrun them.

As they rode into the night, Janis assessed the situation. Mallan was starting to set very quickly and Isllan would replace it soon enough. Looking at the ground, she could see that the trees' shadows were extended halfway across the path, indicating the setting moon. The fog wasn't imminent every night during the moon, but it appeared more often than not.

It would be rotten luck if the fog doesn't show tonight, she thought. Janis wasn't religious, but tonight it wouldn't hurt. She gestured using the common prayer for everything and mentally sent it to the sky.

* * *

They had kept the running pace of the horse for only ten minutes before they slowed. For a moment, Avryn used his strange powers to heal Janis where the arrow had pierced her. Shrell had apparently also taken an arrow to the arm, though in the chaos she hadn't noticed. Avryn's healing Light was indeed handy, but it was so unsettling to her. Though appreciated, Janis hoped that she never needed to be touched by it again.

From then on, Janis opted to travel on foot once again since speed wasn't the priority any longer. She had traveled this path not too long ago and she recalled certain aspects of the road, a tree here, a rock there, things that she used as markers of her position or possible weapons should she be in a pinch. She hadn't taken this path at the same time of day, so most of her memories were bathed in red Light, that of Stellan, the first moon. It gave off an eerie glow then, making everything seem lifeless and dreadful. Blue seemed a much more appropriate light for travel as it was much brighter, and less depressing.

Unfortunately for them, Mallan's time was short and soon, darkness overtook the road. In a moment, a small blue orb appeared a half-handspan from the road, lighting the rocky path just enough to keep them from tripping, but not enough to expose their exact location. It was quite an impressive display that even left Janis in awe, but she wouldn't let it show. Having light at all was stupid, but she doubted that saying anything to Avryn would change things. They obviously had their own way of traveling.

The path was mostly smooth dirt with large stones and rocks jutting here and there that could easily catch someone unaware and pitch them forward. With or without light, Janis was coordinated and could see enough to not fall to that embarrassing fate. Perhaps that is why she preferred working at night; it gave her some nice advantages over opponents or anyone that should try to stand in her way.

The men all dismounted from their mounts and took the reins of their horses. Darkness not only made it risky to be riding the beasts, but the Light obstructed their view of the forest and the high position was not wise, should archers be involved. Unfortunately, they had to take the risk with Marric since he was not aware enough to travel on foot. He was dozing in the saddle and had almost fallen from it a few times, forcing Janis to catch him. With Avryn out of the saddle, he was able to lean forward and rest a bit on the horse's neck.

"There, girl. Take a rest for a bit." Avryn said fondly to the beast.

Janis couldn't understand how someone could grow so fond of such a creature. In her mind, they were merely beasts that were resources or pets, never a friend. She watched with curiosity as he took a moment to touch his forehead to the horse's, then turned and continued to walk down the pathway.

"We'll need to find shelter soon," Avryn said to the group. "Isllan should be on the rise, and if the fog catches us before we can find a good camping spot, we may struggle to find a location."

"Can the Light not pierce the fog?" Janis asked, thoughtful.

"Unfortunately, no. It tends to reflect the Light back to us, making it even more difficult to see."

What an annoying limitation. She had thought that some mystic Light power could debuff something as simple as the fog.

"Pity. I guess I'll have to continue to rely on my own skill in the fog."

He nodded in agreement, seemingly unimpressed with her comment on the situation.

The small caravan turned off into the woods and began trudging there. Just before entering, Janis glanced up at the sky to see that there was an orange hue to the darkness. The tops of the trees began glowing orange as Isllan's orange light shone through the sky. The fog wasn't directly influenced by Isllan, but it tended to show up sometime during Isllan's reign of the night. Oftentimes, the fog would roll in and stay for hours. It had sometimes stayed into the morning, interrupting the normal flow of the morning hours in a town.

They hadn't ventured long before they came to a small clearing that wouldn't allow for perfect sleeping conditions, but there was enough space for at least the five of them to spread out on the ground and get some rest before the sun came up in the morning. Harmel and Avryn led their horses just past the clearing, opting to keep the animals out of the area so that they could use the space for themselves. Shrell offloaded the pack from his horse, which he'd had to carry on his own back, much to his dismay. Finding Marric's belongings, he retrieved Marric's sleeping roll and spread it out in the middle of the clearing. The boy had fallen asleep and appeared beyond full awakening, so Janis and Shrell lowered him off of the horse and laid him as softly as possible on his blanket.

"I hate to have to stop, but traveling at this time of night carries too many risks for our endeavor. We'll rest for a few hours until either after Isllan is past, or the fog clears, whichever is first."

"Under normal circumstances, I would disagree with this, but for now, you are right." Janis said.

Avryn seemed pleased at that, as if he was finally proud to have agreed with Janis on something. He was a strange man to her. Men often were prideful and didn't care what others thought of them, confidence unchanging with their opinions. He seemed the opposite. His display of skill with the blade and obvious authority with the group showed regularly, but in moments without intensity or conflict, he resigned to a more vulnerable person. It seemed a strange combination to Janis, but somehow it worked for the man.

"I'm going to scout the area, make sure that we aren't putting ourselves in the perfect ambush situation," Janis announced.

They all nodded and began working with their own supplies to prepare for the night. She hoped that they all didn't intend on sleeping at the same time. That would just be foolish. She didn't stick around to find out, but slipped into the trees to make her regular rounds for a camping location.

Before she'd made it too far into the trees, she caught wind of the men conversing. Pausing, she positioned herself quietly behind a tree so that they couldn't spot her, but would still allow her to listen unrestrained.

"D'yeh really think we oughta let 'er join us? She ain't exactly someone easy to trust."

That sounded like Shrell. Unsurprising. He still shot her looks even after she'd just saved their hides when she'd warned of the ambush.

"I know that it isn't ideal, but I believe that she means well."

"But S'ren, how can yeh *know*? She's an assassin, for Lanser's sake. I don' like the idea of wakin' up to a knife in the throat. Didn't yeh hear wha' she said? *Watchlight* foggin' paid her for a job. Assassin's go where the money is."

Shrell wasn't wrong in that. It was spot on with how she and most other assassins operated. It made the work easier.

"No. She's more than that, Shrell. I think that her curiosity is piqued enough that her coming with us isn't a sabotage scheme. Though I can't say exactly what her draw is, it's more noble than she'll likely admit."

That struck her like a tree branch ricocheting directly into your face. Did he just label her as *noble*? She wasn't sure if she should be offended or disgusted with the association.

"She did righ' save our hides t'night." Harmel added. "Oi think she might be on our side fer now."

Harmel's voice was quite a contrast to Shrell's, higher in pitch, clear and naturally loud, like you might hear on a professional performer.

"S'ren, if she gets right out of 'and, can we just kill her?"

"I won't deny you your own protection, so defend yourself if you must. But do not lay your hand on her with no justifiable cause."

"What of the boy? D'ye think he right well could survive the awakening?" Harmel asked, genuinely curious.

There was an uncomfortably long pause after the question, indicating that there was a large amount of uncertainty in the answer.

"I honestly don't know, but it would be better for us to be there for it. I really do believe there's a higher chance of it with us here, despite the boy's apparent frailness."

She listened for a few moments longer, but Shrell's question ended that conversation far quicker than she expected. They moved on to less impactful subjects that made it easy for her to detach from the discussion and move around.

Janis had done scouts like this so many times that it took only a short amount of time before she was satisfied with their position. She had quickly set up some purposefully placed sticks to make noise should someone or something arrive through the most likely routes to their small camp. Then, satisfied, she returned to the group to settle in.

By the time she had returned, the orange light of the moon had arrived directly above their heads and thick fog was materializing as if from nowhere. It had a musty and wet scent as if from an old cellar that hadn't been accessed for years. The temperature dropped sharply as it appeared, taking them into what often was referred to as the fifth season. For some unknown reason, the fog always induced the same temperature regardless of the current season, somewhere just below that of the warm season that they were currently in. It was just cool enough to be slightly uncomfortable to any bare limbs that were exposed to it. That was one of the things that made the fog so peculiar and uncomfortable to everyone. It could be right in the middle of the cold season, everything frozen completely, then the fog rolled in and warmed everything again, melting the freeze as if it wasn't there. Then it would leave, allowing the cold season to refreeze the world. The oddity of it was that the temperature change was actually pleasant, for it brought relief from both the heat in the hot season, and the cold in the latter. If it weren't for its association with Isllan and the happenings during that time, people might be inclined to appreciate the fog more. That, and the strange effect on any who were touched by it.

As expected, the fog had an immediate effect on the group stranded in the middle of the forest. Janis felt the hair on her arms stand up and the uncomfortable chill in her spine, making her feel that at any moment they'd be attacked. Their breathing increased and they felt on edge. She had learned to accept the feeling, thinking it a blessing from Lanser more than anything, for it increased her reflexes and kept her on her toes, the way she preferred to be anyway. Avryn and the others clearly didn't feel the same way. Shrell and Harmel breathed in sharply when the feeling hit them, uncomfortable with the sensation. Avryn grimaced as the effect came. It could be very distracting and tiring to have your body put through the 'on-edge' feeling for the duration of the fog.

Avryn's companions murmured a request to sleep through the next hour or so, allowing them to escape the feeling through unconsciousness. He nodded his approval and the two settled down in the bedrolls to rest as best as they could. Though they were uncomfortable with the experience, they appeared to fall asleep very quickly. Even when she could sleep during this time of night, she did so lightly, restless. After the two men had lain down, Janis and Avryn exchanged glances agreeing that neither would trust the other to sleep.

Sighing, Avryn sat back against a tree and stared into the eaves of the trees above, continuing to breathe deeply to try to distract himself from his quickened heart and the sweat that was beginning to break on his forehead.

"It helps if you don't try to relax through it." Janis said to him, staring at him with his head back.

"Hmm?" he responded.

"The fog effect. If you don't try to force it down through relaxing, it actually makes it more pleasant."

He tilted his head back down and looked at Janis curiously, unsure how to take the advice.

"I hadn't thought of that as an option. I figured that the quickening of the heart and breathing should be counteracted for comfort."

"That's why people fail to function in the fog. They push back hard against what is natural. I revel in the feeling and let it take over, making me a bit more prepared for what lurks."

"What an interesting idea," he said, looking at her with an amused expression. It didn't appear that he believed her, but regardless, he closed his eyes and stopped forcing his breaths to stay slow. After a minute, his eyes shot open and his eyebrows knit together.

"Well, I'll be!"

"I told you it would be much better," she said smugly. "In return, I want to know more about your—unusual power."

His expression soured at that. She suspected that he anticipated the conversation, but would rather not address it. Narrowing his eyes at her, he drew his lips in a thin line again. For a man with such skill, she was surprised that he was not better at deceit. All of his emotions appeared on his face, letting her see exactly what he was feeling.

A life as an assassin, or even a simple court actor would not bode well for this man, Janis thought.

"It's rather complicated to explain the exact measures of the power, but even if I could, some secrets are better kept," he replied stiffly.

Very frank, I like that.

"From someone in my line of work, *that* I can understand. However, if I'm expected to accompany you any further, I need to at least know enough that I don't have reason to kill you from behind."

Avryn chuckled.

"You are a strange woman, indeed. Very well, I will answer what questions you have, to the degree that I want to. Deal?"

Seemed fair to her. It was a good response from someone that valued the power of secrecy and understood the danger of information.

"How did you deal with the two bowman back in Wurren? Things were going south really quickly back there, but something happened."

His expression soured unexpectedly, as if he was disgusted by something. That seemed an odd reaction to a question that was relatively harmless in her mind. She'd have thought that someone with his abilities would be more arrogant.

"I should have guessed that your first question would delve into an uncomfortable subject. Regardless, I did say that I would answer and I don't mind satiating your curiosity."

I wouldn't say curiosity as much as wanting to understand what I have to deal with for self preservation, she thought smugly.

"One of the more unfortunate sanctions of my power is what you saw there. In essence, I have the ability to break things apart, destroy them, if you will. When I realized that we were exposed to the bowmen with no efficient way to fight them from a distance, I—for lack of a more eloquent term—blew up the roof upon which they stood."

"*Blew it up?*"

Avryn sighed at her reaction, seeming suddenly sheepish.

"I have a hard time seeing good in the ability, as it is brutish in nature. However, when the situation merits it, I will not deny myself or my comrades protection."

"From an assassin's perspective, it seems like a dream. If it were a bit more stealthy, I'd imagine that would provide more valuable use to me. If you could have, well, disposed of the men directly rather than indirectly, it might have been more discreet."

He winced at her comment, seeming to take a painful blow. She couldn't quite tell in the fog, but his face seemed to whiten and he looked nauseated.

"It wasn't that I *couldn't* do it. I just choose to utilize that function of my power differently than others. Destroying any form of human or animal life directly is distasteful and barbaric."

There was passion in his voice. He had clearly had bad experiences with this in the past. She felt as if she had struck a nerve so deep that she couldn't help but mentally log this away, should she need it as a lever. Seeing this as a strategic piece of information rather than a way to empathize with the man indicated exactly why she wasn't meant for any other profession. It was always a game. You were either winning, or you were losing.

"That's your opinion, perhaps," she replied, pretending to not notice his reaction. "What will happen with Marric?"

His expression softened with that comment. Looking over to where the boy slept, Avryn seemed to contemplate the question with deliberation. There was something there, some attachment that he had to the boy that she couldn't understand. She'd have to make note of that as well. Perhaps that would come in handy at some point.

"We'll take him to our sanctuary, give him a safe home. And provided he can survive the awakening, we'll help him understand his new powers and learn to live with them. It's a scary thing for a boy his age. When you're sixteen, you shouldn't have to worry about such things. Unfortunately, we can only help him cope with the reality of his potential. At Terris Green, there are a lot of us, a lot of young ones his age, people that he can make friends with, perhaps he'll even find one to marry. But, for now, we just have to make sure he survives."

"And if he doesn't?"

The man's head turned and he stared at Janis, eyes boring into her own.

"Then I have failed, and Lanser bless the boy in the next life."

The passion in his answer and behind his eyes seemed dangerous, almost hungry, as if Avryn had something to prove to himself. Once again, she saw something else in him that she could respect. If anything, he had passion, and he was driven by that. The implications of it were unknown, but she knew that he was much more than she had given him credit for.

"Why do they accompany you?" Janis said, changing the subject. "I understand why you are here and what you want for Marric, but why do these men help you in your cause?"

"Ah, yes," he replied, "perhaps for the same reason that you accompanied us here. They have a loyalty to me on a more personal level that binds them to me and our cause."

Janis privately felt this was a gross oversight on his part; he had no idea that she had only joined them for her own preservation.

"Now may not be the time for such a story, but like them, there are many people who have been affected by the truth of Lightbearers, and who have chosen to join the cause. Terris Green isn't only for those that exhibit powers themselves, but for friends and family. You would be welcome there, Janis, if you would like."

Janis chuckled, finding the idea amusing.

"It doesn't sound like the kind of place where an assassin like me could fit in well. I could only imagine the ruckus I'd cause."

Avryn frowned at the comment. He couldn't understand what it was like being on your own for over a decade and learning to be self sufficient, earning your keep where necessary. She had had to gain her own skills and learn to cope with past emotions and experiences and channel that to something that could make her money. The idea of her joining what appeared to be a tight knit and supportive community seemed more comical and impossible than a wolf fitting in among a flock of sheep.

But there was something there. She felt a small twinge of jealousy at Avryn's words. Admittedly, she hadn't ever had a home, not since she was a child and her parents—

She shook her head, clearing her mind of the thoughts and shoving the growing emotion deep again. That wouldn't do.

"Is there anything else to your power? Things that we haven't seen or experienced since we've met?" she said quickly, trying to distract herself.

He smirked at that question.

"I can assure you, Janis, that the powers of a Lightbearer are far more complex than you can imagine. And that is something that I will not answer for you at this time. At least, not until we can know for sure that you can be trusted. In the meantime, know that I mean you no harm and that I will use my abilities only where necessary. I'm not an abuser of my gifts."

She was admittedly a bit disappointed at the answer, but she wasn't the least bit surprised. Once she'd realized that Avryn had some semblance of an understanding of secrecy, she knew she wouldn't get far.

The two of them sat there in silence after that. She closed her eyes and reveled in the feeling from the fog and how it seemed to make her feel alive. It was as if the fog induced the feeling when she was about to engage in battle with someone. Or the feeling she'd get just before the climax of a job, when the actual action happened and the risk was high. It felt like a constant adrenaline rush, heightening her senses and giving her the energy required to survive the next few minutes of the fight. Most people found the experience exhausting, hence why they opted to sleep through as much of it as they could, but she used it as an escape, a way into a world where she felt the most powerful.

Unfortunately, the fog didn't last for very long. After Isllan set, the fog disappeared as quickly as it had come, sweeping into nothingness as if a strong wind blew it all away. This stretch of night seemed more unsettling to Janis because there was no light from any moon. The night became a black canvas that seemed to suck away any light that might exist in flame or other form. It was at times like this that Janis appreciated the fog. Though it was a deterrent in its own way, it also made her feel like she could tackle the world, and it somehow felt like a protection from things around her.

As soon as the fog had passed, Avryn suggested that they start a fire. Not to keep the cold away, since the cool air had warmed now that the fog was gone, but rather to provide a bit of light for those that chose to stay awake. Starting the fire didn't appear challenging for the man, since he was able to do so very quickly. The firelight made the night seem far less foreboding, despite the fact that they probably could be seen from all around. If stealth was your goal, then they were failing at this moment.

Regardless, Janis recognized that she was still human and would need to rest at some point. She decided that she would rather do so with Avryn on watch as opposed to Shrell or his insufferable brute brother. She was confident that should any real threat appear, she would be sleeping lightly enough that she could protect herself. She was well accustomed to traveling in the wilderness on her own and depending only on herself for safety, even in sleep.

Settling in, she laid her head down on her arm, back turned to the fire and the rest of the group there. It would appear to them that her guard was down, but that was just a ploy. In a practiced manner, Janis closed her eyes and instantly fell into a light sleep.

Chapter 6

Marric woke to the sound of talking and packs rustling. He was in such a deep sleep beforehand that the feeling of coming to was disorienting for him. Everything in his vision was blurred color, and his mind seemed to be one step behind the rest of his senses. Before his surroundings began making sense, he felt the crisp air of morning on his face. In an effort to wake up a bit more quickly, he closed his eyes and breathed deeply of the morning air. It smelled wet, clean, and piney from the trees around them. He had no idea how long he'd been sleeping, or exactly where they were, but he knew that the morning air was familiar enough to him for comfort in his disoriented state.

He breathed deeply for a few more moments, just taking in the air, when the smell changed sharply. It took on a more food-like scent, like that of meat cooking. Not strong, but enough to make his mouth water as if it realized that his stomach was almost completely empty. When was the last time he'd eaten? It seemed so long ago that he couldn't even remember it being in the same lifetime.

Opening his eyes, he yelped in surprise as he found a large chunk of salted pork was dangling a half handspan above his face.

Laughter erupted from someone crouching just above him as he lay on the ground. In an instant, the pork dropped onto his face, causing him to sputter and sit upright. Harmel was holding his stomach, belly laughing merrily.

"See, Avryn? Oi told yeh tha' food is the quickest way to wake up a lad in deep slumber!" Harmel said through his bursts of laughter.

Marric grumbled something unintelligible, feeling embarrassed at his reaction to the incident. Looking around, he started. The camp had already been broken and their packs appeared to be strapped to the horses. Marric was stunned that he'd slept through all of this and rose from his bedroll. A pain in his neck announced a stiffness from the night's sleep on the hard ground.

"Yeh righ' well are a good sleeper, ain't yeh?" Harmel teased.

Marric's only response to that was a shrug. Partially because he was still embarrassed by his reaction to Harmel's prank.

The forest was surprisingly well lit considering the canopy above. Looking upward, Marric could see the sun-brightened sky shining through a break in the trees above them. For how strange and eerie the forest was in the night, it made up for itself during the day. The leaves of the trees above rustled in the morning breeze, creating a sound that resembled the constant tumbling water of a waterfall, but lighter. As he watched the trees rustle, a few longbirds flitted through the air, outstretched wings a mere handspan, but bodies long and sinewy, about twice the length of the outstretched wings. No one knew how the silly creatures could fly with such ill-proportioned bodies, yet they did.

Marric took in the familiarity of the forest with a content smile. He closed his eyes and let it take him back to his short venturings from Wurren, suddenly feeling as if he wasn't so far from his home.

He was so wrapped up in the comfort of the forest that he hadn't noticed that the rest of them were watching him. Marric felt heat rush to his face, suddenly embarrassed at his reaction.

"No need to be ashamed, Marric," Avryn said. "I remember my first time venturing outside of my town. Just enjoy it and take your time."

The smile lines on the outside of Avryn's eyes were surprisingly deep as if they had been chiseled by some sculptor into his face. It also made him seem even more aged than he probably was. Marric wasn't sure what made the man so happy, or for what reason he smiled so much, but it was a welcome sight given his current circumstances of leaving the only home he'd ever known.

At that thought, everything came down on him again like a weighted net, the kind that they used to capture large groups of birds, like wild geese or pheasants. It seemed so tangible and real that his breath escaped him suddenly and he had to force himself to start breathing again. Tins was dead. He was headed far from home, probably never to return. His father was left alone and in danger of some cult tribe that he knew nothing about. They'd almost been killed last night by archers and other strange men. Janis had thrown a knife right through a man's throat. His stomach turned suddenly and he almost threw up, even though his stomach had nothing in it. The flood of emotion and memories caused his knees to buckle, gravity pulling him down to sit on the ground.

"Marric! Are you ill?!" a worried voice spoke, seemingly in the distance.

"Oi was just jokin' with 'im," said another.

"He's just in shock, give him some space!" a third hissed, this one was different, higher in pitch.

A strong hand grasped him on the shoulder and forced his head down between his knees. His vision started to clear and he realized he was looking at the ground now, covered in his bedroll.

Blast, Marric thought. *We haven't made it very far to Terris Green and I'm already losing it.*

"Marric, I know that you've seen some pretty nasty things in the past day, but it will pass. Trust me."

It was the higher voice again. As his mind began to clear more, he started remembering details about his comrades. That was Janis. He looked to his left and sure enough, there she was. Short, raven black hair down to her shoulders. Her eyes were dark, but not quite black. They were a dark and deep blue, something he'd never seen before. Staring at her for a moment, he was surprised to see a smile spread across her face.

"You should probably eat something," she said.

"I'm—I'm not feeling that hungry."

"Yes, I bet you aren't. But the one thing I've learned is that through all the action in the world, the only thing that makes it worse is not eating in the midst of it all."

Marric nodded, as if this made sense. Eating did seem logical despite this being his first experience dealing with so many unusual events. He gratefully accepted the chunk of salted pork from Harmel, the same that had been dangling in front of his face just moments before, and started to nibble. They also handed him a bit of bread that he was able to eat more quickly now that the majority of the overwhelming feeling had passed. While he ate, Avryn came over, an apologetic look on his face, and rested his hand on Marric's shoulder. He didn't say anything, but there was something fatherly there as they held eye contact for a few moments. After the brief exchange, the man returned to his horse and made sure the straps were tight.

"We'll want to move as quickly as we can, though it will be difficult now that we only have the two horses. It looks like we'll all be on foot from here on out unless an emergency arises. The horses will still carry the packs."

"Where is this Terris Green? I've been all over Lindrad and haven't heard of such a place." Janis asked skeptically.

"That is, my dear, the point of it. If we were to truly be a secret society, we needed to remain a secret, you see." Avryn said, seeming amused.

Janis made a sour face at the comment, clearly wary of anything that claimed to be a 'secret society'.

"Can you at least tell me how long of a journey we should expect?" she retorted.

"It would take about ten days on horseback, but we'll be on foot. I imagine that if we move quickly, we can be there in maybe a little over a fortnight. If anyone should get too tired with the pace, we can take turns on the horses. For now, we'll just start walking north on the pathway."

"Does it concern you at all to be taking the road? Seems like we'll be easy targets in the open."

Avryn raised an eyebrow at her.

"If you would feel more comfortable, then please stay within the forest. Personally, I don't think that Watchlight, though they are very skilled, has the numbers to put their operatives throughout the forest between towns. We will, however, want to keep our distance from other caravans and travelers, no matter how benign their group may seem."

Marric watched Janis consider her options, then nod slightly.

"I'll stick with you on the pathway, then. Seems like you've dealt with Watchlight more than I have, so I'll trust you. If I were alone, I wouldn't travel on the path, but here I'd rather be closer to Marric."

Marric thought that it was strange for the woman to want to be closer to him, considering that they'd only just met. She seemed to be taking this very seriously, which made him a bit nervous. If she thought that it was better to stay close, then that meant the danger was more real than he wanted to admit. He had seen how quick she was with her weapons a couple times already.

A wave of nausea rolled over him again at the memory. Squinting his eyes shut, he forced the thoughts out of his head, trying to distract himself with his other senses. The air was fresh, smelling like trees. It felt cool on his face, refreshing and invigorating. The pork that he chewed was quite salty, bursting with flavor on his tongue. The rest of the conversation was lost to him as he retreated to his thoughts for the moment.

"Do you think you'll be able to walk?" Avryn asked.

"Hmm?" Marric asked distractedly, realizing that someone was talking to him. He had heard the words, but didn't quite process them correctly.

"Do you think that you are well enough to walk for the time being?" the long-haired man asked again.

"Oh, yes. I think I'll be fine."

Avryn smiled again.

"Good. Then we best be off. We need to get going if we want to reach Terris Green in any reasonable time. Though I don't suspect there will be any immediate danger, I would still like to make it there before—well, before anything happens."

He'd only known the man for less than a whole day, but Marric was realizing that Avryn often dodged subjects that he didn't quite know how to address. It was clear that he was avoiding saying something that might upset Marric more. This only made him more curious and want to question even further. If he had been able to conceptualize the questions quickly enough, he might have done just that. However, he didn't quite feel himself after recent events, and decided to follow along silently.

Shrell helped him roll up his bedroll and attach it to the grey mount, the one Avryn seemed so fond of. That being the last of camp to pack up, they turned toward the path and trudged through the foliage again to continue moving up the wide dirt road. Avryn continued to lead the way with his mount trailing behind him. Shrell and Marric followed behind the grey horse. Janis insisted on positioning herself just behind Marric, which increased the unsettling feeling that he had about his situation. Harmel brought up the rear with his horse. That horse was much bigger, and held a majority of their packs. Marric thought the horse was a beautiful creature, not only in build, but in its coloring. The horse was a standard bay, but sported large light tan patches in various places along its neck and body. He had hoped to examine the horse a bit more as he wasn't used to seeing them, but was too shy to ask and much too nervous to approach the thing on his own.

As they started traveling along the path, Marric was so enthralled with his surroundings that it didn't seem difficult or tiring at all to travel on foot. After a few hours, however, when the scenery didn't make any changes, the monotony of the views started to get to him. The trees on either side of the pathway were so dense and tall that it felt as if they were walking through a tunnel. Occasionally, there would be an animal here or there to observe, but mostly it was just the tall trees and the foliage between. The cool morning air quickly dissipated as the sun rose higher and warm musty air replaced it. It wasn't overly hot, it still being warm season, but the air seemed so wet and dense in the warmth that it felt much hotter than it should in this season. Marric's shirt kept sticking to his back, making him squirm uncomfortably.

Avryn tried to keep the mood light as they traveled by telling stories or singing songs from his childhood. Marric appreciated the tales at first, but as the weather became more humid and hot, he stopped listening as intently and instead retreated into his own thoughts. It was remarkable how the man could continue talking for such a long period of time. When he first began, he had made a point to look back every once in a while to make sure they could all hear, but as they went on, he stopped, making it more difficult for Marric to even hear what he was saying. Harmel was apparently used to this during travel, as he engaged Avryn naturally with questions and comments, chuckling here and there at the errant humor. His other companions were the opposite, staying completely quiet throughout the whole journey.

Soon, much sooner than Marric could have hoped, Avryn called for a break and they strayed from the path just slightly to pull their food out for lunch. Without hesitation, Marric dropped to the ground with a sigh and averted his head to the sky. The sun was just beginning to poke over the clear part of the sky above the road, shining into his eyes. The morning had passed very quickly and it had already reached midday.

Lunch was fruit, still fresh from the day before, dried pork sandwiches, and goat cheese. Avryn had intentionally prepared some fresher foods for them to enjoy at the beginning of their journey before they'd resort to the salted and dried meats, hardened bread, and dried fruit for the remainder. Marric hadn't realized how delicious the fresh fruit would taste after walking for such a distance.

"Yeh doin' alright, Marric?" Shrell asked as he sat lightly on the soft-grassed ground just beside him.

"Yes sir, just a bit tired, is all."

"The first an' second days'll be the hard 'uns, but after that, you'll be right well with the pace."

Marric nodded, hoping that it would be true. Harmel wasn't nearly as graceful as Shrell in most things, and that was very apparent as he plopped himself loudly in front of Marric, facing the boy. The way he came down on his backside, it looked as if it might have been very painful for the man.

"Pish tosh, Shrell, that ain't always true, eh? Perhaps if yeh were a beanstalk without so much weight on yeh." Harmel countered. "Why, it done take me weeks ta git used ta such travel."

"We ain't all as old as yous, Harmel. Or as dramatic," Shrell teased.

"Hey! Oi ain't old at all! Oi just prefer a relaxed pace, is all. Look aroun', enjoy the nature n' things."

Shrell winked at Marric, clearly knowing that he'd targeted his brother in a sensitive place. Marric couldn't help but smile back at the two. He wasn't sure what it was, but these men helped him feel at ease.

"If you don't mind me saying," Marric said to the two, "you don't look much like brothers to me at all. You also don't sound much like kin, either."

"Yeh ain't the first to say it. I think that myself most every day. I think, how could I be related to such a one as this porker? 'E looks like a chunk and sounds like an invalid." Shrell said with a wink.

Harmel was mid-drink when he spat the contents of his mouth out in a spray, sputtering at Shrell's remark. Marric felt the spray of liquid all over his face and hands, causing him to recoil in disgust.

"Oi'm not a fatty, eh?! Oi just am a bit diff'rent in build than yous lanky lot! Yous should count yerself lucky to be my brother, what with my handsome face an' all tha'. Besides, 'oo cares if Oi don' speak proper-like. Oi'm proud of my village and the way Oi speak too. It ain't like you sound fancy, either."

Shrell scowled at his brother and said, "At least I try to be understood a bit. Yeh sound like yeh ain't got no manners."

They were quite different in all ways, except hair color. Harmel was short, stocky, but very strong. His nose was large and flat, and his mouth was wide set. Shrell was tall and very thin, but his muscles rippled in his arm leanly. His hair was wavy and he kept his face clean shaven, making his already sharp and pointed nose seem that much more defined.

Their bickering continued on for a few more minutes, but Marric had shifted his focus to Janis. She was standing near the edge of the forest watching the path while they ate, as if expecting an attacker to suddenly show up. She was quite thin, accented by her tight-fitting outfit. Her trousers were all black and tightly cut, hugging her legs from ankle to thigh. Her shirt was also sewn close to her body, outlining the curve of her waist and upper body. He wasn't sure how she felt comfortable traipsing around in such an outfit, but she seemed perfectly at ease.

"I hate to be the bearer of bad news, but we can't spend a lot of time here waiting. We must eat quickly and be on our way," Avryn said, pulling Marric back to the conversation.

"Oi, S'ren, yeh sure are great at ruinin' the fun, ain't yeh?" Harmel teased.

Avryn rolled his eyes in an exaggerated way, but his face still sported a smile. The break hadn't lasted much longer than the man had said, for shortly after the conversation had ended, the group was exiting the forest back onto the path. Unfortunately, that meant that the sun was shining directly on the party as they resumed their travel heading north.

Though he knew it wouldn't be for much longer, Marric still hated the feeling of the hot sun as it caused him to break into a heavier sweat. In an effort to convince himself that he wasn't the only one that was uncomfortable, he looked at the others to gauge their sentiment toward the weather. His glances, however, yielded no understanding of their feelings. His eyes stopped again on Janis, the one traveling closest to him. There was sweat on her brow and a few drops dripping down her face already. The black clothing was likely causing her to feel even more hot, but she didn't seem phased. Seeing the sweat on her brow seemed strange. He couldn't explain it, but it *humanized* her somehow.

It wasn't like she wasn't human, she just—

"Can I help you with something?" Janis asked cooly without looking at Marric.

He looked away from her quickly, mumbling something between an apology and an excuse. The thought hadn't fully formed, so he wasn't sure what he had meant to say to her.

"I'm not unfamiliar with staring eyes, so don't be embarrassed. I only wonder what you could be thinking."

"I was just thinking that you don't seem to be bothered by the heat, is all."

She raised an eyebrow.

"Oh I assure you that this foggin' heat is terrible. But I've learned that such discomforts are necessary and that complaining about them is a waste of energy."

"Oh . . . well—yes, that makes sense."

What was he to say to *that* comment?

"You can ride a horse if you need."

"No!" Marric said quickly. "No, I'm okay. I am just getting used to the feeling, but I expect I'll be fine."

Janis only nodded at that. She clearly wasn't one for conversation. Realizing that a few words were all he could expect from her, he decided to try another tactic to distract himself. He walked a bit more briskly to catch up to where Avryn was leading his horse ahead. The man turned and smiled at him immediately when he saw him approach.

"Are you doing alright so far?" Avryn asked him.

"Yes, though the break did help me."

"I'm glad to hear it. Are you enjoying the scenery and whatnot?"

"Yes. I really am."

"It's a beautiful place to be, I must say. I've always had somewhat of an obsession for nature and how perfectly tranquil it seems. I grew up in a city, so I didn't get to experience much of this as I grew."

He didn't know what to say to that. Marric wasn't the best conversationalist himself. Not sure how to change the subject in a clear way, he cleared his throat loudly.

"If you don't mind me asking, why do they call you *S'ren*?"

"Hmm? Oh, you mean Shrell and Harmel. Yes, they are a bit odd in that. I don't really know why they feel the need to be so formal, they are technically a bit older than me anyway, but I suppose they do it out of—well, respect."

He looked a bit uncomfortable at Marric's question as if it was something he didn't like to talk about.

"Is it because of your powers?"

Avryn sighed, but nodded in affirmation.

"They treat all of us Lightbearers with reverence. Perhaps it has something to do with their past, but it's not my place to tell you about that. I don't really enjoy them addressing me that way, but I know that saying anything to them won't change that fact. Trust me, I have tried. They are set in their ways and I've just learned to go along with it."

They were both silent for a time after that. The sun had dipped into the other side of the forest and made the journey feel a bit more pleasant. As they walked, Marric stole glances at Avryn, hoping not to draw his attention while trying to learn more about the man. He seemed so perfect. His demeanor was almost always calm, and he seemed to be able to handle any situation with ease. His fierce eyes were bright blue, almost like the sky on the brightest day. It was a bit unnerving at night because they seemed to glow. Perhaps that had something to do with the nature of his powers.

"Avryn, can I ask another question?"

"Please do, Marric."

"Well . . . if I'm supposed to—um—well . . . "

"Please don't be shy. If I don't want to answer, I just won't. Do not be worried I'll take offense."

It was nice of him to say that, but it didn't make it much easier. Marric's hesitation in asking more about the man's powers didn't come from embarrassment, or worry of offense, but more from the fact that he was terrified of his potential death, or the fact that he was being pulled into some war that was far out of his understanding. Not to mention that the past few days had been stressful and tiring, but somehow heartening at the same time. Something about what Avryn said about the nature of Lightbearers and this hidden conflict between rivals—though that didn't seem the right term—seemed exciting. Exactly the thing that he had been wishing for when he went into the forest to shoot yesterday.

By mars, had that only been yesterday? he thought, feeling exasperated.

Regardless of the situation, or the fact that time seemed to be going simultaneously quickly and slowly, he had to learn more about his future. He steeled himself, gritted his teeth, and let out a quiet sigh, trying not to let Avryn sense his emotions.

"Will you tell me more about your powers? I want to know about what I should expect after I change."

Avryn let out a sigh as if he was grateful that the question wasn't something else.

"The correct term is technically *intar'nst*, or awaken, but you are correct in that it will be quite a change. Since you are new to this world and already have a limited knowledge of it all, I'll spare you the deep details and formal terms, for now. Eventually you will need to learn it all, and we'll make sure to educate you as such, but let's start with the basics. Does that sound alright?"

Marric nodded. He felt a thrill in his chest. It was both exciting and terrifying as he felt the anticipation in his whole body.

"Lightbearers, or *Tar'n*, in the old language, manifest in different ways. There are seven known classes of Lightbearers, and each has its own characteristics. They are equal in power, but so very different in their usefulness. We'll start with the simple one, which we refer to as a Lighter. A Lighter is someone that can summon Light in limited forms and project that anywhere. It is quite a useful gift. There is a lot more to it, but going further into details could take quite some time."

"So that is what you did in the forest then, with that little ball of Light and the sword made out of Light?"

"The first that you mentioned, yes, that was Lighting. However, the latter was actually a manifestation of another class, what we refer to in our language as Conjuring. It is similar to Lighting, in that Conjurers create Light out of nothing, but the difference is that it isn't just Light, they are actual physical objects that are made out of Light and are as real as the object itself. That is how I fought with Janis. Lighting, thus, is worthless in a fight such as that, for the Light is just light."

"What can you create, then?" Marric asked, wonder in his eyes. He was fascinated by this and thirsted for more.

"Anything, really. Though, there are limitations. No matter how powerful a Conjurer is, he or she can only create a few things at a time. The mental concentration required for maintaining the objects makes it nearly impossible to Conjure more than four or five things at a time. But let's not get caught in a rut. Another class is the Fixers. These restore things to their prior perfect state. A very common use for this is healing."

"That's what you did to yourself and Janis the few times you were injured."

"That's right. It is a relatively simple class of Lightbearers, but very powerful indeed. I can say that it's saved many lives, including my own."

"How does it work? I don't quite understand that."

"That, unfortunately, is a much larger conversation and it'd be best to take things slowly. Suffice it to say, it is a very good thing. My hope is that my proximity to you and my capacity for Fixing will ensure your safety through your awakening."

Marric felt a lump enter his throat. Avryn immediately saw the effect of his words and cleared his throat hastily.

"Then, there are Movers. These have the power to move physical objects through space. There doesn't seem to be much more to that, other than they tend to have the ability, over time, to move objects that far outweigh them in this world, though it does take much training and practice. Shielders, in turn, have the ability to create a spherical shield that protects any within from any harm. Lastly, there are Seers. You are Lanserian, are you not?"

"Yes, most people in Wurren belong to the Church." Marric replied.

"Then you've likely heard of people seeing the future before. They aren't just things of the past. Seers have the ability to see the future, present, or even the past of specific locations, or people. We've learned that if Seers focus on the events of awakenings, we can locate individuals who will soon awaken, themselves. That's how we knew about you."

"I'm not sure how I'd feel about that. Would it not be disconcerting to be able to see things that haven't happened yet?"

The man only shrugged.

"I couldn't say, for I haven't experienced it the way that they have. My Seeing is much more rudimentary than theirs."

"What do you mean?"

"Well, one thing I forgot to mention is that Lightbearers manifest all of the powers, but in different amounts. When a person awakens to their powers, they have access to each class of powers, but most are weak at best. Each person will manifest only one of the classes in strength, the others are almost dormant. Thus, we've labeled each Lightbearer with the titles that I mentioned, which are rough translations of the terms in the old language. However, each Lightbearer, at least for the most part, has been able to select a second class and develop that over months of time. Though this second gift will not be as strong as the first, it can get quite close."

Marric cocked his head.

"But you have more than two, why?" he asked.

Avryn shifted in his seat.

"Well, yes. That is a bit of a different story, and one that we will get to, in time. For now, let's focus on the basics."

Marric nodded, too distracted by everything to be bothered by Avryn deflecting this particular question.

"You just pick one, then? That's it?" Marric said, continuing to their earlier conversation.

"Well, it's a bit more complicated than that. The best I can describe it is that the second ability sort of picks you."

Marric didn't understand what he meant by that, but all of this information was too overwhelming for him to pry any further. He wasn't quite sure how he felt about all of this.

They walked on for a time, discontinuing the conversation. It was much cooler and pleasant outside, and Marric was really enjoying the breeze and smells of the forest. The pathway had at some point become more rocky and bumpy. He hadn't noticed that it had changed until he stumbled on one of the rocks after slipping deep into thought from their conversation. He had been trying to commit the things that Avryn had told him to memory. His breathing increased as they walked, and he felt his legs start to tire more quickly. Only then did Marric realize that the pathway had become more inclined and they were moving upwards very quickly.

There are Lighters, Conjurers, Fixers, Movers, Seers, Shielders. You only become one of these. . . .

"What's the seventh?" Marric asked, breaking the silence. He hadn't thought about it before he spoke, it just fled from his lips as a continuation of his thoughts.

Avryn stiffened visibly next to him.

"You said that there are seven different classes, but you only told me six. What is the seventh?" He asked again.

"It's one that I try not to speak of, for it is particularly dangerous. I chose not to explain at this time, because it is much more rare for someone to manifest that class of powers."

Silence.

"That's it? You won't tell me? I feel like I should probably know at some point."

"Marric, it isn't something that you need to worry about. You will not likely manifest the seventh, so you probably don't need to know—"

"But what if I do?" Marric cut in. "What then?"

He was surprised at his tone. He'd never been this bullish before, but he felt entitled to the knowledge and was annoyed that Avryn was holding back.

Avryn stared at Marric, observing the resolve in the boy's face. Finally, he sighed and began explaining.

"If you wish." Avryn said. "The seventh class—and, as I mentioned, the rarest—is, for all intents and purposes, the opposite of a Fixer. They . . . *break* things. Whereas a Fixer has the ability to put things back together and restore them, a Destroyer breaks things down or dissolves them. It is dangerous, because in a moment it can level a home, or kill a person, blasting either to bits. The power is a nasty one, and unfortunately, many of the Destroyers that exist have chosen to join Watchlight. They care not for human life, and their use of powers shows that."

Though Marric appreciated hearing the truth, he felt a chill run through him, the hair standing up on his arms and neck. The explanation sounded so macabre. So Lightbearer powers weren't all good. Somehow, that hadn't surprised him, but Lanser's beard, they could disintegrate a person!

Suddenly, he felt nervous at his potential. What if *he* became one of these dreaded Destroyers? Did it alter his mind? Would he think differently? Would the powers take over him?

"Marric," Avryn said sternly.

The boy's eyes refocused on the man.

"I'm sorry," he breathed out. "I got a bit distracted."

"I was hoping to save that last part for a while until you felt a little more at ease with the reality of Lightbearers and their abilities. However, perhaps it was better for you to hear now. I fear that I am a bit too soft when it comes to news like this. That happens to be a fault of mine."

Marric stared at Avryn for a moment, then the realization hit him. He remembered the strange burst of Light as he hid in the forest outside of Wurren, the sound of bursting wood piercing the night. He even heard the men scream as they fell to the ground.

"That's you, isn't it?"

Avryn paused, causing the caravan behind to stop as well.

"Everythin' alright, S'ren?" Shrell called out.

"Yes, yes, it's alright, Shrell."

He then spoke to Marric, "Yes, you are correct. I manifest the powers of a Destroyer, but I do not condone its use, except in times of desperation. I am not proud of the ability, nor of the instances when I've been forced to use it, but it is who I am, and I thank Lanser that Fixing exists to mend what is broken by Destroyers."

Something in his tone made Marric reluctant to say much else. He considered Avryn to be a good man, and to know that he had the power of a Destroyer actually gave the boy hope.

So it wouldn't change me or make me into something evil, Marric thought with relief.

Soon after the conversation, the pathway flattened out and the trees gradually became more sparse along the side of the road. The air began to cool a lot more, and through the now visible space in the trees, Marric saw that the sun was starting to set, leaving them in darkening space. The sky had changed to a brilliant orangish red and the wispy clouds that were apparent shone bright pink. He was caught up in the beauty of the sight. It looked so much as if the sky was ablaze with fire. Surprisingly, creatures seemed to be emerging right at this time as well. He saw a handful of longbirds flitting in the air, snatching the insects that were unseen to his eyes. A herd of deer grazed in the trees a short distance away, heads pointed upwards toward the band of travelers as they walked, though they seemed carefree and unworried.

Movement on the trunk of the tree just next to him around his eye level made him jump. However, when he looked, he saw nothing there. Just when he thought he might be seeing things in his exhausted state, he saw it again. A creature appeared on the trunk of the tree, the same color and texture of the brown bark. It was furry, had six arms, and hands with actual thumbs. Was this the Aperoy he'd heard of from travelers? Its glassy black eyes stared at him, head turned almost backwards to look at the group. As it moved, he could see its limbs and short stubby tail, but the moment it stopped, it was as if it became part of the tree, lost in the grains of the bark itself.

Marric continued to be filled with wonder as the forest teemed with this life. Curiously, they all seemed unafraid of the group of travelers, as if they were very accustomed to people and the sounds they made. It seemed strange to Marric that they hadn't passed a single person on the road as they traveled today, but then again, it wasn't the peak merchant day in Wurren for a couple more days.

An opening appeared in the trees just ahead, almost as if the mouth of a beast appeared and stood gaping, ready to ingest them joyfully. A nervous tightness entered his chest. He could see lights in the distance. These weren't the unfamiliar blue Lights that Avryn had displayed, but normal flickering fires and lamps, scattered along the view in the distance. He wasn't sure he understood how he could see those so easily through the trees. When they reached the opening, Marric's mouth dropped slightly, awe apparent on his face.

The trees ended so sharply that it was a shocking change in the scenery. Looking left and right, the trees continued out of sight for an unknown distance. Straight ahead, there were no trees at all on the landscape. A grassy plain extended as far as he could see ahead of them. The grass stood high, most of it waist-high. The plains were full of rolling hills, appearing as if the land had begun to boil with large bubbles and frozen there, an infinitely churning landscape. The path cut windingly through and over the hills, but more strikingly, it was lined with caravans full of people.

"This is where we'll need to be on our best guard, my friends." Avryn said as they paused and gathered at the edge of the strange plains. "Welcome, Marric, to the Plains of Erisdell."

Chapter 7

Prost hated the sun. It glared down on his head, full of dark grey hair, causing him to break out in a hot sweat as he trudged up the base of the green mountain. It wasn't that the sun itself bothered him, it was just that he thrived in the darkness. Everything was so exposed during the day, much more so than during any of the three moons that shone periodically throughout the night. He could at least appreciate the fact that the sun made the world burst with life. He had always been drawn to wide open spaces and the raw power of the natural world.

Fog, this place isn't half bad to look at, he thought as he made his way up the steep incline.

The base of the mountain was covered in thick green grass that somehow stayed low to the ground. From afar, the whole mountain, where there weren't other bushes or trees growing, looked like a solid green mass that appeared to undulate with the breeze. Rocks jutted up here and there through the grass, making the scene more striking.

Prost stopped for a minute, not because he needed a rest, but because he wanted to take it all in. Closing his eyes, he took a deep breath and let the clear air wash through him as if it was clearing his mind and body of any weakness. He heard a snicker behind him and his eyes snapped open. He spun on his heels and simultaneously whipped out his wicked dagger. The blade was long and wavy, like a snake frozen in a slither. The metal was such a bright silver that it shone even without light reflecting off of it. Without hesitation, he dove on his companion, knocking him to the ground and holding the dagger to his neck.

"You think something is FUNNY?!" he roared at the scrawny man under his grip.

The man wasn't small, but he seemed a lot smaller compared to Prost's muscled body and large stature. Though he stood at about the same height as Prost, Mert was maybe half his weight. That had made it all the easier for him to pin the smaller man under him. Mert kept his whole head shaved, save one thick ponytail of hair that he kept long and died black at all times. He also donned a ring of silver in his nose, thinking that it made him seem more fierce.

He was a Mover, which is why he was often one of the operatives that accompanied Prost. It wasn't that Prost wasn't capable of defending himself, but a Mover was handy when you wanted to intimidate someone or a group of people without having to get close to them.

"Blast, Prost! I was only jokin'!" Mert huffed out, anger contorting his face.

"Let me make this clear, *Mert.* I am your superior, and I can easily outmatch you without the slightest trouble at all."

"Okay, okay! You've made that clear, eh?" Mert sputtered at him.

Prost didn't immediately let him go, but instead narrowed his eyes at the man threateningly. Mert didn't say it, but Prost could tell the thick scars that ran from either side of his nose to each ear unnerved the Mover.

"Prost, git over yerself," a woman standing beside the men said. "Yeh don' have t'always prove somethin'. We know tha' yous could kick our hineys anyday."

That didn't make him feel any better. His admiration of the natural world was often the subject of ridicule by those in Watchlight. Their leader, Riln, hadn't ever indicated that it bothered him, but others in the organization thought it a weakness, as if they shouldn't care about anything other than killing and the destruction of this world. That is where they were *wrong.* The cause of Watchlight was destruction only as a means for their own preservation. Watchlight could not come into their own fully and flourish until the world around them became subjugated to their will. They just didn't understand the higher order.

"Prost, seriously. We don' have time fer this stuff. Riln's waitin' fer the report." Alts said again.

Alts was a fine woman, indeed. She stood next to them, arms folded, and bore a look of annoyance on her face. Her long blonde hair was always perfectly kept, and it contrasted with her almost black eyes. A stripe of her hair from head to end was blue, though how she dyed it that way, Prost didn't know. She was slender, but strong. She too was a Lightbearer, but of the Conjurer class, also handy in combat. She didn't show any indication that she feared him, which normally annoyed him, but in this case, it made her even more attractive. If his calling for Watchlight didn't consume his entire life, he might have even considered trying to court the woman, but that wasn't going to happen soon.

"You're lucky that she's right," Prost growled at the skinny man.

With a grunt, he pushed himself up off the man and started walking back up the incline, not waiting for Mert to stand up and follow behind.

"Yer just lucky that yer a foggin' *dud*," Mert said.

Prost's vision went red and his hand clenched tight next to him. Quicker than ever, he turned toward Mert and punched the man square in the face, knocking him to the ground. He felt his knuckles squish the man's pointed nose and felt it breaking behind his fist. Mert's head was thrown backwards, with his body soon behind. This made Alts curse and run to the man, checking his pulse.

"Oh, fog it, Alts, he's not dead. If I'd wanted him dead, I wouldn't have used my fist. Now get your weak self up and follow me, you bloomin' idiot," Prost growled at them.

The Lightbearers that had joined Watchlight hated Prost. Not just because he was favored by Riln, their leader, but also because their powers were rendered useless on him. For a reason only known by Riln and himself, Prost was immune to all the effects of Lightbearers, both physically and mentally. In his mind, it leveled the playing field. All those that were normally superior to a regular human because of those powers were normalized when they faced him. Unfortunately, it also meant that Fixing wouldn't work on him. That had been a foggin' nuisance, but he'd gotten used to it. In an effort to save face, someone had coined the term 'dud' in reference to his state. Normally, a name wouldn't bother the mountain of a man, but this irritated him far more than he'd like to admit.

His two companions followed behind, Mert breathing heavily from the blow, nose bleeding profusely, soaking the front of his brown shirt and vest. Prost continued on without waiting for them. While he walked, he breathed deeply of the mountain air again, keeping it less obvious this time. This brought him back to his time before Watchlight, before his life had been complicated by Lightbearing. He remembered his combat training for the militia back in the capital, where they experienced heavy rains and beating storms. He had marveled at how a man could train all his life and only have a finite amount of power, but the powers of the earth were unmatched, and unsympathetic. He had always wanted that type of power himself.

It was his last moment to enjoy the fresh air before they would plunge into the mountain where the air was stale and stuffy. They approached a large stone that resembled the shape of a fish fin, pointing up in the air toward the sky. Prost stepped up to the stone and pressed his hand into a portion of the stone that slid inward, grinding on the edges. A larger grinding sound indicated that the lever had worked and a doorway opened inward, revealing a steep set of stairs downward.

Prost took one last breath of the clean air before descending the stairs. Pinkish-red bulbs of Light glowed steadily every five feet or so, about the size of an orange. They looked to be attached to the wall, but actually hovered in midair a finger span from the wall. Watchlight had a number of Lighters that upkept the Light in their gathering place continuously, but this looked to be the work of Neera, their head Lighter. In a fight, her powers were practically worthless, but Lanser's might, it was handy to have her on their side. It meant that there was no trouble living in an underground cavern with no windows or natural light. Fire lamps and torches would be too impractical for such a large network of underground tunnels.

The door rumbled closed behind them as Alts triggered the internal switch. As it thumped closed, the last natural light snuffed out, and with it, all direct access to the fresh air that Prost craved. He was already in a bad mood, but his disposition soured more at the final resounding sound of the door closing. Perhaps the stale air was the cause of his bad mood that gave him such a negative reputation here.

The stairs plunged deeper and deeper in a seemingly never ending sweep. Though the feeling of infinity was present while travelling down the stairs for a time, it wasn't reality, just his perception of the long stairway. He soon stepped loudly onto the landing at the bottom of the stairs. Two sentinels stood at the ready, spears in hand, to the sides of a second doorway. This had no door, but gaped open. They hadn't bothered putting any type of gate or door here, because if an enemy were to breach the top door, the narrow stairway would put them at a disadvantage already anyway. They were clothed in chainmail that looked an eerie red, reflecting the glow of two spheres of red Light identical to those seen above and all along the doorway.

Prost nodded to the men and continued through the doorway into the main chamber. He came immediately to a railing before an enormous cavern that extended both downwards and upwards. Glowing orbs revealed tiers built regularly into the edges of the cavern. The construction of this cavern had taken many years, but having Destroyers in your ranks made it a lot easier to blast out sections and create such an intricate layout.

His two companions, traveling slower than him, stepped up behind him and muttered something about getting Mert to a Fixer. Prost merely ignored them and moved off to meet his master. He was loath to approach the man with the news he had, but he knew that this was his burden to bear, being so highly favored of the master and filling the position that he did. A break in the handrail opened to a set of stairs that ringed the cavern in a spiral from tier to tier all the way to the top. He immediately set out up the stairs to Riln's throne room.

It had not gone well. The plan was to recruit the assassin woman to their side by employing her with the job that they had. Prost didn't know the woman well, but her reputation preceded her, as his did within Watchlight. Talking to her wasn't a way to build trust, but giving her money and a thrilling job that piqued her interest certainly helped. He wasn't sure what had gone wrong, but the fogging woman had disappeared with the boy from Wurren. When he'd approached her in Arrivan, she had seemed promising. He had clearly scared the fog out of her, but admittedly she had proven much more capable than he had anticipated. The loss of her seemed almost as great as the loss of the budding Lightbearer boy.

His thoughts warred with each other as he entered the chamber to Riln. The room was oddly shaped, long, with pillars on both sides, much like a regular throne room in a palace. But the room to the right of the pillars ebbed out in a circular shape, doubling as the strategic war room for their planning. A large circular wood table stood with a map of Lindrad and its townships. A black throne made of twisted and polished wood stood at the end of the long cavern, but Riln was not there. This made Prost break out in a nervous sweat. He was not concerned that his master would—or even could—kill him, but the man was unsettling in a way that he couldn't describe.

"Ah, Prost," a voice said from somewhere in the darkness.

Prost shivered slightly, affected by the strange presence of his master. The air seemed to respond to Riln, chilling Prost as if the cold season appeared out of nowhere in the recesses of this cavern.

"You have returned, far sooner than I would have anticipated."

The voice was high for a man's, but it was smooth and measured. He usually spoke slowly, making his listeners feel like they were on dangerous ground. Perhaps that was what made Prost so nervous and uncomfortable. When he felt emotions, anger, frustration, pleasure, it was apparent in Prost's face and voice. But his master was more often deadpan and rarely yelled—if he ever got that angry, the recipient of his anger was swiftly killed.

"Master, I am afraid the news from Wurren is not good." Prost said hurriedly. With all his thinking and deliberation, he decided to deliver news how he always did: straight and to the point.

"Go on."

A figure slinked out of the dark from behind one of the pillars to the left of Prost. Why his master was occupying that space, he couldn't say, but he was a peculiar man. The man had pale skin, almost as white as bone, and eyes that were a bright blue, bright as the sky itself. His hair, flowing past his shoulders, was also white, even whiter than his skin. He had a fondness for impractical clothing, and currently donned large purple robes, making him more pale in contrast.

"The woman assassin and the boy have vanished. They eliminated most of our operatives in Wurren and fled with soldiers from Evenir. At last report, they headed north out of the town, but their destination is unknown."

Prost heard his master smack his lips and let out a quiet sigh, as if he was straining to contain a tempest of something, though Prost couldn't know what.

Without a word, Riln opened his right hand and a flash of red Light formed into a dagger. It took the shape that it normally did, a bright red glare pulsing at the pommel like a giant ruby formed from real stone. The edge of one side was serrated, the other sharp and smooth. It came to a wicked point at the end. Riln could Conjure whatever he pleased, but he always seemed to revert to this weapon, as if it was something too familiar to forget. Most Conjurers didn't spend so much time on the form of the objects they summoned, unless they were trying to fool someone with their construct, but Riln was very deliberate with his Conjures, especially so with this dagger.

The silence continued as Riln stared into the distance, saying nothing. The garish man extended his hand to the pillar to the left of Prost and opened his palm with the dagger resting there. It launched forward and slammed loudly into the pillar, penetrating the stone deeply. After giving off a few bright pulses of light, it vanished into nothingness, leaving a hole where the dagger entered, and a crack extending on either side.

Prost didn't move. He didn't speak, he practically didn't breathe. He'd found that no reaction was the best reaction to whatever happened while you were with the master. He didn't feel threatened at all, for of course Riln's powers would be useless on Prost, but his instincts shouted at him to run, attack, hide. A conflict of commands shot from his brain, trying to spark him to action.

"That is unfortunate, at best. Do we have a party attempting to locate them?" The statement came out like a drawl.

"We have some leaving north from Wurren in parties to search for them, but with the head start they had, they could have headed in any direction."

Riln tilted his head, face unmoving as it stayed in its passive state.

"What of the Seers?"

"I have not communicated with them at present, for I came straightway to you. I could go now, if you wish and—"

His master silenced him with a few waves of his hand.

"No need. The Lightbearer with them is convoluting the view. I have tried to See them already. I only see snippets of trees and rocks, but nothing to indicate their location or intentions. Their companion is not a Shielder, but he is constantly using his weak Shielding to interrupt our view, which is just enough."

Another pause. Prost considered himself lucky that he was immune to Seeing effects. Normally, one would have to be a Shielder or have a companion with such powers to hide from a Seer's eyes, but he didn't. He would always be hidden from their powers.

Prost suspected that part of his discomfort in the presence of Riln is that the master never seemed hurried in any conversation, leaving him guessing how important he deemed the discussion.

"I would be quite disappointed to lose the young one to *them*. He does show such potential. I have Seen his awakening myself."

"You have Seen it? What is it like? What will his powers be?"

"I cannot See every detail. I can only See the power, the intensity of this boy's Light."

Prost was a bit disappointed in that. He had never, nor could ever, experience the Seeing that his master or the other Seers could, but he was often disappointed in the lack of detail in many instances. Even though he was immune to whatever powers the boy would manifest, it still made him nervous to be close in proximity to the awakening with his other troops.

"Pardon, master. Why is it that we don't know specifics about this boy? Why can we not see the exact time and location?" He had let frustration bleed into his voice, which was a risk.

Fortunately, Riln looked only amused. He shifted his gaze to Prost and cocked his head to the side, looking the strong soldier over.

"Seeing is not as you think. We do not have a window into all the world's secrets at all times. Seeing is better in concentrated power. The more insignificant the event, the easier it is to see in detail. This boy's awakening is too great of an event for us to See it all. Perhaps your normal human mind can't quite capture the concept."

Prost stiffened at the comment. The master had a tendency to highlight the fact that Prost had no Lightbearer powers, but it was something that Prost had to deal with. He didn't follow the man for his kindness, but for his cause. Prost's usefulness was emphasized when he was facing Lightbearers as opponents because of his strange gift, which as far as he knew had not been replicated in any form. Regardless of his usefulness, his past would not allow him to be unaffected by such comments.

"Oh, my dear Prost." Riln spoke quietly. He turned and walked to Prost, who stood almost a foot taller than him. Riln put both hands on Prost's upper arms and squeezed slightly. "I'm confident that you will make this right. Your skill in combat is unprecedented, and you are quite adept at tracking. Go. Take what you need and *find that boy.*"

Even though his eyes didn't show any anger, the sleeves of Prost's long-sleeved jacket smoked suddenly and disintegrated down to his wrists, leaving most of his arms bare. He looked down to see a disappearing glow retreat in Riln's hands, and pieces of his jacket falling to the ground like leaves fluttering down. If Prost hadn't been immune to the Destroying powers, he was confident that he would have left the meeting with no arms. He steeled his face and looked into his master's eyes, trying to show resolve. On the inside, he was quivering with fright.

Perhaps he only likes me as a type of relief mechanism, knowing that he can't actually hurt me, Prost thought to himself.

He took the comment and the destruction of his clothing as a dismissal and turned to head back to the doorway. His assumption must have been correct, for the master made no motion to stop him. As he reached the doorway, Riln spoke again.

"Oh, and Prost."

He stopped, but didn't turn.

"Try not to kill our troops, especially the Lightbearers. Though it may seem that we have many, we cannot afford to lose any to your anger. Poor Mert, though frustrating, needs to keep his life."

Blast, he Saw *that? I thought that I was immune to Sight?!* Prost thought, panicked that his immunity to Lightbearing might have run its course. It seemed like a silly thought, but it was something he had that others did not, something that made him stand out.

"Though I could not See the events of his injuries, I See the poor man now recovering in the infirmary. I can only assume that was your handiwork. I trust that you'll use your best judgment as you carry out this task. That is all."

Relief blossomed in Prost's chest at the comment.

Prost crossed the threshold back onto the balcony overlooking the cavern and set out to gather his troops. He'd need a variety of men, both regular and Lightbearer. Alts would be good to have, and he should probably bring Mert along, with a bit—or a lot—of force. A Shielder or two and another Mover would be good. Fog, he probably ought to bring one of their Destroyers. They were a nasty lot. There was a particular Destroyer that he'd met only a few times. This one had a strange bond to the master, a bit like his own, but the personality of this lad closely resembled the master, which would make it less fun to bring him along, but his passion would be important for the task.

He only had one chance, and he had a feeling that failing would not end well.

Chapter 8

It had been four days since they had left Wurren, and this was the first time the terrain had looked any different. The Plains of Erisdell turned out to be a very popular location for merchants and tradesmen to spend a lot of time. Apparently, it was a well traveled location, though Marric didn't quite understand how that could be. They hadn't seen even one person traveling just south of the Plains, despite the many crossroads they had passed on their way from Wurren. Regardless, the large bustling population of the Plains indicated that the roads had to be used sometimes. There was a strange assortment of not only the wares being sold, but also the types of people that both sold and shopped at the carts. Marric's group had entered the Plains just before the first moon the night before, but hadn't stopped immediately. They traveled for a few hours more, just to the middle of the second moon, before stopping and lodging at an inn-like establishment. Avryn had decided that it was better than being outside again during Isllan. With this many people crowded together, even some walls would be better than none to protect against possible attacks.

The place they had stayed turned out to be a ring of carts that were converted into individual rooms. It seemed a strange concept, considering the fact that the Plains were considered a temporary location, not a formalized merchant town or city. Regardless, the stay had been much more comfortable than the ground, and Marric had slept much better there.

They had risen early and set out again on the path in the Plains, but the path turned a bit more west as they traveled. The breeze rippled through the grass and seemed to flow constantly with the absence of concentrated trees.

Marric was mesmerized by the waves of grass that he imagined likely moved as if they were waves of water undulating in the ocean he'd heard about in stories. The strong wind was welcome, considering there was nothing to block the sun from beating down on their heads and faces.

Marric was struck with how large and wide the Plains of Erisdell were. He was surprised that he hadn't heard much talk of the place, but then again, he hadn't spent much time with anyone outside his sphere due to always being holed up in the fletcher's shop. They had traveled for most of the day and it was late in the afternoon already, the sun dipping to a steep angle, pointing into their faces now that they had turned westward.

Avryn had insisted that if they did a little bit of shopping, they would blend in with the crowd a bit better, so he and Harmel made seemingly frequent stops at odd shops and purchased a few things here and there. The strange brother, for he did seem much more odd than Shrell, turned out to be quite superstitious, and had bought a few trinkets, including a necklace made out of the skull of a longbird. The object was supposed to ward against evil and protect him from spells that could be cast by witches or other beings. Marric had asked Avryn if such beings existed, and Avryn just let out a chuckle. He told Marric to not let the fickle man worry him about such nonsense. His dismissive response hadn't put Marric much at ease.

The rolling hills of the Plains seemed to continue forever, and with the absence of mountains or other trees, Marric constantly felt lost for directions. When they first arrived, he had been fascinated by the scenery and conglomeration of carts and people here and there, but it had quickly turned to monotony.

During their whole time here so far, Janis had disappeared on and off, choosing to take her own path. Though he wasn't sure how, she always seemed to find them periodically to check in and make sure all was well. He could only imagine what she could be doing in such a place. He thought for a moment that she might be off buying things of her own, but when she returned, she was never carrying anything new.

As they were passing another grouping of merchant carts, Janis appeared again, somehow from behind a cart ahead of them.

"It looks like the treeline begins again there in the distance. I suggest that we make for the forest and camp again." Janis suggested.

Avryn nodded, looking grim.

"I suppose you're right. I fear that another night in the settlement is a bit too risky. We'll break here for a time, then make for the trees. I've a few more things to purchase before we leave, and I think that taking a break now might get us to the forest tonight."

He turned to Marric, a smile adorning his face that was beginning to become familiar to the boy.

"Perhaps you can explore the shops a bit, eh? If you see something you like, feel free to buy it."

"But I haven't any money," Marric explained. "Plus, I don't understand most of what is being sold."

"Shrell will be your companion. Just tell him what you'd like, and he'll pay for it. Is that alright, my friend?"

Shrell didn't smile, but he did nod in agreement.

"Well then, I'll be off. Let us meet back here after a time. Perhaps when the sun reaches the tops of the trees, then?" Avryn said.

Janis didn't bother to say anything, but slinked off back toward the cart where she'd appeared. Avryn turned and moved in the opposite direction with Harmel, who was holding the skull on his necklace and seemed to be muttering something.

"Where might yeh like t'go, Marric?" Shrell said, a slight smile adorning his face.

"I'm not sure. I've never seen such a place. It's a bit overwhelming."

"No need ta worry. Yous jus' need t'walk and see, no need ta think much. It's right good t' just wander here n' there."

With that, Shrell gestured back the way they came to a cart that seemed to be selling skin pelts of all sorts. Deciding that it was as good of a place as any, he stepped up to the shop and began looking at what was being sold. The man behind the makeshift table was short and rugged-looking. His fierce eyes were covered by thick black brows. An imposing mustache adorned his upper lip, making his mouth seem nonexistent. Animal skins hung from hooks along the front and ceiling of the cart behind the man, and the table was filled with pelts of all sizes. Most were only pieces of larger animals cut into smaller portions, but some were full animal pelts, complete with heads and paws. Some Marric recognized, but most seemed unfamiliar to him. There was a small and thin white pelt that bore no hair, but had a smooth white surface and a rodent snout. Another was scaly, and had as many legs as an insect. It glowed in the sunlight, marbled red and green scales all along the back.

"What are yeh lookin' fer this fine evenin'? Oi has lots of stuffin' fer yer needs," the man said with a gravelly voice.

Marric hadn't expected the man to say anything, so he started a bit at the offer.

"I'm just lookin', is all." Marric explained to the man.

The would-be salesman pursed his lips, obviously disappointed.

"Are yeh sure, then? Oi've gots plenty of things that might strike the fancy of a nice young one like yous. 'Ere, take a looks at this'n 'ere."

He reached behind him and pulled out a large rabbit pelt that was flattened and stretched out. Marric could admit that it did look quite beautiful and soft, but he wasn't sure what a person would do with something like that.

"Look, sir, I appreciate it, but—"

"It's righ' fine, yeh see. Only one gold frond will git yeh such a fine piece of work."

Marric started at the price.

A gold frond *for just that?! Do people actually pay that?!*

Shrell stepped in behind Marric, appearing as if from nowhere. He must have finished up his browsing and noticed the man urging Marric to buy something.

"Are yeh aright, Marric? Is this man bothering yeh?" Shrell asked in a threatening way. He even put his hands on his sword hanging at his side.

"Um—well, he—"

"Oi was'n doin' a thing!" the man said, throwing up his hands in defense, the rabbit pelt falling back to the table.

"That yeh weren't. Mind yer business, else yeh attract business yeh don' want 'ere." Shrell said with a finality.

The two of them turned away, and Marric looked up at Shrell, aghast. He wasn't completely unhappy with what the man had done for him, but it still made him a bit uncomfortable. Such a display of threat would not have gone unnoticed in a place like Wurren. He felt bad for the shopkeeper. Who knows what he needed money for? Perhaps a family? A home?

"Marric, yeh don' need to feel bad 'ere. 'S all a game."

"Hmm?"

"I'm jus' sayin', that man din' git harmed or anythin'. 'Ere in the Plains, it's all a game. They try to push stuff on yeh, and yeh jus' gotta push back with a bit of force. Don' be feelin' bad about anythin'."

Marric merely stared at Shrell, who grinned at him in an exaggerated way. His green eyes sparkled at Marric as if he had just told a funny joke to the boy, and was holding back a series of laughs. For a mercenary, the tall man did seem to have a sense for what others felt around him. Marric had noticed more instances of his sympathy while they traveled. On one occasion, they had been walking in silence, all five of them deep in thought, when Shrell suddenly sped up his pace to walk next to Avryn. It seemed completely random, but as the man put his hand on Avryn's shoulder, Marric noticed him wipe a tear from his face. He wasn't sure how the soldier had noticed that, but somehow he had.

"Are you a mind reader, then?" Marric asked, dumbfounded.

He just continued grinning at Marric, but gave him a wink.

"Wait 'ere fer jus' a min'. I have to get somethin' fer my sword. Could use a bit of sharpenin'."

Shrell walked up to a weapons stall just in front of them, leaving Marric a few paces back behind him. He just stood there for a time, not sure what else he could look at. Marric was a bit afraid of approaching another shop, lest one of the keepers push him into buying something again. Instead, he slowly turned in a circle and inspected the shops from afar, trying to determine if it would be worth it to approach any of them. Most of the shops were standard. More pelts here, clothing there, weapons, provisions for travel, horse care, and—

Marric froze as he saw that one of the shopkeepers was staring at him. She was a very old woman, with deep wrinkles set in her forehead and around her eyes. Her hair was light grey and stringy. It tumbled over her shoulders messily. Her teeth were crooked and yellow, but she smiled brightly as if she didn't mind who saw them. She had her eyes trained on Marric, steadily and unabashed. Marric immediately noticed that the woman's eyes were pure white, as if all of the color had been sucked out of them completely. He stared at her, perplexed at her steady gaze despite him returning his own. Marric had observed that stares were not an uncommon thing here in the Plains, but this seemed even more uncomfortable than usual.

Not sure what to do, he just kept staring. Though the sight of her eyes was unsettling, it did explain her steady stare. She was obviously completely blind. He relaxed and breathed out, only now realizing that he had been holding his breath the whole time.

What could a blind woman possibly be selling in such a place as this? he thought to himself, curious.

The woman kept staring, a stupid grin frozen on her face as if she were only a statue of an old woman permanently carved into stone. Frowning, Marric stepped forward slowly and made his way over to the wagon shop. Hers was somewhat different from the others. There were obvious themes to all of the other shops, but this one just seemed a random assortment of unrelated objects. There were tassels spaced evenly along the makeshift canvas roof that hung down just a few inches from the woman's head. The tassels were brightly colored in flashy shades of every color imaginable. The table was covered with odd things. Marric spotted a miniature cow skull, somehow shrunk to the size of a mouse. There were an assortment of animal feet, tied to bits of leather as if they were meant to be hung from somewhere. A bowl of green viscous liquid seemed to be boiling slightly, as if it was locked in slow motion. Strangely, there appeared to be some large insect or bird nests woven with string and covered in beads hanging among the tassels above, and drums and instruments littering the empty spaces of the table.

Marric stopped next to the table and continued to observe the collection.

He had almost completely forgotten that the woman was there, until she spoke to him, making him jump at her voice.

"Well, hello, young one." Her voice screeched. It sounded kindly, but also strained and scratchy as if she had just swallowed sharp rocks and was raw from the cuts.

Marric shivered.

"How did you know I was here?" he asked, surprised.

She chuckled at the comment.

"I be blind, boy, not deaf. Yer feet plunk so loudly, I could hear yeh from far away, y'see."

He hadn't thought of that. Of course she could hear him approach her wagon shop. For a brief moment, he considered how he must take for granted his ability to hear. Marric realized suddenly that she had said 'young one' to him. Normally, he wouldn't ask a probing question to a disabled person, but his curiosity got the better of him.

"Beg pardon, ma'am, but how did you know that I was not a grown man, or a woman, or some other sort of person?"

She squinted her eyes and her smile deepened. She did indeed look kind, but her pure white eyes were so unsettling that he almost stepped back in nervousness.

"Well, when yer as blind as me, yeh learn t'use yer other senses to make up fer the gone one. Yous got a way of walkin' that sounds child-like. Yeh breath heavy, like all boys do, and yeh prolly din' hear it, but yeh were talkin' to yerself while yeh walked, an' yeh don' sound like a girl."

Marric blushed deeply. He had always hated that habit. It wasn't often, but he tended to talk to himself when he felt uncomfortable or unsure.

"Ah, don' yeh be worryin'. It ain't jus' you tha' talks to yerself. I right do so meself, now and then. Fer yeh won' righ' find anyone better company than yerself. Now, what yeh be lookin' fer this evenin'?"

He opened his mouth to tell the woman that it wasn't quite evening, merely late afternoon, but thought better of it. She was blind after all, he couldn't expect her to get everything right even though she had known a lot of details about him, despite her lack of sight.

"I don't know that I'm *looking* for anything right now. The other shopkeepers keep pushing things on me, and I was trying to keep my distance lest they try to convince me again."

"An' yet, yeh are right 'ere, talkin' t'me."

He blushed again. Marric was extremely grateful that the woman was blind and couldn't see the embarrassment so clearly displayed on his face.

"Well, I thought you were . . . staring at me, ma'am."

"Ah, I see. I'm sorry 'bout that, m'boy, but I can' right help it. Lost me eyesight awhile back—can' right see where I be lookin' fer the life of me."

Marric smiled at her apology, feeling relieved that she seemed as nice as she looked.

"Well, I don' right know if yeh would like what's I got 'ere, but jus' let me know if somethin' strikes yer fancy, hmm?"

Marric nodded, then continued looking over the strange contents laid out before him. The thought that she was blind suddenly struck him, and he quickly said, "Oh yes—yes, of course, ma'am."

She only laughed.

"I jus' assumed yous had nodded or somethin', don' yeh be worryin'. I've been blind fer years an' years."

Relieved that he hadn't come across rude, he kept looking at the table. For some reason, he felt compelled to find something to purchase, even though he had little interest in anything that the woman was selling and Shrell wasn't here at the moment to pay for it. Something about the way that she spoke to him, or perhaps the fact that she seemed to be alone, living off of her goods only, made him feel like he should just pick something random and pay for it.

"If you don't mind me asking, ma'am, what are you selling? The other shops seemed to have some theme, but I haven't been able to figure out what your shop is for?"

The woman looked contemplative, as if she was thinking about the best response.

"Do all things need t' make sense? Some things need only *be,* I reckon'."

"I'm not sure what you mean?"

The woman's smile deepened, as if she was keeping an old secret.

"My shop is not fer people lookin' fer sense. This'n world can be a nasty place, mind yous. Those that need me wares are those tha' don' think they do. Yeh might find just what yeh never knew yous was lookin' fer."

It was as if the woman was speaking nonsense. Marric wasn't sure what she was trying to say to him, yet the draw to buy something was still strong and completely unexplainable.

A cool breeze blew in, silently rustling the tassels and strange nets above. They danced to and fro, the colors complementing the tassels to either side, making quite a pleasant sight. He hadn't felt too many strong breezes as they traveled today, but this one was strong and cool. It seemed very out of character for what he'd expected the weather to be for the remainder of their trip through the Plains of Erisdell. The air smelled of dried grass and plants, somewhat fresh and relaxing.

Without too much thought, he began picking things up off the table to inspect them further. Though he was tempted, he steered clear of the odd green liquid that continued to bubble thickly in the bowl. There really didn't seem to be anything of value or interest to Marric, but he kept looking. Time seemed to be lost as he gingerly handled things one by one.

Reaching toward the miniature cow skull, his hand brushed the old woman's as it lay near the trinket. She let out a sharp gasp and snatched his hand in a flash, sending a jolt of fear through Marric's whole body. He stared in shock as the woman's pure white eyes began to glow a bright blue. She stared off into the distance past him as she began muttering something to herself. Her grip was alarmingly strong on his hand, which he was frantically trying to pull away, his other hand attempting to pry hers off of his.

The panicked encounter only lasted a few moments, however, as her eyes dimmed and she relaxed her hand, releasing his. Though her grip had been strong and hadn't left his hand hurting at all, he still rubbed it as if it had. Resisting the urge to run away, he simply watched as the woman sat quietly, looking worried.

He wasn't sure what he was waiting for, but he was locked in his position, only staring at her. Without a word, she reached to her left and grabbed the foot of a rabbit connected to a long piece of leather that was open on both ends. It was clear that it was meant to be tied to something, but he could only guess to what.

"Take this," she said in her raspy voice, which seemed to be even more pained than before.

"What?"

"Take this, boy." She was more insistent with her tone this time. "You *must.*"

"I can't just take that," Marric said. "I'll at least pay for it. We just have to wait for my friend—"

"*No!*" she said in a sudden outburst.

This time, he did step back, her tone forceful and intense.

"This be the foot of a rabbit. Only if it be gifted does it reach its full potency." She shoved her hand forward again, clutching the trinket tightly.

"I—I don't understand. I—"

"Hey, Marric. What yeh got there, eh? Is she botherin' yous a bit?"

Shrell strolled up to the two of them, a look of curiosity on his face as he took in the scene before him. He looked at the woman, then back at Marric, not sure what was happening.

"Did you buy that, then?" Shrell asked.

"*No!*" she said again, sounding desperate this time. "I am only gifting this to the boy. Take it, *please.*"

This time, Marric slowly moved forward and took the foot from her gingerly, as if it might hurt him if he touched it.

The woman visibly relaxed when he did so, and a slight smile returned to her mouth. Though her face altogether seemed happy, she still appeared stressed about something grave. Her gaze, blank and yet somehow piercing, continued to point off over Marric's shoulder.

"Keep that on yous, always. It's a ward from physical harm."

Shrell snorted at the comment, inducing a glare from the woman in his direction.

"There be doubters, boy, but know that the foot of a rabbit be righ' effective when it comes t' protection. Don' doubt, just wear it *always.*"

Marric opened his hand to inspect the gift a bit more closely. It seemed an odd thing, but at the same time, quite attractive in its own way. The small foot was full of brown fur, with black and darker brown patches here and there. Marric was struck by how soft it felt in his hand.

"Erm, thanks, ma'am. I think we best be going." Shrell said, breaking the silence between them.

The tall man wrapped his arm around Marric's shoulders and pulled the boy around so that they could move away from the stand. There was a kind of urgency to the way he was walking, as if he wanted to get away before some dangerous thing came. Marric still only clutched the rabbit foot in his hand, dazed by what had just happened.

"An' Marric," the raspy voice called from behind. "You'll have to make a choice where yeh stand 'ere soon. Untold challenges lie ahead. Trust yer gut and what yeh learn, and remember wha' true goodness is," she said with a kind of finality to the conversation.

The hair on his arms and the back of his neck stood up as he heard her.

"But—how did she know my name? I never once said it to her, and she never did ask—"

Marric had tried to turn to look at the woman, but Shrell firmly held him in place, keeping him faced away from her. It didn't feel forceful to Marric, but he still felt a nervous energy blossom in his chest from the way the man was acting, as if he really was in danger somehow.

"Don't yeh mind tha' one. I'm jus' sure that yeh said somethin' to her about yer name. Don' worry, now." Shrell was trying to sound nonchalant, but his tone betrayed the underlying stress in his voice. "Yeh best do what she said, though."

Marric silently tied the leather strings to the left side of his belt, leaving the foot dangling just a handspan down his thigh. He would have guessed that such a thing would look silly, but somehow it seemed fitting with his travel garb. In fact, he felt that maybe it made him look like a hunter or trapper—something he'd always dreamed about as a kid while shooting his bow in the woods.

They continued walking north for a time, dodging people here and there. It was more crowded in this area than the other places had seemed, as if there were more essential things here. A few people bumped into Marric as they bustled to and fro from shop to shop. Based on the location of the sun, Marric suspected that the day was drawing near an end. Avryn had mentioned earlier that they were hoping to make it to the edge of the forest to stay there for the night. The idea of having to stay in the forest again made him a bit nervous, but Marric understood that staying somewhere public might be too obvious, especially for such an odd crew as theirs.

Janis appeared seemingly out of thin air and slid silently to the other side of Marric. She gave Shrell a look of annoyance and gestured to the man's arm firmly over his shoulders.

"Is there a reason that you are holding Marric hostage at the moment? I don't think he needs to be escorted to jail or anything," she said pointedly.

Shrell only scowled at her, but pulled his arm away from Marric. There was an apparent rivalry between the two of them, though Marric couldn't guess why that was. He would have thought that the two of them would get along well, considering they were both skilled in similar things and both seemed fond of him.

During the exchange, Marric's mind was reeling at what had just happened. He felt like he should say something to Shrell and Janis, but he couldn't find the words. He didn't even understand what had happened, so how could he find the words?

The two of them kept their eyes locked for a beat before Shrell looked away sharply and said, "We'd best find Avryn. The sun is goin' down and we ain't got much time afore it gets dark 'ere."

"I saw him over there, buying more food. For someone that should be worried about the time, he seems like he isn't in much of a hurry." Janis replied curtly. "If it comes to it, I'll take Marric myself and head to the forest."

"Yous won't be doin' any of that now, woman, or—"

"Shrell! Looks what Oi gots from over there!" Harmel's voice cut into the argument. It was clear that the squat man had missed the sentiment of the conversation and continued with his usual jovial tone. "They was practically *givin'* this stuff away!"

He held out his hands, which were full of small figurines that appeared to be made of wood. There were human figures mixed with mythical creatures and other creations that Marric could only imagine were some attempt at animals. There were some intricate and beautifully carved ones mixed in with others that looked to be created by mere children. Harmel's appearance didn't completely undo the tension between Marric's companions, but it was a good enough distraction for the feelings of unease to decrease just a bit.

What a curious thing to spend money on, Marric thought to himself. Harmel had proven that he was a hardened and skilled fighter, but outside of battle, he was soft and almost childlike.

"Harmel, please don' say that yeh spent all yer money on *those*. I think yeh got too much stuff like those already in yer rooms back at Terris Green."

"But like Oi said, they were almos' free, theys was sellin' fer so cheap."

The two brothers continued to bicker over Harmel's recent purchases, but Marric stopped listening when he saw the look on Janis's face. She was turned and seemed to be looking at something in the distance behind them. Brow furrowed and lips drawn into a thin line, she appeared concerned. Following her gaze, Marric saw that she happened to be looking in the direction that Shrell and he had just come, toward the cart with the woman there. It had passed out of sight by now, but he had a feeling that he was missing something.

Marric cleared his throat softly.

"Janis, are you alright?"

"Hmm?" she said, still staring into the distance.

"I said, are you alright? Is there something wrong?"

She paused for a moment, before looking at Marric and nodding slightly.

"No, I'm just making sure to know my surroundings. Anything can happen in crowded places like this, and I want to stay on my guard."

The concerned look didn't leave her face as she said it, so Marric didn't really believe that nothing was the matter, but he didn't press her. He didn't know her well, but based on past interactions with her, she wasn't going to provide any more information and if he asked, it would just make things worse. Understanding that, he tried a different tactic.

"Have you traveled alone in the wilderness a lot, then?" he asked curiously.

"You have quite a way of changing the subject abruptly, don't you?" she replied.

Marric blushed at the comment. He did have a habit of awkwardly spitting out comments that were not related to the current topic. When it came to conversation, he admittedly didn't have a lot of practice. He had been somewhat of a recluse back in Wurren. Regardless, the comment had relaxed Janis just a bit. It was noticeable on her face as well as in the slight softening of her shoulders.

"Erm . . . sorry. I was just thinking that you seem very calm for the situation. I think that the only reason I slept the first night was because of exhaustion."

"My line of work requires that I become self-sufficient. Self sufficiency equates surviving in the roughest of situations. Thus, traveling alone in the wilderness and at night are a necessity."

He hadn't expected a response that long. It almost seemed grandiose in comparison to the other responses that she had given him, or even their companions on this journey. Not wanting to kill the progress of the conversation, Marric hurriedly tried to think of a response.

"That seems handy."

Handy?! he thought. *What kind of response was that?!*

He feared that he had blown yet another conversation, when Janis continued.

"That isn't quite the way I might have described a skill like that, but it is useful, I suppose."

Shocked that he hadn't derailed the conversation, he rustled up another question.

"So what exactly do you do, then?"

"I'm an assassin. I kill people for pay."

She said it so smoothly and emotionlessly, as if it wasn't odd at all. Marric was so stunned that he just stared at her, not sure how to react. Somehow, he had forgotten that fact from when they first met. He suddenly remembered her dragging him into the forest the night they had tried to escape Avryn and his companions in Wurren. That seemed so long ago.

Another memory flashed in his mind and he realized that her profession had been obvious another time, when Tins held out a wicked looking dagger and had come inches from killing Marric at his house. Images flooded his mind; the contorted face of Tins as she glared and dove at him with the knife, along with the sight of Janis's dagger thunking into the wall and a knife coming toward his face. It was as if he was there again and he could feel the bite of Tins's blade in his shoulder. Then there was Tins, lifeless on the ground, blood pooled around her gruesomely. The memory of it brought back the thick scent of human blood leaking over their wooden floor, the smell of pine planks and fresh blood mingling unpleasantly. He recalled the stinging in his nostrils, and the nausea suddenly returned as if he were there.

Marric collapsed where he stood. He was only aware of an arm on him, pulling him back up. He felt lightheaded and sick, like he might lose his small lunch on the ground. The world continued to spin for what seemed like a very long time before a face appeared out of nowhere. Dark blue eyes, almost black, stared at him atop a slender and pointed nose. Black hair cascaded around the face and came to a rest on a chin.

Janis.

He came back in a rush, and found himself breathing hard.

"Lanser's beard! I shouldn't have said that. Are you alright, Marric?"

"Woman, what did yeh do to the boy?!" another voice said. It took a moment for him to realize it was Shrell's.

Even though his eyes were still unfocused, he could at least make out Janis's features in front of him. He was feeling nauseous and gulped back bile. At the same time, he was feeling embarrassed that he couldn't be stronger, that he couldn't just stand up to the reality of what had happened the few days before. If he couldn't even handle something as simple as that, how was he going to survive as one of these supposed 'Lightbearers' that Avryn had told him about?

Feeling grim at his current state and his unknown future, he gazed about to see that the others had grouped around him and a crowd was starting to draw at the commotion. His blush deepened.

"I'm alright. I am just feeling a bit tired."

Avryn was suddenly there, and Marric felt the man's hand grasp his upper arm. With a strong pull, Marric easily stood. Holding each shoulder, Avryn stared him right in the eyes, his face looking serious.

"Marric, are you feeling ill? You collapsed so suddenly, I'd have thought that a marksman had dropped you where you stood. I almost panicked when I saw you fall." Avryn said.

"No! No, I'm okay. It was just something Janis said. It made me remember—well, anyway. I'm fine. I don't feel ill at all!" Marric felt desperate with the statement.

"If you need to take a break, we can do that. I don't fancy the idea of staying here in the Plains for another night, but I'm willing to if you need it."

Harmel and Shrell had taken the liberty of shooing passersby on their way, making up some excuse for Marric's strange behavior. Janis didn't appear to be interested in helping their effort, but seemed to be almost more effective by giving her sharp glares to those that dared to ogle. As someone's gaze aligned with Janis, they received the nonverbal message of, 'get out of here now'. A few younger girls even yelped when they locked eyes with Janis. She continued to stand there, arms folded, a look of challenge on her entire visage.

"No! I will be okay," Marric assured him. "Let's just keep moving."

Avryn narrowed his eyes at Marric, but said, "If you say so, but if you ever need to rest, do not hesitate to tell me. We'd best be moving. Evening is near." He said that latter part more loudly, addressing the whole group.

Without a word, Janis hefted her pack and turned north. She seemed bent on leaving the rest of them behind. Marric couldn't understand what she thought. It was as if she was completely uncaring about the others, and sometimes even about their situation in general, but the way she had reacted when Marric collapsed indicated that there was some amount of care, albeit small.

"Aw, yous sure we can' stay 'ere? Oi thinks that Oi could get a bit more o' great stuffs fer real cheap-like." Harmel said, sounding disappointed.

"*More* stuff?" Shrell said incredulously. "Where do yeh think yous would put all that, eh? I sure ain't gonna carry nothin' fer yeh."

"Oi'm more 'an capable of carryin' me own stuffs. Don' yeh be worryin' 'bout tha', brother."

Shrell rolled his eyes, but shouldered his own pack. They continued on with this conversation while they retrieved the horses and packed the rest of their provisions, new and old. Despite their quarreling, Marric supposed it seemed an iconic example of brothers that had lived together their whole lives. Shrell complained about his brother's tendency toward hoarding, while Harmel griped about Shrell's lack of care. There was something about it that made Marric regret his lack of siblings. There was Crents, but that was all he'd had that might have been close to a brother.

Before long, they were walking through the last lines of carts and tables, headed toward the treeline. The breeze seemed to cool with each passing minute as the sun dipped lower and lower toward the horizon on the west of the Plains. It had adopted its normal orange color, darkening as it lowered. Colors seeped through the surrounding clouds and sky as the sun set. The yellow orb was over halfway covered by the horizon when they met the treeline and plunged themselves into the darkness of the tree shadows. The wind seemed to be funneling through the pathway, intensifying instantly. It wasn't overly uncomfortable, but it did make Marric's eyes dry out. He blinked away the feeling as his fellows discussed where they should camp for the night.

"I don't know that it matters much, for most people will have assumed that we would travel through the night. Let's just walk a bit more, then veer off into the trees like we did once before." Avryn suggested.

"I say we just keep going for a few more hours. We're too close to the population back there." Janis countered, without any apparent emotion.

"Though I understand your hesitation, I assure you that we didn't alert anyone to our identities or purpose. I'm sure we're quite safe here."

Janis snorted at that.

"Any good predator would make their prey feel exactly just that. That way, their guard is down, making them easier to best."

"Maybe with beasts, but we are human." Avryn sounded dismissive when he said this.

"Pssh. It's all *instincts* in the end. Man is far more animal-like than we want to admit. Regardless, if you have a death wish, I'll do my best to set up the necessary precautions."

With a wave of her hand, Janis stalked off ahead of the group with her head held high. Though it seemed to bother Avryn, her apparent confidence in herself comforted Marric to a degree. It wasn't that the other men didn't make him feel safe, but Janis had a way of just being right about these things.

"We should keep moving. I don't anticipate that we'll need to move much further, but some amount of distance will make us harder to find, should someone actually be tailing us."

They continued walking for a short time, but soon enough, it became too challenging to see the way. After tripping at least a dozen times, Marric heard Avryn call the halt and saw him lead the party through the trees on the left, plunging them into an even deeper darkness. Once again, a small ball of bluish Light appeared, blinding Marric with its brilliance until his eyes adjusted to the newfound radiance. He could see that Avryn was holding the small Light aloft and trying to walk sideways, almost backwards to provide the Light for those behind him. Realizing that their progress was too slow, he concentrated and let his hand fall. To Marric's amazement, the orb remained elevated. Seeming satisfied, Avryn turned and continued walking while the bit of Light followed after at the same pace.

The glowing orb was mesmerizing. Marric stared with his mouth slightly open. Thoughts raced through his head as he tried to reason with himself how such a thing could work. The staring caused him to trip on a rock and he was brought back to reality once more. He didn't have the excuse of darkness this time, so his face flushed deeply at his clumsiness.

"It's so unnatural, isn't it?"

A voice from Marric's right side made him jump. Janis had materialized out of the forest silently. He still didn't understand how she was able to do that so easily, but somehow, she just did.

"It's ridiculously convenient, but so unnatural. I hate how it makes it hard to see into the forest. Too many shadows for my comfort."

Marric just walked on, head down, not sure what to say to that. For a moment, they simply continued forward. It was then that Marric realized she was trying to strike up a conversation with him. The thought of this was so jarring, that he said the first thing that came to mind.

"Yes, it does."

Janis's mouth pulled up slightly at the side as she heard his reply.

Blast, I sound like an incompetent fool! he thought to himself.

"Well I'm glad you agree," she replied, "Do you feel uncomfortable, then? Being so close to such a thing?"

Marric shrugged before answering. "At first, it made me uncomfortable, but I guess I'm just getting used to seeing it. Well—" he corrected, "I'm not *used* to it, but it doesn't seem as unsettling as it used to. Now that I know Avryn isn't here to kidnap me."

Janis raised an eyebrow at him.

"An interesting point, but not altogether true," she said, seeming smug. "For kidnapping involves taking someone away from their home to an unknown and hidden location. Now, normally, it would be against the person's will, but in my opinion, a kidnapper that's smart makes the person they're kidnapping *think* that they aren't."

His mouth fell open slightly. What did she mean? Staring wide-eyed at her, he didn't say anything for a time. Janis looked back at him, a twinkle in her eye.

"But who knows? I guess we'll see what happens when we get to this Terris Green place. At this rate, I'm not entirely confident that we will make it there alive or in one piece."

This, as with the previous comment, struck Marric hard at the realization. She spoke so matter-of-factly, that the gravity of the statements seemed to affect him stronger than they might have if she matched her tone to the seriousness of the words.

Marric stared at her again, mumbling something like an 'uh-huh' while they continued on. Janis didn't appear to notice his stare, her eyes scanning this way and that through the trees, as if trying to find something. As he stared at her, his foot caught on another branch and this time, he lost his balance. Falling forward, the ground seemed to rise up to his face so quickly that he didn't have time to think. Before his face could collide with the surface, his shirt became taut against his chest, and his fall halted. By then, he had closed his eyes for the impact. Instead, however, he felt something pull him backwards until he was on his feet again.

It had happened so fast that he wasn't sure exactly what he'd just experienced. His shirt became slack again, and he stood there, slightly shaking his head.

"It's a wonder you didn't kill yourself jumping from roof to roof back in Wurren." Janis commented.

"Unfortunately, I almost did a few days ago. As I fell though, it was like someone—"

Marric's eyes widened and he spun his head to look at Janis.

"Was that *you* who pulled me back onto the roof?"

Janis just smirked, but didn't say anything else.

"But *how*? I didn't see anyone else on the roof and—"

"In case you haven't noticed by now, Marric, if I don't want to be seen, I make sure that I'm not. It's a skill that has saved my life on many occasions. Perhaps you ought to learn it yourself." she replied smugly before noting, "It looks like Avryn means to stop here."

At that comment, she slipped into the trees and was gone in an instant. It was as if she herself became the shadows. Sure enough, as soon as she disappeared into the trees, the party stopped walking.

"I think this ought to be as good a place as any for us to camp for the night. No fire tonight, let's just set up our bedrolls, then eat our supper in the dark. I don't want to risk being found by our firelight." Avryn said.

A groan escaped Harmel's throat at the comment. They were all hoping to get at least a warm meal before having to sleep on the forest floor. That idea had been dashed quickly by Avryn's comments.

"Oi guess it's the salt pork *again*. Least this time Oi gots me some sauces from a place back'n there."

They began setting up their bedrolls, and this time there didn't seem to be any order to it. The last time they had camped in the woods together, there had been a fire, so they organized their sleeping arrangements in a circular pattern around it. Without a fire, there wasn't a reason to do this. Marric attempted to find the flattest part of the ground for his roll. The fact that he didn't have much experience sleeping in the woods meant he had to guess at a good sleeping location. Before long, he realized that the others were intentionally setting up their rolls around him, as if he was the fire and reference for the camp. He wasn't sure if this made him feel better or worse.

Marric finished unrolling his bed and sat down with a thud on the soft earthy ground. He glanced around the camp, mostly expecting to not see Janis there, but hoping that she was. She was indeed a peculiar woman, someone that he'd never expect to meet in his lifetime, but something about her felt familiar to him. Though he couldn't explain why, he felt much safer when she was near.

By the time he saw Janis coming toward them, the night had fully enveloped the camp and Marric wouldn't have been able to see even his own hand in front of his face if it weren't for Avryn's magic. The small blue ball glowed softly and steadily, giving enough of a view with its glow. He had reduced it to the size of a needle eye, but because of the inky blackness of the night, it provided plenty of illumination for the whole camp, despite its size.

Janis strolled up to the camp casually, as if their situation were a normal day in her life. Though she walked so smoothly and without care, there was not the slightest sound from her footfalls. With disbelief clearly on his face, Marric stared at her feet. He wasn't able to see anything on the ground, but he knew there had to be branches, rocks, and other things there that would make any normal human being's position obvious. It was as if she was floating, not in the way that she walked, but by the sheer silence that persisted while she moved.

"As usual, I've set up the necessary precautions around the camp," she said as she stopped in front of the group. "Before any of you try to wander off to relieve yourselves tonight, please warn me first. You wouldn't want my knife in your back because you sprung one of my traps while I dozed."

Shrell snorted at the comment.

"I think that yeh underestimate the likes of us. We ain't gonna git stuck in one of yer traps that darn easy."

Janis stared flatly at him, unamused by the response.

"If you feel that confident in yourself, then by all means, do what you want. But I will not make any promises nor apologize for anything that will inevitably happen if you stalk off like an idiot without waking me."

At that, the assassin lay down on the bare ground, slid both arms behind the back of her head, and closed her eyes without another word.

The rest of the party stared at her for a moment, and there were a few glances exchanged among themselves, but her comment had seemed the final horn announcing that it was time for the camp to be quiet. They all ate their dinner quickly and without any conversation.

After finishing up his food, Marric lay down on his bedroll, intentionally not pulling his blanket up over his chest. The temperature wasn't hot, but nor was it cold. He was confident that if he did pull them up, he'd get too hot and wake up with a nightmare. During the in-between of the cold and hot seasons, he would often misjudge the air and pull his blanket high when he didn't need to, fending off a cold that wasn't there. That's when the dreams would come. His father had said that it was common. Something about bodies overheating and the imagination of the brain running rampant. Marric had never understood why that would be the case, but it was unfortunately a very true thing. He had learned from too many bad dreams that it wasn't worth not taking the time to feel out the air before settling into bed. Marric just couldn't stand reliving that night.

He shuddered at the thought. Part of him liked entering dreams because he often got to see Jord again. The dreams were never the same at first, but they always ended with his best friend crumpling to the ground and the scar-faced man grinning at him from a handspan in front of his own face and the sick feeling that he wouldn't make it through the night alive.

Shaking his head quickly, he banished the thoughts from his head and tried to focus on something else. The night was quite beautiful. It was still, almost no sounds at all. The dark blackness that surrounded him somehow made him feel both protected and exposed at the same time. Avryn waited only moments before extinguishing the Light and settling into his own bed.

Though he was feeling tired, Marric couldn't relax himself well enough to fall asleep. Crickets chirped in a surprisingly loud and hypnotizing rhythm around him, though the sound really didn't bother him. He found it comforting. It was like a blanket of sound that was helping shut out the rest of the world, allowing him to think to himself without any other interruptions. Once again, he was forced to shake his head to get horrible memories out of his mind before they overtook him. Suddenly, he heard whispers.

"S'ren, it was such a strange thing. I wasn't right close to them, but I was sure I'd seen it 'afore. She was Seein' him, or summin about his future."

Marric's mind focused sharply on the whisper. They weren't extremely loud, especially not over the sound of the chirping crickets in the trees, but as soon as he'd realized someone was awake, his ears strained to hear.

". . . do you think he knew?"

"I can't be sure, but he knew somethin' was up. He got pretty shook."

"What else did she say? Her words might—"

A breeze blowing through the leaves interrupted the words and Marric scowled in frustration at the disturbance.

"—summin about keep it on 'im always. I think she meant the critter foot."

"What she Saw must have been a crossroads for Marric—a choice he will have to make."

A pause.

"We must be ever diligent in keeping him safe. I'd hate for him to not even make—"

Another breeze came. It took all Marric had to not jump up and demand that they talk to him directly about the events of the day, but he knew they'd stop the conversation if they knew he could hear. For an almost unbearable time, the wind continued. Finally, it broke again.

"—a decision. She said somethin' about Marric needing to trust himself with a choice. Not sure what that meant."

"She Saw something that even our Seers haven't. We only got a small view of his awakening, but that's it. Whatever she Saw must have been troubling. I wish I'd have been there, I'd have asked about what she Saw so that we at least know what he'll be deciding and—"

This time, the interrupting sound was a rustle. Janis was rolling over near him and the noise of it covered up the conversation once more.

"Should we tell *her*?"

"I don't know that I trust her. But regardless of her knowledge, I suspect she'll do what she can to protect him anyway—for what reason, I can't say. Thank you, Shrell. This is important information. Sleep so that we can move more quickly tomorrow."

There was soft rustling and padding footfalls on the soft earth, and Marric suspected the two men were settling down into their own beds. He wasn't sure who would be up for watch first, but whoever it was stayed quiet as they sat down in the dark.

Marric was perplexed by the conversation, and their references to what had happened earlier. It was something that they were familiar with, but he'd already guessed that based on Shrell's reaction to the situation earlier. Avryn was obviously concerned about it. The forest suddenly felt darker and colder as he recounted what he had heard. They thought he would be in danger, and this woman somehow knew it was coming. Perhaps the decision he was to make would put him in the danger.

If he had any hopes of falling asleep before, they were dashed away almost completely by what he'd just overheard.

Chapter 9

People were far too trusting with their conversations when they thought that others were asleep. That was obviously the case with Avryn and Shrell, as they spoke as if completely alone, despite their companions lying closeby. Janis wasn't certain that by feigning sleep she would actually hear anything useful, but it had turned out to be a good decision. She would rest in time, but not until she was confident that all conversations were completed.

The air smelled clear and unpolluted, and the almost continuous breeze through the trees kept it that way. Though the wind impeded her ability to hear everything as freely, it did provide additional protection from approaching danger by way of smell. She hadn't spent her previous years attuning each of her senses for no reason at all. If there were a threat anywhere upwind, Janis was confident that she would be able to notice the slightest change in scent.

What had happened to that old woman? she thought to herself.

Whatever had occurred, it was something beyond any normalcy that Janis had experienced, and that was saying a lot. In her profession, she had seen a fair amount of unusual things. A man with more than one head—or was it two men with only one body? That was certainly unnatural. She'd known a breeder who crossbred animal species in ways that had never been imagined. Suffice it to say, Janis was not unfamiliar with strangeness. But this was different.

She recounted the images in her mind again, trying to determine what exactly had happened. While Marric had wandered around on his own, Janis had kept her distance to see more clearly anyone that might be paying too much attention to him. Janis spotted the woman quicker than Marric had, as she was most obviously staring at him. She was blind, that was clear the moment Janis noticed her, but her gaze followed Marric with an uncanny accuracy, and this was alarming. Her body language didn't suggest that she meant any harm, so there had been no need to stop him from making his way to the shop.

Janis hadn't bothered to get anywhere near the table because she hadn't expected anything extraordinary to happen in their conversation. As she watched, she saw the woman's eyes light up with a bluish Light, bright and piercing. Then the woman snatched Marric so abruptly that Janis had promptly slid a dagger from a sheath hidden in her bodice and prepared to throw it. She remembered how the hair on her entire body stood on end as she saw the old woman stiffen, eyes wide with—had it been fear?

In not even a moment, the old lady's eyes dimmed. Something was said, and Janis had begun moving that direction, staying in the shadows. Shrell's advancement had also caused Janis to pause and maintain her distance. Though at the time she couldn't hear what the old woman said to Marric, overhearing the two men's conversation just before entering her in-between state had cleared things up about the event. She strained to hear the last words from the decrepit woman in the memory.

"You'll have to make a choice where yeh stand 'ere soon. Untold challenges lie ahead. Trust yer gut and what yeh learn, and remember wha' true goodness is."

It had sounded like something that a crazy fortune teller would say, but the seriousness in her voice wasn't forced. There had also been a kind of sadness to the comment, like it pained her to say such a thing to him.

After the strange encounter, Janis had made a point to slip toward the shop quickly and snag one of the trinkets from the woman's table. She had only gotten a slim view of what the woman had given Marric, but it was enough for her to grab one almost exactly like his, save in color.

Janis lay in the dark of the night as she recalled the events, trying to understand what it was that she'd gotten herself into. The only thing she had been able to assume from the situation was that this old woman had some type of power like Avryn's, which was confirmed by the conversation only moments before. What that meant, she wasn't sure, but it was significant, at least in their minds.

Reaching to her side, she withdrew the rabbit foot and rolled it between her palm and fingers. She couldn't make it out completely in the dark, but she could see the fuzzy outline and the leather tied to the end of it, trailing off in two strands. It didn't seem to be anything valuable, but the way the woman had treated the one she'd given Marric led Janis to believe that she was missing something.

For a time, she considered what the men had discussed and how they thought that something was coming soon that would put Marric in danger. Fortunately, she was confident that at least tonight, that danger wouldn't come. Or, rather, it couldn't come without her having enough time to prepare for its approach.

The night drew on, and Janis thought it might be best if she rested at least during the time of Isllan and the fog. Even now, Mallan's light was starting to wane in the sky and the eerie glow on the trees was beginning to shift to the orange of the third moon. The air had begun to grow warmer, ever so slightly, announcing the approach of the fog and its strange effects. Closing her eyes, she relaxed to the point where she could slip back into the in-between—that's what she called it—the place where she was not quite asleep, nor was she awake.

It had taken numerous years for Janis to be able to get to the point of the in-between, and even then a few more years to master passing her consciousness in and out of the state smoothly. She wasn't exactly sure who had been the first to discover it, but she remembered the time that Macks told her about it.

She felt her thoughts shift momentarily to the man, dressed in all black, like she did herself. Hair light brown with flecks of grey, bangs hanging down heavily just above his eyes. His wicked grey eyes hiding infinite secrets as his thin lips spread into a soft smile, making them seem thinner still. His clothes clung to him tightly, revealing muscles that were somehow bulky and lean at the same time. Something inside of her stirred at the memory of him, and Janis's consciousness balked.

Concentrating, she removed the image from the forefront of her thoughts and drifted back into the in-between. The state she had so fondly named the 'in-between' was a great tool for any assassin hoping to become successful, not to mention any other person working in a combat profession. This was a place between sleep and consciousness. When she had first begun learning to be an assassin, she had hardly slept, almost getting herself killed when she fell asleep while climbing up a wall to escape authorities. The in-between was the perfect solution. Keeping the key senses such as sound, smell, and feel engaged, a person in the in-between could rest their body without actually losing consciousness. It was perhaps only half as restful as actually sleeping—she had to do that occasionally when necessary—but usually, this was sufficient. Finally gaining the ability to do so had been far worth the time it had taken to learn it.

An unexpected side advantage to the in-between was the ability to access one's sub-consciousness and even manipulate things when needed. It was almost as if you could hear the things that you heard, but didn't notice before, or see things that you couldn't before. Janis had learned from this that one's brain processes far more information than a conscious person can handle, thus packing it away to the dark recesses of the mind.

She couldn't actually *see* anything from her reality here, but at the same time, she had some perception of visual queues. In her mind's eye, she perceived the inky cloud of grey that accompanied entering the state. Getting into the state hadn't been the hardest part of learning this, but rather controlling the thoughts that came. It felt the same as dreaming; thoughts impeding your mind without control. In learning to navigate this part of her consciousness, she had encountered far too many bad memories, which incidentally always pushed their way to the forefront first. Fortunately, that was no longer a problem for her. Naturally guiding herself to the memory that she was seeking, the fog cleared and she heard the conversation that had ended only moments before.

"S'ren, it was such a strange thing. I wasn't right close to them, but I was sure I'd seen it 'afore. She was Seein' him, or somethin' about his future."

Recalling conversations like this was always so strange. Her mind went beyond the actual words and listened to what else was happening while the two men spoke. She could hear the forest alive with sounds of the night. A night owl hooting in the distance, the slight breeze rustling leaves, Harmel mumbling to himself in his sleep, and Marric—

Ahhhh, clever boy, she thought to herself.

"*. . . do you think he knew?*"

"*I can't be sure, but he knew somethin' was up fer sure. He got pretty shook.*"

The men continued their conversation in her memory, but she wasn't focusing on them for the moment, for she could hear how uneven Marric's breaths were, and she even detected slight gasps as he held his breath unintentionally to try to keep quiet. The boy was very clearly awake and listening to the conversation as well.

I suspect the lad is more capable than I thought. He heard the entire exchange too. A slight smile spread on her face. Anyone on the outside of the in-between would think she was having a fond dream at the moment.

Parts of the conversation were lost on strong breezes in the wind, but Janis was still listening to the forest, hearing nothing out of the ordinary.

"*. . . somethin' about keepin' it on him always. I think she meant the critter foot.*"

"*What she Saw must have been a type of danger.*" There was a pause. Then, "*We must be ever diligent in keeping him safe. I'd hate for him to not even make—*"

Janis could hear an unsteadiness in Avryn's voice that was so subtle, but here she could tell. The man was nervous. Actually, he was scared. It wasn't the fact that this woman saw something, or not *just* that. Avryn was made uneasy by the fact that she could See something with her abilities.

"*She Saw something that even our Seers haven't. We only got a small view of his awakening, but that's it. Whatever she Saw must have been troubling. I wish I'd have been there, I'd have asked about what she Saw so that we at least know what he'll be deciding and—*"

A rustle interrupted the conversation and Janis remembered rolling over toward the sound, slipping her hand into her side pocket for her dagger. She honed in on the sound and heard the distinct padding of four paws. Thum, thum, thum, thum. Her memory flashed with sight (she had opened her eyes then to make sure it was all okay), and she saw the small fox padding softly in the forest just outside of their camp. The sight vanished again as her past self closed her eyes again.

The memory finished out with the men discussing whether or not to tell Janis what had happened, but she only half listened as she concentrated on shifting her focus to the actual memory of the old woman earlier that day. Instantly, her vision cleared and she could see Marric approaching the woman at the table. She extended her hearing and her peripheral vision to take in the surrounding area as the earlier events played out again in her mind.

A majority of what she heard in the background was dialogue of shop owners and customers bartering or discussing their items at tables close to her. Most of the information was not helpful and not worth listening to. She hadn't anticipated that she'd see or hear anything useful, even with the added benefit of her focused senses while in the in-between. Janis just figured that it wouldn't hurt to replay the memory, just in case. It helped her convert things to her longer term memory, so it was worth the time. She didn't have much else to remember or focus on at the moment, anyway.

As she focused again on the woman's eyes as they began to glow, she couldn't help but feel like she had seen this moment already. This was common in the in-between though, she had found. Technically she *had* already seen it, so it never bothered her much. Shaking off the feeling, she continued to watch the woman's eyes. At first, she thought that they shone steadily and unwaveringly, but as she looked closer, there was a soft pulsing rhythm to the glow, as if it was following her beating heart. Suddenly, the woman's eyes went dark and she stared at Marric, wide-eyed. Then her eyes flicked to the side, so quickly that Janis almost missed it. In fact, she *had* missed it earlier. The movement was so fast that without recounting the memory, she wouldn't have remembered.

What did she just look at? she thought to herself.

She couldn't actually move the memory's view since she was only recounting the events, but she honed in on a part of her periphery to the left where the woman's eyes had gone just moments before. The shopkeeper to the left of her was staring at the two of them, eyes narrowed as if he suspected something. She maintained this focus, needing to exert her mental capacity to do so. He leaned in closely as if for a better look, definitely noticing their interaction with a suspicious stare. When Shrell interrupted the two of them, the man slipped into the tent behind his table, and came out with a birdcage. She watched as he scribbled something on a paper and attached it to the bird's leg. Unfortunately, Janis had started moving again, this time toward the table of the woman, so her peripheral vision shifted and she lost sight of the man.

That was a carrier bird! she thought.

What had he written on that paper?! He clearly was sending a message about Marric. Janis doubted that the old woman was the subject of the writing, that would be too coincidental. As much as she didn't want to, she decided that it would be best to tell Avryn what she had discovered. Though how to tell him without letting him know about the in-between, she had to figure out. Before she could pull herself out of the in-between, her senses piqued.

A loud rustling burst into her ears, followed by thumps that she couldn't just hear, but feel in the ground. There was loud grunting and breathing in sync with the two.

Janis's eyes shot open and she pushed hard with her hands against the ground, launching her body onto her feet. She was instantly alert and she focused on the sounds with full consciousness to gather her bearings. The sky had already started to lighten with the morning sun, so visibility wasn't as much of an issue.

In a flash, she whipped out two of her daggers, her favorite long one and another half its size. The sounds that had been so overwhelmingly loud and the vibrations so heavy in the ground were less so while she was conscious. Somehow, the in-between amplified her senses, which though handy, was extremely disorienting when she woke up and her senses were dulled to their normal levels. It had taken another long bit of time for her to learn how to ignore all of the normal sounds of life and only focus on the out-of-place or unusual ones.

Another unfortunate thing about the in-between was that real time went by very quickly when she was in the state. She had merely been recounting memories that were a few moments long, but the sun was already on its way up, brightening the sky in anticipation of the full blaze of sunlight.

Tilting her neck side to side to crack it slightly, she felt herself click back into reality and locate the sound that she had heard only moments before. It was coming from her left, and it was coming fast.

Any moment now. . . . she thought. *You're bound to hit it soon.*

A loud snap rang through the air suddenly, followed by the screaming and wailing of an animal.

Janis smiled to herself and began to advance toward the sound. Before she got to the edge of the camp, however, the rustling intensified from a small concentrated area to a broad area in the same direction. Her smile faded quickly as she felt the ground begin to rumble and vibrate in conjunction with what sounded like hooves beating loudly on the ground.

"EVERYONE UP! NOW!" she shouted to the sleeping party.

The men stirred slowly. Her shout hadn't had the effect that she had hoped it would. Immediately, she ran to Marric and yanked him by the arm. He sputtered awake, confusion in his eyes and his body still sluggish from sleep. His eyes focused on Janis and he tried to jump back, but couldn't with her firm grip.

"Wake up the others, quick!"

He nodded and ran to rouse the other men. Shrell appeared at Janis's side only moments after Marric retreated, and she wondered if Shrell had also achieved the in-between because he looked refreshed and awake, as if he hadn't just been woken up by her shouts.

The screaming of the trapped animal persisted, but was soon drowned out as the stampeding and thunderous sounds got closer. A few more snaps indicated that her traps had found more unsuspecting creatures like the first, but there were still at least a dozen approaching.

Janis crouched in anticipation of the coming wave of animals and Shrell drew his sword, preparing his own way by shifting sideways in a very obvious sword stance. She wasn't familiar with this one, but then again, she hadn't trained much with swords. They were too long and unwieldy for an assassin, although her favorite dagger was technically considered a short sword.

The sound reached deafening status and bushes just outside their camp burst about as a blood-red creature crashed through. In a flash, a red spine flew through the air at Janis and she dodged just in time to see it fly right by her face and thud into a tree behind her. Without hesitation, she sped forward toward the creature and swiped her long knife into its face. There was a sound like an axe hitting wood and the animal recoiled. She hadn't swiped with the sharp edge—that would have gotten her knife stuck and would have had little effect.

At least a dozen other creatures, identical to the first with the exception of size and color pattern, filed in behind their leader. Each stood firmly on four hooves, snouts held proudly high in the air as if they owned the place. Bright red spines, some as small as her little finger, some as thick as tent stakes curved backwards all along their snouts, running down their backs. Their legs sported similar spines, only pointed downwards, as if the gravity pulled them that way. All in all, spine hogs were terribly ugly, and looked more like pincushions than pigs. Unfortunately for the travelers, spine hogs were quick and lethal.

As if in unspoken sync, Shrell and Janis both leapt forward at the line of animals, not giving them time to react. Janis feigned a slash high with her dagger, causing the lead animal to release a set of spines toward her descending arm, instead, she ducked low and cut the creature's front legs clean off, making the animal pitch forward, face hitting the ground hard. Shrell had attacked the hog just to the left, and though his attempt hadn't been as clean as hers, he had managed to stab the creature through the eye, which did the job.

It was clear that Shrell had experience fighting spine hogs, because he intentionally avoided using the sharp edge of his blade when striking anywhere besides their weak spots, which he seemed to know pretty well.

Janis wasn't sure what was happening behind her, but she and Shrell fell into rhythm, blocking spines and attacks from the hogs while taking them out periodically. The biggest challenge was being faster than their ability to launch their spines, and to not lose your blade by getting it stuck in their hard hides.

The spine hog to her right shot a few spines and she bent backwards to avoid them, at the same time sliding a small dagger from her belt. As she straightened, she let it fly, lodging the knife into its left eye. It wouldn't kill it immediately, but it bought her some time.

A gasp behind her made her turn sharply. Marric had somehow been in the line of fire and two of the spines had lodged into him, one in his gut, the other in his thigh. Wide-eyed, he fell to his knees. A few of the animals saw this and launched spines in his direction. They always teamed up on anything vulnerable, helping them collectively take down prey much larger than themselves.

Janis cursed as she watched them fly toward him, too many to count. A flash of light appeared out of nowhere and the spines clacked loudly in the air, ricocheting in different directions. It was there and gone in an instant. Whatever it was hadn't blocked them all, as she saw a few more spines in Marric's arms and legs. A second flurry of spines flew toward him and this time, Avryn appeared like a human shield in front of Marric. Another blinding Light, and more clacking. A few spines lodged into Avryns legs, and his face was sliced by another that had just missed him.

Satisfied that Marric had sufficient protection for the moment, Janis turned and continued her work on the hogs nearest her. She had dropped another to the ground, blade in the soft exposed flesh of its body just above the front legs, when the group of hogs behind it exploded in a cloud of flesh and blood. Instinctively, she ducked low. Two more flashes announced the explosion of the remaining hogs, and then all was quiet.

Whatever just happened, she wasn't sure, but the quiet that followed the event seemed unnatural. She stood quickly and did another scan of the horizon. There was no sign of other spine hogs approaching, and no sound other than the hogs that had been captured in her forest traps. Turning, she saw Light pulsing from Avryn's hand just above Marric as he lay on the ground.

Her heart thudded heavily and she worked to make her breathing even. An adrenaline high like that was often helpful in situations where quick action was required, but she couldn't let it distract from her senses. One threat was taken care of, but that didn't mean there weren't more. She turned again and looked at Avryn working on Marric.

At least we have a nice contingency plan if any of us gets hurt really bad, she thought as she watched from afar.

Marric was still unconscious from the pain and shock, but she knew that he wouldn't die. Although uncomfortably unnatural, Avryn's strange healing powers had proven very reliable on multiple occasions. Rather than just stand there idly and watch what the other two men were doing, she figured it would be best to silence the creatures in the traps. They were making quite the ruckus hung up by their hooves.

While Janis walked, she tried to recount what had just happened. Fights were normally fast like that, but things had happened that she wished she could have observed more closely. She wanted to, no, *needed* to understand what powers Avryn had and how they worked. What were their limitations? What was their scope?

She thought back to the fight and recalled the bright flashes of Light at the end and the explosions of the hogs. How did he eliminate so many of those spine hogs so quickly? She would have to analyze that fight from the in-between at some point. Maybe there she could get an idea of what was possible through his Lightbearing.

It wasn't just curiosity that drove her to thirst for the answers, but from a natural survival perspective. If it ever came down to her fighting one of these Lightbearers—fog it, if she ever had to fight Avryn himself, she was not equipped to do well in that match. That fact made it difficult for her to get too close to the man in any way. Knowing that at any moment he could use one of these powers to destroy her and that she wouldn't be able to put up much of a fight irked her more than anything at the moment.

Her feet crunched on fallen leaves and pine needles as she walked. That was soon drowned out, however, by the squealing of the hog hanging from one of her loop traps. With a quick stab in the right place, the hog fell silent. Fortunately for her, spine hogs didn't handle being caught well. It could easily have launched flurries of spines at her, but it was too panicked to even consider such a thing. Once caught, they went into a panic mode that made them easy prey.

It didn't take much longer to silence the other two hogs. After they were all taken care of, the forest returned to its quiet and calm state. Janis took the moment to close her eyes and breathe deeply through her nose. The smell of the forest filled her lungs and her mind cleared instantly, allowing her to open her senses further. Birds chirped in the distance, their happy song announcing the morning. A woodpecker pecked loudly at the top of a tree to her left. The wind blew the clean and fresh air through her hair and rustled the leaves quietly. As usual, the forest was alive and thriving in its own noisy way.

"Marric, are you feeling alright now?" Janis heard Avryn say as she stepped back into the clearing.

The boy was sitting up now, and though his clothing showed holes surrounded with drying blood, he looked altogether healthy and energized.

"Yes, I think so." Marric replied. "I can't believe I just passed out so easily. I've proven useless in all our skirmishes so far." He sat there shaking his head while he said it.

"Marric, there is no way you could have done better. If you hadn't woken us all, it could have been much worse."

"But I didn't even help fight at all! I just got skewered who knows how many times. I brought my bow for a reason, but I've only used it to practice."

Avryn looked at the boy with softer eyes, a slight smile on his face.

"Fighting spine hogs is not something that you can just do without proper instruction and training. Even if you know what you are doing, you almost inevitably end up hit by some of their spines. You just have to make sure that they don't strike you where it could be lethal."

Marric didn't look completely satisfied with the man's answer, but he dropped the subject anyway and let his eyes wander to Janis.

"Doesn't look like she got hit by any."

The three men turned to look at her. Both Avryn and Harmel looked shocked at the revelation, but Shrell's eyes narrowed as he scanned her body, noticing that she indeed hadn't been struck even once. Shrell had been struck by a few spines during the encounter, but Avryn was already working on his wounds, so she couldn't tell if there had been more. In her mind, it wasn't *that* unusual to come out of a spine hog encounter unscathed, but apparently to a normal person, it was unheard of.

"Well, I ain't so sure that she's a human, that one." Shrell said indignantly.

Janis only grinned at him.

"Regardless, a stampede like this doesn't happen without some type of cause. How did this happen? Spine hogs don't normally travel in groups of this size. Perhaps four or five, but this group looks to be at least twenty, and that's not including the three that Janis stopped with her traps."

Janis looked around at the carnage and shrugged. How anyone could estimate a number based on the remains was unknown to her. She and Shrell left the carcasses pretty well together, but that couldn't be said of Avryn's work.

"Oi dunno, it weren't terrible a thing. Oi thinks tha' Oi've seen some groups be large-like." Harmel shrugged as he said it.

That man has an annoying way of making serious situations seem completely normal.

"You're right, Harmel, large groups have been seen before, but these were too organized, like they'd been taught what to do."

"Nah, theys was jus' spine hogs. Seemed dumb as ever ta me."

"No, this was somethin' else. I could tell that it wasn't right. Like someone trained 'em fer that." Shrell agreed with Avryn.

They all looked at Janis as if she was the determining vote in the conversation. Rather than answering, she puckered her lips and stared off in the direction the hogs had come from. This was far from a usual spine hog attack. There were definitely too many, and they were more organized than usual.

In response, she only nodded, continuing to stare in that direction.

Without another word, she launched herself into the forest toward where the spine hogs had come. She really only had moments before she might be able to find some evidence of what had happened. If a person had been involved, they were likely not smart enough to stick around too long, especially if they saw their attempt to kill someone had failed.

The wind whipped through her hair, flapping it in the air behind her as she dashed side to side through the trees. Running at full speed had always felt so exhilarating to her, but it was even more so in the thick of the trees, as if she was dodging the attacks of enemies surrounding her on all sides. This had actually been a part of her training on surviving exactly that—attacks that were quick and on all sides. Macks had told her that she should imagine each tree as a person that she could not kill, but only avoid. She remembered more than once running headlong into a tree, or clipping an arm or a leg on a branch here or there. He had pushed her to run as fast as she could without letting up.

A sense of sadness and longing constricted her chest and stomach and she forced the thought of Macks out of her mind once again.

Why do I keep doing that?! He's gone. I can't let him distract me anymore!

Janis burst into a clearing that had to have been large enough to hold all of the hogs. Sure enough, there were at least two dozen or so harnesses tied in groups to trees there. Whoever had been here hadn't bothered to collect all of them and had merely fled the scene. The harnesses were bright red rope, somehow dyed that color with a plant or other dye. They were thick and oiled, likely to ensure that the hogs couldn't launch volleys at their ropes and chop them in half. The oils would make them slippery, but they would be lodged beneath their spines so that they couldn't slip out.

Determining that whoever had been here no longer was, Janis crept around the camp, searching for signs of retreat. He was apparently fairly adept in his care to remain unfound, because Janis wasn't able to locate any tracks indicating which direction he might have fled. Of course, she wasn't completely sure that this had been a man, it very well could have been a woman.

After finding no tracks anywhere, she elected to look upwards, making sure that he hadn't tried to fool her by climbing up in the trees. As she did so, the perspective made her vision tunnel slightly as the trunks of the trees created a silo view and the sky peaked through the canopy. It was a bit disorienting at first, but she focused on each tree, ultimately finding nothing.

Janis turned and headed back to the camp. Just before leaving the clearing, she spotted something that seemed out of place. Reaching down, she snatched a piece of fabric half buried in the leaves and brush of the forest. As she pulled it free, she saw that it was a peddler's cap, clearly left behind by the perp in haste. Something itched in her mind as she stared at it.

Narrowing her eyes, she focused on why this seemed familiar. She had seen this before, but she wasn't sure where. All at once, it came to her. She hadn't *seen* this per se in reality. No, this was seen by her subconscious. This was the hat of the man that she only saw in the in-between, the one at the shop next to the old woman's. It was the man that had sent the carrier bird.

* * *

The group was on its way again shortly after Janis had found the harnesses and the hat. When she had returned, she told them that there was nothing out of the ordinary, but she had shot Avryn a look that suggested they had to talk. Normally, she wouldn't want to share what she had found with anyone else, largely because no one could be trusted. However, this whole Lightbearer business was something beyond her understanding, and she needed Avryn's insight.

They had been traveling for a few hours before Janis slipped to the rear of the party, allowing Marric, Shrell, and Harmel to move to the front of the group. She had remained at the front of the group should any trouble arise, but once the time had passed beyond the third hour, she figured it was unlikely to have any trouble from the man that had sent the hogs, or anyone else that might have been near them during the incident.

Avryn remained in the rear, an unspoken agreement from the two made earlier that Janis was concerned about what she had found and that they should take position on the borders as an added protection. Whether Avryn wanted to admit it or not, she was as capable a protector as Avryn, if not more so.

She had made it back to Avryn's position without too much suspicion from the other three, except for Marric, who had glanced at her curiously for a moment as she first began to fall back. There was something odd about that boy and his innate need to know where she was at all times. Janis could tell that he made attempts to hide the fact that he was trying to keep his eye on her, but he wasn't very good at it. It was somewhat endearing to her in a strange way, almost cute.

I really hope the boy doesn't get too *fond of me. It won't last long in the end.*

Marric and the two men talked and laughed as the brothers told of their experiences with each other growing up and working together, both before and after their time with Avryn and their band of Lightbearers. It appeared that they had no limit of stories—or even time that they could spend talking about them—so Janis took the liberty of getting out before she was too stuck in listening. Besides, she had to talk to Avryn at some point, and now seemed as good a time as any.

A brief nod was exchanged between the two as Janis took position to the left of Avryn, his horse occupying his right side.

"You found more than you let on earlier, didn't you?" Avryn said bluntly, not bothering to let her start.

"Yes. The attack earlier was not a force of nature. There was someone involved, though I can't be sure who," she replied. "Let me ask you this, what types of resources does Watchlight have at their disposal?"

"I'm not an expert on their economical conditions, but based on past experiences, it appears that they have pretty much whatever they need to get whatever they want."

"Is it possible that they were involved in this?"

"That depends on what you found. Normally I like to speculate only *after* I hear what evidence we have."

She glared at him for the comment.

"There were harnesses tied to the trees in a clearing. They were obviously intended for the hogs, based on their construction and well-oiled state."

"*Harnesses?!*" Avryn said, aghast. "By Lanser, someone kept those things as *pets*?"

"Harnesses don't always indicate that what was tied to them was a pet. These could easily have been trained for war."

"Regardless, it's lunacy. I suspect that you didn't find a person there, otherwise you'd have brought back a body."

Avryn said it like it was a joke, and he had amusement on his face as he said it.

"Of course I would have, but there wasn't a person."

The amusement on his face fell at her remark, changing to more of a worried and sick look.

"What?" Janis questioned.

"That was meant to be a joke."

Janis shrugged, but kept the conversation going.

"I found a peddler's hat, one that I had seen before. While I was trailing Marric in the Plains of Erisdell, I saw from afar what had happened with the strange woman with the glowing eyes."

"Wait, you saw— "

"Nevermind that!" she cut him off, waving her hand in the air. "I also saw the shopkeeper next door watching. Soon after the event, he let loose a carrier bird with a message. The look on his face suggested that he didn't think fondly of the situation."

Avryn went silent at the comment, eyes staring forward and unmoving. For a time, he just stayed that way, the sounds of chattering and laughing from the others in front being the only thing to occupy them.

"Why did you wait until now to share this?" Avryn finally said, suspicion in his voice.

Janis rolled her eyes in a show of annoyance.

"I'm not going to betray or kill you. If I was, I would have done so already; I don't bother making relationships with people if I intend to kill them. Espionage isn't my style. I didn't realize until this morning that what I'd seen could be related."

Avryn clenched his jaw, clearly not satisfied by her excuse, but unwilling to press the issue further. He breathed deeply for a time before continuing.

"This must be Watchlight. As far as I know, there are no other parties that would be interested in Marric."

Janis knew that wasn't true. She thought back to the job that she had almost taken from Luden. For some reason, he wanted Marric dead, though that was a problem for another day.

"Thank you for this news, Janis. We must be ever vigilant in our journey."

She nodded, then slipped into the trees to get a better vantage of the group. Her gut didn't tell her that they were in any immediate trouble, but she still preferred to keep watch in her own way. If the man with the carrier bird was associated with Watchlight, they likely had eyes everywhere; and the only way to combat that was to keep your eyes everywhere, too.

Chapter 10

Prost stood facing the forest line, a strong wind whipping at his clothing. He had sensed the storm much earlier today, and he had been right. There was something in the air, a thickness that had accompanied them as they moved through the Plains of Erisdell. It was usually hot and dry here, so the storm would be very welcome to him, except for the inconvenience of its timing.

He turned to face the south and saw the dark and thick clouds rolling toward them rapidly. There were flashes inside, revealing the lumpy texture that was hidden in the darkness of their color. The sun was on its way down, so the storm would hit early in the evening.

Prost cursed to himself. He had hoped to travel through the night as much as possible, but the storm would not allow them to do so. Closing his eyes, he breathed deeply of the sticky and wet air, reveling in the power of the approaching storm. As a child, he had always been able to sense storms like these at least the day before. His friends had called him crazy whenever he predicted the arrival of one, until they realized that he was accurate every time.

They were late. It had been three days since he'd received the letter from Iridan saying that the boy had been by his shop. That meant that Marric and the assassin had three days to get ahead of them, and they still weren't sure where they were headed. Whoever their companions were, he still didn't know, the reports only told of 'soldiers' accompanying them. The only thing that he did know was that one of them was a Lightbearer with the powers of a Destroyer. Apparently, they had Destroyed the roofs of a few houses to eliminate Watchlight's archers back in Wurren. Either this was a lone wolf Destroyer, or it was someone from Evenir, those opposing Watchlight. Evenir didn't have too many capable Destroyers as far as Prost knew, at least from reports he had received in the past. Most of the Destroyers aligned with Watchlight. It was something about the power that they possessed and wanting to use it to break everything. They often left a trail of destruction and fear in their wake.

Prost scoffed at the thought. Maybe he would feel the same if he were affected, but being immune to their powers revealed how measly Destroyers could often be. They put way too much stock in their powers and didn't spend nearly enough time training with the sword or any other useful weapon. That left them almost defenseless against him. With the exception of one Destroyer, at least.

Yes. The reports had said that the Destroyer in Wurren had been capable with a sword as well. That could only be one person: Avryn.

Prost narrowed his eyes as he thought about Avryn. It had been a long time since they had encountered each other, but if it were true that it was him back in Wurren, then Evenir had gotten to Marric first, and he was likely to be accompanying them, wherever they were going. The thought of fighting the assassin and a few measly soldiers had sounded easy to him. But if Avryn was with them . . . well, that would change things.

A feeling of regret, pain, and anger filled his body, and he felt the sudden urge to punch through a wall or tackle the closest person to him. Breathing deeply, he forced back the feeling and closed his eyes again, focusing on the air and the approaching storm. This cleared his mind. The rain always did that for him. It was something that had kept him from letting his anger rule him.

"There he is, day dreamin' again in all this *wilderness* stuff."

Releasing his breath, Prost opened his eyes and bared his teeth.

"Fog it, Mert. Don't you have someone *else* to bother right now?"

"I prefer to live on the edge, playing only with the lion rather than the lamb."

Prost turned slowly and stared flatly at Mert. The man had chosen to wear a shirt that was far too short for him and his bare stomach was showing a few inches above his pant line.

"Playing with lions might be smarter if the person doing so didn't dress so much like a foggin' imbecile. Your stomach flesh is asking to be stabbed by even the smallest of blades."

Mert made a show of looking at his midriff, a look of shock showing on his face.

"Oh no! I'm *so* nervous."

To prove his point, Prost whipped a dagger from a hidden pouch on the right side of his body and launched it at Mert, directly at his stomach. Without hesitation, Mert thrust his hand to the side and Moved a wooden plate from the shop table to his left. The dagger connected with the plate with a thunk just before it could pierce Mert's stomach. It stayed there, glowing with a reddish glow as if frozen in time.

"Now, now, Prost. You'd best be keeping your daggers pointed at the enemy, not your companions. Wouldn't want to make daddy Riln angry, now would we?"

Prost's stomach twisted at the comment, his innate fear of Riln being stirred from below.

With obvious poise and a desire to make a show of it, Mert Moved the plate up in the air so that it hovered a few armspans above his head. He then held his right hand out slightly and let a small ball form there. Once satisfied with the size of it, he threw it at the plate, causing it to explode into a dozen pieces with a loud crack. Prost's dagger flew straight into the air and landed on the ground far behind its owner.

Mert let out a whistle, obviously impressed with his own display.

"Now *that* is what I call some power. Eh, Prost?"

Mert was awakened as a Mover, but he had a passion for Destroying powers and had chosen that form as his secondary power. He wasn't up to par with someone awakened with the ability, but even Prost had to admit that he was making progress. Many Lightbearers in Watchlight adopted Destroying as their secondary power, almost as if it was some rite of passage for the group. As much as Prost hated it, he did envy them. There was raw power in that class of Lightbearer. The only thing that helped him cope with his envy was the fact that their powers, no matter how strong, were useless on him.

"Fog off, Mert."

"If you *had* killed me, Riln wouldn't have taken it lightly. No matter how annoying I am, we can't afford to lose even one Watchlight Lightbearer."

"I would have just let you suffer until you were almost dead, then let Yanlin Fix you up. There's a lot I can do to you without killing you."

Mert feigned fright on his face, then rolled his eyes and walked a few paces to the shop table there. This was a shop for eating wares, plates, and utensils. He took a seat on the table, inspecting his nails as if he didn't have a care in the world. The shopkeeper looked annoyed at the man, but with Mert's overt display of power, the man didn't dare say or do anything about the situation. After a few moments, the merchant shook his head and retreated inside his tent and away from the men.

"Are yous twos fightin' again?"

Alts had walked up carrying her side sword in her hand and a pack of food in the other.

"Prost started it."

Prost's entire body tensed as he resisted the urge to slaughter the man sitting idly on the table. The weasel of a man was close enough that Prost could end him so quickly, but he didn't dare. Mert acted like a child, not someone that could be trusted, or even someone that a person could work with.

Alts looked back and forth between the two of them before deciding not to talk more about it.

"I gots the extra fruit and foods for the next leg, Prost. Neera's got some more, but she had to make a quick stop a'fore comin'."

Prost stared at Alts flatly, trying to keep emotion out of his gaze. She really did look quite stunning today, as usual. Her long blonde hair was braided in a single plait down her back. She had changed the color streak in her hair from blue to a bright red. Alts had a strange obsession with changing the stripe of color in her hair, though Prost couldn't understand why. It made her stand out too much. She looked at him with a slight smile on her face, as if she were amused by what had just happened between Mert and himself. Her dark eyes threatened to mesmerize him.

He pulled himself out of his reverie and nodded to her before scanning the crowd for the rest of the group. They had agreed to meet where he stood now just before nightfall so that they could begin their trek during the evening. It wasn't quite the time yet, but he hadn't expected them all to be gallivanting through the shops until now. The crowd was still bustling, despite the approaching storm and night. That's how it was here in the Plains of Erisdell. In some ways, he liked how lively it was, but in other ways he hated how on edge the crowd left him.

As he looked about, his eyes fell on a hooded figure standing across the way. A chill went through him as he recognized the boy. He couldn't see his face, but he knew who it was. Riln's 'pet destroyer'. Prost made a point to not talk to him or interact with him except when necessary. So far, it had worked out just fine. The Destroyer reminded him too much of Riln and his slinking creepiness. Perhaps that was the product of all the private sessions Riln had held with the boy for as long as Prost could remember. It didn't surprise him that he was hooded and hiding, that was usual for him.

"Master Prost, I'm sorry I'm late! I—"

Prost held up a hand and the voice behind him cut off.

"I don't want apologies, Iridan, I want answers. We'll address your tardiness in just a moment."

"Yes, master."

Prost turned and stared down at the little man. He wasn't actually that much shorter than Prost, but he seemed to shrink down in his presence, making him appear so much smaller. Iridan wasn't old, he was middle aged, but he was balding. The look was unbecoming of a man his age. Despite the condition of his hair, Iridan was quite fit and muscled, his arms bulging through his tight shirt and his neck thick as a tree trunk.

"Where is the boy? Your first letter placed them here three days ago, but your next said they had moved on."

"Y-yes sir. They went north, straight north without much deviation. After they slaughtered my pets, I had them followed for a time. That's what my informants told me, at least—"

"And who is following them now?"

Iridan paled at the question.

"Why master, my informant stopped following a day ago so that he could tell me where—"

"You didn't send anyone else?! You imbecile! They could be anywhere!"

The shopkeeper shrunk down further at this outburst and looked as if he were trying to hide behind a table that wasn't there.

"No! Master, I didn't send a *person* to follow them. I sent a bird! She's right good at tracking people! Never you mind that!"

Prost wasn't completely satisfied at the thought of an animal tracking the party, but at least the man wasn't overly incompetent and had continued tracking them.

"Why did you not stop them? You were told to capture them, or at least stall them as best as you could. Yet here we are, and here they are not. How did you fail?"

Iridan looked offended at the comment.

"I *did* send my spine hog army to at least kill some of 'em, but they had a Lightbearer with 'em. He right blew up my precious pets with a mere hand flick. I've never seen anything like that. I managed to skewer a few of 'em pretty quickly, and I thought that I had the best of 'em, before they blew up my hogs."

Prost glanced to the side at the Destroyer they had brought with them. He had seen firsthand the power of a full Destroyer, and it wasn't something you could prepare yourself for. Mert was a fledgling in comparison, as were all second-birth Destroyers.

"With their injuries, I figured I had stalled 'em for a time, but the foggin' Lightbearer *healed* 'em quicker than I could do anything about. I didn't stay around much longer after that. They'd have sure caught me and killed me.

That was it. It confirmed that Avryn was with them.

Fog it! That is going to complicate all of this.

"You were told to do *everything* that you could to stop them. It sounds to me like you did not. Our partnership depended solely on the keeping of our deals, and you have failed me, Iridan."

"But—no. I—I—didn't fail. I'm tracking them now, see? They won't get much further without you knowing where they'll be and—"

"When will your bird return?"

The man sighed, realizing that any explanation was going to be lost on the powerful man before him. Prost liked that he had that effect on most of his 'partners'. They never were quite that, more like his inferiors, and he made sure to make them feel that way. It made working with them a lot easier when they feared him.

"She'll return on the morrow. She comes to my shop every two days to see if anyone's ready to follow. You can go with her after that to their position."

"And what's this bird's name?"

Iridan paused at the question, clearly perplexed that Prost needed to know such a menial piece of information as the name of the tracking bird.

"Speeker, that's her. Why would you—?"

His knife cut the man's throat cleanly, Iridan's eyes open in shock. Prost stood there, a fire in his eyes as he watched the man clutch at his neck, blood pouring through his fingers. Without much of a thought, Prost turned to the north and began walking. His murdering of Iridan would likely cause a commotion soon, but they would be gone before that. Stopping just a few shops down, Prost leaned against the pole of a tent and watched as a crowd gathered around the body of the man.

"Lanser's beard, Prost. Couldn' yeh have waited till dark at least?" Alts said as she came up beside him.

"I didn't want to listen to his babbling or excuses anymore."

Mert came and stood next to Alts, an annoyed look on his face.

"Well, now what are we gonna do? We have to wait until tomorrow for the bloomin' bird to show us where to go."

"Shut it, Mert."

The rest of the group arrived shortly, each of them skirting around the crowd as they approached, a look of concern on their heads. Prost hadn't worked directly with all of them, particularly Yanlin, their Fixer, but they seemed to understand right off the bat not to mess with him. With unspoken communication, they all seemed to know that Prost was the cause of that chaos.

"Vint, I need you to See Iridan's bird. Tell me where she is, and how she got there."

A man with brown hair cut very close to his scalp stepped up to him. He was short, much shorter than Prost, and very bulky. Vint looked to be almost twice the width of himself, which made him look disproportionate in nature. The man and his twin sister, Lathe, were both Shielders, but Vint had chosen Seeing as his second-born power and was actually quite gifted, from what the other Seers had said.

"Tell me about him." Vint said. His voice had an accent that clearly marked him from the mountains in the southeast.

"I only got her name, which is Speeker. And she supposedly makes her way to the shop of that dead man over there every two days. His shop is just over there, not too far from where he died."

Vint raised an eyebrow at the brazen comment about another human's death. He was too soft of a man in Prost's opinion, but he was very gifted.

"You know that I work much better with more of a description. Why did you not get one?"

"Your reputation precedes you, Vint. Now, *See*."

Vint scowled, his thick brown eyebrows framing his eyes, making his wide set nose seem much larger than it was.

Breathing in deeply, Vint closed his blue eyes and exhaled slowly. He did this a few more times before his eyes snapped open suddenly. Instead of the normal color and white of his eyes, his entire eyes were glowing brightly with a reddish sheen, characteristic of all Lightbearers from Watchlight.

Prost stared at Vint who stood there, unmoving, while his eyes Saw things that no one else there was able to. Though it seemed like an eternity before the glow in his eyes left him, it had only been a short time. As quickly as they had started to shine, his eyes faded and he gave Prost an apologetic look.

"I'm not a full Seer, Prost, I'm only a second-born. I can't See the present and past as well as I can see an actual future. I either need more information about the bird, or we need to create a future that I can See more easily. You should not have hastily killed the man."

Annoyed at the limitation of the man's powers, Prost growled softly, thinking about a possible solution.

"Idiots." A voice cut in, interrupting Prost's trail of thought.

He turned, anger flaring in his chest, and glared at the woman that had spoken up. Vint's sister, Lathe, was inspecting her nails casually, acting as if what was happening was little concern to her. She was Vint's twin, and they looked frighteningly similar, despite the differences in their gender. She also kept her hair cropped so close to her head that you could see the shape of it. Her build was the same as Vint's, wide set, bulky, almost fat, and her eyes the same striking blue. The only difference was her unusually large breasts that poked out heavily in front of her. That, and her disposition was almost the exact opposite of the considerate and kind brother of hers.

"You said the bird comes back every two days to the dead man's shop? Just leave someone here and let them follow the bird. I vote Mert, he's the most annoying one, anyway."

Mert, hearing the comment, merely grinned and made a hooting noise as if to validate her claim of his annoyance. She rolled her eyes and spat on the ground. Lathe didn't like people in general, and she often thought that she was far better than those around her. It was a fascinating event, finding twins that had awakened on the same day and had both awakened as Shielders. The two were inseparable since then. The party didn't really *need* two Shielders, but Vint had chosen his second-born power as Seeing and she chose Destroying. That would come in handy, at least.

"This would work, actually. Though I don't think leaving Mert is wise. His Moving will be needed, should conflict arise."

Prost hated to agree with Vint, but he was left with no choice. Mert, no matter how stupid and bothersome he was, could actually be handy in a fight. He was their only Mover in this party, and they couldn't afford to leave any of their Lightbearers. That is why they had brought a few normal soldiers—they were expendable.

"You." Prost said, pointing to a plain looking soldier that they had brought along. He was fairly new to Watchlight, so Prost hadn't bothered to get to know him, let alone his name. "Head to the merchant's shop, wait for the bird to come back, then follow it to where the boy and the wench have gone. It's just over there." He gestured to where the dead man's shop was located. After a brief description of the shop, the man set out to hold the post until the bird arrived.

"Now, is *that* sufficient of a future for you?"

Vint nodded, seeming satisfied. Once again, he concentrated and his eyes began to glow, their reddish gleam casting a grim look on the faces of those standing around him. The clouds had gotten close enough to partially block the setting sun, so the darkness became stark against the glow.

He was in the trance for a bit longer this time, and a smile spread across his face.

"I See where they are now, yes. The bird will return tomorrow, and she'll lead our soldier north a few days. They seem to now be in a glade, a day from Arrant Falls. I cannot see their destination, but they will be at the falls by the evening tomorrow."

Prost cursed to himself. They were quite a distance away. He didn't like it, but they would have to travel in the storm and hope that it would delay Avryn and their group enough that they could catch up and intersect at the falls.

The light faded in Vint's eyes again and they all stared at Prost. As much as some of the people in the group didn't like it, they knew he was in charge and the call was his.

"Get the horses. We move out, now."

Mert let out a whine at the decision.

"But it's going to be stormin' soon! I *hate* getting wet in the storm."

"If I cared about that Mert, I would let the boy and Janis get away and let Riln's wrath fall on us. But I don't, so get your foggin' behind on your horse and let's *move*."

Mert feigned offense at the comment, but did as he was told. The rest of the group followed suit.

“Neera, in the storm we’ll need you to Light the way as much as you can. I wouldn’t worry about being seen by anyone, the storm’s going to be a bad one.”

“Very well, sir.” Neera replied.

She was always overly polite to her superiors. No matter how gruff or rude Prost was to her, she maintained her coolness and used honorifics when addressing him. He didn’t particularly like it, for it made him feel old, and a bit more hard in nature than he actually was, but he couldn’t hate Neera for it. It wasn’t just to him that she was kind, but to everyone.

“Do you think you can?”

“I awakened years ago as a Lighter—this will be no problem, despite the storm.”

She was confident in her abilities, that was good. Neera stood tall and lean. Her skin was dark, so dark that when night came, she blended in well, something Prost could only manage by wearing black clothing. Her hair was thick and coarse, black as night, cut around her shoulders. She hailed from the northern mountainlands, characteristic of which was her dark skin and hair.

“Good, let’s move.”

In a few moments, the whole group had gathered their horses and tied on the new things they had purchased. Prost lurched himself into his saddle and kicked his horse into motion. By the time they had reached the forest line, the clouds had reached over their heads and a slight rain had begun to fall. The wind hadn’t picked up yet, but he could feel it. It wasn’t far behind them.

“Neera, now.”

Neera breathed in and held her hands out before her. In a flash of brilliance, a large orb of red Light burst into life in front of her. Spreading her hands, the orb multiplied into a dozen others of the same size and flew to the edges of the group, hovering a few feet above their heads and surrounding them in a tight circle, some extending into the forest to show the way, should anything dangerous try to approach.

“RIDE!”

Prost kicked his horse into motion and it began running. The Lights closest him followed at the same pace, illuminating the whole area. Just as he began the run, the wind picked up in fierceness and buffeted his clothes. The torrent that followed left him soaked to the bone in mere moments. He gritted his teeth against the cold of the wind and rain, but felt a thrill within himself. He loved the rain. Instantly, he felt a burst of energy and excitement as he led the party north, toward Arrant Falls.

Chapter 11

The rain pummeled the ground, roaring loudly enough to drown all other surrounding sounds out easily. It was morning, that was evident by the dull grey light that filtered through the pouring rain, but what time in the morning, Marric couldn't tell. Wet earth and plants produced a smell that was actually quite nice, had he not been soaked and cold at the moment. He sat with his legs up to his chest, trying to fend off the uncomfortable feeling of coldness. It really wasn't that cold outside, but the strong wind and rain seemed to cut directly through his clothes and touch his skin with its kiss, making it seem freezing.

"Well, at least we git ta take a break, righ', Mar?" Harmel said cheerily, also keeping his legs curled up to stay warm.

Marric stared at him incredulously. The man had a strange way of staying cheery in the worst of situations. Just a few days ago, he had cracked some joke about being just like their dinner of meat on a stick after being skewered by multiple spines from the hogs.

"Oi'm jus' sayin', we could be a lot worse, tired'n all tha'."

The deluge hadn't let up all morning. It had started in the middle of the night and woken them all up with a start. With urgency, they had tried to prepare a shelter of branches, roots, and other plants, but it was mostly washed or blown away with the strength of the storm. Where Marric and Harmel sat now was a sad excuse for a shelter—all that was left was a branch of considerable size propped up against a tree slanting down at a steep angle. It did little else than cause the rain to run down its length and create a pool down at the bottom. There was some foam spinning idly as the rain-created river flowed into the puddle. What created the foam, Marric couldn't tell.

Well, I guess he's not wrong. I was getting pretty tired with our pace. Though I wouldn't count this as rest, Marric thought.

Though the comment about rest was a strange one, not to mention that it was delivered at a really strange moment, it did seem to warm Marric up a bit.

"Why do you say things like that? It's like when things are completely horrible, you seem to see the good in it all."

Harmel produced his famous giddy grin that he showed ever so frequently. His smile was a bit crooked, the left side of his mouth pulling up a bit higher than the other.

"Well, yeh see," he said matter-of-factly, "Oi figure Oi have th'right to be 'appy, no? Life 'as a way of gettin' yeh down, bu' tha' don' mean Oi 'ave ta feel th'same, hmm?"

Marric smiled back at the man's stupid grin.

"I think you're a bit strange, but it's nice that you can feel that way."

Barely audible through the pouring rain and wind was the yell of someone approaching. Harmel's face hardened into an uncharacteristically serious form as he reached for his sword. Avryn appeared through the sheet of water, hair pulled back in a ponytail to keep it out of his face. His clothes drooped off of him, their water-filled weight yanking them down to the ground.

"I take it you didn't hear me, did you?" Avryn shouted again, a grimace on his face. "We found a place to hole up for awhile. Let's get the bags."

Marric felt a small flame of hope in his chest at the sound of that. Perhaps they could light a fire and warm themselves for the first time in what seemed like an eternity. When the rain had first woken them, they had opted to wait out the storm as a group, then continue on as soon as it broke. After their makeshift shelters gave up the ghost and they saw that the rain wasn't changing its pace, Shrell and Avryn decided to search for more adequate shelter. Janis didn't say much, but she slipped into the rain herself. They could only assume that she agreed with them and was doing the same.

"Is it far?" Marric asked, trying not to sound pathetic in asking, even though it's how he felt.

"Not unreasonably, no. Fortunately, it is quite deep so we should be able to stay dry from the rain.

They didn't talk much more after that; the need to yell over the rain expended too much energy for them to waste. Plus, what could you talk about while you were trekking through pouring rain and wind? It wasn't a good time to bring up the weather, at least.

Avryn hadn't been wrong, it seemed the perfect place for a group like theirs. The hole in the wall stood above the trees, but the rain made it look like a different color of stone, which wasn't unusual in these mountains. There were often patches of rock that took on a different color tone than the surrounding rock, which was the normal grey.

They passed into the hole in the wall and entered a dark cave. Without hesitation, Avryn summoned his small ball of Light and let it fly toward the roof of the small cavern, which turned out to only be an armspan above Avryn's head. Marric suddenly felt a bit claustrophobic. However, being a bit cramped was far better than being wet and miserable. Already he felt a significant difference in the temperature of his body as he left the pelting rain outside.

Janis and Shrell were already in the cave at opposite sides, though that didn't put much distance between them, since it only was about as deep as the height of nine or ten men, and as wide as six. Because of this, the horses, unfortunately, had to stay outside in the rain. There was probably enough room to fit them, but with a fire, it wouldn't be safe for either them or the others to stay in the cave together.

"I see that you are playing nice already." Avryn said lightly.

Shrell stared at Avryn flatly and Janis just ignored the comment. She was sitting near the mouth of the cave and scanning the trees and area around.

"Anyway, how about we get a good fire started, hmm? I think we could all do with a bit of warmth at this moment, and my Light is too small to be of much use. A Lighter would be good right about now."

In no time, they had a fire raging in the center of the cave and Marric had shed his outer clothing and set them near the fire to dry. Janis had warned against starting a fire, but Avryn made the final decision to actually start one. It was deep enough in the cave and the rain was strong enough outside that the firelight wouldn't attract unwanted attention. Regardless of the results of the conversation, Janis kept her post at the mouth of the cave, watching.

"It really is a shame that we have to pause, we are getting quite close to our destination."

"Where exactly are we going?" Marric asked.

"Unfortunately, even if you knew the surrounding area, I wouldn't want to talk much about where we are going. Some things are best left alone. Needless to say, we are going to a place of refuge for people loyal to us."

"So there are a lot more of you, then?"

"Oh, Marric, far more than just the three of us. We were just an escort sent to fetch you. Our leader warned us that coming to get you was too risky, but I didn't want to leave you to Watchlight. They aren't as forgiving if you don't do what they ask."

Marric gulped loudly, though no one else would have been able to hear.

"Anyway, enough about that. Is anyone getting hungry? It's about time for a bit of food."

"Blimey, it be about time, S'ren! Oi'm so hungry Oi could eat one of them 'orses!" Harmel blurted, sounding desperate.

They took advantage of the fire and made a warm stew with collected rainwater and some of the ingredients they had saved from the Plains a few days before.

As they ate, Marric was trying to build up the courage to ask more about Lightbearer gifts. They hadn't spent much time talking about them since the first conversation, and Avryn always seemed sheepish about the subject. Not to mention that he hid his powers more often than he used them. It was only in combat or desperate situations that he used them somewhat freely. Since nothing eventful had happened in the last few days, there had been no show at all of the powers.

He glanced up warily at the ceiling where the small ball of Light hovered. It was dim now against the roaring fire, and yet, it did seem to cast away some of the shadows in the corners of the dark cave.

"Do you think we still need that?" Marric said out loud, pointing to the ceiling.

Avryn followed Marric's point and a surprised look flashed on his face.

"Oh, I forgot about that."

In an instant, the orb snuffed out and the places where the small Light touched went dark around them. It didn't seem like much of a change with the fire, though.

"You don't have to think about it, then? It just stays there?"

Avryn eyed Marric warily, but clearly didn't want to disappoint the boy.

"With Lighting, that is the case, yes. The tricky part is summoning the Light effectively, but once it's there, little concentration is required to maintain its form, unless you are being attacked or otherwise distracted, then it gets a bit tricky."

"Is it the same with the other powers, then? The ones we talked about before?"

The man let out a loud sigh. It seemed that he realized he couldn't avoid the subject much longer.

"Perhaps I should give you what you deserve, Marric. If you are to become one of us, you should be privy to the powers and their respective restrictions. Where to start, then?"

He seemed deep in thought for a time before continuing.

"I think it's probably best to start with what I'm most familiar with: the powers that I've manifested. The three that I'm most acquainted with."

"Hang on, *three*? I thought you said awakening only gave one and then another could be chosen—or whatever." He remembered what Avryn said about the power selecting the person and that made him amend what he said.

For some reason, the comment made Avryn look troubled.

"Yes, you see, I'm quite an anomaly. In very rare cases, a person manifests not one, but three powers instead. I am one of these. Hence, the process of my awakening nearly killed me. But my theory is that because of Fixing being one of mine, I didn't perish."

Avryn made that last comment so nonchalantly that Marric almost didn't register what he had said. His own awakening had almost killed *him* as well? This made the boy more nervous than ever about the whole thing, but he worked to hide it, fearing that showing so would cause Avryn to stop telling him more.

"Anyway, first things first, the three I know most. First is Conjuring, then Fixing, as I just mentioned, then—then, there is Destroying."

A silence followed that made the hair stand on Marric's arms and neck.

"Well, this is fascinatin' an' all tha', but Oi'm pretty foggin' tired, so Oi'm gonna sleep a bit. Nigh', all."

Harmel had a way of intervening with odd comments when things started to get awkward. For that, Marric was actually grateful. The stocky man lay back where he was and rested on his back, hands behind his head.

Avryn stared at the man with a smile, seeming to appreciate his timing as well. Then he continued.

"Conjuring is a very useful skill, and one that I use very often. As I noted before, a Conjurer creates a physical item out of Light. It appears in Light form, but is very much tangible and can even be stronger than the real thing. There are technically no restrictions in size, shape, or hardness of the object, but to summon something very large or many objects at once is difficult, even for an awakened Conjurer. The most handy part about this power is that the weight of the object can be modified."

A Light flashed in Avryn's right hand suddenly and the sword appeared, the one from the night he and Janis had fought. It wasn't intricate, but there were wavy designs on the pommel. It was a standard sword length, but despite it being made of Light, Marric could sense its sharpness.

"Here, hold it for a bit."

He held out the blade and Marric hesitantly took it. He had never been good with a knife, let alone a sword, and even holding them made him uncomfortable.

"Do you feel that?"

For a moment he hadn't noticed, but he suddenly realized that it was almost weightless. His eyes widened at the revelation.

"That's amazing! It's so light, I can barely feel it."

"Slice that log next to you."

Marric looked concerned, but took a breath and swung at the log. It cut clean through it easily.

"Wow."

"Yes, it is just as hard and sharp as a normal sword of steel."

The sword rapidly got heavier and heavier until Marric had to drop it because of the weight. It clattered loudly to the floor, making a sound all too much like a metal sword.

"It just changed!"

Avryn smiled.

"Yes, I just made it heavier. I can modify the weight, size, sharpness, pretty much anything about it, without having to touch it. Of course, the ability to keep it Conjured and modify any physical attributes does have a distance limit. With practice, I've been able to extend it to one hundred armspans away, but most can only handle about fifty away. Once the object gets too far away, you can't modify it, and once it breaks the limit, it snuffs away."

A flash of Light in each of his hands revealed an axe—a woodcutting one—and a tall mug used for ale or spirits. Marric glanced down to see the sword was still there.

"I can Conjure multiple things. I can handle six or seven really easily now, but I'm working up to an eighth. And, as you can see, I can Conjure *anything* physical. It comes in handy if I've forgotten a fork or plate for my trip."

Marric stared in amazement at the three different objects, looking between them all. The axe and sword puffed away, but the mug remained.

"Shrell, be a good man for me, can you collect some water, please?"

Shrell nodded, not saying a word, but he took the mug and walked to the entrance of the cave and held it out in the rain.

As he did so, Marric saw Janis eyeing him warily. She then moved her gaze to Avryn and there she held it. She was able to do so without having to turn her whole head, so Marric himself could barely tell that she was. Avryn didn't notice, however. It was clear that Janis was taking in as much of the information that she could, just like Marric.

What are you thinking, Janis?

Shrell stalked back and sat down again beside Avryn. It seemed that he already knew what he needed to do, so he tilted the mug sideways and poured out rain water he had caught.

"As you can see, it works exactly as a mug should. Thank you, Shrell."

The man nodded and let the mug fall from his hands. Before it could strike the ground, it disappeared.

"Though the gift is handy, it can easily give you away in the night. It happens to be less obvious during the light of day than at night. This is why I don't use it so openly as we move around at night, however useful it may seem."

Marric was dumbfounded by all of this. He had assumed that the sword was the only thing that Avryn could make out of Light, but this was astounding.

"I take it from your silence that you don't have any questions."

Marric only shook his head slightly, obviously overwhelmed enough by what he had just seen. He couldn't even imagine what kinds of questions he *would* ask right now.

Avryn gave his characteristic warm smile at Marric's reaction, then let it melt away.

"Good. But feel free to ask any at any time, I won't mind. Though this does feel a bit strange. I don't often share as much information about Lightbearing unless we're in the safety of our stronghold, but this time is as good as any for you."

Marric took that moment to glance at Janis, a look of concern on his face. She still had her face toward the mouth of the cave, but that was just a facade. Her head was turned slightly so that her ear could catch every word of the conversation, and more often than not, Marric knew that she was watching from the sidelines, taking in all the information that Avryn was sharing.

She is just as curious as I am, but she won't show it. Unless her interest is for some other reason. . . .

It was too much for Marric to think about at the moment. He focused his attention back on Avryn.

"Let's move on to Fixing, hmm? As you've seen, Fixing is a remarkable restorative power that, to my knowledge and experience, can work on anything or anyone. It essentially restores an object, or person, to their perfect state before any imperfections, erosion, or other type of destruction affected it. The most common use of this, as you've seen, is healing a person that has just been injured. Fixing, as you recall we discussed before, is how I restored the floor of your home not long ago. A Fixer can restore something to its previous state, but that means it needs to have existed before that. For example, a Fixer could not take materials for a home, or a piece of clothing that hadn't been organized, and turn it into that thing. It would only Fix the materials themselves. Some people misconstrue the power in this way."

He paused a moment, giving Marric time to ask something. When no questions came, he continued.

"A Fixer has better influence over an object if he or she is touching the thing that they are hoping to restore. However, that isn't always necessary. If something is broken to pieces, with concentration, a Fixer can still Fix the thing from a few paces away, though they can't be too far in distance, or it won't work. The bigger the thing that they Fix, the more difficult it is. It is possible to Fix, say, a wall surrounding a city that was broken in an earthquake, but the Fixer would have to be very practiced and powerful to do so, and it would expend a lot of energy, making them very tired after the fact.

"As I mentioned a little while back, Fixing is effective and quite useful, but sometimes it can be too powerful, taking the restoration a little bit further than you expected. There have been times that a Fixer has restored a home made of wood, but rather than just Fixing the wood, it caused some of the wood to sprout branches and leaves and extend roots into the ground. Or, like you saw at your house, the wood became a little bit too brand new. The most challenging part of Fixing is knowing when to stop. Though it isn't necessarily dangerous to Fix too far, it can have an unintended effect on the object."

"Does it require a lot of concentration?" Marric blurted, surprised at his own question, and how suddenly it had come on.

Avryn didn't look the least bit taken aback by his question, but rather looked pleased that Marric was starting to ask for further details.

"Fortunately, in most cases, Fixing does not. It just feels natural, like it's *right* for things to come back together that were previously not. I am, however, an awakened Fixer and not a second-born, so I can't speak for what it takes for them to Fix things, but for me, it is very easy. On occasion, I have restored a home, or something else far larger than myself. Though *concentration* isn't what I would call it, I do have to be a little bit more focused in what I'm doing, and I can feel more energy expended, as I mentioned before."

Marric's eyes seemed hopeful and bright. He blanched at the thought of having to learn to fight more aggressively—it made his stomach turn and anxiety fill his whole person. But perhaps he could be useful with his future powers, if he just became a Fixer instead of one of the others.

Oh Lanser, I pray that I can be helpful and not a burden when I awaken.

Avryn's eyes crinkled at the sides as he saw Marric's reaction to his thoughts. Immediately, however, they turned to concern and he cleared his throat loudly, seeming uncomfortable.

"And though I don't enjoy having to do this, I am an expert in the opposite force. I am somewhat an anomaly in that regard."

A pause followed, and Avryn seemed to be gathering the courage to move on.

"Fixing, unfortunately, came with an opposite power, called Destroying. It's not something that I am particularly fond of, but desperate times sometimes require my use of this class of Lightbearing. Destroying breaks things, exactly opposite of Fixing. It is a very potent power that also requires little concentration to use, which makes it that much more dangerous. An object—"

Avryn paused again, obviously deliberating how to choose his next words. Sighing indignantly at the inevitability of the conversation, he continued.

"—or even a living being touched by the power will, in essence, break into pieces, often in a very explosive manner."

They sat there in silence for a time, Avryn studying Marric's reaction to the news. In all honesty, Marric didn't know how to react. It wasn't that the thought of a living being, a *person*, falling apart in an instant didn't disturb and bother him, it was just that he was a bit numb to this after the events of the past few days. Deep within him, he could feel his subconscious squirming, and even a sickening feeling growing in his stomach, but he was just too emotionally exhausted for the feelings to overwhelm him. He was grateful for the timing.

"That's what you did to the hogs, then."

Avryn leaned back in surprise, not expecting Marric's cool and frank response.

"Why, yes."

Avryn cleared his throat again.

"We were in quite a situation and I didn't know what else to do. You were hurt and we didn't have much time. As I mentioned, I don't enjoy calling upon this power unless it's in a time of need."

A realization came to Marric at that moment.

"But wait, if Destroying is like Fixing, wouldn't you have to be touching the object for it to work?"

A look of surprise flashed on Avryn's face.

"A wise question, indeed. That is one area where the powers differ in an unfortunate way. Destroying can be utilized through touch, but a Destroyer also has the ability to create a ball of Light infused with the power that can be thrown from afar. Upon impact, the power Destroys the thing that it touches. This makes it a very lethal force, and the reason why when facing a Destroyer, you need to be vigilant. These balls won't have as powerful of an effect as when passed through physical touch, but it can still be dangerous and deadly."

In an obvious attempt to change the subject, Avryn continued hurriedly.

"But any power, even Destroying, can be blocked by a Shielder. Admittedly, not being an awakened Shielder myself, I am not an expert in that force. However, a Shielder's ability can block any ability used against it. A Destroyer cannot break through it without using more force than the

Shielder's power. A Seer cannot See through a Shield, a Conjurer cannot use an object summoned to break through. As you can imagine, this is quite a useful power, and one that is highly sought after by those that know of Lightbearing."

The wind howled in an unexpected frenzy outside, causing the entrance of the cave to moan loudly. Marric shivered at the sound. He knew that ghosts were not real, but the state that he was in still left him affected by the sound.

"You may not have noticed," Avryn continued, ignoring the eerie sound that preceded his next words. "But I've tried to maintain my weak Shield for most of our journey."

Marric started a bit at the revelation. He looked around, confused.

"Look just there." Avryn said, pointing to a spot above their heads a few feet up. It was hard to make out, but there was a small bit of whispy Light, a very slight glow, hovering there. It wasn't bright enough to provide actual help for someone in the dark, but looked more like a trick of the eye. As he stared more closely, he could see that it wasn't just above them, but it extended out and around most of the group, Janis being the only one outside of it. It wasn't a wonder that Marric hadn't seen it, it was practically invisible.

"I can hardly see it at all."

"Yes, that's because it's actually quite weak. A real Shielder's power would be made of blazing Light. If I were to retract the Shield to be small, you'd see that it was lit quite nicely. Here, see."

At that, the practically invisible wall of Light shrunk quickly to just around Avryn. The Light did intensify, but it was nothing compared to anything that Avryn had Conjured just moments before, or even the small ball of Light that he could summon, which was very intense indeed. With it holding its place there, Marric could at least see that it was a thin sheet of Light that surrounded Avryn in a round shape, almost like an eggshell around him. All at once, the Light expanded again and returned to its almost invisible state around them.

"But why have you been doing that?" Marric asked, curious.

"I don't expect that my Shield will do much for any physical harm that may come our way, in fact, it was practically useless in the fight with the spine hogs. The best it was able to do in that fight was misdirect some of the spines shot at us. The spines easily broke through the Shield, but I suspect that it threw them off course enough to miss our vital areas. It very well could have saved your life."

"Anyway, I mostly keep it up because it disrupts Seers' visions. A strong Shielder can block a Seer completely, but with mine, I at least have the ability to make it very difficult to See us. Watchlight has many Seers, some of which are very strong. Blocking their vision means that they can't locate us, or see where we are going. Unfortunately, I'm not adept enough to keep it up while we sleep, so they may catch glimpses of us while we sleep, but with us sleeping in odd parts of the forest, they can't locate landmarks of any kind, so they just get to watch us slumber."

The thought of that unsettled Marric more, and suddenly he didn't want to sleep outside anymore, as if the security of walls of any kind might make him feel more sheltered against unknown eyes.

"Seers can see anywhere?" Marric asked, his voice wavering a bit.

Avryn grimaced at the question, seeming a bit sorry for where the conversation turned.

"I'm sorry to make you nervous, but I assure you we are taking precautions, and I am confident that they haven't located us. Really, I've gotten used to the idea of an enemy Seer watching me at any time of the day. They can't do much harm from a distance, other than watch. At our base, however, we have strong Shielders that block it from view at all times, so we are unseen there."

This didn't make Marric feel much better. Though he was almost dry from the heat of the blazing fire, his barely damp clothes seemed to hug tighter to his skin and the cold of the wet intensified. He shivered, reacting to the feeling.

"Admittedly I'm not overly familiar with the ins and outs of Seeing, but I do know that they must know what they are searching for fairly well in order to See it. Also, they can extend their view into the Future and into the

Past, so from what I hear, time is a bit nonexistent for them. They are often an odd lot, those ones."

Hearing that last part solidified the feeling within Marric. However useful Seeing was, he didn't want to be that person spying into other people's lives without their knowledge or permission. It wouldn't feel right at all. Not to mention that it sounded like they were outcasts, without actually being cast out.

Oh Lanser, please don't make me a Seer. Marric prayed to the god.

"Movers come to mind next," Avryn continued, not seeming to notice Marric's reaction to what he'd said about the Seers just before then. "In essence, what I said before is what they do. They have the ability to move objects external to themselves. What they manipulate glows with Light and they can shift it physically. I'm not sure what limitations exist for a well trained Mover, but I do know that it takes training to be able to Move something that is larger or much heavier than yourself. Also, there is an element to proximity, though perhaps not as much as Conjuring. From what I know, Movers must be able to see what they are trying to move. Regardless, a Mover is challenging to fight as they can just throw you away if you try to get close."

He said the last part a bit absentmindedly, as if he was imagining something from his past—an experience that he had.

"Well let's not get into that, if you end up being one of the classes that I don't have, we'll make sure to have you trained well enough by someone who is more expert than I."

There was a nervous and excited feeling churning in Marric's chest and stomach, one that was a bit exhilarating and the other exhausting, the combination making him feel sick. Though he appreciated the information and the ability to ask questions about these strange powers, it seemed to drop a heavy weight on his shoulders, as if he was picking up a large sack of grain and leaving it there for no reason. The pouring rain and wind continued, but there was more flashing now, as if lightning was creeping up on their location, trying to overtake them like one of their enemies.

"How will I know which I am?"

"Oh, don't worry, it's a bit obvious. Perhaps not to you as much as it will be to me. As I mentioned a while ago, there are external effects to a person's awakening that reveal that instantly."

Marric nodded, but he didn't really want to talk about the awakening, at least, not now. The only thing that he felt when he thought about it was that he might die. He had to shake his head to not allow himself to dwell on it.

Janis was less obviously listening to the conversation now that they had moved on from the actual powers themselves. Her fascination in them was not unusual, but the fact that she didn't include herself in the discussion was a bit strange to Marric. If she was that interested, why not ask questions herself? Avryn was more than willing to answer Marric's, so why not hers as well?

"Wait a minute." Marric said suddenly, "What about the seventh?"

"Hmm?" Avryn said, looking at him.

"There are seven, so I think we are missing one."

He went through them in his head again, then said out loud, "Lighting."

"Oh yes, how could I forget? That is the class from which we all relate, as our powers come from Light. A Lighter is very handy, indeed. They can generate Light that is so blinding and piercing that they can illuminate a whole village for a very long time. The Light of a Lighter is more potent as well, seeming brighter than the other classes. Our entire sanctuary is lit by just one Lighter. We have a few of them, but keeping up the Light in the entire structure isn't difficult, so they take turns so that the others can have time off. Unfortunately, the most I can manage is this small bit of Light."

He held out his hand and the small ball appeared again, indeed very bright and piercing, the blue hue making it seem even brighter.

"I've tried to extend my Light, but I haven't had much success. Though I could likely spend more time, since I don't technically have a second-born power yet."

Avryn adopted a look of deep concentration, then the ball split into two of them. However, they weren't balls of equal size, they seemed to be about half the size of the first.

He sighed and let the two balls snuff out.

"As you can see there, I can only manage the one ball, and if I try to split it, they just get smaller and smaller and—"

"What did you mean by that?"

"I'm sorry?"

"You said something about a 'second-born', what do you mean?"

"Oh, yes, that is the term, though I'm not sure why, that we use when a Lightbearer chooses their second power, I believe we talked about it a few days ago when we first started discussing this."

"So what's yours? What did you choose?"

The long-haired man looked sheepish suddenly, as if Marric had caught him taking food from the pantry before supper. It seemed a very childish look for a man of his age, but it was genuine. His cheeks turned a bit red, a slight blush forming on his face.

"Well—I haven't quite chosen yet. I've been too busy developing my three powers and I haven't had time to actually choose and develop another. In fact, I'm not even sure that I can. Some of my fellows think me a fool for procrastinating, but someday I'll work on that."

Beside him, Shrell suddenly tensed and put his hand to his sword. Marric looked at him, not sure what he was doing. Then he saw that Janis had her hand up and was staring intently out the cave, body tense.

"Put out the fire! Now!" she hissed at the group.

Without hesitation, Avryn held up his hands and a dome of Light flashed into existence above the fire. It fell with a bit of a clang and engulfed the burning logs instantly, plunging them into darkness again. Marric felt a stab of fear and shrunk to the ground. No one had said to, but he lay on the ground as if that would protect him better.

All was quiet except for the crackling logs of the extinguished fire, though that threatened to be covered completely by the pounding rain outside of the cave.

His eyes adjusted, and he could see Shrell shake Harmel awake and the two of them moved to the cave entrance quietly, swords sliding out of the sheaths slowly. Avryn's face seemed intense and he moved into position between Marric and the opening of the cave.

No one had said it, but Marric could tell. Someone was coming.

Chapter 12

Avryn's explanations of the powers were not only intriguing, but essential for Janis. The one thing she had learned right off the bat when Macks was training her was that knowing the enemy, even the fine details, could mean the difference between a live assassin and a dead one. Listening to Avryn and Marric had caused her to rely on her sight for monitoring outside the cave, though the intense storm rendered her hearing almost useless anyway. As soon as Janis had spotted the lamplight and movement with it, her ears snapped back to the cave entrance and the flood gate of sound rushed in. The stark difference made the storm seem even louder. Now she stood, both hands occupied by her wicked daggers as she watched the people approaching.

At first, she thought that it could be a larger group, but it turned out to only be two people. The taller of the two was carrying a lamp that was miraculously still lit in the wet of the rain. It appeared that they had prepared this lantern for weathering conditions such as this. Glancing to the side, she saw that Harmel and Shrell were there at the entrance, weapons drawn and at the ready.

Though I appreciate their sentiment, they are more than likely going to be in my way! she thought in annoyance.

The two people were covered in clothes head to toe and it wasn't easy to distinguish anything about them. At least, it wouldn't be easy for someone who wasn't Janis. She could tell by the gait of the two that the taller one was a man, one without much coordination at all, and that the other was a woman, far more controlled. They were together, not just in person, but romantically, for the man was slightly behind her and was softly pushing on her back.

Janis snickered at this, for the woman was far more capable of moving through the storm than the man, but he did this anyway. When they were close enough, she examined their bodies for any signs of weapons. She did spot a protrusion from the man's cloak on his left side that looked like the handle of a blade, perhaps a short sword.

Before long, the two individuals stumbled to the opening of the cave. Janis bent down and prepared to pounce on them, when Harmel quickly shifted his sword in front of Janis, blocking her path. She turned and glared at him, frustration burning in her gut.

Just then, Shrell spoke.

"Who goes there?!"

The two figures froze and stumbled backwards a pace. Though their faces were covered in hoods, she could see them look back and forth, only now realizing that there were people in the cavern. Without hesitation, the taller one pulled back his cloak, revealing a man well past his middle age. His cheeks were starting to sink and his face was showing wrinkles, but his body indicated that he was much stronger than a man would normally be at his age.

"Oi—Oi'm sorry, sir. Oi sure din' see no one 'ere, see? We's jus' lookin' fer a place ta git away from the cold an' the wet, see? My wife an' I jus' lost our cart an' horses an' we need a place ta rest."

Is that really *what you need?* Janis thought, reeling.

Harmel seemed as if he knew her intentions and he pushed his sword against her chest as if to emphasize the point. The anger boiled again in her gut, but she held still.

"Well, yous are welcome 'ere, then. I think that yeh better get in 'ere quick." Harmel said.

Shrell took the woman by the arm and helped the two into the cave. Harmel's eyes caught her own and he smiled. Though he didn't say anything, she knew what he was thinking.

Janis got the message: hold off, they don't seem to be threatening right now.

She slid the larger of her two daggers back into place in the hidden holster down the left side of her body and switched the smaller dagger to her right hand, watching as Shrell guided the woman to a place next to where the fire had been only moments before. Seeing how the man's wife reacted to the sudden change in lighting solidified the notion that she was not likely a threat to them, for the woman seemed to trip on practically everything that lay on the ground. Having been in the cavern herself for some time, Janis's eyes had adjusted, but it was clear that the man and his wife needed a while to let theirs adjust. He had chosen to stand there for a bit while his eyes did just that, looking wide-eyed at how dark it was.

"Tis a shame you ain't got a fire burnin', 'tis mighty cold right now," he said, eyes staring past Avryn and Marric.

"Well, my good man, we can have one up and burning again in no time."

The fire indeed lit very quickly, given that it was very much alive not too long before. They all gathered around the fire, sitting close and letting the two warm themselves from the wet and the cold. Janis, however, chose a position behind Marric that allowed her to see the faces of the travelers. It would help her to see if they lied as they talked. Avryn sat next to Marric protectively. His face indicated that he wanted to ask the newcomers some questions, but it seemed he didn't want to disturb them just yet. Instead of just sitting there in silence, Janis decided to take matters into her own hands.

"So how did you know where to find us?" she asked, voice hard.

The old man looked up, startled.

"Oi'm sorry?"

"How did you know where we were sheltering from the storm?"

Clearing his throat loudly, Avryn cut in.

"She means to say, how did you know the location of this cave? It is quite hard to spot through the storm out there."

"Oh, well, yes. Me wife and Oi have been merchants fer quite a long time, see? We been passin' this place 'ere for many years now, and even had ta stay 'ere a time or two. We well know it's righ' hidden well. That's why we din' expect no one t'be 'ere 'afore the likes of us."

Avryn and the others seemed satisfied by that answer, but skepticism was something Janis always adopted, especially when strangers were closeby. Despite not feeling completely satisfied by what he said, she didn't press the issue further. Mostly because she wanted to hear more about where they were hailing from and where they were going. He had also mentioned something about losing their horses and cart. Deciding that it wouldn't be worth her time to drive the conversation, (these people weren't wealthy and didn't seem important enough at the moment for her to intervene any longer) Janis slunk back into the shadows of the cave and made her way back to the entrance. The rain continued, seeming unchanged.

"Well, I must say it is a good thing for merchants like you to have places like this to stay should you run into trouble." Avryn said. "You mentioned that you are merchants, but where are you keeping your belongings? You seem to have come here empty handed."

The man looked at his wife, a sad look on his face. She had since pulled back her hood and was letting her hair and clothing dry by the warmth of the fire. She too was older, but her appearance was younger. Her youthful face was almost free of wrinkles, and it was only her completely grey and white hair that gave any indication of her age.

"Tha's jus' it, sir. We was ridin' along down there by the road," he gestured out the cave as if the others could see where he was talking about. "A few hours ride down from 'ere, when some men all dressed in black came out of nowhere. They 'ad horses, but theirs were all worn out like, or so they said. They forced me and my wife righ' off th' cart, rummaged through, and galloped away with our horses and cart. Course they left their horses, which we tethered to a tree in th' rain 'afore we set out 'ere. The poor beasts were tired to the bone, an' they likely ain't gettin' no rest in the wet, I think."

He has a tendency to ramble, I see. Janis thought, annoyed. She wondered why he hadn't put up any sort of fight. It wasn't as if he showed any signs of abuse or a scuffle, so did they just submit that quickly? If he'd been a merchant for this long, wouldn't he have had to learn how to defend himself and his wares?

As if in response to her thoughts, the merchant shifted in his seat and let out a gasp of pain. The woman put her hands on his shoulders, a look of worry on her face. For a moment, he held his breath, then seemed to have to steady himself before he finished his previous movement.

"Are you quite alright?" Avryn said.

"Oi'm a bit bruised, is all. They roughed me up qui' a bit, as thieves often have a way of doin'." But when he said this, there was something else. He stared off into the dark of the cave, deep in thought. His wife's brow was furrowed, concern showing deep on her face.

Janis stared at him, trying to understand what he wasn't saying. Avryn seemed to notice too, but he didn't speak right away. When the man spoke of being beaten before he was robbed, she wasn't quite sure in the dim firelight, but he seemed to turn a bit pale and a shiver had run up his spine, the kind of shiver you get when you remember something frightening, or feel like someone is watching you.

"Do you need bandages? Are you bleeding anywhere?" Avryn asked, now seeming more concerned than he was before.

"No, no. Oi'll be fine. Bu' they sure did knock me qui' good 'afore they took our things. Oi'm only glad they left me sweetheart without harm."

His wife remained quiet, sitting there with the same sad look on her face.

"My apologies, madam, I never had the chance to introduce myself, I'm Avryn," he said, extending his hand towards her.

"Ah, sorry. Eh . . . me wife is a mute, yeh see? Since she's a kid, she ain't much able ta say much. She can 'ear you righ' fine, though."

The woman looked at his hand, her face shifting from worry to a longing one, though no one could be sure why. She did, after a pause, take his hand and shake it lightly.

"'er name's Lydia, jus' fer yer knowledge."

Just then, the woman, keeping eye contact with Avryn, made a series of hand gestures, some small, some sweeping. It happened so fast that it made Janis tense up. Her husband just nodded, then interpreted, "She says it's nice ta meet yous, and thank yeh for sharing yer fire."

Avryn smiled more brightly and just nodded to the woman.

Janis had heard of mutes and deafs often creating hand gestures and signs to communicate, but she'd never met one, let alone one that was married. Of course, none of what the old woman did made any sense to her, but it seemed to work fine for the two of them.

"Are either of you hungry, by any chance? Without your provisions, I suspect that you don't have much to go on, food wise."

The old man chuckled a bit.

"Well, see, on a good stroke a' luck we was eating our supper when t'all happened. I'm still feelin' qui' full from tha meal. What about you, dear?"

The woman shook her head. Something about her unsettled Janis, as if whatever secrets she held were far beyond Janis's capabilities of retrieving. There seemed to be some thoughts lurking in her mind and without her ability to speak, they were locked away, not accessible to anyone, not even through torture. Of course, Janis didn't love using torture; she preferred to get her information through intrigue and spying, but even in this instance, she could gain nothing from this Lydia.

"Me name's Milnarin, by the by. I see yeh have a lot of people 'ere with yous."

"Oh yes, how rude of me—these are my two traveling companions, Shrell and Harmel." Avryn gestured to each in turn. Shrell gave a sullen nod, not seeming overly happy, while Harmel waved enthusiastically, characteristic of his normal cheery disposition. "The boy here is Felrin, and over there, his sister Marivel. We're helping them return to their home up north."

Janis started inwardly, but not indicating it in any obvious physical way. She had trained herself to hide emotions, even the normal physical responses that often came with them. For a very brief moment, her eyes caught Avryn's, and he nodded very subtly to her. Despite his friendly tone and kindness, the man knew the importance of anonymity, even in situations that seemed harmless. Even if these two merchants hadn't heard Marric's and Janis's names through their network, they would eventually, and leaving any trail would lead trouble back to the party, albeit unintentionally.

"Well, it's nice ta meet yeh. Seems a bit coincidence though, the men tha' took all our things said they was lookin' fer a boy and a lady wearin' all black. It was a bit odd, if Oi say so. They dun ripped our cart apar' first, lookin' fer stashed people."

Avryn's face betrayed him, and Janis saw it. His mouth turned down slightly, and so briefly, eyebrows lifting up quickly in surprise. He hastily corrected his expression. Janis eyed the old man, but he was looking down at the fire, not seeming to notice. His wife, however, was staring at Avryn, a curious look on her face. She shifted her eyes to Janis and the two looked at each other for a time. It seemed the perfect time to adopt whatever persona Avryn had assigned to her. She grinned openly and waved at the woman, who responded with a smile of her own.

The fire danced between them all, casting strange and twisting shadows of all those sitting around it. To Janis, the light of the fire exposed her far more than she liked, and she resisted the urge to plunge herself back into the rain to get away.

"Well it's righ' bad luck fer yeh Oi s'pose, t' be travelin' when there be people searchin' fer ones lookin' like yeh."

"It has actually been a nuisance, admittedly." Avryn said. "We were stopped numerous times along the road, soldiers seizing these two and interrogating them. In the end, they were disappointed. I haven't yet understood why they are looking for these two individuals, for when I asked, they ignored my requests completely. Did these men say why they are looking for them?"

"Oh, they sure din' tell us much. But Oi heard them sayin' somethin' about the boy wakin' up or somethin' 'afore they found 'im. Perhaps the boy is sick an' sleepin'? Oi'm not sure."

"That seems odd. I'm not sure anyone could sleep well in rain such as this." Avryn said jokingly.

The old man chuckled a bit. Janis was quite impressed by Avryn's responses. He was very quick on his feet. By not admitting that Janis and Marric obviously matched the description, he would have made it seem obvious that they were hiding something. She particularly loved the bit about them already being harassed for the same reasons that the two merchants were.

"Well whatever the reason was, they were motivated t'find 'em fer sure. . . . "

The man trailed off, eyes staring into the fire now. The same worried look came over his face that they had seen earlier when he mentioned the men attacking and stealing their things.

"Are you quite alright, my good man?" Avryn said. "You look like you've seen Ugglyn himself."

Milnarin shivered slightly, but not from the cold.

"There were strange things, is all. Oi'm not sure how t' say it all, righ' well enough."

"I would be lying if I didn't say that I was curious, regardless of how strange they may be. Did something else happen when the men took your things?"

Milnarin and Lydia looked at each other, uneasiness showing in their body language and on their faces. Janis moved closer to get a better look at their reactions and to make sure she didn't miss anything from the conversation. The lightning and thunder outside had increased, and the booming became too loud for even her to drown out with her mind.

Just then, a wicked flash lit up the mouth of the cave and not a few moments after, a loud crack echoed through the cavern. Janis had a feeling in her gut that what the two merchants had seen was important. Before she got too close, she realized that she had taken on an intense gait that was uncharacteristic of this 'sister' person she was supposed to be. She smiled again, and slowed her pace, making herself seem more curious than passionate.

Lydia was signing furiously to Milnarin and he was nodding. He signed a few things back to her, before the old man sighed deeply and turned back to the group. His mouth was turned down at the sides, and it looked as if he was going to cry while he composed himself.

How could I have possibly felt threatened by these two just earlier? They are just fragile and sensitive old people, she thought to herself.

"There weren' tha' many of them, really only two, see? Tha' we could see, a'least. Now Oi'ma tell yeh tha' we were quite ready for such a thing, merchants have to be, see? Oi had me crossbow out in a min' and had fired a warnin' shot righ'tween the legs of one of them men. Then, quick as the wind, me bow was gone, flown through the air by who knows wha'. All I remember was a brigh' flash of somethin' Oi thought was lightnin' at first. But no. Oi had a bad feelin' in me stomach after it."

Bright flash of Light, moving bow, uneasiness in his gut. Janis felt her own insides buzz to life with a mixture of excitement and discovery, as if a great secret was about to unfold.

"Course Oi couldn' just let 'em off tha' easy. Oi pulled out me knife, but Oi felt it pull away from me, covered in Light or somethin'. Boy, the man was an ugly fella. All long braid and crooked teeth. Oi stood up and shouted, but Oi felt some—" Milnarin paused and shuddered, taking a moment before he could move on. ". . . an invisible force or somethin' push on me chest and Oi flew through the air. Oi hitta tree somehow, twenty paces away."

The old merchant reached back and winced, remembering the pain on his back when he struck the tree. Lydia stared at him, seeming embarrassed, though Janis couldn't understand why. Avryn was looking at her too. It was clear that he knew what had happened. This was the same power that he manifested, perhaps not exactly the same, for Janis remembered that he couldn't move objects with his Lightbearing. But he knew all too well, and his face had hardened after he heard. Milnarin's wife made a few more hand gestures, and he nodded.

"Then it righ' happened again, all odd like. Oi started—well—to *glow,* and Oi felt the force pick me up and hang me on th'tree. Oi saw the man, the ugly long-haired 'un, holdin' his 'and ou' and he looked righ' wicked. He asked me abou' th'boy and the woman in black, 'course Oi don' know such a thing 'bout them, then Oi blacked ou'."

Lydia gestured again. Milnarin watched her, but it was clear the two of them had recounted the things over and over because he didn't seem to need her guidance while he continued.

"Lydia told me that while Oi was ou', the man dun' kicked me a few times 'afore lookin' at 'er. She ran ta me side, 'course, and watched as the two men rummaged in our cart, takin' this an' tha'. The one of 'em din' take off his hood at all. They untied our horses, left their own, and then—"

He shuddered.

"Then, well, my Lydia tain't no liar, see? Bu' she said the hooded one had a ball of Light in 'is 'and, then, well . . . "

The hairs on Janis's arm stood up as if she knew what was coming. Though all of Avryn's powers made her uneasy, there was one she had seen that made her body tense, knowing danger was near. The blue-eyed man's face seemed to harden deeper, as if he also knew the next words.

". . . He threw it righ' at the cart, and it exploded."

The silence that followed seemed deeper and darker than normal. This one didn't bring the peace that silence often did. Shrell shifted in his seat, Harmel looked out of the cave, face distant. Marric just looked sick, and he appeared to be paling slightly at the description of the events.

"Of course, me darlin' tain't one ta go down without a bit of a fight. 'Afore the cart was destroyed, she got her blade into the side of one of the men, the hooded one. He was right mad she said, but when the ugly one went to get her, the hooded one dun' stopped 'im, an' they left her alone. Odd bit, there."

It was silent again for a moment, and most of the group avoided eye contact with each other. Except Lydia, who was staring at Janis with a curious look on her face, as if she knew her from somewhere. Janis smiled sweetly at her again, but the woman's eyes narrowed slightly, her mouth open in thought. Suddenly, Lydia's eyes were aglow. Brightly shining into the darkness of the cave, wide with surprise. They glowed a bright blue for only a few beats before she let out a loud gasp. In a flash, she held a small dagger pulled from inside her robe and she turned towards Avryn.

Avryn, Shrell and Harmel jumped to their feet and backed away. The old woman had gone from sweet mute to what seemed like a feral animal so quickly. Janis didn't feel threatened, for Lydia was staring at Avryn. Milnarin rose to his feet as quickly as he could, meaning not very quickly at all, and he held out his hand to his wife.

"Lydia, wha' happened? What did yeh See, eh?"

She glared at Avryn, eyes wide with fright, and while still holding her dagger to Avryn, she used her free hand to make gestures to her husband. Though she couldn't understand what they meant, Janis could tell that using only one hand was awkward and made it more challenging to say what she had to. Regardless of the difficulty, she was able to deliver the message to her husband.

"No . . . " Milnarin turned slowly and stared at Avryn, who suddenly looked embarrassed.

"Milnarin, please, I—" Avryn started to say.

"No! *Who* are *yeh people*?!" The old man had drawn two of his hidden daggers and had moved closer to his wife. "Are all of yeh these monsters like the ones we seen in the forest?!"

Regardless of the weapons that they held, or the obvious angry expressions that adorned their faces and their bodies, Janis stood still, looking curiously at the two. She didn't actually feel threatened, for their age and frailness had shown through since their arrival, and she was confident that she could take care of them both without even drawing one dagger. Instead, she just looked back and forth between them and Avryn. She was very curious to know what had happened, and even more about what would happen next.

"I'm not evil, I swear to you. I—"

"Save it! She Saw yeh, killin' those poor beasts, blowin' up the rooves t' kill men. Yer jus' like the ones tha' stole our stuff."

"I swear to you, I'm not!"

"How can we trust yeh?! Yer a Destroyer, yet here yeh are, talkin' to us like friends and all tha'! We are leavin', now!"

Keeping his knife between himself and the rest of the group, he bent down and grabbed his few belongings as well as his wife's, and backed away toward the opening of the cave. The rain continued, hard and relentless. It looked as if Milnarin and Lydia had just recently dried off, the fire performing its function very quickly as intended, yet the old man's resolve was firm. They were headed back into the deluge, regardless of getting wet again. As they neared the entrance, a voice stopped them.

"Wait."

This actually did stop Milnarin. Harmel and Avryn turned in surprise, and Shrell stiffened. Marric was standing, chest out, full of confidence. Janis tensed as well, concerned at what the boy was about to say.

Fog it, if that boy reveals what he shouldn't, I'll wring his neck myself!

"What you Saw, about Avryn . . . " Marric looked at Avryn, not sure if he should continue. Marric spoke again. "It's true. He does have the power to do what the hooded men did to you. But I promise you, he is a good man, and so are his companions. Please—if you don't trust them, at least trust me."

The air about the group stayed tense, but no one moved. Instead, they all continued staring at each other. After a time of Milnarin looking at the boy, the anger on his face started to melt away and he relaxed. Lydia remained behind her husband, fear still adorning her features. Her hand was tight on the handle of her knife, knuckles white with the effort.

"Well boy, Oi jus' might actually trust yeh. Bu' the thing is, Oi have a feelin' tha' if we stick around, it won' be righ' good for either of us, see? Whoever yeh are, Oi hope that yeh git where yer goin' righ' safe. We'll keep yer secret, if yeh keep ours."

He pointedly eyed his wife, and his message was clear. If you don't tell anyone about her powers, we won't tell anyone about you. Milnarin slid his knife into his robe, then urged Lydia to do the same. She finally did, after some coaxing, then the old man put on his hat while she donned her own.

"Wherever yous are goin', Oi hope yer lucky, and tha' yeh don' run into trouble."

With that, he smiled at the group and made eye contact with each of them, his smile deepening when he got to Marric. It was then that Janis noticed Lydia was staring at her, and had been for who knows how long. She looked almost curious as she nodded slightly to Janis. She didn't seem afraid or angry, just intrigued.

Without another word, the two plunged themselves back into the storm, leaving the group alone in the cave.

Chapter 13

Well, Oi'd say that went well, din' yeh think?" Harmel remarked.

Shrell rolled his eyes at the comment. Shrell, the man of few words, didn't say anything, but instead went and sat next to the fire again, seemingly unaffected by the events just before. Marric stared outside into the storm, concern on his face.

Avryn heaved a large sigh.

"I can't say that I agree with you, but at least no one ended up hurt. I would have felt very badly should that incident have ended differently."

He turned to Marric, an appreciative look on his face.

"Thanks to you vouching for me, at least."

Marric blushed at the comment and looked down at the ground.

"I was just telling the truth."

Avryn came over to Marric and put his hand on his shoulder, squeezing it slightly.

"I think your genuine manner is what saved the whole situation. Thank you again."

The blush appeared to deepen, which didn't seem possible to Janis. She stared at the interaction between the two of them for only a beat before she felt like she had to look away. Watching it all had made her very uncomfortable, as was the case with all situations like that. Situations with so much 'feeling' made her squirm and want to escape more than sitting in a vat full of snakes—poisonous ones.

Janis moved to the mouth of the cave so that she was just out of the pouring rain, though the wind blew drops and splatters onto her face. It felt refreshing and cool. There was nothing to sharpen your thoughts and invigorate you more than being wetted with cold water. It was often why she used a freezing cold bucket of water to coerce people into telling her what she needed when she interrogated them. She smiled to herself, enjoying the feeling of the rain. She could have kept moving in the storm—it didn't bother her being soaked to the bone, but she did recognize that it would disrupt her abilities should they run into their enemies, especially ones wielding powers such as Avryn's.

Closing her eyes, she imagined what had just happened. It wasn't as clear as when she entered the in-between—she would recount this experience again later—but for now, it was sufficient. Watching it again, she tried to notice the subtle things that she hadn't before. The way Lydia had kept her body turned slightly to the cave entrance, so that she could keep her eyes on the whole group, as well as the outside. The way that Milnarin seemed to aid Lydia in walking, sitting, standing, but the woman was more fit and able than him. The way that she had stared at Janis, brows furrowed, as if she knew something about her. She suddenly felt exposed, and her eyes snapped open.

She would certainly have to go over the events again later; there was far more there than she could have noticed the first time. Until then, however, she moved to the exact place that Lydia had been to gain vantage over both the whole cave and the opening. When she sat down, Harmel grinned at her and handed her a bit of food.

What a strange creature he is, Janis thought as she took his offering.

"What do yeh think she Saw, S'ren?" Shrell asked.

Avryn looked troubled at the question, but shook his head in response.

"I honestly can't say for sure. I suspect that she must have seen some past event of me using my powers. Unfortunately, it sounds like she specifically witnessed my use of Destroying."

He winced at that.

"Well, it's rotten luck, it is. I felt we was getting somewhere good with their story. Who do yeh suppose attacked them?"

"Though I can't speak exactly to the attackers' identities," Avryn said,

"I think we can be relatively sure that these aren't rogue Lightbearers on a rampage. Watchlight is responsible, and it sounds like they are close. And while this troubles me, I fear that we'll have to wait out the storm until tomorrow. It doesn't appear to be letting up anytime soon."

There were nods of affirmation, and equally troubled looks on most of the others' faces, except Marric, who looked pale and terrified. Janis suddenly had a strange feeling of pity and worry for the lad, which caught her so off guard that she almost had to physically shake it off.

Fog it, there it is again. That fogging feeling that I'm getting attached to the boy.

As if in response to the thought, Marric slowly turned his gaze to Janis and gave her a wry smile. It was obvious that his capture was the goal of Watchlight, and he knew it too. She had already learned to come to terms with someone hunting her so it didn't bother her much, except perhaps making her feel like she couldn't ever let her guard down. She wanted to tell the boy that at least they likely weren't trying to find him to kill him, but she suspected that wouldn't be the best thing to say to him at this moment.

"I do find it interesting that they specifically mentioned Marric . . . " he paused and looked at Janis. ". . . and you. Why on earth are they so bent on finding you, Janis? How did they know that the two of you would be together?"

She stared at him, saying nothing. Her lack of response actually seemed to trigger a memory in him.

"Oh, that's right, didn't they pay you to protect him or something?"

She didn't particularly want to get into the details of how she had received the job from the horrid man in front of the bakery.

"Well, it sounds like their displeasure in your progress has reared its head, doesn't it?" Avryn said, seeming amused.

The fire flickered and cracked, casting their shadows around it and making a scene. Rather than play into Avryn's comments, Janis took a different route in the conversation.

"If we are to stay here for the night until the storm hopefully passes, we must extinguish the fire as soon as possible. I would imagine the visibility of this cave will be stark in the dim gloom out there. The rain will provide some cover, but if these men are as close as the merchants described, we'd best be cautious."

Avyn frowned, but nodded affirmation.

"She is right. We should finish up our meals and be prepared for a colder night without the fire. It's not the cold season, but that wind blowing outside is enough to make it chilly here in the cavern. I'll take first watch. I'll wake Shrell up after a time, then we can switch off periodically as usual. However, should the rain let up in the night, no matter what time, we move forward. We are close to our destination, and I think we can make it quickly if we move swiftly. Objections?"

There were only head shakes from the party, though it was only a curt nod from Janis herself. She admitted that she was curious as to their destination, but she was unsettled at the thought of some hidden location housing other people with powers like Avryn. Janis never liked feeling unsafe or inferior combat-wise to those around her. Even if they were 'allies', she felt like she was walking on thin ice, ready to be swallowed up at the drop of a coin.

The conversations were small after that, as if the group didn't want to discuss the grave danger that might lie just ahead, or the seriousness of the events that had occurred not too long before. Janis's discomfort increased further by the fact that a benign situation and conversation had turned so hostile in a mere moment, and the subject matter of the contention was Avryn's powers that Lydia had also manifested. She got the feeling that she had gotten herself caught up in something bigger than she liked.

Marric finished eating relatively quickly, then muttered something about 'tired' before retreating to the side of the cave. She did notice that he purposely selected a spot behind Avryn, putting the man between himself and the cave entrance. She cocked her head, slightly annoyed, but at the same time, impressed. The boy's survival instincts were a bit better than she expected. She wondered when and where he had gained that. The boy clearly recognized that their best line of defense against other Lightbearers was their dreadfully positive companion.

Well, Avryn isn't nearly as annoying as Harmel.

Janis looked at Harmel, and he caught her gaze. His characteristic crooked grin spread on his face and he tapped the side of his head, as if to say that he knew what she was thinking. She merely stared at him, brows furrowed.

Deciding that she'd rather not have a 'moment' with Harmel any longer, she resolved to get some sleep. Before she could, however, she ensured that the fire was taken care of properly and the light extinguished. Selecting her vantage point—further from the entrance than she liked, but in a place that she could see each man—and be near Marric all the same, she sat against the wall and closed her eyes.

It was quick. She had learned to relax and let go very fast. Her body lightened and her mind sharpened, as if some of her senses were drawn into her thoughts to add extra focus there. Of course, before she ventured off into her memories, she took a moment to check her lines of defense. She could hear the rain, pounding outside the cave. She could feel the ground and lack of vibrations, other than the rain and wind shifting plants outside. She could smell the rain, and the wind, fresh and cool. Feeling satisfied, she thought for a moment where she'd like to go first. She obviously wanted to recount the events of the cave just moments before, but for some reason she was drawn to the memory at the Plains of Erisdell. She wanted to revisit the moment she had seen the old woman's eyes glow, and Shrell disrupting the conversation between her and Marric.

In a flash, the blackness of her mind shifted and there she was, in the tall grass hidden between shops across from the woman's. Marric was looking at the woman's wares and she was smiling at him. Unsure of why she had come back here, she shifted her gaze away from where she was looking in the memory, and scanned her peripheral vision. There didn't seem to be anything out of the ordinary. The woman's eyes glowed and she snatched Marric's hand. Still, nothing strange seemed to be happening around the woman's booth. Her eyes faded, and Shrell interrupted. To the side, she saw the man write the note and retrieve his carrier bird. Once again, she lost sight of the man as she moved in the memory toward the woman's table. Her eyes were on the woman now as she delivered the final message to Marric.

"You'll have to make a choice where yeh stand 'ere soon. Untold challenges lie ahead. Trust yer gut and what yeh learn, and remember wha' true goodness is."

Shrell took Marric by the shoulder and pulled him away. She had stared at the woman for a moment before she watched the two walk away, and she checked all the side shops for signs of trouble. She was behind the shop next to the woman, but well within her sights. As she watched, there wasn't any reason to think that there was trouble. Then she felt it. Eyes were watching. Though the memory stared at her two companions retreating from the shop, she focused on her right peripheral vision, and saw the old woman watching her with a troubled look.

Janis felt her stomach lurch and her chest tighten. The old woman stared on. It wasn't a glance, she had stared at Janis the entire time she had stood and watched the men disappear. Then, just before she retreated back behind the shops, the old woman raised her hand up, and looking the in-between Janis directly in the eyes, waved.

Her mind went black then, the memory ending. She stayed there, in that moment, feeling uneasy. The strange old woman had waved at her, when she wasn't looking, as if she knew that Janis would see her later. As if she knew everything. About the in-between, about Janis recounting events. She suddenly felt very exposed, as if she was being watched everywhere, even here, in the in-between.

Through her numerous encounters in the in-between, never before had any other person indicated that they were also aware, like she now was. Not even Macks himself, the one that had taught her about the place.

Taking a moment to recover in the blackness, she pushed the thought aside for further investigation at a later time. That was something that she could think about and consider when she wasn't here in the in-between. For now, she had to move on and use the time that she had. As usual, time here would increase ten fold and she likely would only have time to go through the night's events before she was woken up for her turn at the watch. Feeling resolute, she imagined just what she needed, and the blackness faded into images and sounds. She was at the mouth of the cave again, the rain was pouring and the thunder booming. It was admittedly a bit disorienting with the *actual* sound of the rain going on outside of the in-between, but she focused her senses and was able to keep the two separate. Mixing the two sounds would make it harder for her to wake up, should she hear something outside of this place.

As she remembered, she was listening to Avryn talk about Lightbearing and the various powers, but she moved through this quickly, wanting to get a better look at the man, Milnarin, and his wife, Lydia. Fortunately, she had the ability to do that. The memory seemed to increase in speed, until she saw the flash of lamplight in the rain in the distance. Standing, she told the others to put out the fire.

Shrell and Harmel joined her quickly at the mouth of the cave, Harmel just to her right, Shrell to his. They looked very intent and ready. It was a surprising look for Harmel, as he almost always had that dumb smile on his face. She was a bit struck by how attractive it made him look.

She shook her head—not physically, for she couldn't change her past actions—because the thought was absurd. Harmel was a creature far below anything that could be deemed attractive. He was far too bubbly for her. Not to mention that the last time she had begun to be fond of a man, it had turned out costly. It almost meant her life.

The two figures came out of the rain, and she remembered doing her initial assessment of them. It was clear that they were romantically involved, and that they had traveled a distance, for their postures looked weary. Though the woman looked strong and able, regardless.

"Who goes there?!" Shrell said, breaking the silence.

The two merchants froze at the comment, and though she'd missed it the first time, the woman discreetly pulled her left hand into her sleeve just enough to hide her weapon.

Clever woman, taking advantage of those baggy cloak sleeves. Likely had a knife at her ready, Janis thought.

The man stumbled back a bit, indicating his genuine surprise, but the woman didn't—she stood firm, ready to engage. Janis did remember this piece, there wasn't anything new. It was the reason Janis hadn't relaxed so easily when they came. Shrell and Harmel were too enveloped in the reaction of the larger figure to notice the smaller. Fortunately, Janis had better sense in these things. After the brief exchange, she recalled Harmel stopping her with his sword, but she quelled the annoyed feeling she had.

Though the talking continued, Janis wasn't paying attention. She was observing as the two newcomers moved to their seats. Sure enough, the woman was more graceful and walked with the finesse of either a dancer or a fighter, or perhaps both. She wasn't sure if the husband was completely unaware of his wife's capabilities, or if this was a practiced ruse. Janis settled on the latter when, for only the briefest moment, the woman turned around as if to look outside the cave, but her eyes shifted to her husband and, once their eyes locked, she gave two curt nods. He responded with his own, so slight that in the dark you wouldn't have seen it, in fact, she hadn't before.

"Tis a shame you ain't got a fire burnin', tis mighty cold right now."

Commenting on the fire got the obviously intended result. Taking advantage of the light, Janis tried to observe as much as she could about the whole situation. Lydia, though names hadn't been exchanged yet, had removed her hood, and Janis was watching her face. It remained hard, yet weak and tired. She was definitely playing a part, though what exact part, Janis wasn't sure.

"So how did you know where to find us?"

This comment induced an interesting reaction from the two. He, of course, looked surprised, and responded questioningly. Lydia, however, stared flatly at Janis. Her hands were clasped in her lap, but Janis saw the woman's arms move just slightly as she clenched them together, anxious.

Lanser's beard, she knew. She had *to have known that I was a threat. I can see it in her gaze, in the way her body reacted to my comment and my tone.*

The man, however, was dense. He did not pick up on anything. At least not according to his body or facial expressions.

A flash of Light suddenly interrupted the memory. It wasn't directly behind the old woman, Lydia, but close enough that Janis didn't have to push into her peripheral vision to see it. It was subtle, yet it felt unnatural, for it wasn't a part of her normal memory—she would definitely have remembered a flash of Light such as that before now. The event seemed even odder than usual, for she felt that for some reason there should have been a sound that accompanied such an event, but there was none.

After it passed, she gasped and dropped into the ready position, low to the ground, muscles taut. But Janis then remembered that this was a memory, and she couldn't actually manipulate her body in that way. Her reflexes were so ingrained that she could hardly feel that her precautionary crouch hadn't actually occurred. Regardless, she stood there and stared in disbelief at what she saw.

There was a man.

Somehow, there was a man there. She had to think for a moment to understand what was happening, for this man had not been there in the cave earlier when these events had occurred. Her gut wrenched and tightened in nervousness as she stared at him, now through her peripheral vision as her memory body had moved its gaze to the side, looking at Milnarin.

The new man was of medium height and average build. Despite that, however, he looked sickly with pasty white skin, like someone who hadn't seen the sun in years. His nose was sharp, his mouth a thin line, but that was emphasized by his shining red eyes, which were glowing like the other people she had seen. The man was not muscular by any means, but instead was skinny and frail, as if he hadn't bothered to do anything physical in his life. The hair on his head was stark white, like that of an old man, but his face was less aged, perhaps only ten years her elder. What added to the oddity was that he was wearing a deep crimson robe, thick and large, which appeared to hide most of his body and skin. Thick rope-like cords hung around his neck, one purple, one gold, as if they meant something to him.

What horridly impractical clothing, Janis thought to herself.

She didn't really care about his clothes, but she was trying to distract herself from the panic she felt at seeing him, for the fact that she saw him there, with them, in the cave, meant that either he had been there, unseen, during all the events there around the fire, or that he was here now with her, in the in-between. She suddenly felt the desire to escape as quickly as possible, but Janis pushed that feeling away. Both the possibilities meant something grave; the group was in danger. For either he had seen them and what they discussed, or he was about to.

After a few beats, it became apparent that he hadn't noticed her presence there with him, for he stared at the woman, Lydia, in the memory. His gaze shifted from Lydia, to Avryn, then to Marric. He didn't seem to care about anyone else in the group, which Janis resented a bit. Couldn't he see that they weren't the only ones that could pose a threat to him?

Why those three? she thought.

By now, she had completely forgotten about observing the memory, and was instead focused entirely on the man. With another stab of regret, she realized she had lost focus on her outside senses. Panicked just a bit, she reached out with her senses and felt the floor of the cave where she lay; she heard the storm and the rain—the real storm, and felt the cold air of the wind on her face outside of the in-between. Nothing seemed amiss, so she returned her attention to the memory, and the man.

Janis shifted her gaze to the man again and froze, her gut wrenching again. For the dead-looking man had stopped observing the others, and was now staring at her. There was a moment of strange surreality as they stared at each other, confusion on his face. She couldn't actually be sure what her face looked like at this moment, for she could only see from her own eyes in this state.

Behind the red glow, his eyes were piercing blue like the sky. For some reason, she got the feeling that her action of reaching out to her senses had given away her position, but that was ridiculous. How could he sense such a thing?

His stare persisted for a time, but then his eyes narrowed, and his thin mouth became a thinner line as he pressed his lips together. Then he spoke.

"So, I'm not here alone, then."

A chill ran up Janis's spine at his voice. His voice was not deep, like a man's ought to be, but higher in pitch, though it wasn't high like a woman's. It was sharp, and seemed accusatory, as if he was catching her in a crime. But it wasn't just his voice that made her shiver, it was the fact that it sounded echoey and murky, like they were underwater, piercing her soul and mind, as if he weren't actually using sound to talk, but instead entering her mind directly. It was unnatural.

He stood there, expecting her to respond, but she didn't. Come to think of it, she wasn't sure that she even *could* respond. Never at any moment had she been joined in an in-between by another human being. His eyes narrowed again and he spoke once more.

"Are you incapable of speech, woman?"

He didn't sound angry, but instead bitter, as if his whole life was terrible and he had never been happy before. She felt that she was actually incapable, but if she had been able to speak, she wasn't sure what she'd say. She would rather have the ability to move, for that was her better form of communication. When she didn't respond immediately, he hissed slightly. But the sound was loud in her mind, and echoed like his speech did.

"No matter. I'm not sure how you are Seeing this, but your little Avryn's Shield isn't enough to block *my* Sight completely. I've been watching you and your little band of miscreants every day."

Everything felt wrong. Normally she felt so comfortable and safe in the in-between. It was like the small and cozy closet a child could use to hide from the worries and the cares of the world. She never felt vulnerable, but instead powerful, like she could see more, understand more. She hadn't thought being there was any type of magic, but it made her feel stronger regardless.

Today, it was different. She felt exposed—open, like she couldn't get away or hide anywhere, even if she tried. She wanted to run, attack, at least pull out her daggers for Lanser's sake, but she couldn't do any of that.

The strange white-washed man bared his teeth like a wild animal. He slowly began walking toward her, and the memory around them slowed down. A stab of worry and fear blossomed in her chest and gut as she watched Milnarin telling about something, though she couldn't hear it anymore. His hands were moving so slowly, as if they were trapped by something thick and viscous. Then it happened, a strange pulling sensation spread on her body, and she fell to the ground. Shaking her head in confusion, she looked up to see her body, her *full body* sitting there and listening to Milnarin without her.

Blinking for a moment, she tested her grip and found that she was able to move. Instinctively, she reached to her side for her dagger, but found it empty.

Janis cursed. Apparently, weapons weren't transferred to the in-between like the rest of her. Dazed and feeling horribly strange, she got to her feet and faced the stranger in her memory. Something had happened to her just now. It was as if her consciousness was forcibly separated from the memory body inside her head. With another stab of fear, she realized that she couldn't sense her body, her outside senses seemed to have been left with her actual body, locked in a place that she couldn't reach.

Fog it! What is happening?! she thought, exasperated.

She would have to deal with one problem at a time.

Spinning to the side, she saw that the man was watching her, looking amused. She was at the ready, anticipating a fight, but he only watched her. For a moment, nothing happened. They just stared at each other. Then he smiled eerily, his teeth looking remarkably white and clean against his pallid skin.

"I must say, you have some fight in you. You needn't worry, there are no physical forms in this place."

At that, he held out his hand and a dagger appeared. It was reddish, and shined as if it was made from—

Light, Janis thought, *he's a Lightbearer.*

The dagger was surprisingly intricate for being made out of Light. It had ornate designs not only on the small pommel, but also running up the blade. Without any warning, it launched itself at Janis, right at her heart. She gasped, attempting to jump out of the way, but was not quick enough. It just missed her heart, and instead passed through her right shoulder. Then—nothing.

Looking down in shock, she saw that there was no blood, no pain. Nothing.

"I tried to tell you, I can't kill you here. Which is such a shame, if I do say so myself. It would be a perfect time to slay you and your little band of—whatever you are."

Janis was breathing hard, adrenaline rushing through her limbs and making her ears roar. He hadn't even moved a muscle at all. Such movement would have given her more time to dodge, but it was as if some invisible force had launched the dagger at her. Yes, she wasn't bleeding or dying, but if this was any representation of the power this odd man had outside of the in-between, Janis didn't stand a chance.

"Who are you?" she said forcefully.

Her voice shocked her, as if it came out of a place she didn't know. It sounded far away, once again resembling sound underwater.

"Oh, so she *does* speak, then? I can tell that you are not accustomed to viewing the world in this way. I suspect you'd be full of idle threats had you been able to speak earlier."

"What did you do to me?"

A small smile spread across his face, and he seemed more amused than ever.

"So many questions. This isn't an interrogation, my dear. You're lucky that I separated you from your body. So many limitations exist in this place if you're stuck there."

Separated from my body?! What the fog is going on?! she thought.

"Oh relax, my dear. You aren't dead, and I can't kill you, so you might as well enjoy our time here. Now, it's my turn to ask questions. Where is the boy?"

Janis didn't relax, despite his comment, but instead bared her teeth. She remained low in her ready-to-fight position. Then, without warning, she yelled and launched herself at the man. Throwing a fist right at his jaw, she aimed to knock him down. Unfortunately, she was disappointed in this as her hand passed right through his face. Cursing, she spun to look at him again.

"Are you quite done, my dear?"

He was pleased, and his face was practically dripping with the emotion. The shadows continued to dance on the wall, but they were slow, which felt odd and unnatural. Well, no more odd and unnatural than what she was experiencing now.

"Where is the boy, woman? I have strained and tried to See where you and your little friends are, but I cannot See. Now that I have you here, *tell me.*"

Janis smirked. "Or what?"

She felt nervous, and a bit afraid, but also very confident now that she knew he couldn't hurt her, and that he couldn't find them.

The confident look on his face melted away and was replaced by rage. His lip began trembling and he was growling slightly. Bone white hands clenched at his side and she sensed that he had just lost his leverage on her.

"Blasted woman!" he shouted, anger boiling out. "No matter! I'll have *her* to talk to."

Confused, Janis looked to where his bony finger pointed. He was fixed on Lydia, and just then, still in slow motion, the woman's eyes began to glow. All at once, there was a ripping sound and the woman's body separated, a second version of herself sliding out behind the glowing-eyed version sitting by the fire.

The older woman looked puzzled for a moment, standing just behind herself in the memory, then her face twisted into fear as she took in the scene around her. She stared at her body sitting by the fire, then looked up to see Janis, or rather, the in-between Janis, standing a bit back behind herself, and the strange robed man.

"We haven't much time, woman! Where is this happening? Where are you and this little band of so-called warriors sitting around this fire?!"

Her gut twisted inside.

Where is this happening?! she thought. *Why in Lanser's name is he speaking in the present?*

She suddenly felt very small, like she didn't know anything real in the world. It was the feeling that she got when she felt like she was breaking laws of nature. A similar feeling had overcome her the first time she'd entered the past in the in-between, and that had taken time to come to terms with. Laws were being broken. Janis didn't know why or how, but she got the feeling that time was blurred here, and it made her almost lose herself to its strangeness.

It took a lot of her strength and focus to push the feelings aside and refocus her mind. She had heard accounts of men and women breaking laws of nature and going mad because of it. However, even more strange, this odd man and Lydia seemed unaware of the strangeness.

Janis almost yelled at the man that this had already happened and that Lydia had left the cave a while ago. She opted to say nothing so as to not indicate her lack of knowledge about the situation. Besides, he was oddly adamant that this was happening in the present.

Lydia looked scared, but also resolved.

"You have no power over me here."

She said this quietly, and her lip trembled slightly.

"Blast, woman! We haven't the time for your *games.* Your vision is about to end! TELL ME NOW!"

Her mind raced. It felt as if it was spinning faster and faster, trying to take everything in before it ended. She only recognized now that the man's eyes glowed eerily, as did Lydia's, though hers were blue, and his red.

They must be using some Lightbearing of some sort. He mentioned her 'vision', so is that what is happening right now around the fire? Is Lydia Seeing them?

Janis looked at the memory of Lydia sitting by the fire, eyes aglow.

That's right! Her eyes only glowed for a time. What happens when it ends?

"Do you know who this man is?! He can't be trusted! He also is one that can Destroy. He has powers beyond your comprehension, woman! Come to me, and join my forces. I can protect you from people like *him.*"

Lydia's body stiffened and her face hardened. She glanced over at Avryn, looking worried.

"Yes, I Saw him, and I am Seeing him now. He can Destroy, and he has killed. But I can See you, and you are no better than he."

Janis felt proud of the woman's resolve, and suddenly felt self-conscious about her own cowering before this man.

Her words carry more power than she expresses with her stature—

Then it hit her. Lydia shouldn't have been able to talk. Without realizing it, she spoke.

"But—how—" Janis said, interrupting the exchange. "You can't speak."

The old woman shifted her gaze to Janis and she narrowed her eyes.

"I know not how you join us here, girl, but this place is different from the real realm. It's a place of Seers, and information. Your eyes don't glow, yet you hear, and See."

"Forget the assassin! Tell me where you are! NOW!"

The man was roaring now, not even attempting to add pleasantries.

"You cannot hurt me here, Seer." Lydia said with an air of finality.

Growling, he summoned his dagger and launched it at the woman. She gasped and attempted to dodge, but it passed right through her chest and disappeared behind her. It was clear that the woman knew she couldn't be harmed, but instinct would always get the better of a person.

"You know not what power I hold! I will find you, *Lydia,* and I will exterminate you and your plain little husband!"

Janis soon got the answer to her question before, as Lydia's past self, or rather, the fire-sitting self, relaxed and her eyes returned to normal. The second Lydia's body faded to mist and quickly combined itself with her real body, then the memory continued, albeit slowly.

"Assassin! Mark my words, you cannot escape your fate. I *will* find you and the boy, and you *will* die at my hand."

At that, he swept his hand to the side and vanished himself. When he left, the tugging sensation returned to her gut and she was pulled back to her sitting position by the fire. Her vision was restricted again, and she had to peer only out of her peripheral vision to see where the man had stood moments before. Sure enough, he was gone. She once again had access to her outside senses and she relaxed a bit feeling them, so familiar and safe.

Her attention was lost completely. She paid no more attention to the memory. All that stood out to her was the last look that Lydia gave her just before they left the cave. It was a knowing look. The look carried a much deeper message than Janis could have imagined. Lydia knew that Janis had seen the strange man with the red glowing eyes. She had known that Janis met her in the in-between.

For the second time that night, she felt exposed to the world.

Chapter 14

Janis's eyes snapped open and her full senses took over again; the crispness of the night air felt colder without the fire to push it back. What struck her the most was how quiet everything seemed. The stillness of the air almost felt uneasy. Then she realized that the strong torrent of rain outside had stopped, almost. There were occasional bursts of wind and sometimes a rumble of distant thunder, but it had turned from an overwhelming volume to a small, dull hum. She turned to the hand that had awoken her and saw Harmel smiling at her in the dim light. With the absence of the fire, it was strangely lit in the cave.

Looking over her shoulder, she saw a very small ball of Light, about the size of her thumbnail, hovering against the wall near the sleeping form of Avryn.

Seeing her gaze, Harmel answered a question that she didn't know that she had.

"Yeah, 'e can hold it up jus' a wee bit while 'e sleeps. Can be righ' useful, tha' thing. Why, Oi don' remember the' last time Oi had t'stand watch without the bit o' Light."

How remarkable, Janis thought as she stared at the small bluish Light. *What else can this man do while he sleeps?*

That thought reminded her of her recent experience, and she shivered to herself. Though she was no longer in the in-between, she still felt lingering feelings of exposure and insecurity.

"I guess it's my turn then, hmm?" she said idly, still staring at the Light.

"Mm-hmm."

"Did I miss anything?"

"Yeh mean, other than the fact tha' yer a noisy sleeper? Nah."

Harmel moved so that he was between her and the small ball of Light. As he did so, he noticed that Janis was still staring at the ball of Light.

"Yeh know, it ain't goin' nowhere. Yeh gots plenty o' time ta watch it, if yeh like."

A grin spread on his face, the stupid grin that he gave when he told his terrible jokes, which happened far more often than Janis enjoyed. She was honestly surprised that she put up with his comments and jokes, for they lacked all intelligence in her mind. There was something about this man, though, that made her want to feel something. Happiness? No, it wasn't that.

Pushing the feeling aside, she merely sighed and stood up, shoving the grinning man to the side slightly. He hadn't actually been in her way, but it felt natural to brush off his dumb happiness with a physical rebuff. It was a language that she spoke better than any emotional nonsense.

"What's the time? I can't quite tell with the clouds in the darkness."

"Wha'? There's somethin' tha' the all-talented assassin can't do? Fog me good. Din' see tha' comin'."

Janis rolled her eyes and suppressed a biting comment. He was just joking, but she really didn't have the patience for it, especially with how she felt right now.

"Couple hours is all, till sunlight. Avryn came after Shrell, then me, so Oi reckon' it won' be long now."

Janis nodded to him, indicating that she understood, *and* that the conversation was over. Harmel seemed to get the idea. He settled in next to where the fire was, just a few paces from Avryn and Marric, and closed his eyes. The man had a remarkable knack for falling asleep on the go, for it seemed only a few breaths before they slowed into the rhythm of sleep.

The rain drummed on the ground lightly, making a hissing sound rather than the pounding that she had grown accustomed to in the last day and a half. She was glad that it appeared to be slowing down. There was something about the power of the storm that made her uneasy. The mountain weather was so unpredictable, especially this high up. It was lucky that the cave hadn't flooded with the quick rainfall and that they hadn't met any man or beast already sheltering in the cave. It seemed almost too good, now that she really thought about it.

Despite her last thought, nothing *had* happened, so she sat on a rock and stared into the waning storm. Closing her eyes, Janis breathed in deeply the fresh, rain-filled air, and let it calm her. As much as she didn't want to, she recounted the events of the in-between, trying to make sense of them.

The pale man with the robes was filled with a power that she didn't understand, though she knew that Avryn might have the knowledge himself. She had to resist the urge to shake the man awake right away to interrogate him. Something about the encounter made her hesitant to provide too much information to Avryn. She got the sense that he would have too many questions for her if she let on too much, and she wasn't willing to let him know about the 'in-between' or the fact that she could go there.

For reasons unknown to her, this man was after Marric, and he wanted him very badly. Though he couldn't reach her in the in-between, his threats of killing her did make her more uncomfortable than death threats usually did. Based on their encounter, she sensed that her skill as an assassin wouldn't stand much of a chance if they were to meet in person. That is exactly why she had to learn as much as she could about this Lightbearing. All of its strengths, weaknesses, and especially its limitations.

At that thought, she launched into recalling what Avryn had told Marric about the different classes. He had said that they get only one power, besides the second that they choose and practice using. That meant that she just had to identify what power they had so that she could play on whatever limitations and weaknesses they had.

So, what is this robed figure's power? she thought to herself.

Well, it was clear that he had the power of Sight, for how else could he have gotten to the in-between? Also, the eerie glowing eyes gave it away pretty quickly. That meant that Lydia was one of these as well.

Janis started suddenly, realizing that she had overlooked the obvious until now. Lydia probably had another power that she was hiding dormant. She cursed herself for being dense and not remembering that when the woman had still been in the cave with them. Janis didn't suspect that the old woman meant them any harm, but she should have remembered that and been on guard, should something have happened. At least it was when there was no threat that Janis got the reminder to watch out for two abilities.

Clearing her mind, she returned to the original question at hand. The strange robed man was a Seer, and he seemed to create something out of thin air, a blade of some sort. Though it couldn't actually hurt her, she suspected that the blade was normally solid and she would have known that quickly if they hadn't been in the in-between.

So, you are a Conjurer as well, hmm?

Satisfied with her revelation, she began to remember the information that Avryn had been giving Marric the day before. Seers can See into the past and into the future, but not when a Shield is up.

Well *that* wouldn't help her much, she didn't have one of those. That is, unless she stuck close to Avryn. Her eyes wandered over to the ball of Light and the sleeping man. As much as she wanted to stick close to him against other Lightbearers, she couldn't rely on him her whole life. This thought made her feel less secure. Now that she was known to this Watchlight group, she suspected that she'd be under the watch of their Seers for the rest of her life.

Janis decided that she couldn't dwell on that problem for much longer, for she didn't have a great solution other than staying with Avryn, which was the plan, at least until they got to wherever Terris Green was. She still felt uncomfortable with the fact that she didn't have any idea where that was, but Avryn and his fellows had proven useful and painfully loyal, so she just let her mind work on other things.

Moving on to the Conjuring. Avryn had said that a Conjurer couldn't create too many objects at once, though she was sure they could create enough to keep one person occupied. There had been something about range.

A Conjurer can't sustain their creations over too much of a range, or what they create will disappear.

This was a helpful bit of information, but it did make things tricky for her.

She wasn't very practiced at range weapons. Perhaps now would be a good time to learn one.

Janis was skilled at throwing her daggers and knives, but she suspected that the range in which she could hit a target with a dagger was well within the range of a Conjurer's ability to sustain their weapons. Also, she had a distinct limit of daggers on her person. There wasn't a perfect solution to this one, but at least she knew that getting distance between a Conjurer and herself would provide some level of protection. Also, a Conjurer could create weapons, but that didn't mean that combat was their skill. Once again, distance seemed like the best option for her.

Not overly happy with these conclusions, but likewise not disappointed, Janis sat in the quiet and let her mind wander for a moment. It wasn't often that she allowed herself to do this, but things were quiet enough, and the terrible feeling she was left with after her encounter in the in-between made it necessary to put off some unwanted emotions. Her mind wandered to Macks.

Janis felt the familiar fondness burning in her chest, spreading to her whole body at times. Macks was handsome, strong, and extremely skilled as an assassin. She had him to thank for not only her skill, but her survival.

The more you know about your enemy, the better chance you have to best them in a fight. Even intimate details like their hobbies can aid you in a match.

His voice hummed in her mind through a memory that had a deep and lasting impression on her. Why this man had taken in an orphan girl, skinny and weak, Janis couldn't say, but his lessons made her what she was today. That, and all the fights and jobs she had survived. She recalled times when she was bloodied beyond what she thought she could survive, yet somehow, she pulled through. There was no better way to learn survival than to have to figure a lot of it out in real situations. Janis was grateful that she hadn't sustained injuries beyond flesh wounds for a long time now. Feeling helpless and dying was unnerving.

Then Macks had just gone. Her gut tightened and she felt sick, forcing her to gasp quietly to push the feelings away. Betrayal was something far worse than mortal danger. She couldn't stand the feeling. Her mind worked to undo the thoughts and feelings that had just overwhelmed her and she pushed it away. She was back to the trail of thought where she met the robed man.

Fog it, thoughts of Macks are surfacing too much these days. Traveling with this group must be getting to me.

She was mentally rehearsing situations where she had to face off with a Conjurer and playing them out. It helped her prepare for real situations if she could think of everything. After thinking through a few scenarios, some in which she did get injured, some where she died, and others where she succeeded, she thought of the Seeing. There had to be another way to combat the Sight, to hide from it. Though she wasn't sure what it could be, she was confident that there had to be another way besides the Shielding power. A Shield would also come in handy should a Conjurer hurl one of their constructs at her.

She froze. A memory, sharp as a knife, jutted into her mind. With every object that Avryn had Conjured, he had to use his regular skill and muscle to utilize them. But the robed man hadn't.

Janis recounted the events in the in-between, and she saw the dagger, beautifully intricate and stunningly red, created from Light. The robed man had opened his hand and the dagger had flown straight and true.

Lanser's beard. . . . Janis thought.

The robed man hadn't moved his arm, he hadn't moved much of anything. Even Janis had to train hard to move her arms specifically to achieve that kind of straight and true dagger throw. How had that happened? It was as if he—

He Moved it. That had *to have been what he did.*

How could that be possible? Was Avryn wrong then about a person only being able to have two powers? Or was it that this robed man was an exception? After all, Avryn himself was an exception. Without any comparison to other Lightbearers, she couldn't determine how powerful this robed man actually was. Perhaps Avryn was lying about how common a Lightbearer with more than two powers was.

But then, why would he lie about that? He didn't have anything to gain from it, other than making himself seem more important. She still didn't quite understand what Avryn's motivations were, but he seemed painfully genuine to her.

All she knew was the feeling she had while facing the strange robed man. It had been a long time since she had felt scared. Just remembering the encounter made her want to scramble deeper into the cave to get away from the man who wasn't even present.

As she sat there watching the slowing rainfall, her thoughts moved to how different things had been the past few days. She wasn't sure she liked where she was, but she also wasn't sure that she hated it, which was perplexing to her. Ever since she had left training with Macks all those years ago—or rather, when he left her—she had been mostly on her own. Sure, she'd banded together with a bounty hunter here, a peacekeeper there, but mostly it was just her following the biggest jobs. It wasn't like anyone had ever shown interest in working with her before. Avryn and his companions didn't seem overly thrilled to work with her. It was more like they tolerated her presence so that they could better protect Marric.

Well, except Harmel.

Janis looked at the sleeping man. It wouldn't be long before everyone would wake up and they would move out and continue toward their destination. What would happen then? Part of her didn't really care. Technically, she could just leave Marric when they got to this sanctum place that Avryn had talked about, then she could be rid of the boy and the insufferable man Harmel.

But why hadn't she already left? Avryn and his companions would have been well off without her. Whether or not they reached their destination with the boy was not her problem, nor should she care about their welfare.

And yet, she did care. At first, it was just the boy. Marric had latched onto her in a way that she hadn't experienced before. Janis didn't quite understand it, but she actually cared about his safety. She had realized it not long into their journey. As much as she hated to admit it, she cared for him and wanted to make sure that he would be alright. She was loath to admit it, but she couldn't leave the boy until he was really safe.

Her thoughts paused.

Is anyone ever really in a place where they are fully safe? Janis thought.

She had an unfortunate suspicion that she wouldn't be leaving the group soon, at least not soon enough. It wasn't just her odd and frustrating fondness for the boy—she was drawn to Lightbearing. Learning new information had always been a draw for her, and this was such a big area of knowledge she lacked that she couldn't shy away. How she'd worked all over Lindrad and not come across this before, she didn't know, but now that she had, her appetite had grown strong.

No, Janis wouldn't leave them until she at least understood how she could stand up against one of these Lightbearers. Everyone had a weakness, and finding theirs would be paramount to—what? She hadn't come up against any of these people yet. Why would she now?

She narrowed her eyes, staring into the forest, which was now getting lighter and lighter. The draw to understanding these strange things wasn't overly unusual, but it somehow felt different to her. Maybe when they got to the sanctuary, she could learn exactly what she was hoping to about Lightbearers. Avryn may not be open to discussing these things, but Janis believed that one could go to the heart of something and learn all you needed from just being there. This was often the reason she visited hometowns and sometimes even houses of those that she hunted.

Understand your enemies, and you cannot lose.

His voice echoed in her mind again. Macks. Fog that man. Janis hated that she kept thinking of him these days. She switched all of her attention from inside her head to staring into the forest as the treeline became more defined in the dim sunlight. The sky was still grey, but not nearly as dark as it had been. The wind had all but stopped, and the rain was no more than a drizzle with small bursts here and there. With the clouds less darkened, the sunlight reflected along the whole sky, lighting it to a dull grey. Despite the clouds, it would be very bright outside. With the rain stopped, they'd be able to move on.

Sure enough, it wasn't long before her companions stirred and awoke. After peering out into the forest, Avryn declared that they could move on and that they would likely reach their destination tomorrow afternoon, possibly evening. The rain had not stopped altogether, so they would still get wet while trekking through it, but they all agreed it would be best to start moving again, especially knowing the two merchants were aware of their location. Only Janis knew that the bone-white man knew about Lydia, and was likely en route to extract their location. In short, Janis couldn't get out of the cave fast enough.

As they stepped into the forest, Janis immediately scanned the area for any movement. When she didn't detect anything, she felt a bit more at ease. Normally, rain would bother Janis if she was hunting down a mark, but this time they were the ones being hunted, so the rain kept their tracks hidden. Her stealth and speed was possible on her own, but rain such as this would have slowed them down too much.

While they traveled, Harmel talked about his past adventures and Shrell cut in to correct gross overstatements. Shrell seemed to disapprove of his brother's attitude toward life and his reactions to all situations, but that only seemed to fuel Harmel's levity more.

Janis remained quiet. Of course, she normally did while they traveled, but for her, the quiet was not because of her normal reason of disliking people and conversation in general. Instead, her silence was from the lingering feeling of her encounter earlier that previous night. She was haunted by the knowledge of one thing.

If the robed man ever found her, he would kill her.

Chapter 15

Marric was tired of being wet. Ever since they had left the cavern, it seemed that the rain was just teasing them. As they walked through the forest, there would be a lapse in the rain, just enough to make them think it had passed, but then it would start up again. Of course, it wasn't a terribly hard and fast rain, but it soaked them well enough.

The boy wrapped his hands around his chest and shivered to himself. When they first started, Harmel had been able to keep the mood light in the group by telling his silly tales and making jokes, but now even he remained quiet as they trudged through the rain. Janis had stayed quiet the whole time, and Marric was a bit worried about her. She was normally quiet, that was true, but this time, there was a look in her eyes that was just wrong. The woman was usually so confident and strong, but now she seemed withered, almost worried about something. It made him wonder what had happened while he slept.

Shaking his head, he focused on taking one step at a time. They had just walked through a swampy part of the forest, so his boots were covered in mud, as were his trousers almost up to his knees. The group had been forced to pause to scrape off their clothes and shoes after making it through so that the extra weight wouldn't slow them down.

What a silly notion. As if I wasn't weighed down with exhaustion already.

The daylight was reaching an end, and Avryn had declared that if they just pushed a bit further, they could reach a stopping location that was much closer to their sanctuary than he could have hoped for. He also said it would provide a much safer place for them to sleep for the night, and that it was quite beautiful.

At this point, Marric didn't care much for how beautiful their campsite was, he just wanted to sit.

Marric forced himself to not ask Avryn over and over when they would get there. He knew that wouldn't help. Not to mention he was a bit nervous to find out what Janis's reaction to his constant questioning would be. It wasn't that he was scared of her. Well, normally he wasn't, but something about her made him feel like he should keep his distance. Though, it might have just been him making something up, for Harmel seemed to keep himself quite close to her.

In time, the group paused for a small snack before they moved on. There wasn't time for a full supper, but they did need to eat.

At least Avryn is human enough to let us pause for a moment.

They chose a thicket of trees with many low-hanging branches that sheltered them from the rain just a bit. It still dripped through in some places, but overall they were able to avoid the brunt of the rain. Of course, the poor horses had to stick it out in the rain, so they didn't find the respite they likely deserved. In a way, Marric felt really bad for them. But that was technically what they were for, to endure hard conditions to make travel more comfortable for humans. He respected them for that. Though, it did irk him to know that all the contents of their packs were likely soaked through. He hadn't wrapped any of his things in oilskin.

"You know, for being rainy, it isn't really so bad out here. I quite like the journey here, I've made it so many times before." Avryn said.

Marric and Shrell gave each other a look before Shrell rolled his eyes.

"Oi think it's jus' tha' Avryn took a likin' to bein' wet. E's got some weird 'obbies, tha's fer sure."

Avryn made a face at Harmel, but it was clear that he knew his friend was joking.

"Why, S'ren, hows abou' we take yeh righ' out ta the river and throw yous in? Oi bet you'd quite like tha', eh?"

"In fact, I do quite like swimming. Plus, it's not like I could get any wetter anyway. It is an odd sensation being underwater when it's raining outside. Have you ever experienced that?"

"The only time that I've done tha' was when I was tryin' to run from some nasty beasts. I don't remember it bein' a good sensation then." Shrell said.

Harmel laughed loudly at this, though Marric didn't think that it was a joke.

Marric just shrugged at Avryn's question.

The group had all huddled pretty close together under the thicket, since it was a small spot. Janis, however, remained standing out in the rain. This of course wasn't unusual for her, but Marric couldn't conceive how she just stayed in the rain all the time. There really was something odd this time, though. She wasn't looking around and scouting the area like she usually did. Marric realized that she was staring very intently, and it was directly at Avryn. The look on her face was one of confusion.

This struck Marric even more. She hadn't expressed anything other than fierce determination for the majority of their traveling, but now it was clear that there was something on her mind. What it was, Marric couldn't even come close to guessing.

For a moment, he thought about asking her what she was thinking, but then he thought better of it. She was a private woman, and that was likely not going to change.

"I thought you said that having more than two powers was rare." Janis blurted out, seeming hostile.

Well that was unexpected, Marric thought. The whole group stared back at her. Even though the attention of the whole group was on her, she kept her eyes locked on Avryn.

"Excuse me?"

"You said that Lightbearers manifested only one power, and developed another, but what of you? You claimed that having three powers was unusual and rare, but how do we know that's true?"

Avryn's eyebrows knit together. He stared back at her.

"Yes, it is quite rare. But why are you—"

"If it's so rare, then why does the man with the bone-white skin have more than two powers?"

Their leader's expression changed, and a look of graveness replaced the one before.

"How do you know about him?" Avryn said, calm and measured.

Shrell and Harmel stared at her, and their expressions seemed angry at her comment. This was a very unusual thing for Harmel, so Marric knew that what Janis had said carried a lot of weight, though he didn't understand why.

Silence. No one seemed to want to say anything, they all just stared.

For a moment, no one moved at all, and nothing was said. Then the woman's eyes flicked to Avryn's companions in turn and she narrowed her eyes.

"So they know about this man as well, huh?"

Avryn's face held the look that it always did when he was considering deeply how to answer.

"It seems that there is information on both your part and mine that should be shared if we expect to move forward together. I'm not sure how you know of him, but we'd best discuss this privately."

At that, he got to his feet and nodded to his companions. There was some silent exchange of understanding that was beyond Marric, then he and Janis moved off into the trees. It wasn't difficult for them to leave his range of hearing, for the rain was pittering enough to cover sounds not immediately near him. He could see them, though not enough to glean any information about the tone of the conversation.

After a time, Marric wondered if they would have to sit in silence for the rest of the break. As if sensing this thought, Harmel broke the silence.

"Well, Oi tell yeh wha', Oi sure can' wait to have a nice bed and some decent food fer once. Oi feel like we've been eatin' kitchen scraps fer over a week. It's righ' too bad tha' we couldn' 'ave packed a game hen, hmm?"

Shrell scoffed at the comment.

"Brother, if yeh spent half as much time practicin' somethin' important as yeh did eatin'—like fightin' perhaps—yeh might actually be more useful."

Harmel covered his mouth in a feigned shocked expression.

"Are yeh sayin' that' Oi'm worthless, then? Tell tha' to the spine hog Oi killed righ' 'afore it gutted yeh."

The stout man gave Marric an exaggerated wink at the comment. Marric had to admit that traveling with the duo definitely made things more fun. The dynamic between the two of them was beyond anything that he could comprehend. Perhaps that was because he didn't have a brother, or even a sister for that matter. Crents was good company, but he was no brother.

Regardless of how the men made him feel, he didn't feel like he could ask them what Janis was talking about. She had mentioned some 'bone man' or something, and the comment had a strange effect on all of the men. He tuned out Harmel and Shrell's conversation as he looked back at the dark outlines of Janis and Avryn in the distance. They were moving, likely using hand gestures as people often did while talking, but this told him nothing of the conversation. Still, it wasn't long before the two ended their huddle and made their way back to the rest of the group.

"It seems that Janis has had an encounter with our enemy, Riln." Avryn spoke shortly.

Shrell and Harmel didn't react to this any more than they had earlier at first mention, which made it obvious to Marric that they already knew who this was, and what that meant.

"The encounter itself is what troubles me most, but let's get moving before I give more information to you all."

Without asking further questions, they finished packing up and hit the path at a brisk walk. Avryn stuck close to Marric while keeping Harmel and Shrell within earshot, and began his explanation once they'd been moving for a quarter hour.

Avryn looked the most serious Marric had ever seen him. He took a deep breath, then started explaining to Marric in a resigned tone. "Riln is the leader of Watchlight. He is volatile and very dangerous. You see, Riln is even more of an anomaly than myself when it comes to Lightbearing."

He paused, then continued, "Riln has somehow manifested all of the Lightbearer powers."

Another pause, to let that sink in. For a moment, Marric wasn't sure what he meant. Then he understood and he felt the hairs on his body stand up as if there was some spirit just behind him. He didn't really understand why this news made him feel this way, but it somehow did. Perhaps it was the tone of Avryn's voice, or the meaning of the comment. Regardless, Marric suddenly felt all feelings of security and safety leave. It was as if a truth he had finally settled on and had become comfortable with was ripped from him. That was a silly comparison, however, since he'd only been exposed to Lightbearing for nearly two weeks.

"Riln contacted Janis through a vision while she was—" Avryn glanced her way, eyebrows knit together, but continued, "—dreaming. It appears that also in this dream was the woman Lydia, the wife of the merchant man we met in the cave. It seems that Riln had targeted her, knowing that she was a Seer and that he could talk to her and extract our location."

Shrell cursed to himself and performed the warding off hand gesture common in those of the Lanserian religion, hand in the form of a cup, fingers extended, swiping up across his body. Harmel was just quiet, walking along resolutely and looking uncharacteristically tough.

"Riln made an attempt to extract our location from the woman, but fortunately—according to Janis's report, Lydia revealed nothing to him."

"Well tha's righ' nice of 'er, eh?" Harmel said brightly.

Avryn nodded.

"I must say, I am a bit surprised at Lydia's decision to not disclose our location, especially considering the circumstances when they left us in the cave."

"That hadn't happened yet." Janis spoke quietly from the front of the group.

Avryn paused and peered at her.

Marric stared at her, mouth slightly open at her sudden comment. She was a bit of a brash woman; cutting off another person's sentence wasn't that unusual for her, but this felt different. The tone of her voice and the way she stared off into the distance as she said it looked like she was lost in a sea of thought.

"Pardon me?" Avryn said, actually sounding a bit annoyed.

Janis paused her walking and turned around. "In the dream, when the bone-white man—Riln, you say? When Riln spoke to her, Lydia had only just determined that you were a Lightbearer. However, she was much more afraid of Riln than of you. The way she looked at me there . . . and time just felt—*wrong.*"

She shook her head as if she was trying to shake the thoughts away before continuing.

"No, she wasn't afraid of you yet, Avryn. She hadn't determined that you were a threat. I don't know how, but she was in the past, even though I wasn't."

The silence that followed burrowed into Marric's chest like a worm. He wasn't fond of *any* long silences in conversations, but this one seemed more grave and daunting, likely because of the subject matter.

Finally, Avryn spoke out.

"Let's not worry about the specifics. At least we can be sure that my Shielding is performing its function partially as he hasn't yet been able to locate us at this time. Now that we are nearing our destination, I feel confident that we'll be just fine. Regardless, we are almost to the place where we can spend the night. Then we will reach our sanctuary before lunchtime. We must keep moving, now.

Shrell stared at Avryn with a stern look, clearly not happy with where they were leaving the conversation, but he didn't press the matter. The group pressed on, feeling strangely gloomy—and not just due to the weather. The rain may have stopped, but the clouds persisted, leaving the forest around them bathed in a dull gray that deepened in shade. Marric knew that was just the sun getting close to fully retracting behind the horizon, even though they couldn't see the sun itself.

The forest was waking up around them, now that the storm was over. Birds flitted through the trees; rabbits and other creatures skulked and hopped around the bushes. It wasn't until now that Marric realized the forest had been somewhat devoid of life during the storm. It wasn't unusual for that to be the case, for even animals didn't enjoy being out in the wet, but their emergence seemed a beautiful thing to him. The world was suddenly like a wonderful work of art, changing with the times and circumstances without actually changing much at all.

Lanser bless us, this is a wondrous place.

As Marric walked, he wasn't paying too much attention to his companions. Though Avryn had said that he thought they wouldn't meet any trouble, the gravity of the conversation just before seemed to slice through that notion like one of Janis's blades through a man's arm.

Marric winced at that thought. What a macabre thing to think.

But was that what he was meant for? How much violence and fighting had he been exposed to in the last few weeks? Far more than he had *ever* had in his entire life so far. By the mere nature of his association with the power that Avryn described, it was as if he was subject to a life of violence, danger, and uneasiness.

The twist in his gut forced him to move on in his thoughts. It wouldn't do him any good to dwell on the past, or to be unsatisfied with his future. He might never know exactly how things would turn out, but he resolved to not let his guard down. In a strange way, Marric felt like an outlaw that sooner or later would get caught. Something told him that getting caught by Watchlight wouldn't be as pleasant as living in a jailhouse.

Imagining himself behind bars seemed so ludacris that he actually chuckled to himself, awarding him a sidelong glance from Shrell and a look of disdain from Janis. She never did care for levity.

She's the real outlaw. She doesn't want to be caught unaware.

This thought actually made him appreciate her and her ways more than he had in the past. Her paranoia had saved them on more than one occasion. Whoever Janis was, she was passionate about her safety.

His thought was interrupted by a roaring sound in the distance. The sound wasn't a big one, but it seemed loud in the quiet of the forest. Based on the depth of it, the source was big, and it sounded like water was running. It wasn't long before the mystery sound was identified as a large waterfall. In the waning light, Marric could see a large cliff, dark and brooding, and from it, a torrent of water was rushing down and pounding the rocks below.

The waterfall was majestic and powerful. Marric stared in awe as they approached the monstrosity. How could something like this even be formed? There was so much water that the sound was overwhelming, not to mention the sight. All other sounds were drowned out by its flow. Even his companions had to shout very loudly to be heard over it.

As they got closer, however, Marric was perplexed at the noise, for though the waterfall was large, it seemed to be loud from all directions. Breaking through the final trees near the base of it, he realized that it wasn't actually one waterfall, but three that flowed into the same large pool of water. The two falls on either side were hidden from view, for the water expelled from the deep point of the cliffside, and the other two fell from the two taller peaks of the v-shape. The noise of the tumult was amazing and emphasized the power of the flow.

More perplexing still was the fact that the heavy flow of water had no output to be seen. There wasn't any river or water flowing away from the falls in any direction, it merely fell into the pool, then disappeared. Marric stared wide-mouthed at the view, trying to come up with a conceivable solution to the riddle. As he scanned the cliff looking for an answer, his eye caught Avryn, who was looking at him endearingly.

"It's quite amazing, isn't it? There's something about these waterfalls that make me feel at home and safe."

Avryn had to shout over the sound, of course, which made it seem strange that such a situation would make him feel safe. At the same time, however, the sound and the view enveloped Marric in a cocoon of pleasant sensations so that he couldn't help but understand the feeling of security Avryn claimed himself. Marric wondered suddenly if the effect had come over the others. Shrell and Harmel seemed contrite, but that could be just because of the familiarity of the place, rather than the wonder of it all. The boy's eyes fell on Janis, and to his surprise, she seemed unimpressed. In fact, the woman seemed more tense, as if the waterfall and all its glory put her more on edge.

She was a strange woman, indeed.

"I'm not sure if it's because of their beauty, their sound, or the fact that it means we are within a few hours of our sanctuary, but I am more than happy to stay here for the night. We should be safe now."

Without any warning, Janis dove toward Marric, knocking him to the ground. Shrell cursed and pulled his sword on Janis, looking to skewer her right then, until his eyes focused on something in the tree just behind Marric: a long dagger with a silver pommel was wedged in the wood.

Jumping to her feet, she shouted something at their companions and instinctively, they formed a ring around Marric, Janis and Avryn in front to either side, Shrell and Harmel doing the same thing just behind.

It had happened so fast that Marric wasn't sure what to do. His mind was still foggy from the effect of the view, but his body ached from the hard tackle just moments before. Making the decision to be more resilient, he stood on his feet and looked through Janis and Avryn's forms. There stood two men, neither of which looked even remotely familiar.

* * *

Janis's blood boiled. Her body felt like a hanging line for clothes, taut and ready to spring at the slightest touch. She knew that stepping into this place was a death trap. Not only was the sight distracting to those of a weaker mind, but the sound of the falls debilitated one of the most essential senses to an assassin, their hearing. It was the perfect place for an ambush. And here they were, facing the man that had threatened her life and had given her the gold to 'protect' Marric just weeks ago. Although the forms facing them were hooded, she recognized his clothes and his stature.

At least now I can see him, and he doesn't have a crossbow with him.

As much as she didn't like to admit it, having Harmel and Shrell behind her actually made her feel more prepared for an encounter with this man, for last time, he had bested her with a companion poking their knife into her back. That shouldn't be a problem here.

The two men were black clad, meaning they intended to blend into the darkness. They had been waiting for them. The fact that there were only two wasn't a comfort to Janis, for an ambush that was this well prepared normally meant reinforcements, though they couldn't be seen. She'd been in this situation before, on both ends of the fight; the ambusher and the ones being ambushed. Fortunately, that meant that the men's colleagues were still fanned out, waiting for either the targets, or the signal. If they could just get away before the signal.

Just then, one of the men put his hand in the air and a small reddish ball of Light shot into the air. It was about the size of Avryn's when he created his, though the color was off.

Fog it! We only have moments now!

Avryn made a sound that sounded like a growl. Janis knew then that he was aware of their situation. They had been caught, and there were more coming.

As if sensing their dismay, one of the figures pulled back his hood, revealing the wicked scars running from his nose to his ears. Marric gasped loudly behind her. She glanced back to see his eyes widen and his face pale.

It seems our scar-faced friend has had experience with the better part of our group.

"PROST!" Avryn shouted suddenly, "You have no claim on the boy. Leave, or perish!"

The scar-faced man just smiled, unaffected by the comment.

Instead of Conjuring a sword, Avryn pulled his own steel one from his side, pointing it at the man whose name was apparently Prost.

For a moment, nothing happened, they just stared. Janis knew time was running out and that they couldn't wait. There was something off about the other robed man, and Janis didn't know what, but she didn't have the luxury of finding out. In a flash, she whipped out her two long daggers and dashed toward Prost's companion. She didn't think she would actually be able to run them through as she would have liked, but she did hope that her action would at least enlighten her companions to the gravity of their predicament.

Sure enough, as she ran, Avryn called out orders to his companions to take Marric somewhere, though she didn't catch where, and rushed toward the two with her. As she neared them, the other man stood there, motionless, until he put his hand in front of him, palms out. A sudden burst of light flashed in her eyes and she watched as a globe of light spread out to cover the three of them, shielding them completely from her.

Though she wasn't unaffected by the surprise of the situation, she charged toward it anyway, striking the sphere with one of her daggers. Instead of piercing the sphere, however, her dagger bounced off of the thing as if it were solid. Janis shifted to the side and stabbed it with another, but the same thing happened; it only bounced away. She looked up to see the other man had removed his hood. He was short, stocky, and had short hair cropped close to his head. The strangest part of it all was that his eyes glowed red.

Lanser's beard, he's a Lightbearer!

She dove to the side, expecting some other attack or blast of power, but none came.

Avryn was not far behind, letting out an unholy yell that you only hear from a determined soldier in battle. He rushed forward and slammed his hand hard into the Shield. When nothing happened, he rammed his hand again, and this time, an explosion of blue Light was followed by a sound similar to shattering glass. Blinking repeatedly to remove the burned spots in her vision, she saw that the Shield was gone.

Whipping her head to the side, she saw that Avryn had engaged the man Prost in a sword fight. Determined, she dove at the other man, who wasn't actually prepared for her. The look on his face indicated that he hadn't expected his Shield to break so quickly or so easily. Without hesitation, she dug her knife into the man's stomach and kicked him away.

Grunting, he fell to the ground, but still managed to pull out a sword of his own. Not letting him gain footing, she rammed the side of his head with the hilt of her dagger and he crumpled to the ground.

Janis looked toward Avryn to see that he and the scar-faced man had moved quickly away in their engagement. Avryn wasn't using any of his powers, which was strange to her. Why not use something that puts you at so clear of an advantage? It couldn't be chivalry, could it? That would just be stupid.

A tug in her gut and a flash of Light in her peripheral vision told Janis to dodge, and she did, just as a dagger made of Light slammed into the ground just past her.

She cursed.

The reinforcements had arrived.

* * *

Marric was terrified.

His mind spun and his heart raced while a strong hand pushed him forward quickly. Someone was shouting. No, there were a few people shouting, though he didn't recognize the voices of some. What they said, he didn't know.

That man, he thought.

There had been so many nightmares of the night Jord was taken, and it always ended with the scar-faced man smiling at him before knocking him out.

He was here. That man was here. Marric knew that the man was here for him.

All at once, his senses shifted and he escaped the trap of his mind. Harmel was before him, sword raised and rushing toward the treeline. Shrell was behind, strong hand gripping Marric on the shoulder so hard that it almost hurt. His friend was pushing his body forward with urgency, which made the boy even more nervous.

As they neared the treeline, a pair emerged from it. They were both hooded, but were of vastly different sizes. One of the figures was tall and so skinny that Marric wondered how it was humanly possible. The other, short and stocky, was actually shorter than himself.

If it weren't for the circumstances, Marric wondered if he could feel worried facing a pair such as this, for they seemed odd, indeed. That thought was soon relinquished as Harmel engaged with a roar, one that Marric hadn't ever considered coming from a man such as himself.

Harmel's sword swung in for a swipe, but was wrenched from his hand with a flash of Light. The sword spun to the side as if it had a mind of its own.

What the?

One of the figures, the tall and skinny one, had his hand outstretched toward Harmel. A feeling struck Marric and he knew suddenly that they were facing Lightbearers. The dread deepened in his gut.

Harmel, taken aback only briefly, whipped out two more swords and charged forward, more determined. The sword in his left hand glowed brightly and it was pulled in a direction to the side, but with gritted teeth, he held on tight. Though his determination saved the sword there, the sword in his right hand was torn from his grasp easily. He kept running.

Suddenly, the first sword that was flung away came rushing toward his head, glowing with red Light. Cursing, Shrell lunged from behind Marric and blocked the sword with his own, causing it to clatter away. By then, Harmel had reached the two men.

A flash of red Light was followed by a crashing sound and Harmel falling to the ground with a loud grunt. Marric stared in awe at the sphere of Light that surrounded the two black-clad and hooded figures. It was reddish, and seemed menacing as it made the trees and ground around it glow. The tall and skinny man pulled back his hood to reveal a sallow and an equally skinny face behind it. He was bald, except for a thick ponytail of hair sprouting from the center of the top of his skull. He was baring his teeth.

"SHIELDER! And a Mover!" Shrell screamed as he parried a sword that was hovering in front of him. Harmel was battling his other sword, also flinging through the air with unseen hands.

***

Janis turned to see a woman with blonde hair, long and braided down to her waist. Her eyes shifted up and down the body of the woman, assessing the threat. Janis noted the same tattoo, and eye in a beam of light, on the inside of the woman's left wrist. In an odd sense of fashion, the woman had somehow managed to color a bit of the hair running from the scalp of her head all the way to the end of her braid. Janis thought it looked silly and very impractical.

The assassin didn't have much time to entertain those thoughts as another pair of daggers, made from the same red Light, appeared in the woman's hands, just before she heaved them into the air toward her. Janis easily dodged the throws, rolling on the ground and stopping a dozen paces away from the woman. She wasn't alone, though her companion, a ridiculously short man with blond hair, stood there, slightly behind the woman, as if he needed protection.

This made Janis smile.

Of course, he isn't a fighter, so he is hiding behind the blonde woman.

The revelation made Janis feel like she might actually be able to gain an advantage over the two of them if she could just throw a well placed dagger. Or if she could get close enough, she could incapacitate them.

An arrow pierced Janis through her shirt, inches from the edge of her body at her waist. Gasping, she dove to the side, narrowly missing another three that followed. She came to a stop and glared at the woman, only to see that she was holding a bow weaved from the same red Light. Holding out her other hand, she created another arrow out of Light and nocked it.

Blast! She can create anything!

Getting closer to them would prove far more difficult than she imagined. Janis hated bowmen—they were such cowards, staying far from the fight like a bunch of children. Despite her lack of respect for them, she knew she couldn't last long against the blonde woman, not with that bow.

A thought struck Janis like a wall. *She must be a Conjurer! What are the limitations?!*

An arrow swished through the air near her head and she ducked, rolling backwards to avoid a few more.

A limited number of objects . . . and—

Distance.

Janis turned and dashed toward the treeline. It was a gamble, but just before she entered, she turned to see a volley of arrows flying toward her person. However, just before they landed, they disappeared into the air, becoming nothing.

Janis smiled.

The look on the blonde woman's face was not pleased. She dismissed the bow and summoned swords, knowing now that ranged weapons would do no good if she had to continually chase Janis just to get close. Janis was surprised by this. The strange blonde woman had instinct, and she knew not to waste her energy any longer on trying to hit her from afar.

A formidable opponent, indeed.

She gripped her long daggers and rushed toward the woman and the squat man.

* * *

They were losing, and badly.

Marric watched as Harmel and Shrell battled the haphazardly floating swords. It wasn't as if the swords were being wielded by trained combatants; rather, they swung about violently and with no seeming pattern. Despite their lack of technical direction, the Light-controlled swords were worthy opponents. Harmel and Shrell were almost skewered more than once. Marric stood there, watching as if he was a bystander observing some theatre production. But this was real. All too real.

Harmel dodged a swing from his sword but got nicked by the second, a cut opening on his upper arm. Shrell seemed to be doing better, but he was getting tired. All the while, the two people—one unhooded and baring his teeth like a fiend, stood protected in their Shield of red Light. At that moment, Marric noticed that the shorter figure, arms outstretched, was a woman. Her breasts poked out through her black robe as she stood there stiff, focusing.

His mind raced. There had to be *something* that he could do! What was it?!

Without any warning, Avryn ran into view, racing not toward his companions, but instead to the Shield. He swung his hand and a fist-sized ball of blue Light shot out toward the red sphere. It collided with a loud crack and exploded in a blast of blue Light. The woman shrunk a bit when that happened, but the Shield held on.

Avryn kept running, directly toward the red sphere.

Marric shouted a warning to Avryn, but instead of ricocheting off of the sphere, he held his hand out and the sphere shattered, making a sound between glass breaking and wood splintering. He continued onward and whacked the short woman with the flat of his blade, knocking her backward. Before he could reach the skinny, animal-like man, he was thrown backwards, body wreathed in red Light. Avryn flew twenty paces, colliding with a tree.

It seemed just the momentum they needed, however, for Marric heard the clash of steel behind him and turned to see Harmel and Shrell engaging the tall and skinny man. Just as what had happened to Avryn moments before, Harmel was lifted off his feet, surrounded by the same reddish Light and thrown backwards, not getting back up. Unfortunately for the skinny man, this focused attack on Harmel left him open to Shrell's attack, and he took a sword right in his stomach.

Groaning, he clutched his gut and fell to the ground, blood spilling out over his hands.

Shrell, in a seemingly heartless move, kicked the man in the face, knocking him out. He then moved to Harmel's side to make sure his brother was okay.

Avryn! Marric thought suddenly. But when he turned to see if Avryn was there, he was shocked to see that the man was up and fighting again, this time with the scarred man. Janis seemed engaged with a couple other people a dozen paces to the right of them.

And I'm useless.

"I guess we got lucky then, huh, Destroyer?"

Marric froze, fear gripping his entire being.

Chapter 16

Janis dodged the swing of the blonde woman's sword and jabbed with her daggers. The woman danced away easily, as if she knew exactly what Janis would do. This deepened her admiration for the strange woman's skill. It wasn't everyone that could withstand her speed and fighting prowess.

Regardless of her admiration, she couldn't let this go on much longer. As she engaged the woman again, Janis positioned herself to the side to see how the others were doing. Shrell was bent over the limp form of Harmel, and Avryn was fighting with Prost still. It seemed those two were evenly matched, which was surprising to Janis considering Avryn's skill with Lightbearing.

Where is Marric? she thought, scanning the trees. *There. He was standing there facing—*

A shiver went up her spine and she somehow knew that Marric was in trouble. They weren't fighting, but the two black clad figures stood before Marric, brooding and strong.

Her fight had to end *now.*

Knowing this, she decided to employ a trick that would almost certainly best the woman. Unfortunately, the trick wouldn't end the woman's life, which would provide the finality to the fight that Janis preferred. Leaving the blonde fighter alive could prove costly, but based on the woman's own skill with fighting, Janis didn't have the luxury of time.

Dropping low, Janis rushed the woman head-on. This, of course, made the woman step back in surprise. Before long, she realized that Janis's course of path would make her vulnerable to a swipe with her blade. Taking the bait, she swung her blade right at Janis's sides, ready to slice into her midsection. Knowing and expecting this, Janis dove onto her stomach and slid right through the woman's legs. Flipping around, she took her dagger to the back of the woman's knees, slicing through the tendons on the back of them, dropping her to the ground.

Then she ran straight toward Marric.

* * *

Marric stood there, frozen for a time, looking back and forth between the two new people before him. One of the figures was hooded, and didn't seem to be that much larger than himself. The other was a woman. She wore black, like the rest of them all seemed to be wearing, but her hood was back. Her skin was dark brown, and her hair as black as her clothing. It was cut short, and was so wavy that it seemed unnatural, for he wasn't sure how anyone could work their hair in such a way. The sight of them, under normal circumstances, wouldn't have made Marric all that nervous. It was what the woman had just said.

She called the other one 'Destroyer'.

Marric could feel his palms sweating. His ears roared and he shook. It was slight, so he doubted that the two facing him could tell, but he was terrified.

"I suppose it's just a grab and go then?" the woman said to her companion, smiling at Marric.

Marric stared at her, confused. She looked so kind. He knew why they were here—at least, he *thought* he did. But her face. On any other day, when he didn't feel like he was in so much danger, this was the kind of woman your mother would tell you to trust. In fact, she even made him feel like everything was okay.

But it wasn't.

Grab and go . . .

This brought him back to reality.

He suddenly was acutely aware of the bow and arrows that he had been carrying the entire journey. Until now, he hadn't even been able to remember that *this* was the reason he brought them along in the first place!

In a fluid motion, and to his own surprise, he quickly and smoothly pulled his bow out and had an arrow nocked as if he was an expert bowman. It was like his mind was shut down, but his body was acting on memory, shifting into protection mode.

Mind numb, he raised his bow, aiming at the woman's chest.

Marric's mind screamed. He'd never hurt a person before so intentionally, let alone killed one, but his instincts took over.

The smile melted from the woman's face and her eyes widened.

He released the arrow.

The bowstring sang its familiar springing song and the arrow flew straight and true.

Crack!

Splinters flew in all directions as the arrow exploded before it made contact with the woman.

Marric sank, realizing that his attempt at assault was thwarted, and it had happened in an unimaginable and incomprehensible way.

The woman's companion stood with their arm outstretched, hand open.

That can't be good.

Despite his confusion and frustration, he quickly nocked another arrow, though stumbling a bit while doing so. This time, he aimed at the hooded figure.

Before he could release his arrow, another black figure blurred in his vision to the side, coming from behind him. He turned his arrow on the newcomer, but stopped when he saw it was Janis.

Relief blossomed in his chest as he realized she was there. His instincts broke and the fear took over.

Janis placed herself between Marric and the two before them. This seemed odd to Marric, for Janis didn't normally wait in such a manner. Her speed and skill normally pushed her to action, not waiting. Something was wrong.

. . .

* * *

As she ran ahead to Marric and the two figures facing him, something in her stomach told her to not rush them. She wasn't sure why, but her instincts weren't often wrong. Janis somehow knew that she would die if she didn't handle this with a little more pause. She suspected that it had something to do with the fact that she'd just seen Marric's arrow explode into bits accompanied by her new least favorite thing, a flash of red Light.

Janis could hear Marric breathing shortly behind her, obviously terrified. She was impressed that he had been able to fire an arrow at all, but was disappointed that it had not connected with its target.

Breathing hard, she stared at the hooded figure. It was a man. Well, more of a boy, really. His stature wasn't large, and he didn't appear like he had grown into his full adulthood yet. He had lowered his hand, but seemed to hold it at the ready.

"Hmmm," the dark-skinned woman said. "It doesn't look like it will be as easy as I thought."

Marric gasped suddenly and whispered to himself before shouting, "Destroyer! Janis, watch out! He can—"

As if in response, the boy flung his hand out toward her and a red ball of Light flew towards them.

Janis kicked backwards with her leg and knocked Marric to the ground, then jumped on top to shield him from the danger. The red ball of Light flew over them and she heard an explosion of something behind them.

Blast it all! What in Lanser's name am I supposed to do about this?!

She rolled to the side, hoping that Marric would have the sense to stay down. Her dagger supply was almost out. She was still clutching her forearm-length dagger in one hand, but she only had a small one left hidden.

This she grabbed, and mid-roll, lobbed it at the woman. The boy saw it and tried to intercept it with one of his balls of Light, but he wasn't fast enough. It sunk into the woman's thigh and she shrieked in pain. Once again, an explosion sounded where the red flash had gone somewhere to her right.

Unsure of exactly how to handle someone that could throw Light that made things explode, Janis charged right at him. This tactic appeared to be effective, for nothing blew her up. Instead, she slammed right into him, knocking him to the ground.

* * *

Marric lay on the ground, stunned from the sudden blow from Janis. His mind was foggy, and for a moment, he wasn't sure where he was or what was happening. It felt as if he was dreaming, staring up at the tree canopy and the now black sky with beautiful stars shining brightly.

All at once, a sharp pain pierced through the brain fog and snapped reality back into place. He had landed almost flat on his back, and he was feeling it. He wasn't sure why, but he didn't dare move an inch. Seeing Janis fling her dagger into that woman's leg was enough to make his stomach heave, but the thought of one of the Destroyer's balls of Lights hitting a person made him freeze in terror.

Marric's stomach turned. He was never able to handle the sight of violence and blood well. Emotionally, he could feel himself losing it. He wished he wasn't here. He wished he hadn't ever found out about Lightbearing. He especially wished that he wasn't destined to become one.

But then I wouldn't have met Avryn, or anyone here.

He had grown fond of his companions. Even Janis, in an odd way.

A grunt made Marric flinch and pull his limbs in close, expecting someone to see him lying there and attack him in his defenseless state.

What in the blazes am I doing?!

The dazed boy rolled to his stomach, tucked his knees under him and jumped to his feet, back to the Destroyer and the wounded woman. Without much thought, Marric bent down and snatched the bow that had fallen there. While turning around to face the attackers, he fluidly reached back and pulled an arrow free. Nocking it in turn, he turned to see the dark-skinned woman on the ground holding her leg and groaning in pain, and a jumble of fabric that seemed to be undulating on the ground.

It took Marric a few moments to realize that the undulating fabric, all of it black, was Janis wrestling with the other black-clad figure. This was also the source of the grunting that had aroused him from his deep and panicked state. Not sure what to do, he just stood there, bowstring pulled taut and ready, pointed at them. Fearing he would strike Janis with his arrow, he pointed the bow at the wounded woman next to them. She was so busy looking at and tending to the knife in her thigh that she didn't even seem to notice Marric.

For some reason, this made him feel guilty. He could easily have hit her with the arrow, possibly even killed her without so much as a little resistance, but it didn't seem right. After a short pause, Marric resolved to not shoot the woman. He turned once more to see Harmel and Shrell combating with the Mover still, though without much success. They just kept getting thrown back by his powers. However, working against the two soldiers, he was having a difficult time keeping up. Marric recalled the same Mover having been stabbed not too long before.

They must have a Fixer with them! Marric thought, more nervous now.

Marric looked to see Avryn still fighting the scar-faced man, and neither seemed to be making any progress against the other. Avryn's sword slashed and stabbed through the air so quickly that Marric could barely see it at all. The scar-faced man moved to match the pace so easily that the fight between the two looked almost like a dance. It might have been beautiful if death wasn't the outcome to the one who missed a step.

Movement in his peripheral vision made him shift to see another pair; the blonde woman and an unnaturally short man, standing twenty or so paces from Avryn. From the looks of it, she appeared injured, for she sat on the ground with a pained expression, holding her legs. The short man next to her seemed to be recovering from something himself. If it weren't for the man's girth—he was round around his midsection—Marric might have thought he was a child. The man moved to his blonde companion, and held his hand over her legs. Light glowed from his hands, intense and bright. All at once, the pained expression left the woman's face and she smiled.

Chills ran up Marric's spine. Another threat was just restored to their group, and they didn't have the numbers to keep up. His eyes flashed to each of his companions, each fighting their own battles. He realized then with a jolt that he was the only one left.

With dread in his chest, he released the arrow, missing both the woman and the man, instead hitting the air between them. Their heads snapped in Marric's direction and they sprung into action. The man turned and began to head in the opposite direction. The woman, instead, came right toward him.

Marric nocked another arrow.

* * *

Janis grabbed at the boy's hands, trying to restrain them, but she was unable to, for he moved very quickly, and she wasn't in a position to do much about it. Normally, she wouldn't grapple with someone so closely. Wrestling and hand combat were not her forte. Sure, she could defend herself in a fight, and she probably could even win one, but being so close made her feel more exposed than experienced. Unfortunately, it was her only option. Once Marric had revealed the true nature of this person, she knew that distance fighting would get someone blown up by his powers. Such a small ball of Light could cause so much destruction.

Instead, Janis came to the conclusion that being so close to the boy himself would make him hesitate to release his Destroying powers. She had a feeling that he wasn't immune to the effects of his own powers. This appeared to prove true, as she wasn't dead yet. For the duration of their grapple to this point, he hadn't used his powers.

The bad side of this idea was that she didn't know what to do about it. She didn't have hand restraints, so even if she did subdue him, her hands were the only thing she could use, but if she was trapped there holding his wrists, she couldn't contribute to the fighting or even protecting Marric. The thought crossed her mind to just strangle him, but that would take too much time.

Glancing to the side, she saw that the woman she had pierced before wasn't a threat, for she was moaning and nursing the knife wound. She was inspecting it very closely. Bright balls of Light were hovering behind her, and on either side of her leg.

I see . . . Janis thought, *she's just a Lighter. No wonder she isn't being overly helpful in the fight.*

Finally, Janis was able to sprain the boy's wrists and he gasped, growling in defeat. She still couldn't see his face, but she could imagine the indignant look as he realized he was bested in the grapple.

Now what? she thought.

Fortunately, this fight, though potentially more lethal, wasn't very difficult compared to the blonde woman. Remembering the results of that skirmish, she turned to see that she was no longer where Janis had left her, but instead vaulting towards Marric, who stood with his bow ready.

How in Lanser's name is she up and running? Those wounds should have kept her down, possibly even permanently.

Cursing, she did the only thing she could think of. Without releasing his hands, Janis headbutted the boy in the nose so hard that she hoped to knock him out. She would have rather put her dagger in his gut, but it was off to the side, and reaching for it would give him enough of a window to push her off, or even blast her to pieces with his power. A crack sounded as their heads collided, and she sprung up to engage the approaching woman.

She turned to see Marric release an arrow that took the woman in the shoulder. This caused the woman to scream out in pain, but it didn't stop her.

Of course it didn't. That type of wound wouldn't slow Janis down much, either. Another pang of respect came to Janis at seeing this. She was also impressed that Marric had actually struck someone with an arrow. He'd been carrying that bow the entire time they had been traveling, but he had not once shown the ability to use it during their prior fights.

Seeing that he had struck her, he stood still, shocked. After a pause, he reached for another arrow, but it would have been very much too late, for the woman already had two glowing long daggers summoned and would have reached the boy before he could nock another one. Of course this wasn't a problem, for Janis parried one of the daggers easily and kicked the other out of her hand. It spun into the air and dissolved. Marric staggered back at the sudden appearance of Janis.

How's about round two, eh?

* * *

Janis flew into Marric's view and blocked what likely would have been fatal blows to him. After disarming one of the blonde woman's knives, Janis lunged with her wicked long-bladed dagger to strike the woman in the heart.

Without coming close at all, the other woman stepped out of it and swung her remaining Light-blade toward Janis's side. She also side-stepped out of this, and then they sped up.

Marric lost track of what was happening. How they moved so fast was a wonder to him. He could only stand there and watch with awe as they blocked, parried, dodged, lunged, and performed other maneuvers that he couldn't even name. With the blonde woman's summoned Light-blade, it seemed more beautiful. The glow danced and flickered off of the trees and the two fighters' own faces.

Things seemed to be going well until the blonde woman held out her empty hand and another blade flashed into existence. Marric shouted a warning, but it was too late. The enemy fighter slashed down with the new blade and Janis just had time to take the blow in her arm rather than her neck.

Despite the likelihood that the wound hurt, Janis made no noise, but instead just gritted her teeth, and jumped backwards.

How do you fight someone with infinite weapons?! Marric thought.

They were outnumbered. They were losing.

Marric felt completely useless.

The blonde woman didn't allow Janis much time before she lunged with her twin blades. She was moving too fast to really see, but it seemed as if the knives grew in length, becoming short swords in an instant.

Unbelievably, Janis dodged and parried each attack from the swords with ease, though she couldn't last much longer with the cut on her arm. Marric couldn't see the wound itself, but he could see the splatters of blood that came from it on the ground around them. How long would it take for her to bleed out?

A voice behind him spoke. "You can't win! We will take you, and your friends will die."

A chill ran up Marric's back and his body turned cold. Spinning around, he saw the Destroyer getting up, recovering from whatever state Janis had left him in. Marric had an arrow nocked and he raised it to the chest of the man, ready to let the arrow loose, ears pounding from his quickened heartbeat.

His hood had fallen back, revealing blond hair cut close to his head. The stranger looked up.

Marric froze. The world suddenly went silent around them.

"Jord. . . . "

* * *

Janis didn't have much time, and she knew it. The blonde woman had caught her off guard and sliced open her upper right arm. Normally, a cut like that wouldn't have worried her too much, but that was when she knew the fight would be over soon. Even an extremely skilled fighter and assassin would run out of blood. It was bleeding quickly.

She dodged two consecutive slices from the woman's blades and knocked one of the swords free with her open hand. Of course, a new blade sprung to life, brilliant and red, replacing the one that she had just lost.

She isn't even bothering to stop me from disarming her, Janis thought.

It was clear what was happening now. The woman was just keeping her busy until her energy ran out and she became easy prey. Janis had been there so many times that she couldn't count, but she was always on the other side of the fight.

Knowing that she didn't have much time, she decided to act quickly and get to safety. An idea came to her, and she hoped it would work. It was crazy enough to free her of this situation, and the blonde woman would not expect it.

Janis pretended to lose energy. It wasn't that difficult to fake, considering she was indeed losing energy. Dramatizing it was easy.

She lunged at the woman, who easily blocked her quick knife slashes. Janis lunged again, acting to stab the woman's mid section, but once again, she easily blocked the blow. Stepping back, Janis paused, and shook her head. It was only a slight pause, anything longer would have been obvious, but the woman took the bait, a smile spreading on her face.

Thinking Janis was running out of energy and this was her chance, the woman lunged with both blades. In her mind, the assassin knew how to accomplish her plan. She couldn't have anticipated exactly how the blonde woman would take the bait, so she had to think fast.

Quickly, Janis turned to the side and cut one of the woman's hands clean off. The other blade grazed her back as it barely missed her midsection. As expected, the force of cutting off the blonde woman's hand made Janis lose her grip on the dagger and it was ripped free of her hand. At once, Janis spun and kicked the woman in the chest while snatching her remaining Light blade by the crossguard. Continuing the motion, she took the Light blade and slammed it into the blonde woman's gut.

The blade dissipated into thin air, but it was too late.

Eyes wide, the blonde woman scowled at Janis and fell to her knees.

Shouts caught Janis's attention and she turned to see Harmel on the ground. He looked unconscious, but Shrell was outnumbered, facing two of the black clad figures. Avryn and Prost were still fighting, but neither appeared to have the upper hand. The blonde woman's other companion was up and running toward her. Spinning around, she saw Marric standing there, facing the Destroyer boy. He had an arrow nocked, but he was frozen.

Suddenly, the bow and arrow dropped from his hand and he fell to his knees, arms wrapped around his midsection.

Janis tensed. She hadn't seen anything strike him there, but he acted as if he was struck by some invisible force.

What's wrong with him now?

Feeling her energy waning, she pushed forward toward Marric, bending down in time to snatch the long dagger. It was her favorite one. Probably because it always seemed to be the only one that made it to the end of all of her fights.

* * *

Marric felt sick. He knelt on the ground, pain bursting in his stomach as if he'd been stabbed there multiple times. His mind was locked on the last image that he had seen.

Jord.

His childhood friend, standing there, as if it was a memory. The boy's hair was longer, and he did seem to have matured a little bit, but he looked the same.

The image soon left his mind as the pain in his stomach started to run into his legs and push its way into his chest. He stopped breathing. Or at least, it felt like he did.

Jord's face left his mind as the pain overtook him. He felt like he needed to throw up, his body felt like it was being ripped apart. Marric lost all trail of thought and only felt pain. For a moment, he thought he saw bright lights, but then his vision darkened.

Am I dying? Marric thought in a panic before he couldn't think anymore.

Images filled his vision and mind. Janis and Avryn's faces loomed over him, as if he was waking up from a dream. Then it changed; it was Wurren, only there was a fire. The vision zoomed in and he saw his house burning. Once again, the images changed and he was looking at a majestic mountain, sun blaring through the blue sky; grass, tall and beautiful, blowing in the breeze. As if he was flying, the vision zoomed into a hidden doorway in the mountain and through a terrible looking, red-lit set of caverns before halting on the face of a man.

His hair was white, and he was pale. So pale that Marric might have thought he was looking at a dead man. Eyes blue, standing out on his white face. The man grinned.

Then, everything went black.

* * *

Janis stumbled back as Lights appeared around Marric. There were what appeared to be four blue rings of Light circling and stacked evenly surrounding Marric as he knelt on the ground. The appearance of the Lights in the darkness was so sudden, it blinded her for a moment. Blinking away the effects of the Light on her eyes, she squinted to see through the columns.

What in the fog is happening?!

She gripped her dagger tightly and moved toward Marric cautiously. The rings of Light didn't appear to be harming Marric, but it was unnatural seeing them, and Janis knew it was some Lightbearing power. Perhaps a Shield?

Seeing Marric frozen in a state on his knees, she moved slowly and deliberately. Despite the strange sight of the Lights, she looked to see the boy she had headbutted helping up his companion. They moved into the trees *away* from the kneeling boy.

As she got closer, she saw that Marric's eyes were glowing and he was looking up to the sky. The scene was odd, and very uncomfortable to see. It was as if he was bewitched by some unknown magic and frozen in time.

She heard Avryn shout something in the distance. Ignoring the shout, she got closer. A new Light joined the ones already existing, and she looked closer to see the rabbit foot, starting to glow on Marric's belt. It started small and then intensified, glowing gold and bright.

"Janis! *Get away, NOW!*"

Janis heard Avryn's shout and her stomach lurched. He knew something, and he was trying to warn her.

Without warning, a pulse of Light flew out of Marric in a dome and struck Janis. She felt herself flying through the air before blacking out.

Chapter 17

Prost smiled to himself as he watched the pulse of Light strike the assassin, throwing her into a tree. She didn't rise after that. His own companions were also struck back by the force, most losing consciousness in the blast. Avryn, who had kept him busy for the length of the engagement, flew backwards as well, blown away by the bluish dome that came from the boy. During the last moments of their fight, Avryn was forced to turn away to warn his wench assassin. He sprinted away. Prost could have likely killed him in that moment, but it wasn't the time. Avryn would die by his hand, but not now.

The dome of Light connected with Prost, but as expected, nothing happened. He was left unaffected by the powers of the new Lightbearer. A second dome of Light burst from the boy, and this time, the other Lights, including the one in his eyes, snuffed out as the blue Light dome flew outwards like the first. Prost watched him slump to the ground on his face, fully unconscious now. Those that were still conscious from the first blow likely failed to remain so with this second blast, as they were all thrown back once again.

His smile deepened as this happened, for he knew that this was the one thing that gave him an advantage over others. He may not have their powers or even their respect, but he had something even more unusual. He felt confident as he walked toward the boy lying on the ground. There wasn't really anyone to oppose him anymore.

For a slight moment, the man had a twisting feeling in his gut, the one that reminded him of the betrayal he felt as Riln treated him with contempt, and his brethren treated him like he had a disease. Now would be the perfect time to hit them back. He could simply kill the boy and pretend like the mission failed, to spite his master. He could even run off with the boy, starting his own army of Lightbearers with the boy's gifts. Based on how his awakening had happened, he was clearly a Seer, as well as a Mover, which explained the domes of Light that had thrown the others away. He didn't turn in time to see everything, but he thought he had seen the rings of a Conjurer as well.

So he does have more than one Lightbearer class, Prost thought. That could come in handy if they were to build an army together.

No. That wasn't enough. Prost knew that his time was coming, but it wasn't yet.

Prost paused just over the boy and stared down on him, envy filling every part of his body. It wasn't because of the boy's nature, for he didn't know much about him. No, the anger boiled inside because he knew that this little cretin was already more desirable and dear to Riln than he ever could be. This weak-looking whelp already had the admiration of his master just because of the powers he now manifested.

Well, that is if he survived it. I'll admit, that was a pretty rough one, Prost thought.

His scars itched.

It really didn't make much sense for them to itch like they did, but they did whenever he was reminded of his past—the dark days that led up to him joining Watchlight, and how he'd gotten the scars.

The large man reached down and felt the neck of the boy lying there on the grass. He really was a pleasant looking youth, Prost had to admit that. A heartbeat pushed slightly back at Prost's fingertips, and he was confident that the boy had survived the awakening. Satisfied with the result of the skirmish and that the boy was still alive, he reached down and lifted the boy over his shoulder. He probably could have carried him in his arms, but this was more practical especially should an unknown enemy emerge from the woods. It was clear that this was a small party, but he didn't know for sure that there weren't any of their allies hiding close by.

As he lifted the limp form of the teenage boy, he spotted a black spot on the ground. Reaching down, he lifted the blackened trinket that smelled strongly of burnt hair. He rolled the object in his fingers a few times before realizing that it was a rabbit foot.

Prost snorted.

They really are a strange lot, these peasants, he thought in disdain.

Prost thought that it was an odd superstition to have. How anyone could fall prey to such ridiculous beliefs, he didn't know. People with such superstitions often died at a very young age. For him, it indicated weakness. Only those with no fears or worries could stay alive. Though how the rabbit foot had been blackened, as if it was burned in an intense fire, he couldn't know.

Tossing the charred rabbit foot to the ground, Prost turned and made his way to where their horses were hiding in the forest not too far from here. He passed Neera and the little Destroyer who seemed so favored by Riln. The thought occurred to him that he could just kill Jord to be rid of him now, but that wouldn't do. Riln would know. Technically, Riln wouldn't be able to See the event as Prost was immune, but his leader was too clever to believe that the boy fell to battle. Riln would have seen Jord up to now. Prost had only just approached him.

For some reason, Riln's Seeing had been blocked by the boy's awakening, for he couldn't See the event itself, other than some unconscious people, nor could he See any other events from Marric's future at all. It wasn't the first time this had happened, though it did make Riln insufferable when it came to new budding Lightbearers like this boy. When his master's Seeing was blocked in this way, it meant that the new *Tar'n*, as was the real name for the Lightbearers, would be powerful once awakened. Unfortunately, they mostly died in the process, their power overcoming their hearts once they manifested.

The limp body of the boy over Prost's shoulder made him scoff. How this weak looking thing had survived, he couldn't know, but at least it would please Riln. It didn't happen as often as Prost would like, but this time, his master would be satisfied.

Prost kicked Neera softly in the side, checking for life. The dark-skinned woman groaned and her eyes fluttered open. Eyeing her thigh, he saw a knife jutting out as if it had sprouted there like one of those quick growing purple flowers that grew near their lair.

"Neera," Prost said loudly, "wake Jord up, we must move. Now."

Neera didn't seem to indicate that she had heard him speak at all. Instead, her eyes were far off in the sky, searching for something that wasn't there. Sighing to himself in frustration, he bent down, gripped the hilt of the knife, and yanked it free.

That did the job.

Neera gasped sharply and her eyes focused immediately. Nothing could bring a person around better than some good old pain.

"Wake Yanlin to Fix your leg, then rouse the others. We must hurry before Avryn and his companions wake up."

At that moment, the assassin stirred softly near them, as if saying the words made it happen. Prost cursed to himself, and kicked Jord awake. After seeing Neera rise up and hobble towards Yanlin, their only Fixer on this job, Prost rushed to his horse. Placing the limp boy on top of the horse, he jumped up on the back and kicked him into motion. Surely the sound of his horse hooves would wake some of them up, but he couldn't risk wasting time engaged with Avryn in combat again. Distance was what would help him the most.

As the horse bounced up and down, Prost recounted the events of the fight near the falls. It was his custom to think back on engagements so that he could learn from mistakes and plan better for the next time. His engagement with Avryn had been less than ideal. Under normal circumstances, he would have been able to best a Lightbearer with ease, seeing as how their powers were rendered useless against him. Unfortunately, Avryn had been a skilled sword fighter before he had come into his Lightbearer powers. He had never really become dependent on his powers like *Tar'n* so often did. Prost suspected that his own swordsmanship was really the only thing that made those in Watchlight respect him.

No, not respect. Fear.

Prost had spent the entire fight engaged with Avryn. No matter what he had done, Avryn was always there, somehow faster. While he rode, flashes from the fight came to his mind. He saw himself stab towards Avryn's stomach, only to have the sword knocked away. His opponent's sword reciprocated with a jab of his own, but Prost blocked that and swung at Avryn's arm, the closest exposed body part. The man only danced backwards easily.

The memory changed then. He was still fighting Avryn, but the man was young, in his teenage years. His blue eyes were framed by his long blond bangs, and they were sparkling with happiness. Avryn's hair was shorter, like he had always kept it when they were young. Prost jabbed him, but Avryn dodged. Nostalgia blossomed in Prost's mind and chest.

Growling loudly, Prost clenched his teeth and urged the horse forward more quickly. That was the past, and he'd never see it again. Things had changed. No longer were they the simple youths with nothing better to do than to spar and waste their time staring at the clouds.

Though he had forced such thoughts from his mind, there was a piece of him that missed that time. The time when they were young and innocent. That was also the part of himself he hated. The part of him that was weak. The part that would destroy him if he wasn't careful. Riln had given him strength, power, an army for fog's sake. He didn't want anything else.

Prost inhaled sharply, hoping the smell of the chilly evening air would clear his thoughts. Fortunately, it did just that. He could make out the distinct smell of the water wafting from the falls he'd just left. Grateful that it had worked, Prost shifted his mind to Riln. He hoped that at least once he would gain the approval from his master he craved. Sure, Riln *claimed* that he was pleased with Prost's work, but no, Prost could tell that it was a ruse. Lacking powers at all seemed to disappoint the Watchlight leader more than anything.

The sound of horse hooves behind him made him pause his thoughts for a moment. His hands clenched the reigns and he almost kicked his horse into a mad dash, but he waited tensely. Turning around, he strained his eyes to see not one, but two horses coming up behind him. Fortunately, they bore a distinct feature that put the man at ease: a brilliant red ball of Light hovering above them. Neera and Jord rode up to Prost and nodded to him.

"Yanlin Fixed me up good, and he was working on the others before we rode out. Alts took a bad beating. She lost a hand and took a sword to her stomach. He said it would just take a while to get her all Fixed up right. Vint and Lathe stayed back just in case our . . . *visitors* woke up and attacked again, though they hadn't stirred a mite while we were there."

Prost grumbled his assent, but didn't say more. He did like working with Neera, she was less insufferable than that horrible Mert, whom he was very disappointed to hear hadn't died. It would have been the perfect way to be rid of the dolt without killing him himself. The three horses' hooves clopped together for a time, and no one said anything until Neera broke the silence again.

"That was a rough awakening for sure. What is he, then? Didn't see anything but the Mover blast that threw me far."

Jord spoke this time.

"I think I saw 'im glowin' in the eyes a bit. Likely a Seer as well."

Neera whistled softly.

"Well that's right nice, I'll say, a Mover and a Seer, could be handy for sure. Riln will—"

"Conjurer." Prost said bluntly, interrupting whatever thought she had.

"Hmm?" Neera asked.

"He's a Conjurer, too, I saw the rings floating around him before his Mover blast knocked you all to the ground.

A soft but high pitched whistle came out of Neera's mouth.

"Well, I'll be. He's got three of 'em. No wonder Riln sent so many of us this time. He'll be quite an add to Watchlight." Neera said.

Prost looked down at the form of the boy slouched forward on his horse. The boy was already special to Riln, and for that, he hated him.

* * *

Marric felt as if the world was spinning, a blur of unrecognizable colors flashing through his mind. Without any pattern or explanation, the blurs would stop abruptly on something; a person, a place, some event that he didn't understand or recognize. It was as if he was traveling great distances in a matter of moments. Fortunately, some of the images that he was seeing were good ones. However, some of them were terrible.

All that he could recall just before now was seeing Jord, and then collapsing from the blinding pain that filled his whole being.

Then he was here.

The vision of his home burning lasted a moment longer before shifting to the forest. There he was with Avryn and the others, standing ready to fight. All at once, a large group of spine hogs attacked them, coming hard and fast. He saw Janis flashing through the mob, dropping some of them easily. He saw Avryn blow a few up with his Destroying, his face serious as he did so. Then there was the flash of light, a Shield of brilliant blue, only thrice the size of a dinner plate, blocked spines headed for Marric. He felt his leg burn with memory pain where the spines had pierced him simultaneously as they struck him in the strange vision-memory.

Blurs overcame his vision once again and he found himself facing *him*—the white-skinned man—staring at him with a smile that chilled Marric to the bone.

"Well, well, this will be much easier now that we can save some time." Riln said.

His voice was much higher pitched than Marric would have guessed, though he couldn't describe why he thought the pale man's voice would have sounded any different. With a start, he realized that he could see more than he had the last time he'd seen the strange man. They were in a throne room of some kind, with stone pillars that lined the hall both left and right. There were no others in the room, just the white-skinned man and himself. Marric wasn't sure where he was at the moment. For all he knew, his body was still by the falls. Or maybe Avryn and Janis had brought him to their destination. He couldn't even tell how long he'd been unconscious, but he knew for sure that he was at this moment.

"What? No greeting from my visitor?"

Marric looked around the room for another person, but found none. Staring at the strange man, he inspected his choice of clothing. He wore a really thick and bushy robe of a deep maroon color. The sleeves were wide and hung down by his sides, even when he clasped his hands together. It came to the floor, so Marric couldn't see his feet at all. Where the style had originated, Marric couldn't say, but it was odd indeed.

"Marric."

The boy's skin crawled. His eyes snapped to the face of the strange man and he stared, eyes wide.

"Yes, yes, I know that you are here. Seer visions can be a bit jarring for some time after your awakening. Rest assured that we can help you control them and use them for your own benefit. We have a lot to offer you, in fact."

Seer visions? Marric thought. *What is he saying?*

"Of course, Seeing is not your only gift, from what I gather? Let's have a look, why don't we?"

The man lifted his puffy-sleeved arm and waved it once through the air. The columned throne room melted away around them. All Marric could see was darkness, everywhere. Just black. Above him, around him, even under his feet. It was as if the world became nothing.

Suddenly, after a pulling sensation, a deafening roar filled his ears, making him flinch. There was ground under his feet again, grassy and soft. There were trees all around them, and Marric saw two black-robed figures standing near the treeline, hoods pulled back. A blond boy stood facing them, bow ready with a nocked arrow, bent over in apparent pain, but frozen, unmoving. And there was . . .

Janis, he thought, surprised.

She was frozen in time somehow, rushing toward the boy, it seemed. Chest tightening, he realized who the blond boy was.

It was himself, facing the dark-skinned woman and . . . Jord. The friend he thought he'd lost years ago. Jarred by the sight of himself, he stepped back, uncertain.

All at once, his surroundings became familiar. The loud roaring was the giant waterfall, three-sided and dumping the torrent of water. He saw

Avryn, engaged with the scar-faced man. There was Harmel and Shrell, one of them on the ground and the other engaging another black-robed figure with his arms outstretched. But something was off.

Besides the fact that everyone he saw was frozen as if time had stopped itself, Marric realized that the waterfall had also stopped moving. Yet the roaring in his ears persisted.

But how . . . how can I hear something that isn't moving?

Additionally, he realized that he could see in the darkness. That wasn't true of just this interaction with Riln, but he had been able to see during the past events as well, and hadn't tried to figure out how and why until now. Looking upwards, he saw at least a dozen large red Light orbs. Each was just slightly bigger than his own head. They were scattered around the clearing, shining down on all the frozen figures. Each cast its own eerie red Light on the ground.

Lightbearer orbs. Someone had lit the whole area, Marric thought. It couldn't have been Avryn, for he said that he could only create a small one. Also, his were blue, not red.

The voice next to him made his body chill.

"Let's watch it over again, shall we?"

Marric didn't turn to the side, for fear of seeing the man up close. Instead, he saw a thick sleeve pull upward and a hand wave in his right peripheral.

Everyone moved again. He saw Janis moving quickly toward him, while the blonde woman collapsed to the ground behind her, left in Janis's destructive wake like most things were. Looking toward himself, he saw himself collapse to his knees.

The memory of the pain blossomed in his own body and he grimaced at the thought. The pain had been so intense that he had lost all sense of the world around him, and instead had passed out into instant dreams.

Without warning, a blue light, bright and piercing, appeared from that direction. Lifting his hand to shield his eyes, Marric tried to locate the source. When he did, he gasped.

Short beams of Light were shooting from his—or his past self's—eyes. Marric didn't understand it, but there it was, the Light piercing the dark treeline and the figures around him. He looked eerie and unnatural, kneeling with his head elevated and arms outstretched.

"There it is. Seeing is the first to manifest itself during the awakening process. That very power is what makes us have such a strong connection at this moment."

Marric stood there watching, dumbfounded by the sight. He was so enthralled with the scene that he hardly heard the comment from the white-skinned man.

While he watched, four rings of Light appeared, surrounding him, followed by four columns. They weren't *full columns* like you might see in a home, but rather short columns that capped off a few handspans above his head while hovering above the ground a bit as well. Twirling slowly around him, it seemed like he was being watched over by four stone guardians.

"Conjuring. Useful, but then again, we have many of those already. Alts, as you can see there."

Marric's attention was lost as the pale man moved into view, almost blocking the sight of his awakening. Turning to see where his strange companion was pointing, he saw the blonde woman, a read streak in her hair somehow, lying on the ground, incapacitated by Janis. There was blood coming from an open wound in her stomach, and she appeared to be missing a hand.

His stomach churned with sickness.

A flash in his side vision brought him back to himself. He turned to see a dome of Light, very faint, yet distinguishable, moving outwards from himself. As soon as the Light hit Janis and the duo of black-robed people, they were all thrown backwards. Gasping, the present Marric reached out his hand as if he could stop it. Nothing happened, of course, and Janis slammed into a tree. The dome expanded, hitting everyone and everything, knocking them back, swaying the trees.

He was dying. Somehow he knew that. Marric realized that he was unconscious by this point, so he'd been seeing visions and images that spared him from this whole experience. The past Marric's body began to droop, face pale, life draining from him, while all at once another bright flash, pure white this time, pierced his eyes, causing his present self to flinch away.

Just as he opened his eyes, a second dome of blue Light pulsed and knocked everyone away again. Except . . . movement to his right drew his attention and he saw that the scar-faced man was standing, as if unaffected.

"Ah, yes," the robed man said, "Prost cannot be affected by any Light-bearer. It is a strange anomaly, but can be quite useful. Though we are of the Light, he seems . . . of the void."

The look on his face as he said this was disgust with a mixture of annoyance.

"But what *I* am more interested in, is how you didn't die. Awakening with three powers, such as you did, often kills the person. Perhaps it was the doing of that bright white Light we just saw, from your lower person."

A memory hit Marric's mind, rough and quick. Instinctively, he reached down to his belt but felt nothing there.

The rabbit foot. From the old woman!

It was clear that the man was trying to force Marric to tell, but the boy played ignorant.

"I—I'm not sure. But—what do you mean *three* powers?"

Scowling at his response, the strange man turned back to the now frozen image of Marric lying on the ground, scar-faced man looming over him, then looked at the present Marric again. His displeasure was obvious, but he wasn't going to press the issue.

"Seer, Conjurur, Mover. That is you. Your new identity. And it is how you will be recognized as a champion in my court."

The words seemed even more strange and unfamiliar than any he had heard before. He hadn't thought of his awakening as giving him a new identity, nor did he really want that to be the case. Also, he never thought that he could be considered a champion of anything, save perhaps the champion of being useless in any fight.

"But how? I don't even know how to use them and—"

"We shall teach you, don't you see? I have trained and helped countless new Lightbearers to harness the powers that they possessed to become great. I have seen sniveling children become strong and powerful warriors in half the time it took for their parents to teach them any responsibilities at all. You are no exception to this."

He said this last part with a sneer and looked Marric up and down disdainfully.

"Of course, there is no forcing you. Should you feel the desire to move in a different direction and *not* accept my offer to train you, take you under my wing, so to speak, your other options are far less . . . liberating."

At the last bit, he held out his hand and a flash of red Light appeared there. After the initial burst, Marric saw a dagger made of red Light, clutched in his unnaturally white hand. It was exquisite, intricate, and quite beautiful. How Marric could see such detail in something made from Light, he couldn't tell, however, it was enthralling.

The white man made a point of lifting the knife up and brandishing it before Marric. The threat of the act was lost on the boy though, because he was locked on the beauty and majesty of the thing.

Perhaps it wouldn't be such a horrible thing to learn from him. It's clear that he knows how to use his powers well, and perhaps he'd be more open and forthcoming about my new powers than Avryn has been.

This thought caused his gut to twist and writhe. How could he possibly just abandon his friends? How could he give all that up to join a group that had just tried to kill them all, for Lanser's sake? Marric scolded himself for even thinking that it could be a viable option.

Oh, but that beautiful dagger. Avryn's Conjures bore no such beauty or finesse.

Without warning, the man thrust the dagger through the palm of his other hand, then twisted the red dagger. Blood gushed down his white arm and ran to the floor where it pooled, making a red puddle.

Marric's stomach twisted and he wrapped his arms around his body, unable to move his eyes away from the macabre scene before him. The man smiled at the boy's response, and pushed the dagger slightly further, acting as if it caused him no pain at all.

"As I mentioned, your other option is far less agreeable. In short, we will kill you. We can't have you sharing information about us or where we are located. Once my warrior delivers you here, the choice must be made. Progress, or meet an end. Grow, or simply die. The choice is yours."

Finally, Marric was able to tear his eyes away from the horror before him. He crouched down and put his hands on his head. Fear gripped his very being and he was unable to think of anything else.

"Oh, and Marric. Remember that all wounds can be healed. Pain is but a teaching method."

A slowly pulsing light in his side vision caused Marric to look upwards and see that the man had removed the knife and was holding his cut-free hand over the other. The blood had stopped, and instead, the hand was knitting back together very quickly. In an instant, the cut was gone and the blood with it.

"Power comes only to those that sacrifice the things that make them weak. We will break you, Marric, but we will make you strong as a result. You approach quickly, and once you arrive, you must choose. Greatness, or death."

The sides of Marric's vision blurred and he got tunnel vision, the bone-white man being the only clear image for a moment. Then he shrunk, moving into the distance as if he was being sucked away. A horrid smile was all that adorned his face.

Marric knew at that moment that he couldn't possibly choose to join such a person.

But he felt like he had no other choice.

* * *

Janis kicked the horse into action, urging it forward more quickly. She couldn't make it run as fast as was possible, for that would make it too challenging to track their quarry. That frustrated her. Under normal circumstances, she wouldn't feel so rushed, and she could track her target with a little less urgency.

This was different.

The forest seemed more damp than usual, as if she'd just missed another drizzle of rain in this part. The air was more dense and wet, but not so dense as to indicate that heavy rainfall occurred, most likely just a mist of rain. That smell mixed pleasantly with the earthen smell that often accompanied a forest, creating an aroma that most would find very pleasing and relaxing.

Janis didn't have time to consider such pleasantries. After being knocked back by the strange light force, she had lost consciousness. Waking up had been more difficult than usual, likely because of the nature of the cause of her unconsciousness. This bothered her—she could normally wake up very quickly. By the time she had awoken, most of the others were stirring or awake already. Avryn was healing her cut arm when she came to, noticing that Marric was gone, along with a few of the black robed figures.

It was fortunate, however, that one of them had just made it to their horse and was climbing on. Janis had ripped him down to the ground and taken his horse. He looked both perplexed and bothered by her treatment of him, which made her laugh internally, considering the black-robed group had just assaulted the lot of them. This made forcing him to the ground and taking his horse that much more satisfying to her.

The sound of the horse's racing hooves clopped on the ground, muffled by the greenery and fallen leaves. Though muffled, the silence of forest and night seemed to amplify the sound, making her feel like she was announcing her pursuit. Stealth was definitely her strong suit, but at this very moment, it would do her little good. The further ahead Marric's captors were able to go, the less likely she'd be able to find him and bring him back to—

She cursed.

Janis just realized that she had no idea where Avryn was planning to take them. She knew that they were close, but based on his description of the place, and the fact that it hadn't been discovered by Watchlight and all their Seers meant that she had little chance of locating it on her own.

With a huff, she pushed the thought out of her mind. This wasn't an oversight or a mistake, the urgency required that she not take the time to discover that information. The moment she had realized that Marric was gone with Prost, she had immediately locked onto her objective: to get

Marric back.

Janis strained her eyes, looking for signs of tracks, and she was able to see some. It was fortunate that the moon seemed to brighten suddenly, as if the rain clouds from before had just disappeared in a moment, without cause at all. The hoof prints were deep in the ground, which made her think about how additionally fortunate she was that a rainstorm had just passed, but stopped seemingly the moment her quarry's horse passed through.

Not knowing how far ahead they may have gotten, she clicked her tongue and pushed the horse to a quicker pace. Time was definitely not a luxury right now. She only hoped that the horse wouldn't keel over dead before she was able to catch up to them.

Once she caught up to them, then what?

She couldn't be sure how many of the black-robed figures had managed to wake up and move out before her. Probably at least two or three, she guessed. Also, Janis wasn't even sure if they were all together, or moving in the same direction. There were indications of multiple hoof tracks that wove in and out of trees here and there, but they always seemed to come back to the one that she was following. This is what led her to believe that she was following the right one.

That, and her gut.

Even though she disliked riding horses so much, she was quite skilled at the practice. Macks had always taught her to be a master of all trades. Admittedly, this had been the *least* amount of fun to learn, especially compared to dagger fighting and knife throwing, but she had learned it. Despite her dissatisfaction of the practice, her mind seemed to sync with the horse, the thrum of the hooves on the ground bringing clarity to her mind and her mission.

Her mission.

Janis couldn't describe why she was even following Marric. She likely could have just let the boy go join Watchlight, or possibly even die, and be on her way. She imagined that Watchlight would even leave her alone after that. The danger of Watchlight *was* the original reason she had joined the escapade in the first place, but it no longer seemed to be a problem. Perhaps it was the opportunity to learn about Lightbearers and how to fight them that kept her here.

Something had changed and she couldn't quite describe what it was. All she knew was that she couldn't let the boy die. Janis somehow knew that a group like this wouldn't take no for an answer. Based on the softness of the boy, she knew that he would decline their invitation to join them.

Then, they would kill him.

* * *

Marric could feel cool air blowing on his face, yet somehow he wasn't awake yet. He could feel sunlight, which felt warm and inviting on his skin as well. The last thing he could remember was a pale face and a wicked grin. Then, just blackness. This was the first physical sensation that he had felt since then, and he wasn't sure whether or not it was a good thing. Little by little, other senses attuned to wherever he was. He could hear grass whooshing softly in the field. The smell of fresh morning air mixed with wildflowers filled his nostrils. The harsh but rhythmic and almost intoxicating feel of the up and down motion of his body pulled him out of his sleep, or whatever he was doing at the moment.

He didn't *feel* like he was asleep, but there was no other way to describe what he was at the moment. The strange man he presumed was Riln had mentioned that Marric was on his way there now, yet Marric had no awareness of traveling. The feeling that the pale man left him, plus what he had said gave Marric the impression that his intentions were not good. With how Avryn's moral reasoning was, there wasn't even the possibility that the two were associated. Though Riln hadn't said it, Marric now knew that this was Watchlight, and if he was on his way there now, that meant he would soon be facing the man he'd heard Janis and Avryn talking about—the man he'd just Seen.

Forcing his eyes open felt really difficult to him. Eyes feeling heavy, it was as if the pull of the earth had grasped his lids and was forcing them downward. With what seemed like an inordinate amount of effort, Marric forced open his eyes just a crack and winced away from the light. It was so bright that it almost hurt. However, the sweetness of the air and the peacefulness of the sounds around him made him too curious to keep them closed.

After leaving his eyes slightly open, they adjusted to the bright sunlight and he was able to push them open further until he could make out the horizon. It was slanted, which, for a moment, seemed to make him feel a little bit of vertigo, until he got his bearings and realized that they were climbing a steep hill. He remained still for now, only moving his eyes. For some reason, he didn't want to alert anyone around him that he was awake. Marric could feel the body of someone behind his, but he couldn't quite tell who they were.

The world around him was beautiful. He had to force himself not to gasp at the sight. It appeared to be morning, for the sun was still low, but it was rising into the sky, its light shining on a vast field of green grass—this was what was causing the swishing sound he had just recognized a moment ago.

It wasn't the grass blowing that caught his attention the most, but instead the vibrant flowers that sprung up in the midst of the thick, tall, grass. There were so many colors. Blues, reds, oranges, purples, yellows, even flowers with brown petals, which Marric had never seen before. They all danced in the wind as the grass did around them. The smell of the flowers filled his nose and warmed his body up in a familiar way.

Marric subtly tilted his head back so that he could see who rode behind him. It was obviously a male, whose black robe seemed stark against the wilderness background. Out of the corner of Marric's eyes, he saw the face of the man, and his blood froze. Instantly, nausea gripped his stomach and he could feel his face pale.

Twin scars, gruesome and wicked, pulled at the edges of a nose, nostrils flared, up to his ears. The familiarity of the face was not a welcome sight. Prost likely knew his prisoner was conscious, but refused to acknowledge it in favor of not having to converse with him. Forcing his eyes away from the man, he focused on the scenery around him, which had dulled now that he realized who he was with. He was reminded where he was going, making his chest constrict with fear.

Suddenly, the world around him took on an even sharper familiarity. It wasn't the familiarity that he had been experiencing only moments before—that was merely his mind reminiscing of similar places and sights he had seen throughout his life. No, this was different.

He had been here before.

Somehow, though he didn't know how, he *knew* this place. This was odd, for he was sure he'd never been to this place before, let alone this exact place on this very mountain. Yet, it was as if he knew every little feature and characteristic of the mountainside around him. He looked slightly left, and sure enough, there was a large boulder, bigger than himself and even the horse that he rode on, that was shaped like a small mountain, cone-like, almost pointed at the top and sloping down all sides.

He shifted his eyes to the right, and as he'd Seen before, there were some mountain goats, grazing together, regal with their large and twisting horns. As if he knew what would happen, he watched them slowly move closer, grazing all the time.

That means I'm about to see the jutting rock, Marric thought.

As expected, there was a passageway opening jutting out of the mountain just before them. His stomach wrenched. He wasn't sure if it was the oddness that he knew exactly how and where everything was in this exact spot, or the fact that this was their destination. The knowledge that he had to join a group that attacked and murdered people, and likely did all sorts of other deplorable things, didn't help matters. He knew that through the passage were red-lit halls, filled with guards and other people, and that man, Riln. The man that would either change his life, or take it.

A moment of realization hit him as the doorway, filled with a regular-sized stone door, grew larger as they moved toward it. In the forest where he and his friends were attacked, just after his body was wrenched in terrible pain, but just before everything went black, he had seen this exact thing. Somehow, he had seen this very moment in time, which is why he felt like he had been here before.

A Seer vision. That's what happened when I—

Marric didn't want to think the word, for it brought both excitement that he had received his powers, but also fear because he hadn't had any time to learn them or be taught them by Avryn. That meant that he would either use them for ill, or not use them at all. Looking up, he saw that they had arrived at the doorway.

Chapter 18

The doorway and the hall that lay behind it were far more imposing than they seemed in Marric's vision the night before. Everything was made of stone and bathed in red. Orbs of red Light, about the size of his own head, hovered near the tops of the walls periodically throughout the hallway. They were spaced six or seven paces apart from each other, but that wasn't far enough to break the constant Light as they traveled between two orbs.

Prost had shaken him before pulling him roughly off the horse. The boy considered himself lucky that he'd already been awake and just feigning sleep, for he was confident that this man wouldn't have let him take the time to fully wake up before shoving him into the stone doorway. That would likely have resulted in him pitching forward down the stairs that stood just beyond the stone door, and inevitably injury, for the stairs were very steep, and seemed to go down forever.

After reaching the bottom of the steep stairs, they came to yet another doorway, though this one had no door. Passing through, they came upon two guards standing still to either side. Both were clothed in black, like the others he had encountered before.

Why do they wear black clothes so much? Marric thought.

One of the robed figures had their hood up so their face couldn't be seen. The other had his hood back. When they got closer, Marric gasped in shock. The man had spikes, at least a dozen, jutting through each ear from lobe to the top. He also had a spike through the bridge of his nose. The sight looked so horrible and frightening that Marric stopped for a moment, unable to move. Even more surprising was the reaction of the guard to Marric's stopping. Rather than growl, roar, or even glare at the boy for reacting in such a way, the man smiled and winked at him.

Unsure what to think of that, Marric resolved to just keep moving. Prost surprisingly hadn't noticed his pause, nor had he scolded him. For a beat, Marric thought he might have a chance to turn around and run away, but that thought didn't last long. He had no hope of outrunning the large man, and he expected the guards, despite the wink and smile from the one, would stop him and likely kill him. He had a distinct feeling that the guards weren't just to keep things out, but to keep people *in*.

After a short hallway, they passed through another doorway and into a chamber. Marric's eyes immediately widened and his mouth dropped open slightly. The 'chamber' that they'd entered wasn't so much a chamber as it was a chasm. The ceiling extended far overhead, creating what looked like a red-starred night sky. When they moved forward, he could see over the edge of the pathway that they had just come from. The ground, like the ceiling, was so far below that it looked like an identical starry night sky, gravity being the only tell that indicated the direction as down versus up.

Marric was immediately overcome by vertigo and he wobbled on his feet. Before he could pitch forward and fall down the deep pit, a firm hand gripped his shoulder and pulled him backwards.

"I can't have you dying before we see Riln. Your life isn't worth much to me, but he would not take your death well, which means it wouldn't end well for me."

The comment came through what sounded like gritted teeth. Anger exuded from his captor, so much so that it was almost palpable in the air. Fortunately, despite Prost's obvious and apparent anger toward him, the man allowed Marric to sit for just a moment before he urged them on. After the vertigo passed, Marric could see that tiers of ramps spiraled around the chasm up, and also down, leading to landings and other doorways or terraces lining what seemed like the entirety of the chasm.

He wasn't sure how Prost knew where he was going, but without any hesitation, the man turned and started making his way up the ramp to the right. This shouldn't have surprised Marric, for he suspected that Prost had been familiar with this place for some time, but he couldn't understand how anyone could keep their directions straight, let alone know where to find anything in this lair.

Marric started to feel claustrophobic. The cavern to the left of him was enormous, and even the pathways that lined the cavern—especially the one that they walked on now—were large, so the feeling seemed out of place. Looking up at the ceiling just above him, he recalled how deep underground they were. A pit in his stomach formed and he realized that his claustrophobia wasn't completely unreasonable.

As they walked, he started paying attention to those around him. Most of them were black robed, but there were some people who were not. Besides the strangeness of the wardrobe, everything seemed normal, like what you'd find in a normal city or town. Some shops were set up on the sides of the wide pathways, where people sold various things; there were people talking, laughing, and even some children playing along the way. Marric didn't really know why this seemed strange, but it felt wrong. He hadn't known what to expect coming to Watchlight's lair, but it wasn't this.

They didn't continue upwards very long before they turned away from the large cavern and stopped just outside a stone archway. Prost stiffened when they arrived, which made Marric even more nervous to be there. There was a distinct feeling of finality that exuded from the archway, despite the fact that he didn't even know where they were or what lay behind it. Regardless, Prost stood up a bit straighter and stalked into the room without a word. Not sure what to do, Marric just followed, slumping his shoulders in nervousness.

Stone pillars loomed just on the other side of the stone archway, framing a long hall. At first, Marric thought that it was just another hallway with more adornments, but this one was distinctly darker, which made it feel less like a passageway and more like a dungeon. The pillars were massive, but well made, evenly spaced, and mirroring each other to each side. Everything was stone. Scanning the room a bit more, Marric's eyes caught on a throne that stood at the front of the room.

Oh—so this is the throne room, Marric thought, somehow pleased that the puzzle was revealed. *But where is the man that I Saw?*

As if in response to his thought, a voice sounded from the shadows.

"So . . . you've finally come."

The voice was high, raspy, and slow. Chills ran up and down Marric the moment he heard the voice coming from the darkness to his left. It was one that he recognized, a voice that brought dread at what was coming.

Slinking out of the darkness came the man that he'd only seen in what he thought were dreams. It became apparent, however, after their most recent encounter, that they weren't imaginations of his mind. As the sickly looking man approached, Marric was even more disturbed than the first time he'd seen him because his skin carried a reddish tone. Then again, everything had the same coloring in this whole place. Eyes flashing upwards, Marric saw a lone red globe of Light hovering directly in the middle of the ceiling, high above. Of course that was the reason for the man's red features. However, the whiteness of his skin made the red seem to seep into it more brilliantly.

Marric shivered at the sight.

"Riln." Prost said with reverence, inclining his head to the pale man.

He wore a heavy robe once again, though this time it was a dark purple color.

No, not purple . . . . the boy thought.

The robe was actually a deep blue color, but the red glow above made it seem purple. Marric wondered if anyone ever got used to the red Light here. If it was merely a supplemental illumination, the sun being the primary source, it might not be so bothersome. However, there appeared to be no other source of light in the caverns.

Marric examined the man's clothing and found that there seemed to be far too much fabric. Ruffles ran from the shoulders of the robe down each sleeve to the cuffs. In the dim Light, he couldn't quite count, but there had to be at least seven layers on the robe.

Lanser's beard, isn't that hot *to wear all the time?!*

"We can make you one just like it, if you please."

Blinking, Marric took a step back, not sure what to say. The strange man was staring directly at his own eyes, unwavering, a slight smile adorning his face. As if to emphasize the design of his robe, he brought his hands together, letting the wide sleeves fall toward the ground, the edges pushing together.

"Umm . . . no thank you—sir." Marric said.

Using 'sir' seemed awkward, yet fitting in this situation. Using this form of address also seemed to make the man's smile deepen, as if he was susceptible to deference, even when offered casually.

"No matter, we shall soon have you made a new wardrobe—you'll not need those clothes any longer. They are impractically made for our purposes."

He waved one of his hands dismissively while he made that last comment. Turning, the man walked back to one of the pillars and caressed the wall softly with his white hand. It was clear that he was remembering something, for the look on his face was dreamlike, wistful. For a leader of such a group, Marric thought he was oddly quiet, and seemed unimposing.

Riln's hand moved down the pillar slightly and rested on a black spot there. He turned and looked at Marric, sizing him up. Marric was focused on the black mark, and squinted in the Light to examine what it was. His eyes widened when he realized it was a hole. It was distinctly a slit-hole, one that matched a sword or a knife.

How odd, Marric thought, *a sword couldn't cut through a stone pillar like that.*

The strange man noticed Marric's gaze and chuckled to himself.

"Yes, you can see that Lightbearing is far stronger than you think."

Holding out his palm, a bright flash of red Light announced the arrival of his ornate dagger. It was just as Marric remembered it from his vision. The boy marvelled at the complexity of the design. He watched as Riln gripped the pommel tightly, then swung it sharply until it connected with the pillar with a loud crack. Sure enough, as the blade met the stone, it sunk in deep, not only creating a hole, but cracking it from the force of entering.

Marric's mouth fell open slightly. Wasn't Riln worried about damaging the integrity of his lair? Perhaps not when he could simply Fix it with his powers. Something stirred inside of Marric at this demonstration—was it excitement? Nervousness? Likely both.

Without thinking about it, Marric held out his hand and stared at it. He had just learned that he was supposed to be able to Conjure things as well; could they really be so strong *and* made of Light?

The boy was so wrapped up in his thoughts that he hadn't noticed Riln closing the gap between them until he felt the man's hand squeeze his shoulder. Marric jumped at the touch.

It wasn't a threatening squeeze, more like an encouraging one—the kind that you give to someone who doubts their abilities, or possibly even to someone that needs comfort.

"Such power is at the tip of your very own fingertips, my boy." Riln whispered, his voice audible only because of his close proximity to Marric. "You have awakened, become something far more powerful than a normal human. We are above all others. In a world of survival of the fittest, we *are* the fittest."

The words made a shiver go down Marric's spine, but not the kind that he'd felt multiple times during this encounter. Was that eagerness he felt, or excitement?

This felt wrong.

Yet he wanted to know more, he wanted to obtain this level of power. Marric hated the feeling he'd had when the others were fighting and he couldn't even lend any aid whatsoever. He had just stood there, not only being unhelpful, but making it harder for the others by putting himself in danger. This could change things.

Except I can only be helpful to Avryn and the others if I somehow make it back to them.

Something inside of him made him pause. He had the feeling that Riln was hiding something, though he couldn't understand where such a feeling could come from. Riln's hand continued to rest on Marric's shoulder, as if the man didn't want to let him go. Marric suddenly had the urge to run, to get out of the man's grip.

For a moment, no one said anything, until Marric could feel the man press his chest against Marric's back, bringing himself closer to the boy.

"As I said before, the very power is just at your fingertips. Shall we test it out?"

Shivers ran down Marric's back, this time, he was sure it was uneasiness. Riln's voice had taken on an urgent and somewhat forceful tone, as if he had asked Marric a question a long time ago and never received an answer. It was impatient. Marric had the distinct feeling that he didn't want to disappoint this man. He somehow knew that it would not end well for him. Not sure exactly what to do next, he figured he might as well just ask.

"What do I do?"

It seemed simple enough, innocent, meaningful, and short, but Riln breathed out behind him, seeming even more impatient. However, despite his apparent annoyance at Marric, he answered.

"The power feels different to each person, so I cannot tell you exactly what you need, but it is there. Just *use* it."

The last part was said through gritted teeth, as if he wanted to yell but was holding back so as to not scare him.

Just moments before, he seemed so pleased with my potential, and now he is so angry.

Marric's eyes flitted to where Prost was standing, aloof to the situation. He doubted that the burly man would do anything if Riln were to kill him, right here, right now, but for some reason, he felt more secure knowing he wasn't alone here with this bizarre man.

Though unsure of himself, Marric followed Riln's example from the moment before and held his hand up, palm open and toward the ceiling. Then, he concentrated. On what, he couldn't be sure. He imagined something there, a ball of Light, simple and small. He tried to imagine the feeling of warmth and comfort radiating into the skin of his palm, strong and sure.

Nothing.

His spirit sank. *Why wasn't this working?!*

Riln's grip tightened on his shoulder and Marric locked his jaw. The man was remarkably strong for how weak and sickly he looked.

"Do NOT play games with me, boy! Did you awaken or not?!"

Marric opened his mouth to say something, but nothing came out. Instead, he gasped in pain as Riln squeezed even harder. A flash of red Light to his left announced Riln's use of his own Lightbearing, and then something happened.

Marric's eyes felt as if he had widened them, opened them up as large as they could go, yet he hadn't moved them at all. The world around him changed. It looked generally the same, but instead with slightly blurred edges. He looked to the left to where the red Light had come and saw that Riln had summoned the beautiful dagger in his left hand. It really was quite exquisite, full of red jewels and ornate designs. He was wrapped up in the beauty of it until he watched as the dagger was whipped forward and plunged into his own side, burying deep into his flesh, blood pouring out around the Light dagger and the white hand that gripped it. He pitched forward and fell to the ground, stunned and dying.

Then it was gone. The blur wasn't there anymore, and Marric was standing there, in the same place, looking forward. However, the red Light was right next to him. Confused, he glanced over and saw Riln's hand, gripping the same ornate and beautiful knife. The hair stood up on his entire body as if lightning had struck closeby. Realizing what was about to happen, he threw himself forward on the ground, just before Riln shoved the knife sideways into the air where he had been standing only a beat before.

His heart pounded, his ears roared, but Marric spun around on the ground and backed away from the robed man in a backwards crawl. Marric wasn't sure how he'd seen that, but he was suddenly feeling unsure about what else Riln would do, a suspicion rising within him that he wouldn't survive this day.

Rather than looking angry or attacking again, Riln only laughed. He raised his white chin to the ceiling in what seemed an overly exaggerated way and laughed loudly, as if laughing at Lanser himself.

"Well, thank the world around us, you aren't completely useless then, are you? I suppose that means you pass the test, since you aren't bleeding at this very moment."

The words were macabre and threatening, but the smile on his face and the crows feet that spread from his eyes looked so pleasant. If it wasn't for the man's ominous presence and hostile emotions, Marric might not have felt so threatened.

That made this whole situation much worse. If Marric couldn't even begin to understand this man's motives or what he might do next, he wouldn't survive long.

"Your Seeing just saved your life, my boy. I'll admit, I was doubtful of your abilities, or that you were even worth our time here, but it seems that you are likely going to prove useful. Stand up."

Without much thought, and before Marric realized what the man even said, he was getting to his feet as quickly as possible. Standing at attention, Marric's whole body was stiff, as if he had to be ready for the next time Riln would attack him straight on. Marric opened and closed his hands, which were hanging down stiffly by his sides, and felt the perspiration that beaded there. This alerted him to the fact that his whole body was reacting in a similar way; sweaty and achy, as if he'd been stiff for hours, muscles becoming sore. He supposed that nearly dying would have that effect on a person.

"Now, Marric. You must show me your other gifts *now*. There isn't much time. The war is happening as we speak and we need warriors—champions. You will be one of these champions ushering in the new times."

Marric's brow furrowed.

"Sir? What new times?"

Riln spun on him, hands clasped together. At some point, he must have dismissed the dagger, for it was nowhere to be seen. This didn't make Marric feel any more secure in the situation. He knew just how quickly the weapon could be back in Riln's hand and coming toward his body.

"Don't you understand, boy? Lightbearers are superior, we are more powerful than normal humans. They should be our subjects, our servants, our soldiers, even. You've been born into the higher race, and it is now our time to take control and rule as we should. Now, *show me.*"

Marric's gut writhed at the words. Just moments before, he'd almost been killed by this man for taking too much time, and now he was demanding it again. Marric was too afraid to ask, but he was also afraid he would fail the test. Unsure of exactly what to do, he just stood there, perfectly still.

"Sir . . . how do I . . . ?"

"Ugglyn's pride, boy! Conjure something! A weapon of your choice!" Riln didn't yell, but his voice was forceful, urgent, impatient.

Trying to not overthink it, Marric held out his hand and thought of a bow, like the one that he'd carried on his journey. Straining his mind, he squeezed his eyes shut and furrowed his brow in concentration, but nothing seemed to be happening. Marric felt sweat at his brow, not from exertion, but from fright. Suddenly, his mind was on the bow and quiver that he'd brought with him. What had even happened to those? Had he left them by the falls? Were they taken from him when he was brought with Prost?

Behind his closed eyelids, the darkness flashed with a light, almost as if the sun unexpectedly rose, quick and bright. Opening his eyes, he saw a brilliant bow made out of blue light, resting in his hand. His mouth dropped open in disbelief. What was even more strange was that it didn't *feel* like anything other than a normal wooden bow, but it was definitely not made of wood. Marric had expected the Conjured items to feel different . . . warm, perhaps? Light often did accompany heat, like fire. But this . . . this was different. It felt like an ordinary bow.

"A bit unorthodox, but a display of Conjuring, nonetheless. Though it would be useless without any arrows." Riln said, raising a white eyebrow at him. He didn't explicitly say it, but Marric knew it was another challenge.

Inside, Marric could feel that something had changed—a doubt seemed to have dissolved. He couldn't describe it, but he held out his left hand, and an arrow instantly appeared, made also of the blue Light.

"Your Light is still blue," Riln said, a look of disgust on his face, "but no worries, we'll take care of that. It will shine red as it should in no time."

Marric continued to stare at the Light-made weapons in his hand, rubbing his fingers over the wood of the bow, the fletching on the arrow. They looked so fake, but felt so real.

"Well? Are you going to shoot the blasted thing or not?" Riln said. "Let's see your work, hmm?"

Jumping to attention, Marric looked at Riln and nodded, still saying nothing.

Marric paused then, realizing that there weren't really any good targets. An arrow couldn't pierce a stone wall or even a pillar.

"Fogging boy, just *shoot the arrow,*" he spat.

Marric reeled inside, but at the tone of Riln's command, fastened the arrow into place and pulled the string back. Gasping to himself, Marric realized how natural this felt. The bow felt exactly like the one he'd used for most of his life. It was as if the bow he knew so well had been changed into Light, the wood form disappearing completely.

Evening out his breathing, he concentrated as he'd become accustomed to when shooting with his bow. Marric was relieved that this had become a habit for him, and it felt natural and comfortable. He released the string and the familiar swish of the arrow flying hit his ears. With a crack, it struck the pillar, the same one that Riln had stabbed just before with the Light-made knife, and bounced off, clattering to the ground.

Riln pursed his lips, but nodded.

"Your Conjures are still weak, but you will learn. In time, that arrow will be able to pierce even the hardest of things. For now, I am pleased with what you've shown. Now, for your final power. Show me."

Marric just stood there. He had somehow forgotten that he should manifest a third power as well, and he wasn't sure what to do. It seemed silly, but he asked the first question that came to his mind.

"But . . . sir, what do I do with this?" he said as he raised the bow up slightly.

Riln stared at him in disbelief. Despite the look of frustration on his face, Riln spoke with a level tone and a calmness that made Marric feel even more in danger than he was before.

"Just *drop it.*"

It felt strange, but Marric did what the man said and just let the bow fall. To his surprise, it disappeared as it left his hands, becoming nothing. Marric felt like he couldn't revel in the wonder of how it worked, though he still paused to take it in, anyway. This was apparently the wrong choice, for Riln huffed again in impatience and clenched his fists to the side.

Raising his hands up, Marric hoped that something would happen, like when he had Conjured the bow and arrow, if he just moved his hands. Unfortunately, nothing did.

For a moment, they all stood there, quiet, watching. Marric could feel a bead of sweat run down the side of his cheek, and it felt alarmingly like an insect moving slowly downwards toward the nape of his neck in the darkness of the space underneath his clothing. It took a considerable amount of control for him to not wipe it away.

Come on . . . please. . . . Marric thought desperately. *Lanser—bless me, make this work!*

Despite his prayers, nothing happened.

Riln, clearly not willing to wait, growled in frustration and summoned his red-lit dagger, but this time, he was too far away to stab Marric. He had started pacing while they waited for something to happen, and had stopped eight or so paces away from where Marric stood, still in the spot where he'd been for the duration of the encounter so far. Thinking that the space would protect him from the sharp blade, Marric was shocked when, without warning, Riln hurled the dagger at him, directly at his chest.

Gasping, Marric dove to the side. He wasn't quick enough, however, and the blade sliced a gash in his arm. The sharp sensation of the cut seemed to pierce his mind, taking his attention away from all else. All he could feel was the pain. Up until now, before he met Avryn, Janis—Riln even, Marric had experienced very few encounters with pain. Yet, in just a matter of days, he'd been hurt so many times as to exceed all other experiences like them in his lifetime.

He still wasn't used to it.

After the initial sharpness of the pain subsided slightly, Marric could feel his fear again. He could feel the panic, the almost loss of control. Pushing through these feelings, he rose to his knees and looked for Riln, finding him in the same place. Without a word, the man gritted his teeth, summoned the blade again, and threw it at Marric.

Time slowed down. The dagger seemed to fly slowly, unnaturally, right toward Marric's face. Then it happened. Instinctively, he threw up his hands to block the incoming danger, and the knife, wreathed in blue light now, ricocheted off of some invisible force and clattered off to the side.

Riln smiled, though it didn't seem a happy smile, more like one that you see on the face of a child with a mischievous plan; a plan that isn't a good one for anyone but themselves.

Marric shook. Seeing knives threaten his life so many times was pushing him past a point that he'd never been to—he could feel himself about to break. All at once, pain in his arm pushed its way into his consciousness and he remembered where he'd been cut only moments before. The warm blood ran down his arm like the feeling of warm bath water, only slower and thicker. Then, he vomited.

He was in shock. Marric had only heard of this sensation from hunters who braved large beasts for the biggest kill. Or warriors that told stories of battles they'd won and even lost, lying on the ground feeling one's body take control of one's mind, and feeling close to death. Each limb felt cold to Marric, which seemed to emphasize the warmth of the blood that ran down his arm. Suddenly it felt comforting, as if it was the only heat he had to rely on. However, when he remembered the source, his stomach churned.

I can't be dying, can I? The cut wasn't that *deep.*

"Remarkable. It's been what seems like ages since I've seen a Lightbearer with multiple functioning powers upon awakening, particularly one that has survived the process. You are a special one indeed, Marric. You will be my champion. You will head the cause of Watchlight. You will usher in the new age, right by my side."

Marric was beginning to get dizzy. He fell to his knees, fearing that if he didn't, he would pass out completely, and this didn't seem like the time or the place for that to happen.

"I will teach you all that you need to know. Your powers will be so great that our enemies will fear you."

The boy listened, but passively. He could hardly understand what he was being told; his sickness, dizziness, and pain overtaking most of his capable senses.

There must be something I can do to control this. What can I do? Marric thought desperately.

Then he remembered something Avryn had said. What was it, exactly?

"*Lightbearers manifest all powers, though some are weak . . .* "

It felt like a dream, and he wasn't even confident that anything would happen, but recalling the memory of Avryn healing his own arm, the first time Marric had seen the man's Fixing, he tried to do the same. He remembered Avryn hovering his hand slightly over the wound and a dull Light flashing slowly, and when he moved it, the cut was gone. Riln continued to speak, but Marric heard none of it, focused only on that very moment that seemed like forever ago, but was only days in the past.

Slowly, he affixed his hand over the cut which seemed distant now that he was lost in memory, and felt his hand warm up slightly, as if a fire finally started to rise and send warmth to those sitting closeby. In his side vision, he saw the blue Light—small and dull, yet strong and pulsing. The pain subsided from his arm almost completely, though raw pink skin and some stinging remained. Then the Light was gone.

Riln stopped speaking and looked at Marric, curious.

"Ahh, well done. You aren't a Fixer by birth, but it seems that you've been able to make use of the limited power you have with it."

He raised a white eyebrow at Marric, clearly pleased, yet surprised at the same time.

Marric felt a thrill in his chest at using his powers. Riln had promised power and training, and he wanted to keep it close, to thrive in it. Before he could revel in his thoughts too long, he heard the words of the blind woman again.

"You'll have to make a choice where yeh stand 'ere soon. Untold challenges lie ahead. Trust yer gut and what yeh learn, and remember wha' true goodness is."

Inside, he knew Riln was twisted. He knew the promised power wouldn't be worth it. True goodness wasn't about just power for power's sake. It was about helping others—and that certainly wasn't the aim of Watchlight.

I have to get out of here, he thought.

"You must rest. But only for a short time. Your training begins today. Come, my boon, please take our newest member to rest." Riln said.

For a moment, Marric thought he was *'my boon'*, until a slim figure, clothed in the common black cloak came out of the shadows to his side. His hood was down, and Marric's breath caught as he saw who it was.

Jord.

So that wasn't a dream, then?

Hearing Marric's reaction to seeing Jord, Riln looked between the both of them, then spoke again.

"Ahh, yes, I had forgotten that there is a history between you two. How very fortunate that you are together again, part of the same family. Jord, take him. Begin teaching him our ways."

Eyes wide, Marric stared at Jord, who nodded curtly to Riln and walked toward him, not making any eye contact at all.

"Come." Jord said.

Feeling awkward, Marric stood up. Inside, he wanted to shout for joy and hug his friend, the one he'd missed for so many years, the one that he'd thought had been killed, lost from this world, but the air around his friend felt wrong. It felt dark, ominous, and unwelcoming. Conflicted, he reached out and grabbed Jord's arm, stopping the boy from turning away.

Immediately, a red burst of Light flashed on Marric's arm with a crack, breaking his hold as the sleeve of his shirt exploded to bits. Pain seared into his forearm from the microexplosion of his shirt, singeing the hair and leaving a red burn mark. Marric shouted in pain and held his newly injured arm to his stomach.

"Don't touch me."

Without another word, Jord turned and stalked out of the door, leaving Marric there, shaking with pain from his new injury.

Seeming even more instinctive this time, Marric Fixed his arm, though it wasn't complete. The slight pulse of the blue light felt so soothing, relaxing almost, and the pain went away completely for a beat. However, a red rash, almost like a healing burn, still ran its way from his wrist to the inside of his elbow.

He heard a chuckle from behind him and turned to see Riln laughing to himself.

"My boon has gained such control over his Destroying. You should consider yourself lucky, my boy. Six months ago, you likely would have lost an arm to his powers. I will have the same pride for you as you gain control over your new birthright. You'll find in time that you have no better family than us. Prost, if you would, it seems Jord is unwilling to wait for you. Please help Marric catch up with his old and soon-to-be new best friend."

Prost, who Marric had forgotten was present, stood with his back to a pillar, arms folded, and though he didn't know it was possible, seemed to have an even angrier look on his face. The anger didn't seem to be directed at him, but rather at Riln.

The burly scar-faced man grunted and nodded slightly. He then walked to Marric, gripped his upper arm, and hoisted him easily to his feet. It wasn't harsh, in fact, it felt gentle and considerate, and suddenly he seemed the least scary and imposing person in the room to Marric. That seemed odd considering how he felt about the man just before they came to this place.

The two of them moved into the hallway and started to walk up another ramp that ringed the large cavern.

Marric's mind raced. He couldn't stay here. This all felt wrong. He couldn't live this way, or with people that treated him so. Riln spoke of family, of friends, of power, but none of it felt right. He had to escape, but the whole place was crawling with black-robed figures, many of whom kept their hoods up, hiding their faces.

How can they live this way? How can they continue being treated like this?

A tear fell from his eye and cascaded down his cheek. He hated crying, but there wasn't anything else he could do at the moment.

One such black robed figure suddenly stepped in front of Marric and Prost, blocking their path.

"What in the blazes are you—"

Marric heard Prost grunt and jump backwards. He didn't see what happened, but a strong arm gripped his own and yanked him back down the hallway before turning sharply to the left and away from Riln's throne room in a different direction.

"Fog it! Stop!" Prost yelled.

His own feet were moving fast, almost too fast for him to keep up. The black-robed figure didn't let go, nor did they slow their pace. The two ran at a break-neck pace, moving down the ramp. Marric couldn't breathe, he felt like he might pass out, exhausted from the travel and the previous events. He thought he should have felt scared, but he was too tired at the moment.

Chancing a look backwards, he saw Prost barreling after them, pushing through people and shouting about intruders. Suddenly, however, Prost fell forward, landing on his hands and knees and coughing.

"Stop . . . them—" then he collapsed.

Marric stared in shock at Prost and then looked at the figure standing next to him. Pulling the hood back, Marric saw raven black hair, dark eyes, and the most cheering thing possible.

Janis had come.

Chapter 19

Janis yanked on Marric's hand to pull him forward faster. It was ironic that someone of his age and size could hinder their progress so easily, but he was clearly out of sorts at the moment. The stone felt extra hard against her feet as they ran, likely because she usually tried to keep to the softest part of the ground in order to maintain stealth. No, it wasn't impossible to be stealthy on a stone floor such as this, it just required more attention and effort. Unfortunately, her companion had no such practice and his feet clopped on the floor noisily.

Pursuing Marric and Prost had been far less challenging or exciting than she had thought, but perhaps she should have considered herself lucky in that. Janis hadn't given much thought to her plan, she just knew that she couldn't be too far behind the two, otherwise tracking them would have been nearly impossible. She *had* run into several hooded figures that were trailing further behind their leader, but daggers had made quick work of them. She felt little remorse considering they ambushed Janis and her companions first. Entering the lair was more risky, given the close quarter. She couldn't leave corpses everywhere anymore. Luckily, she still had some poisons that made victims fall asleep instantly or get violently sick. Just before she slipped into the lair, she had coated her blades with as much as she had.

Shouts continued behind them as the two barreled down the ramp to the next doorway. Fortunately for both of them, the way out was not that far from where Marric had his audience with the pasty man.

As they rounded the corner, Janis honed her hearing to determine how far behind them their pursuers were. Her urgency increased as she realized that they were not too far behind. Echoes of footsteps rang through their cavern, announcing that the feet making them were just nearby. Janis rushed through the door, yanking Marric along and past the first guards. Hovering still near the top of the walls, the red orbs seemed to intensify, making the passageways even more ghastly and disturbing.

A flash of Light appeared in the final doorway and Janis had to dig her feet in to stop their movement. The initial flash then filled the doorway with a wall of red Light.

Fog it, we're trapped! Janis thought.

Spinning around, she saw four or five black robed figures fill the hallway, blocking off their escape. Janis immediately drew her daggers and thanked Lanser that she'd thought to coat the blades with the poisons before coming in here. Crouching down, she prepared to pounce on the closest figure, a man with long hair and pock-marked cheeks.

Just before she was able to slice him, however, the man was wreathed in blue Light, bright and intense, and he was thrown backwards into his companions, creating a fuss of black cloth and shouting. Confused, Janis looked to the side to see Marric, looking determined, with his hand outstretched.

Did he just—? Janis was unable to finish the thought as Marric pulled his hand back and thrust it forward, face hard.

Once again, blue Light surrounded the black robed figure, this time along with a few of his companions, and they were all thrown back again, some through the doorway and some smashing hard into the wall. She even heard the crack of a skull slamming into something. Those that hit the wall slumped to the ground, unconscious, while the others tried to stand up, tripping over each other.

Realizing that this was their only chance to escape the trap, Janis grabbed Marric by the hand and darted back through the doorway they had just come through, dragging the boy with her.

By now, more of a fuss had been created in the cavern as they saw more and more robed figures coming out of the doorways and halls to see what the commotion was. Just as she passed the pile of people Marric had somehow thrown back, she saw one open his hand where a ball of red Light appeared.

Cursing, she shoved Marric to the side and jumped backwards just as it flew between them. It collided with some crates by the nearest wall and they exploded with a crack, splinters flying everywhere. Fortunately for them, it caused a visibility cover and she snagged Marric, diving into the dust.

They were trapped, surrounded by hundreds—possibly more—enemies, many of which likely had inhuman powers with Light that could blast them to pieces in less than a blink. She had to think; what could they do?

Janis considered their options as they ran quickly down the next hallway. Marric opened the closest door and slipped inside, beckoning Janis. After she entered, he closed it quickly behind them. It wasn't the wisest of decisions, but Janis followed only because he didn't give her much of a choice. As they stood there, huffing, they realized that the room wasn't dark, despite there being a lack of windows, as was common in this place. Whipping around, they faced three figures, all black robed, but two with their hoods back. They were playing some kind of game with stones and money.

"Hey, wha' do yeh think yer doin' 'ere?"

Before he could say much more, Janis was there. She could have easily just killed them, but she feared that it would cause too much commotion and leave too much of a trail for pursuants. Instead, her elbow connected with the nose of the man, and he fell over spluttering. Her poisons would do better here. In a flash, she sliced cuts into the cheeks of the other two men, kicking one in the chest just after and punching the other. They all fell over with muffled shouts. One of the men stayed down, while the other jumped up.

A strange feeling came over her and Janis realized that she felt weightless. Looking down, she saw that she was floating, and she was surrounded by red Light. All at once, she flew into the wall, her back shooting with pain. Fortunately, she had tucked her head so that it didn't impact on the wall. She thanked Macks for teaching her such quick reflexes. She'd have been knocked out otherwise. Janis quickly stood up, ignoring the pain, to see one of the men gritting his teeth, holding out his hand. She felt herself start to get lifted again, but the man's eyes rolled back in his head and he fell to the floor, unconscious.

Janis moved quickly to the men and began stripping them of their robes. She removed the black robe she had *borrowed* from a woman earlier since the rushing had dirtied it and cut it in places. Sliding one of the robes on, she tossed another to Marric and nodded to him. Of course, the robes didn't fit them exactly, but they didn't look too off course. Marric looked nervous, but determined.

"They are looking for two people, so we can't walk too closely together, else they might think us suspicious. I will go out first and run across the hallway. I'll stay there, and when you exit, look for a nod. Follow after me, keep your hood up, and don't stop. Understand?"

Marric paled slightly, but he nodded in assent. The commotion seemed to be rising outside, and Janis intended to use that to their advantage. Opening the door, she slipped out quickly and kept her head pointed slightly lower so as to hide her face in the darkness of the hood. Fortunately for her, many of the robed men and women running around still left their hoods up, so it wouldn't look strange for her to do so. She made a show of looking left and right, then began running the same direction that the others were. Before long, however, she veered to the wall and stood there, casually waiting until she saw Marric coming toward her.

Just as instructed, Marric slipped out, hood up, and looked around. Luckily for her, there weren't any other figures standing still, so the boy found her quickly and she gave the nod to follow, then she turned and continued moving briskly in the same direction as the others.

The plan had been going just fine until they had run into Lightbearers. Janis muttered a curse in frustration that she wasn't as well equipped to handle these as she had hoped. Her agility and smarts couldn't help her break through an unbreakable shield, or stop her from getting thrown back by their Moving. Looking around at all the robed men and women, Janis wondered how many of them manifested Lightbearer powers.

She felt vulnerable again.

Gah! This is happening too frequently these days! How is it that years and years of feeling safe and sure of myself can end so abruptly?!

Janis continued to walk with the majority of the flow, until she realized how odd it was that they were all moving in the same direction. It suddenly didn't seem like the wisest of choices to move with the crowd, but they couldn't about face now—it would be too obvious. Plus, Janis realized that Marric might have been lost in the crowd. Against her better judgement, she prayed to Lanser that he had kept up with her.

Eventually, after moving up a few more ramps, the groups broke into two, a majority of people moving into a large hallway on the left, while a few, here and there, went right. Thinking that exiting the large group completely wouldn't be desirable, she went right. After a few moments, she chanced a look backward and was relieved to see that the smaller form of Marric had managed to follow her.

The small trickle of robed figures finally turned into a small doorway and joined a group of maybe fifty or so others, some with their hoods back, some with them up still.

"They are among us," a woman said, nearer the front of the group. "They have donned robes and have moved into our ranks to hide. Clever."

"But not clever enough!" a man said, standing just to the side of her.

These two had their robes back, and their hair matched in a strange way. The woman on the right had her hair cropped close to her head and a wavy design had been cut down, the white skin of her head showing through where the hair had been cut. Likewise, the man had an identical, except mirrored, version cut into the opposite side of his head. It was like a picture was painted on two canvases, both intricate and amazing, but when they were put together, they made something else, something more complete.

Though she thought it was odd, Janis figured it had something to do with leadership, considering the fact that they were the two leading the conversation.

"We must focus our Sight to find them. It will take all of us to locate their exact position here within our crowd," the woman said, sounding resolute.

At that, the members of the group moved in and began linking hands.

Then she realized what was happening, and her stomach sank.

Fog it to Lanser's hall, they are about to find us—a bit too close for comfort!

A hand shot out and grabbed Janis, almost causing her to grab a knife and slice at it, until she realized that it was Marric, standing next to her. He was staring at the back of the robed person in front of him, and he was holding perfectly still. His hood slightly turned toward Janis, and her chest constricting, hair standing on end, she saw that his eyes were glowing blue, intense and imposing.

"Walk backwards, slowly." Marric said, sounding wistful. "Now."

Janis felt awkward staring into glowing eyes and nothing else, but she did as he said and the two of them started backing up toward the door, Marric still holding her hand.

By the time the two of them had made it to the doorway, Janis could see that the group of Seers had already begun to link hands and the main leader of the group had eyes that were filling with red Light.

Then Marric let out a blood-curdling scream, causing Janis to tense up and slip a dagger into the palm of her hand. She spun around, ready to face the assailant that had just attacked the boy—but there was no one.

Marric had collapsed on the floor, holding his chest, but there was no blood, no other people anywhere close to them.

The group of robed figures broke ranks and ran over to see Marric, lying there gasping in pain. One of them knelt down by him and held her hand on his shoulder. Janis could see that this one was a woman with beautiful blonde hair.

"Brother, are you alright? What happened?"

The hair on Janis's arms stood on end and she held her breath. There were a lot of them in the group and any number of them could be hiding a power that she couldn't understand how to face well. Marric's eyes still glowed with the blue Light, making him seem inhuman and strange.

"I—I'm so sorry. I Saw something that frightened me." Marric said, sounding weak. "I'm new here and I heard that my new abilities would be needed. I'm not sure I can handle it right now."

The figure bent down smiled, squeezing his shoulder reassuringly.

"I remember well the day that I first experienced my Seeing. Please, no need to worry. Would you like to try again?"

Janis stood there, not understanding what was happening. Then it dawned on her. Only a few people here knew what Marric looked like. Most people would have heard the alarm and just started moving, panicking. That was probably why these groups of Seers were coming together in the first place, to find them. His shriek had caused them to break their formation. It would take a while before they could begin again.

Clever boy, taking advantage of ignorance when it can be most helpful.

"Oh, I'm not sure I have the strength. Is there a place closeby I might rest? I think a bit of fresh air might help?"

Smiling, the woman gestured to the group behind her and said, "Please, go on without me. I must take our newest recruit to rest."

"Bu' Thalanara, we need all the 'elp we can ge' and w'thout the likes of yous—"

The woman waved a dismissive hand back to the group and said, "If you must wait, then wait, but I don't think that we have much time to spare."

She helped Marric up to his feet and led him into the hallway. Awkwardly, Janis followed. This caused the blonde woman to stare at her, confused. Without a moment of hesitation, Marric spoke.

"Oh this is my sister. She has no powers, but she accompanied me here to keep me safe. I hope you don't mind."

The woman smiled.

"No trouble at all. There are many among us that do not have Lightbearer powers. Though they are beneath us, low of rank, we do need guards and servants. Come."

She said that last part with a gesture towards Janis that the assassin didn't recognize. It seemed old, somehow. Janis just nodded slightly, keeping her hood up. Good thing the practice of keeping one's face covered was accepted here.

As they walked away, Janis could hear the group behind them talking, deciding if they should continue without this woman or not.

They were led up a walkway into a hallway that led away from the large cavern. The hallway angled up steeply and seemed to move on forever. The commotion of people running around faded behind them, as this hallway was abandoned almost entirely. Only two robed figures passed them while they walked. Janis surveyed their surroundings, keeping the pommel of her small dagger in her palm, ready if needed.

Something in her peripheral vision, movement of some sort, caused her to tense again. However, when she looked in that direction, there was nothing.

Is this place making me crazy? she thought, feeling a slight bit nervous with all the unknown here.

"We'll be there soon. From where do you hail—oh dear me. I haven't asked your name yet."

"Oh, it's Daelin, ma'am. And this is my sister, Alain."

Janis smiled underneath her hood. What irony that he happened to choose the exact same false name she'd used when she first came to Wurren in search of Marric. What were the chances of that happening?

"Well, it's a pleasure to meet you. I—"

The woman paused and her mouth pressed into a line.

"Why is your Shield active, Daelin? There's no need for that here, it is quite safe."

Marric squirmed, looking uncomfortable. Janis looked to the side and realized the boy had raised a translucent blue Shield, barely visible compared to the bright red orbs that hung near the tops of the walls around them. It looked similar if not the same as the one that Avryn had pointed out to them while they were in the cave. What had he said?

The Shield can interrupt Seeing.

Clever, clever boy.

"I—I was just . . . practicing my abilities. You see, Riln said I must learn to harness my powers quickly so that I can be ready to serve him and—"

"How do you know that name? You spoke with the divine leader directly? But only the choicest of Watchlight are granted the ability to see him. Who are you?"

The woman's eyes narrowed and Marric paled. Quickly, Janis punched the woman right in the jaw, causing her eyes to roll back in her head. With a quick slash, she cut a shallow wound in the woman's arm, infecting her with the sleeping poison. She didn't rise again.

"I'm sorry, I was doing alright until she saw my Shield and—"

"No time, we must find our way out."

Janis grabbed Marric's hand, then they ran up the hallway, which continued to move upwards steeply. There were doorways on the left and right here and there, but they kept going straight. Then they reached a bigger room with tunnels moving in three directions, all upwards.

Cursing, Janis turned to each one, trying to determine the best way to go. Marric gasped next to her, and she turned to see that his eyes had once again begun to glow, blue and intense.

"They See us now. We have to get out of here."

Her stomach clenched at his words. They couldn't hide anymore. If these people could See what she thought they could, there was no place to hide.

"Let's *move*."

She grabbed Marric's arm and began to move them forward towards the center tunnel.

"Wait!" Marric shouted.

Janis grit her teeth in frustration, but the boy dug his feet in and wouldn't allow her to move him forward. Marric stood still, glowing eyes open and staring forward, until he slowly moved his finger upward and pointed to the left tunnel.

"That is our best option."

"Our *best option*? What in Ugglyn's name is *that* supposed to mean?" Janis said, feeling even more annoyed.

"Just trust me. I can't explain why, but I can See each tunnel and I know that the center one leads to a dead end, and the right one circles back to the large cavern at the center. If we go either of those ways . . . we die."

"And what about the left one?" Janis asked harshly.

"Well, we—"

Shouts in the tunnel from behind interrupted him. Janis, still holding Marric by the hand, dashed down the left tunnel, feeling the incline sharpen even more, though she didn't understand how they could still be going upwards. Sure, there had been a lot of stairs when she followed Marric and Prost down here, but they had to have reached the same level of those already, hadn't they?

The air seemed to grow thicker and more humid as they ran, and Janis could barely hear what sounded like water running somewhere up ahead. Water dripped from the ceiling here and there, and streaks from regular drips lined the walls on either side, creating a striped design all over them. It actually looked quite beautiful, as if the stone walls had intentionally been decorated that way by dyes. Janis also noted that the red orbs seemed further apart from each other than in the other places, as if this was a back corner of the lair that was ignored. This could likely be the case, for they hadn't seen even one person pass as they ran. Doors were also more scarce and continued to be so as they moved upwards.

Marric puffed behind her, slowing down considerably. It was then that she realized that they had been moving at a break-neck pace, barreling up the steep incline. The pathway hadn't been smooth either, but was instead rough and pock marked. The poor boy had tripped a couple times as they ran, but she had just dragged him to his feet and moved forward at the same pace.

Janis stopped and listened to the noises behind them.

Nothing.

Marric dropped to his knees, coughing loudly. His breathing was long and loud, giving away his apparent lack of stamina. Janis examined herself, feeling her heart beat quickly and loudly. She even was breathing a bit hard herself, but she likely could have kept going for quite some time. Thanks to her exhaustive training, she had gained endurance for times like this.

"You may have just a moment to rest. Until I hear sounds behind us."

"I—I—can't—keep—run—ning." Marric said through gasps.

"Just breathe. Don't move, and *try* to be quiet. I'm going to scout ahead quickly."

Marric held up his hand, causing her to pause.

"There's no need, this is an abandoned tunnel."

Janis stared at him, hard. There was no way that he could know that. Even with whatever strange gifts he'd just come into, she had a hard time believing that he could be sure of such a thing. However, she didn't want to make him feel bad, so she said nothing, and instead turned to move off.

"There's no time!" he said harshly.

She raised an eyebrow at him, taken aback by his change of tone. He'd never used that tone before. In fact, Janis wondered if he was even capable of being rude or simply blunt. He was far too kind and patient in situations which required a hardness, even just urgency.

"Move. Now!"

His eyes had begun to glow again, blue and imposing. She really wished he would just stop, it made her skin crawl to see him that way. Regardless, they pushed forward, moving at a quick, but slightly slower pace than before.

She considered their options. If this path didn't pan out, they would likely have to either fight their way out, hide out long enough that they could slip out, or try to sneak their way through the ranks like they had before.

Fighting isn't an option, too many unknowns, she thought.

It really wasn't the number of people that she would have to kill in order to get out that was the problem. She had fought impossible odds like this more than once and made it out alive, even if just barely. No, it was the Lightbearing. No matter how much she thought about it, and how much information she had gathered from Avryn listening to his explanations, she couldn't account for everything. Not only were there hundreds, perhaps even thousands of people here, Lanser only knew how many of them weren't normal.

Glancing over, she saw that Marric's eyes still glowed pure blue Light as they ran. In fact, he wasn't even looking at his feet, like he had been the entire time they had been running so far. He was staring forward, eyes locked on something that she couldn't see. Oddly enough, he wasn't stumbling or tripping at all. This was the most surefooted he had seemed the whole time they had been traveling together.

Janis knit her eyebrows together. She read a lot about a person from their body language and his had changed entirely in just a moment. Before he'd been self conscious, weak, and unsure. Now he seemed like a trained athlete, light on his feet and confident.

The strange Seeing powers seem to affect more than just the appearance of his eyes. This Seeing is much more than I understand right now, she thought.

That's exactly why they couldn't fight. Though Seeing only foiled the plans of those that were hiding, Janis wondered if it could be more lethal than she thought, despite it not being a combat power. The danger wasn't as apparent as a Destroyer, who could disintegrate any object in the blink of an eye, but there was something there, deeper and hidden.

As they ran, the sound of rushing water grew louder and louder, echoing off the stone walls as they ran. The floor felt wetter as well, bits of trickling water now running backwards down the slope and under their feet. This forced them to slow down a bit, needing to ensure they didn't slip and fall. Only then did she realize how odd it was that the water didn't continue all the way down to where they started. It must have run through small cracks or holes in the walls or ground.

The sound of the water was now deafening, and she soon saw why. Just ahead, the walls opened up on both sides, creating a bridge from the pathway, and water ran about a foot below it, coming from the right and rushing left. Janis stopped just in front of the stone-formed bridge and leaned forward to look right. A waterfall, about three armspans wide, fell from a slit in the ceiling, strong and fast, creating the river of water that ran under the pathway and to the left. Looking left, she saw that it fell away somewhere into the darkness.

I've seen more waterfalls in the last two days than I have in the past year.

Janis didn't like waterfalls. Others marveled at them and enjoyed watching them, but to her, they masked her senses. They blocked off one of her precious survival tools, and it made her whole body clench up in anxiety.

"The path looks really thin. We'll go slow, just in case!" Janis shouted to Marric, who looked in wonder at the sight. "Are you ready?"

Marric came out of his thoughts back to the moment, and shook his head.

"This is it. This is our best option," he shouted back, looking grim.

Confused, Janis stared at him, trying to interpret what he was saying. All at once, she realized what he meant. They couldn't go back the way they came, and going forward wasn't an option. Her head turned slowly to the flow of the river, moving off into the darkness away from the path.

"You CANNOT be serious!" Janis yelled.

He paled, but nodded his head, staring at the same spot that she was herself.

"No, we move forward." Janis insisted.

"We can't!" Marric shouted. "That is another dead end!"

Clenching her fists, Janis fumed on the inside.

"THEN WHY IN LANSER'S GOOD NAME DID WE GO THIS WAY?!" she screamed.

It was partially because of the waterfall, partially because of her anger, but she yelled unnecessarily loud. She worried that she had scared Marric or made him uncomfortable.

Marric's jaw locked and he nodded again, seemingly unaffected by her angry shout just moments before.

Why didn't we just take the fogging path that would lead us back to the cavern?!

Too late now. There had to be people pursuing them, moving up the cavern now, and if it truly was a dead end, then Marric was right about it not being a viable option.

They would either have to turn and fight, or hide somewhere, though she didn't know where. There hadn't been a doorway for quite some time, and they couldn't guarantee that there would be any more up there.

Instinct made Janis draw two daggers, one in each hand, and she faced back the way that they had come, half expecting some black-robed crazy person to come barreling up at them wielding red Light-weapons.

Marric, still looking pale and nervous, held up his hand, palm upwards.

He was offering for her to take his hand.

Well, I'll be, she thought. *That is the bravest thing I think I've seen him do yet.*

Marric nodded to her, and she slid her daggers back in their sheaths, taking the moment to button the straps over the knives that held them in place when things got rough.

She figured things were about to get pretty rough.

Though she didn't particularly want to hold Marric's hand, she figured it would make him feel better if she did, so she reached out and gripped it tightly. He flinched at the tightness of her squeeze, but didn't try to pull away. They moved forward until they were facing the left flow of the river, and stood close to the edge.

"Are you absolutely *sure* of this?" Janis asked.

He nodded again, this time looking like he might actually be sick.

Pausing, Janis yelled to Marric, "Can't you Conjure something to float us down? A boat—or anything?!"

Marric shook his head vigorously.

"No time! The tunnel is too steep and they are too close. Let's *go*!" he yelled back.

Nodding resolutely, she turned toward the flowing river.

"Jump in feet first! It's better than landing on your back or your head!! Do your best to push off of any rocks you land on and start swimming—we don't know how deep it is!" Janis instructed Marric.

Janis stared grimly at the river for a moment. Her journey from Wurren had been anything if not interesting so far.

"On three?" Marric yelled, his voice squeaking a bit on the last word.

There was no point in counting.

Janis leapt forward and yanked on Marric's hand, pulling him along with her. She heard him scream in surprise. It felt like time slowed down as the firm stone beneath their feet disappeared and they fell toward the rushing water. Her feet hit first and she pushed them forward, landing on her butt. Sure enough, it did hit the rock and pain shot up through her back. That wasn't the most shocking thing, however, because the water was warm, almost hot. On normal occasions, it would be pleasant to be in water this temperature, but she had expected it to be cold and refreshing. It had been quite muggy and hot as they ran. Being wrong about the water disappointed her. It was also deeper than she thought, with the water coming up to her chest.

She had also slightly misinterpreted the speed at which the water was flowing. Immediately, she was swept forward in the flow, her head being pulled under as the bottom half of the water seemed to be flowing more quickly than the water on the surface. Janis had to exert herself to raise her head above to gasp for air. A gasp beside her, desperate and loud, indicated that Marric was having an equally challenging time staying afloat.

All at once, the small river sped up, moving downwards rapidly. Her head went under yet again and she could feel her chest squeeze up in fright, panic urging to take over her thoughts and body. She gritted her teeth and concentrated. She had been trained for many years, but she was still subject to human instincts and reactions to difficult situations.

Calming down, she was able to push herself upwards enough to gulp some air as she slipped and slid down the steep fall of the water. The water moving rapidly was loud, and she wasn't able to hear Marric. She hoped that he was getting on just fine, but if she was having this much trouble, she had little hope for him. Everything was dark. So dark that she couldn't see anything, not even which way the cavern would turn. Sharply, the way turned and Janis slammed into the bend before being whisked downwards again. Her arm hurt now. Another turn came and she collided with the bend again, except this time she felt something soft between her and the wall. It felt like flesh.

Oh blast, Marric.

Reacting quickly, she grabbed his body, hoping that it wasn't just a corpse now, and clung to him. Using her other arm, she pushed herself up, just getting above the water to get a breath and ducked under, forcing her arms, and Marric, above the water to hopefully draw a breath himself.

Suddenly, as if it came from nowhere, a bright light flashed in her eyes and she blinked. Unfortunately, that wasn't the only sudden stimuli. Simultaneously with the flash, the ground beneath them disappeared.

Her stomach was in her throat, her head felt dizzy, and she fell. They both fell. Blinking, gasping, and holding onto Marric, Janis tried to understand what was happening as the two of them spiraled into what felt like a void. Then they hit a wall again, only this one was just a bit softer. Not soft enough, however, for it to not knock the breath right out of her chest. Pain lanced up the side of her body and she squeezed her eyes shut, dealing with it.

All at once, the vertigo and loss of direction was gone and she realized they were underwater again. This time, however, it was still water. Janis almost sighed in relief that it was over, but pushed back the instinct, given that a sigh would cause her to waterlog at this very moment.

Her head broke the water and she gasped again. She still had to squint, given the brightness of the sunlight from above, but the stillness of the water was comforting enough, even though her sense of sight was impaired at the moment.

Marric was still clutched in her arms, and she kicked her feet furiously to keep them both afloat. At some point, he had gone unconscious, though she couldn't be sure when. This had been far too stressful of an experience to keep track of such things. Pushing forward, she was able to make it to an edge of the pool, which she could now see as her eyes adjusted to the sun above.

Janis flopped on the shore and dropped Marric a bit harshly next to her, fatigue taking over after such an intense experience. She was glad to see his chest moving up and down, showing that he was still breathing himself. After just a moment of respite, she sat up quickly and looked around. They faced a mountain, tall and majestic, standing far above. Out of the mountain, some ways up, but nowhere near the top, came the waterfall from which they came. It wasn't overly loud, but it did make some noise as waterfalls often did.

Scanning the area, she saw that a forest, thick and green, covered a majority of the area behind them, the exception only being five or so armspans from the lake. Janis spotted a place where the water did move away, but it was no wider than the passageway they'd just come through, so the water flowed slowly, coming from the lake in front of them and moving down, hugging the foot of the mountain until it turned off around the bend.

Everything smelled damp. The air was humid; the trees and plants smelled so clean and refreshing, being emphasized by the mugginess and warmth from where they had just come. Catching her breath for a moment, Janis stood up and scouted the treeline, looking for signs of movement or approach, but there seemed only to be the normal woodland creatures and nothing else. Yes, they had managed to escape, but no, she had no idea where they were, or how to reunite with Avryn and his companions.

Emerging from the trees, she saw that Marric had woken up and was now sitting and staring at the water. She moved to his side and saw that he was looking at his reflection in the water, wide-eyed and still shaking slightly from the experience.

"Are you going to be alright?" Janis asked, feeling more genuine than she usually did. What was it about this boy that she was so fond of?

"I just—" Marric said, stammering. "I just can't believe that worked. And I knew exactly how it would turn out. I Saw the whole thing, right up until now."

Still wide-eyed, he looked up at Janis and gave a small smile.

There was an awkward moment when Janis just stared at him, confusion on her face. Then she felt obligated to do something, so she gave a slight smile back.

"I'm sorry to say that we should probably get moving. It seems rather quiet out here, but we can't stay for too long—someone might find us and I don't want it to be an army of Lightbearers."

Helping Marric to his feet, Janis determined that their best path would be to just move into the forest and hope that a landmark of some sort would stick out.

As they walked, an idea occurred to Janis. "I don't suppose that you can use your strange new powers to See where we need to go, can you?"

Saying nothing, Marric stared forward, seeming concentrated. Unsure what to do, Janis kept moving forward in silence. This went on, the two of them quietly walking for some time, before he shook his head.

"I'm sorry, but I don't know much about it. I think it just comes," he said, looking disappointed.

Feeling resolved that moving was better than just sitting, the two just pressed on, the thick foliage of the forest engulfing them as they moved forward.

It didn't take all that long for the sound of the waterfall to disappear, leaving them in the silence that forests often brought. There were of course animals and even a slight breeze that blew through the trees, but all seemed still.

Janis heard Marric muttering and looked over to see that he was staring at his hands. He kept opening and closing them like a baby might when they've just discovered that they are there, and that they can be controlled. He kept on like this for a good while until he sighed in frustration and stalked forward more quickly.

"It's starting to get dark, I think we had better find a place to turn in. I suspect the temperature will drop this evening, but hopefully not too much; today seems a very warm day." Janis said.

Marric nodded.

"Do you know where we are?"

"I do believe that we are moving in a diagonal direction toward where we were separated, based on where the sun is setting. See? Come here."

Janis led Marric to a small, grassy and treeless area where they could see a mountaintop just above the treeline.

"That is where Prost led me, and where they enter their lair. If we keep moving in this direction, we should reach the path that we took to get here. It won't be safe to travel on that road, since that is likely where they are looking for us, but I need a starting point and it's worth the risk. I hope that I can back-track to find where we were. But I imagine that Avryn has moved on now, and he didn't tell us where their safe haven was."

Marric grimaced at the comment and folded his arms. She had to admit that it did look grim, but she figured at some point, things would start to look familiar and she could guide them at least to where they had been before. It seemed like a lifetime, but that had only been yesterday.

And that was only *if* they could get that far without encountering any Watchlight goons. She had been forced to fight them on too many occasions and she felt that another time without rest or training would be pressing her luck. But there was Marric to be looked after, too. And she couldn't keep him safe all by herself, so they had to move.

"Can you make it work?" she said bluntly.

"What?"

"I said, can you make it work? The Lightbearing. Your eyes got all lit and creepy before, so can you control it?"

Marric furrowed his brows at the comment, his mouth becoming a thin line.

"I thought so. Fog it, I was hoping that we could at least even the fight when—" Janis paused, noticing Marric's reaction. " . . . *if* we run into any unpleasants."

Looking down, the boy kicked his feet a few times without saying anything. The sounds of the forest seemed to get louder in the silence, causing Janis to agonize in the awkwardness of the situation. A bird sang in the tree above them, its song sweet and lilting. Bushes rustled, and a rabbit jumped its way out through the clearing and into the forest on the other side.

"I'm worthless." Marric said.

Janis shrugged.

"Freezing under pressure is not uncommon. It happens to most novices. Yes, you are historically pretty worthless in a fight, but maybe that'll change."

Why in Lanser's name am I talking to him like this? I hate talking.

He smiled at her sadly, but just nodded curtly.

"But for now, we must keep moving."

The day passed very quickly, as did the night. Contrary to Janis's prediction, the night was smooth and there was no danger at all, other than not sleeping because of how noisy Marric was when he slept. The fog had seemed extra thick during the night, and it felt even more chilly than usual. All that did was make Janis wonder what was coming. The shifts in the weather and the strange feeling she had in the pit of her stomach made her feel like there was something big coming, though what, she couldn't tell.

They traveled through the day, walking continuously, taking breaks only when Marric stopped or complained of fatigue, but they pushed long and hard.

Finding the path they had taken just a couple days before was far easier than Janis imagined it would be, and soon enough they had made it within a day's foot journey to the waterfalls where the fight had happened and Marric had come into his powers. Each of them agreed that it wouldn't be wise to get too close to the waterfalls, just in case operatives from Watchlight had gone back there looking for them.

During the duration of their travels, Marric had continued attempting his powers, but with no success. It was obvious how frustrated he was getting. Admittedly, she was having a hard time knowing what to do about it, so she just ignored the situation, figuring that to try to encourage or comfort him would cause more problems than it was worth. However, it did stir some long forgotten feelings that she had experienced.

All of the sudden, Janis was back in the streets, following Macks wherever he went. Every now and then, he would turn around and smack her, without warning. Macks had said that she needed to learn to be on edge, always. There was never an excuse to let your guard down. Sure, you could mask it, but you couldn't ever let it down. On more than one occasion that had been true, however, it meant weeks and weeks of abuse. Anger bubbled in her chest as she remembered the last weeks of this unorthodox training method. She remembered hating Macks, but more, she remembered hating herself. Weeks and weeks, and she hadn't learned the lesson. Hopelessness and doubt consumed her. Until one day, it happened.

* * *

Macks and Janis stalked down the road. It had been dark, very dark, as it often was when they traveled to and from the places they stayed. Earlier that day, Janis had failed yet another lesson, though this was on basic survival skills. Janis was confident that if she ever was left alone, if Macks ever left, she would die, and very quickly.

Her trainer led the way to their next escapade and she dreaded it. Not once had she felt like she succeeded, not once did she feel like she could handle the situation. Macks had even smacked her twice already and she just took it with only a delayed and weak reflex.

Janis was tired of it, completely done. Weeks and weeks of frustration were causing her to lose herself to the feelings, the anger.

As they walked, Macks had been saying something, but she wasn't listening. She was only thinking of what she could do, anything, to leave, survive on her own. While Macks went on about who knows what, she was only thinking of how she could beat him up, treat him the way he treated her. She felt like she was incapable of anything useful.

Then, it happened.

Without warning, Macks turned around and made to backhand her in the face. In a flash, Janis blocked the blow with her own arm and swung at his face, missing only by a hair as he stepped backwards. As if by reflex, Macks engaged her again and swung at her with his other arm.

Rage filled her and she may have imagined it, but red filled her vision. Roaring, she dodged that blow, yet another one, and swung a fist at his crotch, her fist connecting with the softness there. He crumpled.

Her anger dissolved and she blushed, feeling ashamed of herself.

"Oh! Lanser's goodness, I'm so sorry! I—"

Macks was laughing. He still knelt on the ground, holding himself down where he'd taken the blow, clearly in pain. Yet, he laughed. This wasn't a normal chuckle, or the kind that you give someone politely to make them feel better, but he was laughing loudly, his shoulders shaking.

"Now, that's my girl."

Janis blushed more deeply. She couldn't believe what had just happened. Confidence flared in her chest and she helped her mentor up to his feet. He hadn't fully recovered, but he had taught her that no pain should keep an assassin from staying in one place for too long in the streets.

* * *

A sound interrupted her memory and she whipped out her daggers. The soft sound of horse hooves, moving slowly, was coming from amidst some trees behind them. Janis pointed at Marric to hide in a bush closeby, and slunk slowly into the trees. It sounded like there were multiple sets of feet moving, though Janis couldn't quite hear how many. It was dark now, so she couldn't make out the figures that she heard. Getting as close as she could, she stood on the other side of the tree where the people were walking.

They hadn't detected her, which was good.

Now let's test your *reflexes, my friends.*

Quickly and as silently as possible, Janis spun around the tree and swung her wicked forearm-length dagger at the chest of the first assailant. He dodged, grunting as he barely missed the cut of the blade.

"Fog it, woman! 'Ow we s'posed t'elp yeh if yer tryin' t'kill us all the time, eh?"

The familiar voice of Harmel cut the tension immediately.

"Well, are yeh ready t'go or no'? We did com 'ere fer yous and whatnot."

Chapter 20

Marric felt his whole body relax, thinking that the sound he'd just heard was the most sweet and amazing thing in his entire life. Against his better judgement, he flew out of the bush and dashed to where he had heard Harmel's voice. Seeing the man, he threw his arms around him and held him there.

"Erm . . . hey, Mar, are yous okay?"

The boy said nothing, but just held the man tightly. He really wasn't sure why he was so excited to see Harmel, but he just felt such relief and happiness that he didn't know what else to do.

Shrell spoke up, cutting the reunion short. "I don' know how yeh got outta there so fast an' all, but we ain't got much time fer that. Get yer bearings, we need to move." Shrell seemed less than happy about Janis's arrival in their vicinity.

The two of them stared at each other for a moment, something passing between them, and then they all turned to Avryn, who hadn't actually said anything yet. He was staring out into the forest, a thoughtful look on his face. Finally, he spoke, though he still looked serious.

"Yes, I am happy that you made it out, though how you did is beyond me. I suspect that there are some Watchlight men following you and they are likely close. Are you okay to begin traveling now?"

Marric nodded, excited now that they had a plan, a destination. By now the sunlight was almost faded completely, and the first moon was beginning to show over the horizon. It wouldn't provide much light until it was higher in the sky, so they would be traveling in the dark. Suddenly, traveling didn't sound so fun anymore. He dreaded the many times he was inevitably going to trip over branches and roots and probably even small animals. Marric felt like his more clumsy self came out in the dark, like some monster from his childhood, creeping out to torment and bother him.

Janis made a sound somewhere between a grunt and an 'mmhmm' and turned to check behind them, looking for something. Seeming satisfied, she turned and stalked over to Avryn and gestured for him to lead the way.

Marric thought the woman was odd, but he liked her. There was something about her that made him feel safe, comforted. Her quirkiness and her amazing skill—pretty much everything—didn't intimidate him, but made him trust her more, as if any horrible situation could be handled by her cool head.

Marric suddenly felt his eyes widen, except he wasn't actually opening his eyes more, or widening his eyelids at all. He wasn't alarmed, however, for this had happened already a few times. Now it felt a bit more familiar. As usual, the sensation was overridden by the vision. The forest dissolved, and so did his companions. Instead, he Saw what looked like another part of the forest. There was a Light moving toward where he was, or rather, where his vision self was, and it was red Light, steady and true.

Somehow, though he couldn't quite tell how, his 'eyes' moved closer to the Light and Marric saw what was causing it. A dark skinned woman with short black hair was using her Lightbearing to create orbs of Light for her whole group of companions. Red orbs lit the surrounding forest with an eerie glow, and Marric saw at least a hundred black robed figures moving quickly, all on horses, in their direction. At their head was a large dark brown horse carrying a bigger black-robed figure. He needed to concentrate, but Marric was able to move in on the face of the leader of the pack, and his own body, whether it was his physical body or some semblance of whatever body he possessed in these strange visions, chilled, his skin crawling.

Prost stood at the head of the group, a look of rage upon his face as he yelled to his companions and urged them forward. Curious, Marric returned his vision back to where he and his companions were and his chest constricted. The Watchlight group was not very far off, and they were moving very quickly.

Marric began to feel very strange as he saw himself with his companions moving quickly, almost running, in the opposite direction from Prost and his goons. It was almost as if he had a twin, one that he'd never known as he grew up, but was now seeing for the first time. When he concentrated and realized it was himself, the world seemed to spin from the oddity of this out-of-body feeling.

Then he fell.

Not in the vision, but in real life. Opening his eyes, he saw worried faces looking down on him. Janis didn't seem too worried, oddly enough.

"Marric, are you alright? I was just asking if everyone is okay to travel and then you collapsed suddenly." Avryn said. "Perhaps we should rest."

"NO!" Marric yelled suddenly.

Avryn jumped slightly and furrowed his brow at the boy's quick outburst.

Marric blushed at his sudden shout and pushed himself to his feet.

"They are coming, and they aren't far off."

Looking confused, Avryn eyed his companions.

"How do you—?"

"I'm a Seer, Avryn, trust me. I just know. It isn't the first time I've Seen something that came true. I—I can't really make it happen, but it just does. Just after you asked if we should travel, I Saw maybe a hundred, possibly more, Watchlight people moving toward us and I think they might *all* be Lightbearers."

Avryn cursed and stood up quickly.

"Mallan's light, I wish we had more than one horse."

Marric winced at the comment.

"What?!" Avryn asked, worried.

"They're all on horseback, Avryn."

With urgency, Avryn moved to the one horse that they had and shifted some of the bags.

"Normally," Avryn said, "I wouldn't condone splitting up. But they had Marric, and they'll want him back. Though this time, I think they won't spare his life."

Marric felt his face turn white and he suddenly felt nauseated. He hadn't thought about what they would do if they caught up to him again.

He shook his head. *If* they caught him.

I need to be positive. I can be more useful now.

"I will ride ahead with Marric and get him to Terris Green. I can then return with an army of our own to assist in facing Watchlight. We have a stock of horses there and we can return quickly, I hope. Shrell, Harmel, you know the way, can you make your way there with Janis?"

"Aye, Avryn." Shrell said.

"If you're intercepted or need to redirect, go to the place where we met for the first time. I'll move straight in this direction, and if I meet the army before you, I'll know where to find you. If I don't see either . . . well, let's just hope this works."

"If it don' work, we'll prolly be dead." Harmel said, levity entering his voice as was common with all things that came out of his mouth.

Janis shot him a death look laced with annoyance. It was clear that she disapproved of his outlook on most situations.

"Janis," Avryn said next. "I am sorry that you have been pulled into this, but I am grateful that you were able to find Marric and bring him back. Lanser knows what would have become of him had you not saved him. Thank you."

The assassin's mouth pressed into a hard line, and she nodded curtly. It was clear that she wasn't going to say anything else, so Avryn nodded back and turned to Marric.

"Come, it's time."

A swelling of sadness filled Marric and, without much thought, he rushed to Janis and threw his arms around her. The woman let out a grunt of sorts and held very still, unsure how to react.

Marric just held tight. He was taken aback at how *hard* she felt. He imagined that she had to be very fit to do what she did, but she also looked so delicate at the same time. However, it was very clear that she was built like a rock, muscle covering likely every inch of her body.

Janis cleared her throat, then wrapped her arms lightly around Marric, looking awkward.

Avryn tried to cover a smile, but didn't do a good job of it. Shrell looked almost as uncomfortable as Janis at the exchange, and Harmel chuckled loudly.

"Well lookie 'ere. She's got some soul then, ain't she? Oi thought she 'ad a black 'eart," he said cheerfully.

Janis scowled at him and took her arms off Marric. Then she lightly pushed his shoulders until he let go.

"You will be fine. Avryn is a very capable warrior and the two of you moving on the horse will be very swift."

He couldn't explain why, but he had begun to cry. Something about leaving Janis and the others behind when they'd just reunited felt too much to handle. Marric knew that it wouldn't be long before he was sobbing, and he couldn't have Janis seeing him that way. So rather than say anything, he just nodded and turned quickly, running to the horse.

Avryn watched him go with a tender look on his face. However, he seemed to understand the boy's urgency. He tipped his head to Janis and jumped on the horse behind Marric.

"Keep each other safe. I want to see the three of you again, and I trust that your combined skill will ensure that. Don't take a straight route there, cover your tracks, and . . . don't die."

He said that last part while looking directly at Janis. The woman just stared at him flatly, saying nothing.

"We're off. Lanser bless your journey."

With a final nod, Avryn kicked the horse into motion. Marric's stomach clenched as it launched forward, barreling through the trees at a breakneck pace. He had made a point to not look back as Avryn had, giving one final wave before their friends were out of view. However, the speed of the horse locked the boy's eyes forward, and very little effort was required to not look back. Fear gripped him as the horse ran past tree after tree. They weren't on any path that could be seen, but somehow the horse dodged the trees as they came. Whooshing sounds filled Marric's ears as each tree passed, some so close that if he extended his arm out to the side, he was sure it would be taken clean off at the elbow.

Memories filled his mind of horseback riding. Before this journey began, it had been a very long time since he'd ridden a horse, let alone at the speed at which they now moved. His eyes lost focus as his memory moved into a field, the sun shining brightly above him.

* * *

He was sitting at the neck of a beautiful light brown mare, her mane flowing down over her neck softly. Marric was only a boy, eight years of age. His father sat behind him, chuckling with delight as the horse trotted through the field, its two riders being its only burden on such a day.

"Should we give it a go, lad? I think tha' yer ma best not know 'bout this, eh?"

Marric turned to look into his father's eyes, the face there seeming so much younger. That day she had still lived, but not for much longer.

"Oi, yes Pa! Me thinks we oughta do just tha'."

"Now, now, son. Yeh ain't goin' t'get far if yeh ain't gonna follow yer proper speakin' lessons, eh?"

He blushed, but rephrased his sentence.

"Yes, father. I think we should do it."

A grin spread on his father's face and he nodded approvingly.

"I think tha' yer lessons are workin' quite fine, don' yeh ?"

He had just started school a few weeks before, and he wasn't enjoying all the rules and properness of any of it. None of his friends had gone to school in favor of learning their family trades. Other Wurren parents didn't seem to care if their children learned to speak and write properly like Narim did. His mind, however, lost track of his preoccupations with school as his father kicked the horse into action, launching them forward.

Marric screamed in delight as the wind rushed through his hair, making a constant roar in his ears. A few insects managed to pelt his face, but he didn't mind. He felt free, and strong. Nothing could get in their way.

* * *

Suddenly, Marric blinked, the sunlight disappeared, leaving darkness, save for the red moon above. His stomach clenched again when he saw where they were and how fast they moved. Somehow, he had lost control of his mind completely, as if he had left the forest and Avryn, and entered into his past. He had been known to get lost in his thoughts, but this was different.

"Marric, are you quite alright? Did you See something?" Avryn inquired behind him.

"Hmm?"

"Your eyes. You Saw something, didn't you?" Avryn asked again. He had to speak loudly, almost shouting, for Marric to hear him.

"I—I'm not sure! I think it was a memory." Marric said.

Avryn made some movement behind the boy, but he couldn't see what.

"Ah yes," Avryn said, "Seeing opens a window not only to the future, but to the present and the past. I'm not a Seer myself, but I hear that it can be quite distracting."

Distracting wasn't necessarily the way that Marric would describe it. The word didn't seem to capture the extent of his feelings. He somehow felt split in half, being in two places at once. Of course the vision had ended, but the feelings he had there persisted. He felt the warmth of the sun, and the cool of the night, the happiness of the fun and the fright of the flight. It made him feel dizzy.

Not wanting the subject to remain on himself, Marric changed it.

"How much longer until we get there?" he asked.

"A few more hours, likely. It depends on how tired the horse gets, moving at such a quick pace."

Marric had expected the conversation to continue, but it was apparent that Avryn wasn't in the mood.

At length, the light of the first moon waned and eventually left them in almost pure darkness, forcing Avryn to conjure a ball of Light, small but bright, to guide their way. The man wasn't thrilled to depend on such, but without it, they wouldn't be able to move at all, for the darkness was thick. Of course, they could have waited until the light of the second moon appeared, but Avryn had said they couldn't spare any time. He wasn't concerned for their own safety, but mostly for that of those they'd left behind.

Marric prayed to Lanser that nothing ill would befall them.

The forest continued without much changing for what seemed like an eternity. The horse had tired out not too long after Avryn had commented on the matter, and they were instead shifting between a quick trot and a regular walk. They were making much slower progress with the pace, but Marric was secretly grateful, for the wind rushing over him while the horse ran chilled him more than he wanted to admit. He didn't want to complain about anything. Something about coming into his Lightbearer powers had made him feel obligated somehow to be better, stronger.

It was eerie how quiet the forest became when all light was gone. Normally, animal sounds and rustling could be heard while they traveled. Now, all was still. It seemed that even the wind had disappeared with the sun. The stillness made Marric's hair stand on end, and his eyes shifted side to side, half expecting an ambusher, or maybe even multiple, to appear and attack them.

Movement in the corner of his eye made him jump, and his hands squeezed the mane of the horse tightly, making Marric's knuckles white. Terror filled his whole being, but when he looked, it had only been the shadow of the trees and the reflection of Avryn's ball of Light off of a particularly shiny tree.

Allowing himself to relax, his other senses came back to him and he closed his eyes, trusting that Avryn would detect any danger, for he felt unfit to keep an eye out himself. That is, unless shadows proved more dangerous than they usually were.

At length, the light of the second moon, Mallan, bright and blue, filtered through the trees above. Looking up, Marric could see that the thickness of the forest was waning, the trees becoming a bit more sparse, though only enough to allow more light to come through. Avryn, now able to see more, dismissed his Light with a sigh.

"I love Mallan's light." Avryn said, seemingly at random.

Marric didn't know what to say to that, so he muttered some sort of response, just so that man knew he had heard.

After a pause, Avryn continued. "The reason I love Mallan's light is because it is very bright, making it easy to see at night. Also, it's blue, just like our Lightbearing."

Another pause. Marric heard what he was saying, but he knew that there was a hidden meaning he was missing.

Chuckling, Avryn clarified his meaning.

"It is a perfect time to practice with our abilities. We still have a bit of time, Marric, and the only way that you will be able to feel comfortable and skilled with your Lightbearing is to practice."

A fog of confusion left Marric's mind and clarity appeared. For some odd reason, the trip had seemed awkward, as if he didn't know what to say to Avryn. This seemed to clear it up.

"Is it safe?" the boy asked.

Rather than saying anything, Avryn removed one hand from the reins, and in a flash of Light, summoned a blue sword, brilliant and true. It appeared without a sound and so suddenly that Marric blinked at the closeness of the intense blue Light. Shocked by its brightness, Marric jumped and scanned the forest around them. However, the Light from the sword was hidden by the blue glow being cast from above. Of course, the sword wasn't completely hidden, but from afar, the gleam of the sword could easily be that from Mallan above.

Marric turned slightly to see Avryn's smiling face. The man gave a nod, then dismissed his sword.

"Do you know what your powers are? I have my suspicions, but I can't be sure."

It took Marric a moment to realize that this was no longer a hidden answer. He had actually received the powers that he'd heard about—seen himself—over the past few days. It was no longer what power or powers he may or may not receive, but which ones he had now received. He had finally gotten them. Or, awakened, rather, according to their term.

Our term, he thought. Warmth blossomed in his chest at finally being able to say that.

"Erm . . . "

The revelation he'd just had caused him to pause for a much longer time than normal, making Avryn furrow his brow in worry. Marric didn't care. This was the first time since his awakening that he'd had the chance to really think about it, really revel in the fact that he was finally . . .

A Lightbearer, he said in his mind, naming the actual term.

Marric was finally able to clear his head enough to talk, though the warmth and elation remained inside him.

"Erm, of course. You've seen it, but Seeing is one of them. It has already proven a lot more useful than I imagined when you first explained it to me."

Avryn hummed in approval behind him.

"I must say that I *am* quite envious of you. I have never been able to develop even what little power of Seeing I have. Most of what I see are fuzzy images with vaguely human shapes."

Marric chuckled at that. It wasn't that he thought that it was funny, but by comparison, his experiences were so clear, sometimes even clearer than his own thoughts and sight.

Another pause.

"So, is that it?" Avryn asked, clearly not wanting to be impolite or rude.

"Oh, no, I don't think so. But I haven't tried the others much. While I was with Riln—"

Avryn stiffened behind him.

"You met Riln directly?!" the man said, surprised.

Marric tilted his head to the side. That was not the reaction he was expecting.

"Well, yes. Before Janis appeared, and—"

Avryn cut him off before he continued.

"You'll have to tell me the full story at some point, but Lanser, am I glad that you made it out in one piece. That man is—" Avryn was choosing his words carefully. ". . . *has been* known to be very dangerous."

Marric nodded. There was clearly more of a story to that comment, but Avryn didn't appear to want to elaborate on the thought.

"Anyway," Marric continued, "He asked me—or rather, forced me—to Conjure something. I was able to create a bow and arrow. Made from blue

Light."

"Ahh, welcome to the ranks of Conjurers. I thought that was the case, based on the events of your awakening, but I wanted to be sure. It is indeed a very useful gift to have. Perhaps I'll teach you myself, once the chaos dies down."

Once again, it was obvious that the man didn't want to discuss Riln further. Avryn pushed forward with the conversation about Marric's powers again.

"I'm a Mover as well, yes?" Marric said, the memory coming back to him. There was a part of him that thought Riln had mentioned Moving at one point, but his short-term memory was a little jumbled at the moment.

Avryn nodded in affirmation.

"Seer, Conjurer, Mover. I'm sure that those three will come quite in handy together." Avryn said, a thoughtful tone to his voice. "At the sanctum, there will be experienced Seers and Movers to assist you in mastering your abilities. Of course, I can help you with Conjuring. Perhaps now is a good time."

Marric felt a thrill in his chest. Ever since he'd learned that he would awaken to powers of his own, he'd been excited for the day when he could actually use them and become trained on how to master them.

Careful not to allow too much eagerness into his voice, he asked, "What do I do?"

Avryn smiled at his quick response.

"Well, the first thing you must know about Conjuring is that it is powered by the imagination."

The man paused there, apparently wanting that to sink in.

Marric felt a bit disappointed, and he let it come out with an, "Oh."

Avryn chuckled.

"No, we aren't going to spend the next bit of time practicing how to imagine, I think that you are probably quite good at that already. I've found that the younger you are, the more natural that part comes."

Marric sighed in relief.

"All you must do, then, is while thinking of that object, whatever it may be, imagine it being real. You may need to hold open your hand like so."

He extended his hand in front of Marric with his palm open and extended. This time, a small flash of Light announced a pair of spectacles. They were small, with round frames, and looked to be for an old man.

"By practice, holding your hand open isn't required, it just helps the process along. In time, you can conjure anything away from your body as necessary. I once Conjured a large rock above the head of one of my enemies. It knocked them unconcious quite quickly and they didn't even see it coming."

Avryn smiled as Marric looked back at him in disbelief. The idea of that actually happening was such a wonder to the boy. Smile lines creased deeply on the sides of Avryn's eyes, which made him look far older than he likely was.

Deciding that it was better to just try, and feeling less overwhelmed without a pale man throwing knives at him, he held out his hand and tried to think of something to create. Of course, nothing came to mind quickly, so he Conjured what he had before. He imagined his bow, the bow that he'd lost during the scuffle with Prost and his accomplices. With shock, Marric watched as the bow sprung into life made of brilliant blue Light. Once again, Marric expected the bow to be hot, painful to the touch, but instead it was pleasantly warm, and felt remarkably like actual wood.

"Very good. I'm impressed with the detail. It also looks quite functional. Though, a bow and arrow is a bit impractical, considering the distance limit that Conjuring tends to have."

Marric had forgotten about that. Avryn had told him, seemingly ages ago, that Conjured items would disappear once they grew a certain distance away from their creator.

Perhaps we should test it, then, he thought to himself.

"Just a moment." Marric said, lifting his leg over the horse and sliding off.

Marric held out his other hand, creating an arrow, and once again marveled at the strangeness, yet easiness of it all. He nocked it, aimed, and shot the arrow at a tree within ten or so paces. It struck the tree with a crack, and hung there, embedded in the wood where it stayed, unmoving.

Cocking his head, Marric wondered why it hadn't disappeared.

"How long will it stay there?" he suddenly asked, still watching the arrow as if it would escape his view if he looked away even for a moment.

"Ah, it will persist until either you grow too far away, you fall unconscious, or you dismiss it. Which, once again, it is an object of the mind. Simply will it to be gone, and it will."

Feeling a bit ridiculous, Marric thought about the arrow puffing into nothing. Regardless of his feelings, the arrow did snuff out, quickly and completely.

The boy looked down at the bow which still seemed to pulse ever so slightly with Light, then looked up at the moon. They were very much similar in color, which seemed like an unlikely coincidence. Regardless, he was glad that he was being allowed to practice. The thrill that he'd felt before returned to him and he suddenly wanted to keep practicing.

Releasing the bow, Marric thought he'd try something that Avryn might not expect. Looking into the distance, Marric imagined Janis, her slight, yet strong and confident stature, her movements, her hair style, everything that he could think of. A sudden flash of Light in the trees ten or so paces away made Avryn stiffen behind Marric. The man summoned a blade of Light and stopped the horse.

"Someone's here. If I tell you to run, take the horse."

Marric wasn't listening, however. He watched with awe as a seemingly perfect replica of Janis, though made of blue Light, stepped out from the tree and started walking toward them. Jumping down from the horse, Avryn moved to the side, away from the Light-figure and toward the trees nearest there.

"Whoever you are, show yourself!"

Avryn wasn't looking at the Light-Janis, but he was looking around the trees. It was clear that he knew it was a Conjure, and he was likely trying to find the person responsible for it.

"Wait." Marric said.

The man paused, looking at Marric with a hard expression.

"It's Janis."

Avryn's brows furrowed in confusion, the blue moonlight from above shadowing them and causing his eyes to look darker and deeper. Then they relaxed and his face took on a more surprised look.

"Lanser's might," he whispered, watching the woman walk to Marric and stand there, looking down at him slightly. "How did you . . . ?"

Marric stared at her, then he held out his hand and she did as well. The two shook hands, and he gasped at how natural the hand felt, not at all like the Light from which it was actually made.

A slight whistle distracted Marric, and he looked away. As soon as he did so, the Light-created woman disappeared in a puff of what looked like mist made of Light. The moonlight above was once again the brightest source of blue Light, save Avryn's sword, which he soon dismissed after realizing it was Marric's creation.

"That was . . . unexpected." Avryn said, clearly choosing his words wisely. "A Conjure of that sort is uncommon in those who awakened very recently. Of course, we can't Conjure real autonomous living things, they are simply shadows of reality. It seems less confusing now why Watchlight was so interested in you."

At the mention of Watchlight, a question suddenly slipped into Marric's thoughts.

"Why is their Light red?" he asked, unashamed.

Avryn released his sword and walked back to the horse. Marric had dismounted and he didn't even remember doing so. When Avryn didn't offer up the answer quickly enough, Marric said it again.

"The Light of our powers is blue, like Mallan," he said, pointing up, "but Riln's, I mean, the robed man, his were red. Very red."

"Ahhh, so that's what you mean." Avryn said, nodding his head. "To be honest, Marric, no one really knows. At least, no one that I've talked to. There is one thing that we *do* know, however."

He paused after that, thinking for a moment.

"I'm sorry," he said after the quiet. "This is very perplexing to me, and I think perhaps it lends aid to our perception of Watchlight as a whole."

Avryn shook his head then, still bothered by something.

"All Lightbearers, as far as we have seen, awaken to Light colored blue, like ours. However, it seems that those who choose to follow Watchlight find that their Light gradually changes to red. It seems very odd and unexplainable, but I will say that it does come in handy to know where allegiances lie."

It was obvious that Avryn took quite some comfort in that idea, but for Marric, it lent him no such feeling. For some reason, that knowledge made his stomach churn. There was something so unsettling, even more so than his first encounters with Lightbearing, about the red-lit powers of Riln and those at Watchlight.

Avryn cleared his throat, apparently noticing that Marric was bothered by the subject. So he returned them to what they were working on before.

"So, perhaps we should continue with your Conjuring." Avryn said. He narrowed his eyes at Marric then, not in a suspicious way, but merely in a curious one. "Conjuring images of people, especially those with the likeness of someone else is very challenging. Have you done that before?"

Marric shrugged. "No, but it felt right at the moment. I'm worried about them."

"Ah, yes. I wouldn't worry too much. Shrell and Harmel are very smart in situations like this."

The man chuckled then. "And Janis has more than proven herself resourceful, to say the least."

The boy nodded, though he didn't feel as confident in their safety as Avryn did. He couldn't explain why, but he had a feeling that something was about to happen and it felt off. The two mounted the mare and set off again.

"How much longer until we are there?" Marric said, suddenly shifting topics.

"To the sanctum? Oh, only a couple more hours. We are quite close."

They both fell into silence, Marric's Conjuring training coming to an abrupt end. The boy was still amazed and full of wonder at his new abilities, but he wasn't in the mood to learn about them anymore at the moment. He regretted asking about the color of Watchlight's powers, but at the same time, he didn't.

The mare on which they rode clopped, the echo seeming so loud, yet so quiet at the same time. It was quiet, save for the hooves and an occasional snort or snuff from the horse. The night seemed to drag on, and Mallan eventually set, leaving them in a dark period before Isllan would rise, and with it, the fog. In his mind, that was the worst part of every night. He'd been out in the fog more than once since they'd journeyed, and no, they hadn't been killed or attacked, but it felt . . . wrong.

Avryn must have sensed Marric's unrest, for he spoke then.

"We are almost there, Marric. We'll probably be in the sanctum before the fog comes out, so try to relax."

That seemed a silly statement to him, for the last time they had been near their destination, an ambush seemed to have been waiting.

Fear gripped him at the memory, and a flash of Light to their left exploded, causing Marric to cry out, almost falling off the horse. Avryn gripped him by the waist and hoisted him back in the saddle.

"What was— "

"Marric, you need to relax. It is all going to be fine."

"—but—"

"That flash of Light was you, Marric."

Avryn spoke softly, trying to keep relaxed. It was clear, however, that the Light had stressed him out. They may be close, but the darkness before Isllan made their powers stand out far too much, and that could give their position away.

"What do you mean it was me? I didn't mean to."

"Your powers, at least until you understand more how to control them, will be triggered by memories quite easily. I suspect you were remembering something stressful, am I right?"

Marric only nodded, trying with difficulty to not let the memories come back, fearing that it would happen again.

A reassuring hand gripped the boy's shoulder and Avryn said, "It happens. For now, may I ask that you focus on where we are going? Our Light is far too bright right now, and I would like to get inside before the fog comes out."

Marric nodded in agreement, though the oppressive memory of the ambush was still imposing on his mind.

The two travelers lapsed into silence once more, which allowed Marric to gather his thoughts and ponder on their conversation and his small amount of training. Fortunately, this seemed to make the time go very quickly. In the darkness, Marric couldn't really tell much about the landscape, and he even wondered how Avryn or the horse could tell which direction they were going, yet they walked on. The air seemed to start cooling, indicating that the fog would soon arrive. However, not a moment after Marric started feeling it, the horse stopped. Isllan's orange light had only started to peek through, and they had left the trees and entered a clearing in front of a great cliff.

The air was much wetter, and Marric could hear the sound of running water somewhere, like the combination of many streams or small waterfalls weaving together into a complex sound.

Strangely, Avryn steered the horse right up to the face of the rock and dismounted, leaving Marric there alone. In the weak light of the third moon, Marric saw the man walk even closer to the wall, so that his face was merely a handspan away. He then held up his hand and slowly placed it there, palm open and fingers spread. A blue glow emitted from his hand, pulsing softly. The boy watched in wonder as he stood there for a few moments, not moving. Then he immediately pulled his hand away and stepped back.

All was quiet, and Marric felt a chill in his spine at the weirdness of the night, and the fact that Avryn had just touched a wall for seemingly no reason. A sound rang out suddenly, like cracking rocks. It started small, then grew to a louder groan and a rumbling as well.

Marric's hair stood on end as he watched with amazement as the rock wall appeared to break—no, *open* before them. A door, about twice the height of Avryn himself and four times as wide, slid backwards, creating a depression, then continued to slide into the wall on the side. The sound of this all happening might not have been significant if it hadn't been for the stillness of the forest and night around them.

In time, the rock door and the sound it made finished, leaving a gaping hole in the rock in front of them. The fog was starting to coalesce around them, just before the door had completed its journey, making Marric feel nervous and exposed.

Avryn turned to Marric and a bright smile was covering his face.

"We're here. Welcome to the sanctum of Terris Green."

Chapter 21

The forest was getting colder, and Janis knew that it was about time for the fog to come out, tickling their skin and heightening their senses. She really didn't mind its effects, but other people tended to be whiny or dramatic about the whole thing, and she didn't particularly feel like listening to this from her two companions.

Just then, a stick broke and she winced at the sound. It wasn't an overly loud sound, but even a small one could give their position away if there were assassins near them on any side. With the impending arrival of the fog, the other sounds of the forest—however few they were this late into the evening, ceased. That was part of the problem with now being the time to make sound. She had half considered telling her companions, Shrell and Harmel, that stopping and keeping quiet would be the best idea, but they were determined to reach some destination that they insisted was close.

Soon after Marric and Avryn had left them, the three of them had decided to shift their path toward a safe place slightly closer than the sanctum. There they could at least hide or make preparations for any Watchlight operatives that were definitely following them. After the ruckus Janis and Marric had made, she was sure they had sent people to find them. Before the three companions left, they had taken the time to cover the tracks of the horse, hoping that Watchlight would instead follow their own. Janis suspected that they would anyway, for when the two of them had escaped the cave, they were on foot.

Fortunately, they had all agreed that covering their own tracks wouldn't be worth the time, but that they should just move quickly and set up defenses, hoping to last it out until Avryn could bring backup. Janis wasn't overly confident that they would last that long, but it was better than getting caught without preparations at all.

Before long, Shrell increased his speed, which was quite noticeable as they were already briskly walking. Traveling had become challenging without Avryn's very useful Lightbearing, but they managed. During dark times in between moons, they just had to slow down and try not to make noise. Janis didn't have much trouble; she had trained to work in the dark, but her companions struggled a bit. Fortunately, it was easy to feel safer in the dark, for if Watchlight was following them, their telltale red Light would have given them away long before they got close in the dark.

"The cave is righ' up 'ere."

Janis heard the words, but didn't believe him for there seemed to be no indication of a rock wall at all. However, to her surprise, the ground inclined suddenly and, after going through some trees, they came to a rock cliff.

She squinted her eyes.

"I don't see a cave here. Are you sure you brought us in the right direction?"

"Aye, milady," Harmel said thickly, his stupid grin filling up his whole face. "Oi am sure tha' yeh aren' doubtin' my skills, are yeh?"

He winked then.

Janis rolled her eyes at the comment. Harmel had of course spent too much of the time telling them about something inconsequential that he thought was funny or meaningful. Thankfully, when darkness came fully, they all agreed to stay quiet.

"Yeh jus' 'ave to look closely, *assassin*." Shrell said, sounding unimpressed. He had emphasized the last word as if it was some type of insult.

For some reason, this only amused her.

Janis turned to the cliff and began looking closely. It looked like a regular cliff wall, nothing to show but rough edges and jutting sharp pieces of rock. She started to move closer to the wall and kept observing. After a moment, she felt something. There was a slight puffing of cool air on her face. It was small, and most people wouldn't notice anything. Holding her hands up, she felt it to her right. Curious, she took a step that way and her eyes widened. There was air coming from the wall.

Moving closely, she drew her long dagger and held it aloft.

"The rock wall ain't gonna kill yeh, milady." Harmel said, stifling a snicker.

She ignored the comment.

As she moved closer, she saw it. There was a crack in the wall covered by a jutting rock that hid it entirely. But, if you got close, you could see around the rock and see a slit large enough for a person to pass through.

Clever, Janis thought.

"Are we sure it's safe in there?"

Shrell scoffed at the comment.

"I am sure, aye. No one has seen the likes of this place. Yeh have t' trust us." Shrell said.

Despite this, he held up his hand for Janis and Harmel to wait, and then he slipped inside, his hand resting on his sword.

Not a moment later, he called for them to enter.

Janis almost felt a strong eagerness to enter, curious to know what it looked like inside. However, she lingered back, wanting to check a few things outside. Harmel entered without hesitation, and poked his head back out, a curious look on his face.

"I'll be there in a minute. I need to set some traps."

The man grinned again, then nodded and disappeared into the hidden crack.

There was no waste in spending a lot of time setting traps, at least that was the way Janis always felt. She took a considerable amount of time setting noise traps, for at the moment that was all she could manage with her meager supplies. She whittled some sticks to points, hiding them well so that she could at least surprise someone with pain. It might also be helpful should she ever be disarmed. Pointed sticks could be handy if knives weren't an option.

The fog had come out not too long into her trap setting, and she felt the familiar increase of her heartbeat, the eagerness to fight, the constant feeling that there was someone there, ready to attack. She reveled in the feeling, for it was familiar to her. In time, she finished what she was working on and moved to the cave. Just before entering, however, she took a deep breath, taking in the fog effects, then she slipped into the cave.

Harmel and Shrell had set up some type of cloth blocking the entrance and she pushed it aside, annoyed. She soon understood why. As she went in, her eyes were hit with a bright light.

For a moment, she stood there, tense, as her eyes adjusted to the light. Finally acclimated, she looked and saw that the 'bright light' was merely a candle. Its brightness was only an effect of her coming from the dimmer moonlit outside.

The cavern inside was actually quite large, which was surprising. Two additional cave openings sat at the rear, one moving off to the right and the other straight back. An alcove was set into the wall on the left, and supplies of all sorts were piled up there. Harmel had already used a lever to pry open one of the crates and pulled out what looked like hardtack. He crunched it happily and came to sit by the candle.

"See? T'was worth the bit o' detour ta make it 'ere for the nigh'. Oi thinks we'll be righ' fine and comfy waitin' 'ere till the morn." Harmel said, taking another clearly exaggerated bite of the food he was eating.

"Right, I think yer right, Harm. Let's just hope that we ain't gonna be Seen by anyone. They'd find us right quick then." Shrell said, a grimace on his face.

Janice felt her stomach clench at the comment and suddenly felt like they were being watched. Though she couldn't be completely sure that she understood how it all worked, the comment reminded her that as soon as Avryn and Marric split off, they had taken with them their only defense against the so-called Seers.

"I set traps," she said, as if to reassure herself.

Harmel looked up from his hardtack, pausing a moment with a half-chewed chunk slightly visible through his partially open mouth. He sat there for a beat, then chuckled and kept eating.

"Good, Oi thinks. Though Oi ain't thinkin' a few traps will do much 'gainst a whole lotta them Watchlight Lightbearers."

He paused a moment, then chuckled to himself about what he'd just said.

"Watchlight Lightbearers, say tha' a bunch fast." Then he laughed a bit more at his comment.

Janis watched him incredulously, trying to understand how the man could possibly joke about such a thing when they were, in reality, sitting like unsuspecting deer about to get hunted. Though not much comforted her at the moment, the thought of her traps were all that gave her a small bit of hope that they could make it through the night.

"Good idea, Janis. Thank yous." Shrell said.

The woman started at the comment, then looked curiously at Shrell. That was the first time he'd said or done anything that was remotely approving of her and her ways. It didn't make her feel anything particularly different about the man, but it was curious. Watching him, she noticed that he was moving constantly. He wouldn't sit for a long period of time anywhere. He had settled for a moment here by the candle, but soon stood up and walked to the supplies, taking inventory, before walking around, examining the walls.

He was nervous.

Despite Harmel's confidence and nonchalance about the situation, it was clear that his older brother was not feeling the same. Shrell had proven quite confident, if not a bit full of ego, ever since they'd been traveling together. Though this was odd behavior for him, it did make Janis more wary about their situation.

"We do 'ave a bit 'o tricks in a bag, we'll just 'ave to be smart 'bout 'ow we use 'em." Shrell said, his accent seeming a bit thicker than usual.

Must be the nerves, Janis thought. The same thing happened to her on occasion, so she understood how it could happen to him.

The three sat down and ate some more of the provisions and determined that sleep would likely be a good companion. Janis, of course, didn't volunteer for the first watch. By now, she had enough trust for the men that she could rest without being concerned for her own life. She had done the calculations and determined that even if Watchlight was following and they had Seers to guide them directly here, they wouldn't be here for a while still. It appeared that Shrell had performed similar logic, for he didn't volunteer either. Thus, Harmel was tasked with keeping an eye out while the two slept. With that, she slipped into the 'in-between', needing some time to analyze what had happened between Marric's abduction and now.

* * *

Terris Green was remarkable. Marric's mouth gaped as they entered the rock wall through the hole that had just appeared. Dazzling spheres of blue Light, bright and intense, hovered near the tops of the walls at regular intervals. Men and women stood here and there, stiffly, acting as sentinels for the entrance, though why, Marric couldn't understand. There was no possible way that anyone would find that entrance. Also, it appeared that a non-Lightbearer couldn't even enter.

As they passed the guards, most of them nodded in welcome, though a few of them had smiles spread across their faces and they greeted Avryn warmly. A handful of them did not, but it was clear that Avryn was a popular figure here. Curiously, Marric noted that only about half of the guards that they passed had visible weapons of any sort. Either the guards themselves were forgetful, or there was something else at play here.

"Why are some of them unarmed?" Marric whispered to Avryn.

Raising an eyebrow at the comment, Avryn gave an approving nod.

"Impressive. Many do not notice such things when they first come here." Avryn said, obviously pleased. "The idea is that we should be prepared for anything. Most of the guard pairs have one combat Lightbearer, and one combat fighter. This hopefully prepares them for any time a Lightbearer's power might be rendered useless."

Marric's blood chilled. He suddenly remembered Riln's words about how Prost was 'of the void' and shivered. *Are there more people like Prost?* He resigned to ask Avryn about it later. Now didn't seem like the right time.

The tunnel continued downwards, but at a small slope. They weren't going deep into the recesses beneath the mountain, but rather into the mountain itself. Before long, they came to an archway and just before they passed through, Marric gasped. Just beyond the archway, the ground was covered in plants bathed in orange light.

His stomach twisted, remembering the red Light of the Watchlight Lightbearers. But then, theirs had been very red. This was more like the light of the moon, Isllan.

Marric soon discovered it *was* Isllan as they passed through the arch. He looked up immediately and found an enormous opening above them, high up in the mountain. Isllan herself was just peeking over the edge of the hole, shining her orange light down. His throat clenched as he saw that the fog had made its way downward, though it had stopped about halfway down from the hole. It also wasn't as thick as it usually was, as if it was not fully being accepted into this sanctum.

Avryn breathed in deeply next to him, and Marric looked over to see the man standing with his eyes closed and his arms slightly outstretched. He was clearly taking it all in.

"I feel like I haven't been here in ages. It's nice to be home."

As if on queue, someone shouted Avryn's name and the two of them looked over to the other side of the strange open-topped cavern to see a woman, or more like a later teenaged girl, rushing over to them. She was of average height, but appeared plump and well fed. Her dark brown hair was tied back with a piece of twine. The girl had a smile on her face and she rushed forward with her arms wide open. There was a soft thud as she ran fully into Avryn's arms and the two embraced.

"Oi, it's righ' good t'see the likes of yous around here, yeh old man." Her accent came through surprisingly thick. It made Marric need to strain a bit to understand what she was saying.

"Kh'areen, how have you been?" Avryn said brightly.

"Oi, t'aint worth talking 'bout the likes of me now, eh? What 'bouts yous? Where's Harm? 'Oos this?" Kh'areen said, pointing to Marric.

She had spouted questions out so quickly that when she pointed at him, he started.

"Ah, yes, this is the boy we were looking for. The world's newest

Lightbearer." Avryn beamed at the comment.

Kh'areen whistled softly, and nodded.

"'E looks a bit smaller than I thought e'd look for a sixteen-year-old. Thistle'll be 'appy t'meet 'im for reals, eh?"

Marric blinked, trying to consecutively take in his surroundings and understand the strange accent of this person. Her name was strange enough for Marric to digest, but the strangeness was further backed up by her odd attitude and way of speaking.

"And how is your sister?" Avryn said, smiling still. He glanced over at Marric, noticed the look on his face, and said, "Thistle is Kh'areen's sister, and the one that happened to have Seen you first of all our Seers."

Marric nodded, though only because he wasn't sure what else to do.

"Meh, she's okay. Nuttin' fancy at all."

The two of them continued to chat with each other, but Marric tuned them out for a minute, opting to give his mind a bit of a break from the overwhelming nature of the space around him. A couple men milled about in the opening, tending to plants and crops that spotted the area. He did find it odd that they were up at all, given how late it was. The clearing wasn't filled with plants completely, but large patches of various things grew here and there, the empty parts forming pathways through the greenery. Marric observed the men, and found them to be quite normal. They each wore very standard clothing, dull in color, but well kept. There were no strange black robes, and Marric suspected that is why he wasn't panicking entirely.

Some aspects of this place remind me too much of where Watchlight housed themselves. Marric shivered at the thought.

"E's a bit out there, eh?" Kh'areen's voice said, startling Marric back to the conversation.

"Oh, I'm sorry. It's just . . . . " he didn't know what to say, so he said the first thing that came to mind. "This place is strange."

Kh'areen scrunched her nose up and made a disapproving face.

"Hey now, it's 'ome to us, strange or no."

Avryn laughed.

"Take no offense to his comments, Kh'areen. It can be overwhelming to take in the sanctum. Let him process it as he needs. Alright? Now, where is Magness? We'd best see her as soon as possible. I have urgent news."

Kh'areen continued to stare at Marric, eyebrows furrowed slightly as if she disapproved of his presence, but she pointed to her left toward that side of the cavern and what appeared to be another opening.

"Thank you," Avryn said. "We'd best get going. Come along, Marric."

Avryn turned and weaved through the various plants on the pathways toward the opening on their right. Of course they were greeted with many more welcomes and hellos before they made it to the cave. Marric was pleased to know that his impression of Avryn as a very friendly and outgoing person was confirmed by all of the people here. It wasn't that he never believed it, but it was still a nice confirmation.

The cave opening shrunk and became a narrow tunnel almost instantly as they entered. Here, the ceilings were lower, which put the orbs of blue Light within touching distance of Marric's hands. An urge entered his arms to reach up and just brush one of them lightly to see what would happen, but he resisted. But the tunnel wasn't ending anytime soon, so the urge got the better of him.

Embarrassed, he slowed down just a bit, putting a small amount of distance between him and Avryn, then he timidly reached up and brushed his fingers through the ball of Light.

He yelped as a tingling sensation filled his hands. It didn't spread any further than his hands, so it wasn't alarming, but it had taken him by surprise.

Avryn turned at the sound and found Marric holding his hand to his chest as if he'd been burned.

"Are you quite alright, lad?" Avryn asked.

"Erm—" Marric said, "Yes, I was just surprised is all. I—"

He paused, his face flushing from his childish experiment on the Lightbearer orbs.

"I touched one."

Avryn lifted his eyebrows at the comment, clearly not understanding what Marric was saying.

Sighing heavily, Marric pointed up slowly at one of the blue orbs. Avryn followed his pointing, and then chuckled.

"Ahh, I see. Yes, I suspect I should have guessed what you meant." Avryn said, sounding pleased. "I forget that most new Lightbearers often get curious and grabby when we go through this hall."

He winked at Marric during that last comment. This just made him flush even deeper red.

"I—I hope it's alright that I did."

The man laughed this time, tickled by the comment.

"Oh yes, yes, of course! Though I bet it did feel a bit odd."

Marric nodded at the comment. Odd was definitely the best way of putting what he felt.

"Lightbearer powers, well—their origin is still a bit unknown, but we can all agree that the physical touch of one Lightbearer's creations to another feels . . . fuzzy, for lack of a better term."

I'd say that was an apt description, Marric thought.

"It's unclear why that is the case, but it is harmless. Touch all you like, it won't hurt you in any way." Avryn said. "Now, come along, we haven't much time."

Relief filled Marric that he hadn't done anything wrong and he hesitantly reached up to touch another Light. Sure enough, the strange tingling sensation filled his fingers and hands, though this time he didn't pull back quickly, expecting the outcome of the touching. Instead, he let his hand linger there, trying to identify the feeling. It felt much like his foot might as a child when he sat on top of it for too long. He almost got lost in the feeling until he looked over to see that Avryn had moved far ahead of him.

He quickly removed his hand and rushed after the man, who seemed to stop for nothing.

Soon enough, the tunnel ended and they entered a normal sized cave, decorated comfortably with couches and fur rugs along the floor and the walls. A few people milled about, reading books and chatting softly. There was a desk to their left with a spectacled woman sitting there reading a book that seemed far too large to be possible.

"Well, hello, Narinda, good to see you again." Avryn said brightly.

For the first time since they'd arrived, a person barely acknowledged Avryn's presence at all. Rather than looking up and saying something welcoming, the woman kept looking down at the impossibly thick book and waved her hand dismissively at him.

Marric stared at her, not sure how to react. She had light brown hair, pulled tightly into a bun. Her spectacles were large circles, extending out over her cheeks.

"Enjoying a bit of light reading?" Avryn said, clearly prodding her.

The woman sighed heavily, clearly not impressed with his joke.

"You know as well as I do, Avryn, that I have quite a bit of free time. I would actually say that this *is* light reading, so take your jibes elsewhere. Perhaps try a few on Magness, you will likely have more success there." Narinda said.

Avryn beamed, obviously finding himself very clever.

"Yes, yes, perhaps I just might, then."

The man turned and began heading toward the only door that stood in the room, other than the entry way that they had just used to enter the cave. Before he'd taken three steps, however, he'd paused, turned, and returned to his former place.

"How rude of me." Avryn said, sounding troubled. "Narinda, this is Marric. The newest Lightbearer to join our ranks. How about you two get acquainted while I mobilize assistance for our stranded companions."

Narinda looked up from her book at that comment and she stared flatly at Marric, clearly unphased.

"I see . . . and what class of Lighbringer do we have here, then?"

Marric looked at her, feeling nervous for some reason. For a moment, they both stared there in silence. Marric looked to Avryn for help, but he was no longer there.

"Well . . . " Marric began, not sure where to start.

At length, he determined that it perhaps would be easiest to just say it without much of an explanation or pause.

"Conjurer, Mover, Seer."

Narinda's reaction was not at all what he'd expected, for she'd appeared extremely dry so far in all of their interactions. Her mouth dropped in shock and she let the gigantic book fall to the table with a loud thud that echoed slightly through the cave they were in, drawing a couple looks from others in the room.

"I see," she said finally. "So you're the one they Saw, then."

Marric just nodded, slightly embarrassed.

"Well then, Magness will be quite relieved to have you here, I think." Narinda said.

Marric's stomach twisted a bit at the comment. It was odd that she spoke of him as if he was commonly known to everyone. Before Marric could think too much into this comment, Avryn interrupted his musings, having just emerged from the intricate double doors he'd left through moments before. A messenger came with him and rushed down the hallway they'd just come through, clearly in a hurry.

"Marric, you may have not realized, Narinda here is one of our Lightbearers."

This made Marric lose track of his thoughts, curious to meet another Lightbearer.

"What . . . um. . ." he paused, suddenly feeling silly. What word had she used when she asked him just a moment ago?

Avryn chuckled beside him and said, "You mean to ask what class she is."

Marric nodded.

Narinda sighed heavily, as if the question was a burden to her soul, but she finally responded, not with words, but by holding up her hand and creating a bright ball of blue Light. Its intensity and brightness made Marric squint and look away slightly. Slowly, it raised up into the room and hovered slightly below the ceiling.

"You have already benefited from my power since you've been here, Marric."

Marric felt confused, not sure what that meant. Fortunately, Avryn spared him with an explanation.

"Narinda is currently the active Lighter on duty—she is and has been the one Lighting the whole sanctum with her powers."

This staggered Marric.

How? How can one person Light a whole network of tunnels?!

Avryn chuckled next to him, clearly sensing his surprise and probably anticipating his thoughts.

"I will admit, when I first met a Lighter that showed me the extent of their powers, I was so taken aback that I fell on my backside."

Narinda shifted her eyes to Avyrn, her eyes showing pride, but the rest of her face showing frustration at their presence.

"There's something else that I haven't shown you yet, Marric." Avryn said. "I was waiting until you bore your own Light to tell you about it. Narinda, would you please?"

This comment meant nothing to Marric, but Narinda seemed to understand. She pulled back the orb of Light that she'd sent to hover near the ceiling a moment ago. Its movement was slow, graceful, unwavering, and all Marric could do was stare in awe at the sheer control of it all.

Finally, it rested in a position a few feet above and to the left of him. Marric had to squint at the proximity.

"Now," Avryn said. "Let's see a display of your abilities, hmm?"

Marric gaped at him.

"You want—what?"

The man sighed.

"Honestly Marric, you need to learn to be less shy about your new powers around people. Just Conjure something. Perhaps something that you've done in the past."

Marric stood for a moment, thinking back to anything he'd actually Conjured. There had only been one object, so he followed the instructions. The bow sprang to life in his left hand. As soon as he did, however, he felt tingling in his hands, similar to what he'd felt when he'd touched the orb of Light when they'd first entered. He gasped at the feeling and almost dropped his Conjured bow. Was the Light . . . *brighter?!*

"You can feel it, can't you?" Avryn said, wonder in his eyes.

"I feel something."

Without instructions to do so, only out of curiosity, Marric raised his bow and a Conjured arrow appeared in his right hand. He nocked it, pulled, and let it fly, right at the stone wall. The arrow struck with a loud crack and entered into the hard stone, burying halfway up the staff.

Marric's mouth fell open.

"But—how? When I'd done that before, the arrow just bounced off."

"That's it, you see?" Avryn exclaimed. "For some reason, it appears that the Light from a Lighter's powers enhances the effects of the others."

What is Lanser's name could that *mean*? Marric thought to himself.

"I'm not sure I understand." Marric felt suddenly overwhelmed, the tingling-burning sensation distracting him.

"To be honest, neither do we. We just recently discovered this and it's been a remarkable revelation."

Narinda sighed at the conversation.

"Can I *please* get back to reading now?" the woman complained.

Avryn laughed at the comment, but nodded.

"I'm sorry, Narinda, I'm just pleased that Marric is alright and that he is finally here."

Avryn beamed at the comment, his smile seeming unnecessarily large.

"Anyway, Marric, let's move on. There is someone that you should meet. We have already started preparing reinforcements for our friends, but let's take a moment to speak to her while we wait."

There was something in his voice in that last comment. He seemed eager, or even excited, which wasn't something that Marric normally noticed in the man's tone.

With that, the two of them walked past the shelf of books to the wooden double doors that stood there. A beautiful image of a tree was carved so that the tree filled up the double doors, the split cutting the tree in half. Images were hidden in the branches and leaves, symbols, seemingly random objects, and sometimes people. The sight of it was mesmerizing and Marric paused to inspect it further. There was so much to see, however, that he couldn't focus on any particular part.

Suddenly, his eyes stopped on a face. It was hidden in one of the branches near the trunk. For some reason, it drew his gaze and he couldn't look away. It was a woman's face, strikingly beautiful and somehow familiar.

Avryn cleared his throat, making Marric jump.

"Sorry," Marric apologized. "It's just that this door is remarkable."

"Oh, it's no worry, I just didn't want to interrupt your view by opening it until you were done." Avryn said.

"I suspect I could spend hours looking, but let's move on."

Nodding, Avryn pushed the door open to the next room. Inside, there was a table with maps laid out, a few sofas, and chairs lining the walls. An older woman with mousy brown hair stood at the table. Her greying hair was also cropped close to her head, like a man's. None of it had turned completely white, so Marric guessed that it had only started to turn recently. Her back was to them and she was inspecting the map that was there. She wore a white dress that fell to her ankles, made of some shiny fabric, perhaps silk. A sword was strapped on a leather belt that was around her waist, which seemed out of place against her white dress.

When she heard the door open, she turned and a look of surprise came to her face.

"Oh, Avryn! You've made it back at last!"

With that, she crossed the room quickly and embraced him warmly. It wasn't intimate in any way so as to indicate that this was his spouse, but more an embrace that one would give to their close friend. She did seem a bit too old for him as well. Marric stood there awkwardly as he watched.

After she had hugged Avryn, she turned to Marric and smiled. Wrinkles at the sides of her eyes dug deep into her face, making her seem even older and somehow even happier. Her eyes were a bright green, warm and inviting. There was something behind them that he couldn't describe, but it was obvious. Was it relief?

"Marric. I am so glad to finally meet you. I've wanted to for so long now."

The boy didn't say anything. He was trying to think of what to say to her.

"Erm . . . yes."

Rather than say something about his awkward reply, the woman just laughed.

"I suppose some introductions are in order. I am Magness, the leader of Evenir."

Marric gaped for a moment.

"Evenir? What does it mean?" he asked.

The woman raised her hands up in front of her and gestured to the door behind him. She looked regal and strong as she did so, and only then did Marric realize how tall she was, standing a half-handspan above Avryn himself.

"*Evenir* means together, or gathering in the old language. It is our 'gathering' of friends and family. It is a sanctum for those touched by Lightbearing that seek to preserve it and its connection to humankind. We oppose those who disavow bonds between Lightbearers and normal humans."

With a start, Marric realized that he'd never thought to ask what they called themselves. Avryn *had* indicated that they had formed a sort of group, but he'd never mentioned that they had a name. Marric supposed that made sense, given that Watchlight had their own name.

"But, you and I share a different bond than others." She said this as her eyes welled up with tears.

Marric already felt uncomfortable enough in the presence of this woman, but now her tears made him feel more awkward. She stared at him for a time, and put her hand on his shoulder, squeezing gently.

"What do you mean?" he asked, still curious despite his discomfort.

She sighed, then spoke again.

"Marric, your mother, Talatha. She was my sister. I am your aunt."

His stomach churned. His mother had a sister? The room seemed to spin slightly. His father had never mentioned an aunt, or that his mother had any siblings at all. It had always been just himself and his father—until Tins arrived. Except Tins was dead now.

Marric's mind was moving so fast that it started to make him lightheaded. It was clear that he didn't have the mind or energy to process this all now, so instead he pushed it deep inside and changed the subject.

"What's your power, then?" he blurted out, feeling overwhelmed. He had said it unintentionally with a bit of bite to his tone. Magness raised an eyebrow at the comment, but said nothing.

Well, that was awkward, Marric thought.

"I have none." Magness said simply.

He looked up at her sharply, feeling confused. Marric expected to see anger, or at least a bit of offense at his comment, but he saw none. Instead, she looked strong, calm, and yet carried a bit of tenderness in her eyes for him. Were his emotions really that obvious?

"I have no powers of a Lightbearer, Marric. One doesn't need to have such things to lead those that do. A leader needs different skills, ones that I've had the opportunity to learn from my predecessor."

She paused then, and eyed Avryn. Something passed between the two, and she stopped there.

Marric thought that the reaction was quite odd, but didn't press the subject. He'd learned in the past with Avryn that the man had good reasons for holding back information and he trusted him for that.

"I hope that doesn't give you the wrong impression, Marric. I am quite able with my sword," she said, patting the long sword that hung at her side. "Regardless, you aren't here to talk about my skills at all. You must have many questions."

Marric blinked, trying to think. All of this was so overwhelming that he couldn't frame any questions. It was clear that his mind was shutting down and he was having a hard time formulating cohesive thoughts. Ironically, there was only one question that he could think of at the time.

"Is that you carved into the door back there?"

Magness started at the question, then pressed her lips together. She looked at Avryn to the side and pursed her lips even more. Avryn closed his eyes and gave a slight nod, as if agreeing with her on something before she proceeded.

"No, Marric." Magness said, apprehension in her tone. "That is Talatha. Your mother."

That struck him.

Marric struggled to keep his knees from buckling, just managing to stay upright.

My—my mother?!

He couldn't speak. It suddenly felt as if his thoughts couldn't accept it. He was at capacity; couldn't hold any more. He was tired, and his stomach had only just reminded him that he was quite hungry.

A warm hand gripped him on the shoulder and he collapsed into the body that had somehow appeared next to him. Marric buried his face into the tunic that was there and wept. He didn't know why, but he couldn't stop. He just cried for a time into the shirt, not wanting to look out.

It took Marric a moment to realize that it was Avryn who had his arms around him and he was wetting his clothing with his tears. His companions said nothing, but let him weep. After he felt somewhat emptied from his sadness, he asked, voice shaky, "But . . . she died when I was a young boy."

Looking pained, Magness shook her head.

"No, Marric, she left to protect you and your father. She was the former leader of Evenir, and hers is the face of beauty that is carved into the door just behind you."

Marric understood now what information they were keeping from him, and part of him wished that they had done just that. He felt empty and hollow, his chest hurting from the revelation.

"Wait, you said '*was*'."

The pain in her face deepened.

"Yes, she was killed in battle only this year. She went back years ago for you and your father, but when she did, she found your father had remarried. She couldn't take you from your father, and she reasoned that you'd be safer living in ignorance of Lightbearing."

As unlikely as it seemed, Marric wasn't too affected by the news. He suspected that he was already deep in pain too far for something like this to make it worse.

"Marric, in time you will learn of your mother. She was a marvelous warrior, and the most skilled Shielder of our time. Not to mention her amazing leadership. Please, take time to grieve, but there is much to be done. I am only happy that you are safe."

Magness scrunched her eyebrows together then, and looked up at Avryn. "We must hurry to Harmel and Shrell."

Avryn jumped in shock as if reminded.

"Marric was taken by Watchlight, but Janis went after him and they were able to escape through her skills and Marric's Sight, but—"

"Who in Lanser's name is Janis?! And why was this strange person the one to retrieve the boy?"

Avryn blushed in shame. This was another odd time that Marric had seen the man show emotion other than complete confidence and clarity. Magness suddenly intimidated the boy.

"Janis is an assassin that was protecting Marric when we found him. She is quite skilled. Regardless, we must get there before they are engaged by Watchlight. I suspect they are sending many. Hopefully by now our men and women are ready to leave."

A familiar buzz in Marric's head prepared him for what was next. His eyes felt like they were opening wide and the world faded away. He was somewhere else, in the darkness. The last moon had already passed and morning would only be a few hours away. The forest was quiet, dark and unmoving. All at once, a flash shone in the distance and Marric's vision zoomed closer to see at least a hundred people, possibly more, moving there. Light orbs floated red and ominous in the air, making their faces red. A man was at the head.

Prost.

His vision turned around and moved forward through the trees a spell, though not far, to a slit in a cave. Moving into the cave, he saw three people. Shrell and Harmel slept, Janis stood watch.

Then it was done.

"They are almost there," he whispered.

Avryn and Magness were still looking at each other and his comment made them turn.

"I Saw it. Prost is almost there. And he has at least a hundred others with him. They know exactly where they are. Janis and the others."

Magness face hardened and she swept toward the door in a rush.

"Come, we must hurry."

Marric followed behind as Magness threw open the doors and rushed into the library that they'd just passed through. She walked so briskly that Marric practically had to run to keep up with her. Her urgency was encouraging, mostly because he was nervous for Janis, Shrell, and Harmel. There were only three of them and he'd seen what was coming.

It struck him that he had no idea if what he Saw was happening right now, or if it would happen in the future. Straining his brain, he tried to remember details about the vision. Anything that could determine the time.

His thoughts were interrupted as the three of them entered a large cavern, this one also full of plants, and Magness shouted loudly.

"Brothers and sisters, it's time to move now! There is no time for delay!"

To Marric's surprise, men and women emerged from all the hallways, in organized groups and prepared with travel gear.

Magness turned to Avyrn.

"I think it's best if you go with them, my friend. It seems your objective is not yet complete."

The man nodded, then turned to Marric.

"You are safe here, Marric. You've nothing to worry about at—"

"'Urry up, love! We ain't got much time y'see!" a voice shouted behind them. A short and plump, yet very muscley man rushed beside them and snatched up a spear that was laying there before rushing into a tunnel.

Avryn continued. "—at all. Watchlight knows nothing about Terris Green."

Magness joined them and interrupted Avryn.

"I'll watch over the boy. Go, Avryn."

He nodded, then ruffled Marric's hair. It made him feel as if he was a young boy, but it didn't bother him. It was endearing to him.

Avryn rushed off through a tunnel and was gone. Marric had a distinct pit in his stomach that it could be the last time he saw the man, but he forced the feeling away. They had an army, they could contend with Watchlight, right?

* * *

Janis sat on a bit of rock that jutted out from the wall at an odd angle. All she could think was how impossible something like this could have been created naturally. It seemed such a strange feature to a cave that was otherwise nondescript, similar to all others she'd camped in.

Harmel snored loudly on the ground next to the dead fire. Embers still glowed from inside the white and black burned wood, a bit of heat still coming off. The two men had insisted that starting the fire during the night was reasonable, considering the black cloth that covered the entrance of the cave. Janis was skeptical, so she instead let it die quickly, opting to not feed it more wood. They had plenty, but with the two men sleeping, she figured that she could do it her way. It bothered her that she allowed them to take the first watch, but she had been getting weary.

Despite her annoyance at the situation, nothing had actually happened during the night, and now it was her turn to take watch. Her thoughts wandered through the events of the past few weeks. There were still some things that didn't add up, and she felt silly for not thinking of them until now. In all honesty, she'd forgotten much about the original job that she'd been given. After all, Luden's men had been killed quite quickly by Prost and she'd slipped into survival mode, practically removing the memory of the moments just before.

Now something seemed odd. Marric was merely a boy. Sure, he'd just become some strangely powerful Lightbearer, but he was harmless. Luden's apparent interest in killing the boy seemed not only odd, but perfectly timed, as if he knew about Marric at the same time as Watchlight.

And Avryn, for that matter.

Perhaps Luden was more than met the eye.

Janis shook her head at that last thought. She'd met the man many times and had even completed numerous jobs for him. Their relationship was not a good one, but he knew she was good at her job, and he didn't need a conversationalist to get his requests completed. He was cunning, that was true. But he was also normal. She'd spied on him too many times for him to be hiding any type of *powers* such as these.

But he had to know. Why else would he have sent her to kill a boy, the son of a fletcher no less?

A breeze blew through the cavern, whipping the fabric of the cave door covering in one corner. It beat loudly as the small part that had come unsecured flapped in the wind. Janis scoffed at the idea that it would cover the firelight completely, considering the one corner that had come undone would have allowed light to peek through.

Standing up, Janis leaned back to crack her spine before moving to the cloth. Signs of the day were arriving and she could see the trees outside through the small crack beginning to change color in the increasing light. Nothing appeared to be amiss, so she began tying the line of the fabric back to the loop of metal that had been pounded into the rock to secure it.

Snap!

A man shouted in pain somewhere outside of the cave. Then there was another *thump* and the sound of a body falling to the ground.

Janis's senses sharpened and adrenaline started to fill her whole body.

Watchlight was here.

Chapter 22

Janis's heart thumped heavily and she backed into the cavern, quickly shaking her companions awake. She hushed them and pointed to the doorway, motioning for them to get up. Shrell immediately drew his swords and moved closer to the opening. Another snap sounded; though the trap hadn't connected with this target, the pointed stick instead collided with what sounded like a tree.

"Lanser's beard," Harmel whispered. "Ow'd they find us so quickly like?"

Neither Janis nor Shrell responded. From where they stood, they couldn't see into the forest well enough to observe their surroundings, or even to discover how many Watchlight members there were, waiting to slaughter them at any minute. Janis felt tense. She'd set numerous traps before she had entered, but they were far apart. The fact that two were hit so closely together in time meant that they likely faced a large group.

Shrell held his finger to his lips, indicating to Harmel to be quiet. Slowly, he moved to the entrance of the cave, likely to peek through a gap for some amount of visibility.

Just as he pulled back the flap a mite, a bright red flash of Light blinded them and a loud crack of exploding rock echoed through the cave. Shrell jumped back at the sound, tripping as he did.

In his haste to back up, he'd ripped down a fourth of the cloth, exposing the cave entrance partway.

Crack!

More red Light flashed into the cave through the now-larger opening created by Shrell just moments before. Rock exploding and breaking echoed through the cavern and Janis felt dread enter into her stomach.

"Blast it all, they have Destroyers!" Shrell hissed at the two of them.

They were outnumbered, not to mention trapped. Neither of the three were Lightbearers, and who knew how many Watchlight had sent after them.

Surprise is the only way we'll survive.

A third crack announced another explosion of rock in the bright red Light, and Janis dove for one of the crates, this one with a bottle of rum. She seized the closest one and ripped cloth from the crate full of hardened bread. She popped open the bottle and began stuffing in the cloth. Harmel stood frozen, a bow nocked and pointed at the entrance.

They wouldn't come in. Not through such a small opening. If they were going to, they would have already. Shrell looked at her harshly, seeming frustrated.

"Fog it, woman! Now is not the time to dr—"

Another red Light flashed and the wall next to Shrell exploded inward, debris and dust blowing at them, blinding them. Rock shards snapped into Janis face, blinding her for only a moment.

Using muscle memory, Janis bent down, snatching an ember from the fire. It was still hot and it seared the skin on her hand, making her gasp out in pain. Without hesitation, she lit the cloth on fire, hoping that the dust from the exploded wall would cover her in case projectiles such as knives or arrows aimed for them. Then she threw the bottle. It flew out of sight into the dust that was beginning to settle. It crashed and flames sprouted behind the wall of dust, a few tendrils of the fire showing a bit through the debris.

Men and women screamed as the fire climbed up their clothes. Janis saw the fire grow in some spots, seeming to spawn fireballs that moved in all directions, voices shouting.

Taking advantage of their surprise, Janis whipped out her favorite knife the length of her forearm and her spare, before rushing through the dust. The dust had apparently blown outward as well, for it obstructed her view a bit as it had done just inside. A shapeless form appeared to her right, which soon sharpened into a person. Not pausing at all, she dug both daggers into their middle and felt the familiar feeling of her sharpened knives entering flesh. She ripped them free and rolled forward coming to her knees just before another person. Again, she slammed her left dagger into the gut of the person and they grunted in pain and surprise, reaching down to the new wound.

Pulling that free, she turned to check her surroundings. Now that she'd come out of the rock dust, everything was clear. The tree just to her left flashed red and exploded into thousands of splinters and leaves. Janis jumped backward, feeling her face sting from a piece of wood that had struck her from the explosion. Light appeared, red and ominous, all around her. Swords and knives of all sorts flashed in the hands of black-robed men and women.

Again, knowing that they were outnumbered and out-powered, Janis chose speed. She rushed toward a black robed figure who raised his own Light sword to block her dagger.

She was faster, however, and knew that her dagger would hit before his parry could catch her own blade. Just before it struck, she felt her body tugged sideways and she flew into the air away from her victim.

Slamming to the ground, Janis grunted and used the momentum to flip back onto her feet. This time, she threw her right dagger through the air, targeting the same person. Another flash announced a red wall that appeared out of nowhere. Her knife bounced off of it harmlessly.

Cursing, she instinctively rolled to her side as a few Light-created who-knows-whats struck the ground where she'd just been. By now she could hear swords colliding, which she could only assume was Shrell engaging enemies to her right and behind her. An arrow flew from behind her and struck a woman in the chest, dropping her to the ground.

Janis felt a surge of relief that Harmel apparently had some skill with the bow he'd acquired.

Didn't know he had bow skills. Good timing to display them, she thought sarcastically.

A burst of confidence filled Janis and she flashed forward, using her spare daggers to slice the arms and legs of those around her. Then pain sprouted in her side and she was shoved to the ground. Her hand groped at the source of the pain and there she felt a knife, wreathed in Light.

No, it was *made* of Light.

Janis ripped it free and stumbled back to where she'd come from. Shrell had finished off the combatant he'd been engaged with and rushed to her side. Before he could reach her, however, he was enveloped in red Light and thrown backwards into the rubble of the former cave wall. His head cracked on a stone and he didn't rise.

Fog it! Fog it! FOG IT!

For a moment, it had seemed like they might actually be able to hold their own, but those hopes had come crashing down.

Janis felt herself bleeding and knew she didn't have much time. Arrows had stopped coming from inside the cave, and Janis suspected that they had neutralized Harmel as they'd just done to Shrell. For some reason, the attacking stopped. This seemed odd, for she was a sitting duck, wounded and bleeding out.

She wasn't scared, merely annoyed.

A figure, dressed in the common black robe of Watchlight emerged from behind the trees and the dozens of people had moved toward her. Twin scars ran from nostrils to ears of the figure, jagged and ugly, a grin set in below them.

"Oh, Janis. Did you really expect to be able to fight us, with just the three of you?"

Prost's voice was more gravelly than she remembered. It made her hate him even more.

"You can kill me if you want, but don't expect that to be added to your list of most honorable kills. Fifty to one isn't an impressive feat."

Prost laughed loudly, almost exaggeratedly.

"You speak of honor, assassin, yet you have killed mercilessly at least as many times as I have." Prost said. "There's no time for playful banter—as you can see, you are outnumbered and dying."

He glanced at her side, blood running through her hand.

"Where is the boy?"

Janis glared at him, but said nothing.

"I said, *where is the boy?!*" Prost shouted this time.

Janis just spit at his feet, glaring at him pointedly.

Roaring in anger, Prost gripped Janis by the throat and began lifting her off her feet. Before he'd made much progress in doing that, however, a thump sounded and he screamed in pain, releasing the assassin.

It took a moment for Janis to understand what had just happened, for almost exactly at the same time as Prost had dropped her, whooping and shouting had sounded in the trees around them, followed by more screams and shouts of pain. Something had struck the man's arm, making him lose his grip. Janis didn't know what it was, but the timing was perfect. She sat on the ground, gripping her wound with one hand and her neck with the other. She was dying, and she knew it.

At least I didn't go out without a fight, she thought, feeling satisfied that she'd killed at least three people and injured more.

Janis closed her eyes and the world around her began to disappear. Slipping into the in-between, she chose to use her last moments reliving the last fight she'd given, just moments before. Before the scene could form completely, a warmth filled her side where the wound was, spreading upwards into her body.

Gasping at the intensity of the warmth, her eyes snapped open and she was almost blinded by the intense blue Light that was suddenly there. Her senses returned to normal and sounds of shouting and fighting flooded in, threatening to overwhelm her. Fortunately, she'd had a lot of practice with this and she focused her mind almost instantly. Unsure what had just happened, she looked to the side to see a familiar face smiling back at her.

"Could you perhaps delay your wound procuring so that I don't have to desperately Fix you to save your life next time?" Avryn said to her.

"Ugglyn's tail, where did you come from?!" was all that she could say.

Avryn chuckled.

"Marric Saw Watchlight coming and we rushed as fast as we could. Seems we've just made it. Where are Shrell and Harmel?"

Janis pointed. Avryn followed her finger and cursed when he saw Shrell on the ground. He quickly moved to the man's side and put his hands over his head. Light started small but grew larger and brighter in intensity until Shrell stirred and sat up.

"By jove, am I glad to see you alive, my friend!" Avryn said.

Breathing a sigh of relief, Janis jumped to her feet and looked around. A new set of men and women wearing simple brown clothing and armor was fighting the black-robed figures. Light flashed left and right, but now it not only consisted of the eerie bright red, but also blue. Janis didn't quite know what it meant, but guessed that these were those that came with Avryn.

"Let's get to work then, shall we?"

Avryn nodded grimly as a sword of Light flashed into his hand and he charged forward. Shrell followed slightly behind and the two ran into the fray, immediately overwhelming a black robed figure that was lobbing Light conjures at a few of their allies. Pulling out daggers of her own, she scanned the scene before her and tried to calculate where she'd be most helpful in this chaotic battle.

A sense of something behind her made her duck, rolling forward just as the sound of a blade whooshed through the air where she'd been a moment before. Kicking herself into the air, she spun around to see Prost, looking angry.

"You can't win this battle, wench. You may have lasted this long, but that will come quickly to an end."

Whipping her hand forward, Janis slashed out with her long dagger, aiming for Prost's neck. He of course stepped backwards, leaning out of the path of the knife. Without a moment's hesitation, she flew into a windfury of attacks, striking left and right, moving through the motions that Macks had taught her so thoroughly years before.

Prost was fast. He managed to dodge each and every attack she launched at him and still managed to attack here and there himself. Determined, she increased the pace of the attacks hoping to get the better of the bulky man, but his stature and appearance did not match the uncanny speed that he was displaying now.

Frustrated, Janis moved closer and made motions to stab with her smaller dagger held in her left hand. He, of course, raised his own sword to parry her attack, but just before their blades would have collided, Janis let it slip out of her hands and she seized his arm by the wrist, holding it tight. This caused the reaction she'd hoped for, and he instinctively reached for it with his other hand. In that moment, she slashed her long dagger forward across his stomach and she ripped a gash in the flesh there. It wasn't the final blow that she'd hoped it would be, but it still felt satisfying.

Gasping, Prost jumped backwards and held his sword ready. He cursed and rushed Janis once again, swinging his sword in an arc overhead.

Knowing that Prost was much stronger than she was herself, Janis didn't attempt to block the blow with her own knives, but instead dashed to the side, letting his sword swing through empty air.

Janis grinned, feeling confident. This man had no powers, much like herself. For some reason, she felt the need to make up for all their past engagements, particularly the first they'd had seemingly ages ago.

It's time to bring down that ego of his, she thought.

Spinning around, Janis made to dig her dagger into Prost's back, but he easily danced out of her reach, moving safely to another position. A flash of Light flew between them and exploded the ground, shooting debris and dirt at their faces and knocking them back. Each, however, took this as an opportunity to best the other, and they dove directly into the dust that had come with the explosion. Slashing, stabbing, ducking, spinning, moving so fast that Janis was shocked at his ability to keep up with her.

Prost came in for a side cut with his sword, aiming for her midsection. Janis, knowing that once again the brute force from the blow would win out against her own, crossed her blades and used the intersection to catch his own sword. Applying the right amount of pressure and speed, she twisted the sword out of his hands.

Burning pain blossomed in her arm and she inhaled sharply at the feeling. Unexpectedly, Prost had procured a small dagger and had stabbed her in the upper arm, the knife almost going through her arm entirely. The dagger that she held there fell to the ground with a thud as her arm gave out to the pain.

Prost bared his teeth into an evil looking grin.

Foggin' hidden blades! How does he move so fast for his size?!

Janis disengaged by jumping backwards while kicking out with her foot, which collided with his crotch. Grunting, he bent forward slightly at the pain, but recovered quickly. All at once, Janis felt pain blossom randomly in her abdomen and she felt nauseous. Sure, the wound that she'd just received was pretty serious, but they had never made her feel nauseous in the past, she merely ignored them. Something felt off. The nausea was combined with an intensifying pain in her gut that just felt wrong.

On top of that, there wasn't much time before her arm would bleed too much, weakening her. This engagement couldn't last much longer if she expected to live.

* * *

"Come, Marric. I think it's best if you rest a little bit. You seem very tired."

"No, ma'am," he said, then he looked down, embarrassed. "I mean, yes, I'll rest, but I actually would like to start training if you wouldn't mind. I'm not sure I could sleep with all that's going on and, well. . . . "

Magness smiled slightly, but nodded.

"I quite agree. Rest is indeed pointless if one cannot rest. Now, tell me, what class are *you*?"

When he'd told her about his three Lightbearing powers, she didn't appear taken aback at all. She merely nodded thoughtfully. She then said as he'd already been delving into his Seeing powers quite readily, that perhaps they should start there. If he was being honest, it was the power that he was least excited to learn, though it had proven quite useful so far.

The rush and hustle of the caves and tunnels around them continued only for a short time before coming to a rest. As they passed through different tunnels, Marric saw doorways to small bedrooms, the mess hall, privies, and even some market-type areas. It seemed to never end. The walls were made of gray stone, smoothed in some places by who knows what, while other bits were jagged and rough. He'd looked to the side at one point for too long and scraped his elbow on one of these, learning that paying attention was important so as to not injure himself.

They ultimately ended up at a small cave with a simple wooden door. There he was left with Tynvel, their former head Seer. The woman seemed too old to still be living, her face riddled with deep set wrinkles and age. Her hair was long, down to her ankles, and it was of the purest white. She was missing a majority of her teeth, so understanding her was quite a feat. Magness stayed only for an introduction, then promptly left.

"Sheet don, boi," the old woman said.

Marric stood there for a moment, unsure what she just said.

Tynvel raised an eyebrow, then spoke again.

"Yeh deaf, shon? I shaid, sheet don."

Unsure what she was saying, but unwilling to offend her, Marric just nodded. This caused the poor old woman to grumble something in an annoyed fashion before she moved behind him. He froze, not sure what to expect. However, she merely put her hands on his shoulders and pushed down heavily. Grunting under her surprising strength, Marric eventually buckled his knees and sat on the ground.

Ahhh, sit down. Blast, how does anyone understand her?

"Sheeing ish about calm, conshentrashion. Relaxsh, breef, and focush."

Marric stared blankly at her.

She sighed again at his reaction, and instead resorted to demonstrating what she intended for him to do. The old woman sat on her backside, one knee up in the air, the other tucked beneath her. Then she closed her eyes and, in an exaggerated fashion, breathed long and deep.

Marric felt extremely awkward seeing how this woman was sitting and how loudly she was breathing, but seeing as how he couldn't really do much else without knowing the directions in the sanctum, he opted to sit down and match what she was doing. He only attempted to sit the way that she was for a moment before realizing that it was far less comfortable than the woman made it look. Instead, he shifted so that both legs were to the side of him.

There they sat for what seemed like forever, her eyes closed completely. He breathed the way that she did, but he could only keep his eyes closed for so long before feeling bored. Wasn't something supposed to happen?

In an attempt to get the woman's attention, Marric cleared his throat. When that did nothing, Marric asked what he didn't understand.

"What is supposed to happen?"

"The vishions will come. Jusht breef, focush."

Fortunately, Marric was starting to get the hang of listening to how she spoke and he could understand her a bit more than at first.

"When? Should I be focusing on something? Someone? I'm worried about my friends, Avryn and them, perhaps if I just—"

"No!" Tynvel said harshly. "You musht firsht learn 'owtta know when yeh Shee. Then yeh learn to focush to somethin'. Let it come. Let it be what it wantsh to be."

He shrunk back at her reaction, and though he wanted to ask more questions, he opted not to.

Sighing, Marric closed his eyes again and matched her breathing. There they sat, eyes closed, breathing in and out slowly and deeply. Rather than clear his mind, it instead fell onto thoughts of Janis, Shrell and Harmel. Marric was worried for them, and he prayed to Lanser that Avryn and those that had gone with them had arrived in time. They had left hours ago, so perhaps that was a possibility.

A sound in front of him made Marric snap out of his thoughts and open his eyes. Tynvel's eyes were open wide and they glowed a brilliant and intense blue Light. It looked unnatural and unnerving, so much so that he got the chills looking at her. Rather than continue staring at the odd appearance of her Seeing, he closed his eyes and breathed again. After only his third breath, it happened.

Once again, he felt as if his eyes were opening up wide, but he couldn't see anything, just black. Before long, however, the vision coalesced into reality. The sun was coming up, revealing a partially lit forest. Flashes of Light, blue and red, prickled the air around him and he saw that this was a battle of some sort. Brown clothed figures used blue Lightbearing to fight the familiar red Lightbearers.

Avryn was among them, using his own powers and fighting alongside Shrell, each engaging the enemy in different but brilliant and skillful ways. Immediately, the vision moved quickly and landed on Janis. She was fighting someone.

Prost.

He couldn't feel his body at the moment, but he was confident that if he could have felt anything, his skin would be crawling.

Watching the two fight was like a dance, a form of art that only the richest among them would pay to see. Looking more closely, Marric saw wet red stains on Prost's midsection, and on Janis's arms. It took him a moment to realize what it was.

His stomach churned.

Marric had never gotten used to seeing blood and now wasn't any different, despite this not even being an experience that he was having in person. He turned away from that scene and observed with wonder the rest of the people. A person here was fighting with twin conjured long swords, each looked long and burdensome, made of blazing blue Light. They flicked and flashed through the air, colliding with a black robed figure's red Light sword, each masterfully wielding their weapons. There was Shrell and Avryn, shuffling side to side and attempting to best a pair of black robed women, one Shielding the other while she threw balls of Light at them which exploded upon impact with whatever they touched. Avryn would spin with his blue Light sword and smack the Shield, dodge a red orb and the explosion of the ground, then lob his own blue orb which connected with the Shield, also exploding with a crack and a flash of Light.

The whole scene itself was mesmerizing, and Marric was having a difficult time taking it all in. He stood fairly close to Janis and Prost fighting, and suddenly a tree just to their left exploded entirely into a mass of splinter and tree pieces, much of it raining down onto them. All at once, Janis stumbled and Prost took advantage of that. He stabbed forward with his sword and it looked like it would connect with Janis's skull, but at the last minute, she shifted her head and barely dodged the blow.

Then an extreme mass of Light flashed near the two and Janis screamed out in pain. The glare was so blinding and intense that Marric couldn't see anything any longer and he was pushed from the vision so forcibly that it was almost painful. He fell over in the real world, his head knocking the ground because he wasn't prepared for it. Tynvel, still sitting across from him, curiously yelped and had the same reaction, falling to the ground.

"What wash a't?" she muttered.

Not a moment after they'd recovered and shaken off the feeling they appeared to both have gotten, a person knocked on the door and pushed in.

"Pardon, High Seer, bu' sometin's jus' 'appened."

"Yesh? What ish it?" Tynvel asked the newcomer.

"Umm, well," the man looked sheepish, seeming to be considering the next words he said, "sometin' 'appened. It looks like every Seer here was jus' knocked over by some force."

Marric's skin chilled. He didn't know what caused the disturbance, but he knew that Janis was in danger.

* * *

Prost observed the assassin's movements and was annoyed at how easily she seemed able to block, parry and dodge his blows. She was quite a crafty woman, but it made his job all the more challenging. He growled in frustration as the pain from his stomach wound flared up, shocking him into action more than debilitating his ability to fight. He hadn't expected this fight to be drawn out for so long, but it appeared that each was evenly matched, though she was a bit faster and he was significantly stronger. Each just played to their advantage.

As his companions fought around him, he considered his current wounds and determined that he had to come up with something fast to take Janis out. Mind reeling, he struggled slightly to continue dodging her jabs to find an opportunity to finish the fight.

Just then, Janis stumbled, likely from the unexpected arrival of the tree shrapnel which she'd taken mostly in the front. Prost grinned wickedly, simultaneously annoyed that he'd been hit by the effects of the Destroying, for if it had hit him directly, he'd have been unaffected, but also pleased that it had given him the opening. He swung his blade quickly at the woman's face. For a moment, it looked like it would connect, but she somehow managed to wiggle her way out of the blow.

Then it happened. A blinding blue Light flashed, extremely intense and bright. Prost could not tell where it came from, but he lost all ability to see. It wasn't a quick flash, but instead persisted, blinding him completely so that the only thing he could do was cover his eyes.

Janis screamed.

A force slammed into him, something strong and large that lifted his feet off the ground and flung him over the tree that had just exploded, eventually smashing into another large trunk that was still intact. He grunted in surprise and pain, then fell to the ground. Trying to ignore the pain, Prost struggled to his knees. Just as he had done so, another force rocked him back again and he whacked into the same tree, but rolled off the side, flying just past it onto the ground.

Fog it! What is happening?! Prost thought.

How could this be? This force was clearly the power of some Lightbearer, but he was k'alek tar'n, he couldn't be affected by their powers. Even Riln himself couldn't touch him with his abilities. Yet now he was being thrown about by what clearly was the power of a Mover.

He looked up, squinting at the source of the Light, still blinding, and watched as a glowing pulse emitted from the intense glow and completely disintegrated anything in its path. Fear gripped Prost as he saw men and women on both sides disappear into dust, Destroyed instantly. Nearby trees exploded into splinters and the very ground below the intense oval of blue Light broke up at its effect. Fortunately, it was a small pulse of Destruction and hadn't reached Prost.

Finally, an even larger wall of illumination appeared around the intense blue Light and flew outward. Its lines were defined, much like a Shield would look, should a Shielder put one up. Prost attempted to rise up and escape its path, but he was weak from the previous two blows and he took the Shield directly in the front, again being thrown backwards. He felt his head hit a hard surface, then everything went black.

Epilogue

The world swirled with impossible colors, full of images that didn't quite take shape, but suggested real world things just enough that they could be made out and understood. Janis floated in all of it, not understanding, yet at the same time feeling quite awake and aware of her surroundings.

It was obvious that she wasn't actually awake, for she knew that the world didn't work this way, yet here she was, experiencing the oddity that it was. What was more confusing than her current location were the events of just before she'd arrived here. She was struggling to stay alive against Prost who had benefited from one of his friend's arrows piercing Janis's other arm all the way through. She thought Prost was more on her level then, and Janis was confident that in a battle of speed and endurance, she would eventually win out.

Just next to her, a scene appeared out of the wispy colors and objects. Marric. He was sitting inside some small room with an old woman who looked like she was not having a good day. They were speaking, though Janis couldn't quite understand what they were saying. It was as if they were just out of earshot. Then it was gone.

As soon as it disappeared, a new scene appeared, this one showing Shrell and Harmel fighting side by side against what Janis assumed was a Shielder, for he had covered himself and his companion with a red wall of Light that resembled a gigantic bubble. The two of them worked remarkably well together, but the Shield was holding effectively.

Once again, this faded into nothingness and to her left, another scene appeared. This was one of her, though she was a small girl, terrified, on the streets, alone, hungry and cold. She squirmed inside, remembering that day suddenly, feeling and seeing the vividness of the experience. She had become something different. Rather than fade away on its own, Janis waved her arm through the scene and it did disappear. She didn't really know that it worked that way, but she couldn't stand—well, *float* there and watch that.

Another scene, this one of her pressing Marric against the wall in the dark, hiding from Avryn who at the time they thought was evil. This she watched for a time, considering how her sentiment had changed toward the boy and even Shrell for that matter. She worked alone, and that had always been the way it was. At least since Macks.

Macks, she thought.

As if in response to her thoughts, a scene of Macks training with her appeared in the color and mist. He was strikingly handsome, which frustrated her. His cheeks creased inwards just at the corner of his mouth as he spoke, his smile was infectious, his stature strong, lean, and hard.

Pain blossomed in her chest and she again pushed that image away with her hands, making it disappear into nothing.

What had brought her to this strange place? She recalled fighting Prost and feeling her life draining out through the hole in her arm. He could clearly tell that her energy was running out and she was fighting more desperately. She had begun to feel sick to her stomach, which was not a reaction that she'd ever experienced during battle, not even when seeing grave injuries and blood.

Then what? Janis thought, struggling to remember.

A tree had exploded. There had been a flash of red Light just before it, so she guessed that it was the result of a Lightbearer aiming their power incorrectly. She didn't actually mind the wood shrapnel that she'd taken from the blast, she only remembered the relief that came when she saw that the distraction had affected Prost and left her an opening. But then—a memory of the pain flashed through her abdomen and she clenched her teeth. Before she could make any moves and take advantage of the situation, her stomach wrenched in the most horrible pain she'd felt. It very quickly spread to the rest of her and then—blinding light, searing pain, and here she was.

This place, albeit very strange and unfamiliar, seemed also familiar. It took a moment for her to make the connection, but she eventually realized that this felt similar to what going into the in-between felt like. It wasn't the same by all means, but the feeling was alike in ways. The notion wasn't a completely irrational one, for she was seeing scenes from her past, though they weren't fully formed. There were also other images, other scenes, that she knew were not from her past. They didn't even seem related to her in any way at all, yet here they were.

Janis strained to think back to the moment before she was here, hoping to find some evidence or some idea of what might have happened. There was the possibility that she had died, but that didn't feel right. She was pretty confident that death wouldn't have such a strange and unorganized result. Though she wasn't religious at all, she had a feeling that there was more to life after death than this.

Something gripped her hand and she yanked it sideways, trying to get away from whatever it was. However, when she looked in that direction, there was nothing, no one. Shaking her head, she continued to observe things around her, trying to understand patterns, ideas, even how she might be able to control what she saw and experienced.

Then something strange happened. Symbols appeared out of nothing, each as large as her own head, and each unique in its own way, but each carrying an element that matched them all, brought them together. They looked old—ancient even—and Janis wondered if perhaps she was going insane, for she didn't understand what they meant, but at the same time, she knew what they were. This was the ancient language, and each symbol carried power. One by one, each symbol pulsed and an image appeared next to it, portraying a faceless person wearing a simple brown robe.

The first showed a woman, hand held to the side, palm upwards, an orb of Light hovering just above her hand. Janis stared, unnerved by the faceless rendition of the woman. The second showed a man holding what looked like a ladle in one hand, and a dagger in the other, each was made from white Light. The third showed a man straining, holding his arms out, palms glowing with the same white Light, just next to him a stone, wreathed in Light, floated off the ground.

It didn't take long for Janis to see the pattern. She didn't know why, but she knew that these symbols represented Lightbearing. Each of the seven powers was here. There was another man, still without a face, but eyes made of white Light glowed there. Another, covered in the odd gigantic bubble shield also made of Light. Then, a woman, holding her hand aloft towards a house that had exploded, the pieces flying in all directions, then another woman, hand outstretched and the same house being knit together and Fixed.

Janis took account of what she knew. Lighter, Conjurer, Mover, Seer, Shielder, Destroyer and Fixer. Why she was being shown this she didn't know, but she internally and mentally memorized the symbols on the off chance that they could provide a solution to her current circumstances. Finally, after the last image appeared, each symbol glowed more brightly and a line of white Light, originating from the center, grew inward so that they met in the middle. Together, the seven formed a symbol that emanated with power.

Then an image of a person formed there. It was a woman, faceless once again, but oddly wearing clothes very similar to her own. In fact, the hair on this woman was very similar, even so that it felt as if she might be looking into a mirror.

The hair stood up on her whole body at the eeriness of the image just before her.

All at once, the symbols and the faceless lookalikes disappeared into nothing, and the world went black. Janis started falling and she gasped in surprise at the sudden movement, the sensation feeling unnerving.

* * *

Janis opened her eyes and squinted back at the intense Light that shone in the room. Immediately, she felt her senses flow through her body, returning to their acute awareness as she had trained them to react. Someone held her hand and she ripped it free, moving it to her side where she normally kept one of her blades. She found none.

Trying another spot, she was disappointed to find that that dagger was missing as well.

"Avryn said that we should probably take them away." Marric said to her side.

She looked at him and relief filled her at the sight. It wasn't a feeling that she was normally accustomed to, and she balked a bit at the sensation. Yet, at the same time, it felt almost nice. Immediately after her eyes adjusted to the light, she examined the room they were in. The walls were an uneven dull gray stone. Janis recognized them to be cave walls. Even if she hadn't been familiar with spaces like these from her whole life as an assassin, the last couple weeks would have given her plenty of experience with the likes.

The bed on which she lay was made from a simple wooden frame, and filled with animal pelts of all kinds. That explained why it felt so soft beneath her. Luxury of that kind wasn't something she was familiar with, and she wasn't sure if she preferred it over the normal hard ground that she often slept on.

"Where are we?" Janis asked. "More important, where are my daggers?"

Marric said nothing, and the pause made her look expectantly at him. She was shocked to see that his eyes welled with tears.

That made her stomach twist.

Oh Lanser's beard, he's getting emotional.

Before she knew it, Marric threw his arms around her and squeezed her tight. Unsure of how to handle the situation, Janis merely did nothing. The awkwardness that she felt apparently wasn't translated to the boy, for he stayed there for quite some time.

Perhaps it was wise to remove my weapons from me. The only way I know how to deal with things is by using daggers.

In time, he pulled back, sniffling and wiping his nose.

"I wasn't sure if you'd make it. I mean, your heart never really stopped, but it's been so much time, and when Avryn told me what happened, I just couldn't believe it— "

"Wait. What do you mean *so much time*?"

Marric blinked.

"Oh, I suppose you wouldn't know. You've been unconscious for almost a week now. They've tried all the herbs and tonics they could to wake you, but none worked. If the doctor hadn't verified, I'd have thought you were dead myself."

"Well I'm not. So there isn't a reason to blubber about it. No?"

Marric nodded, blushing slightly.

Blast, I shouldn't be so harsh.

"Can I know where we are now?"

"Oh! Of course! This is Terris Green. The sanctum of Evenir."

Janis stared flatly at him, emphasizing the look a bit to make a point.

"Right. That means nothing to you, I guess. Terris Green gets its name from the actual lush setting outside of the cave. There are these beautiful waterfalls just outside, you really should see them."

That would explain the humidity.

"Daggers. Evenir. Keep talking."

"Ah, yes. Your daggers are just here."

Marric pulled from a bag behind him the straps she used to hang and store her various daggers on her body and limbs. This was the most welcome sight of all of them, though it was more of an empowering relief than the relief she felt when she had seen the boy.

"And Evenir. It's a place where Lightbearers seek to be in harmony with non-powered folks. Regular humans. It's a sanctum that's safe for us."

Janis nodded, thoughtful. She'd have to verify the 'safety' of this place herself, but it seemed to fit his description so far. She wasn't dead, after all.

"I'm glad that you found a place where you can be safe from Watchlight."

"You mean where *we* can be safe."

Janis looked at Marric, not understanding. She didn't plan on staying long at all. In fact, after doing a safety check, the first thing she was going to do was leave and get back to her old life. Dig into Luden.

"Yes, where you can be safe," she repeated.

"No, Janis. *We*, as in *you and me*. People like *us*."

She continued to stare, not understanding.

"Janis," Marric said, "you awakened."

*Liked it? Hated it? Leave a review!

Get Shielded, Prequel to this series FREE at dankenner.com!

Transformed: The Lightbearer Chronicles Book 2: Prologue

Fire crackled in the corner-set fireplace of the lodge room. Among the tables and chairs, people milled about in a spirit of merriment. Women in colorful dresses roamed with trays of spirits and other fine foods, stopping to allow the people to eat and drink as they pleased. It was hot and dry, the air devoid of moisture due to the roaring fire. Nearly a hundred conversations caused a loud hum to thrum in the ears of those in attendance.

Luden sat in his high-backed leather chair, staring at the corner and the fire there. His hair was bright blond, curly beyond normalcy, and cropped close to his scalp. He hated growing it out to any degree, for it sprung about like an unruly pet, tickling his ears and making him look like a cherubic baby. He was of average build and had green eyes the color of the Veruvian sea.

His men never understood why he liked to face the corner. They assumed it opened him up to assassination and showed weakness that would make him vulnerable.

Luden knew better than they did.

There weren't many people in the world that would dare attack him. He found that money had given him an incredible immunity from any who might seek his demise. That, and anonymity. As of now, there were few who knew the numbers of his men, the locations of his warehouses, or even what his intentions were. The fact that he was rich allowed him to keep all these things secret and still maintain his followers, who didn't necessarily *trust* him, but obeyed him all the same.

The power of money is unnervingly effective in this world, he thought to himself.

His thoughts immediately shifted to when he'd first hired Janis to kill the boy, Marric. She was one of the best, and money controlled her easily. Unfortunately, this no longer seemed to be the case.

Now the deadly woman is likely brainwashed by the lot of them, Luden thought, seething.

Footsteps sounded behind him, barely audible above the loudness of the room. In fact, by the time he'd heard them approaching, they were nearly behind his chair.

"Master, I gots news of the wench," a burly voice said.

Luden didn't answer immediately. He wasn't in the mood to hear about Janis and the happenings of the boy named Marric.

Sighing heavily, he tore his eyes from the flickering flames and spoke in a lazy voice.

"Oh joy, share with me the news of your failure *again,*" Luden said, displeasure thick in his tone.

"We still 'aven't 'ad any luck findin'em. They were righ' slippery, they was."

Luden growled inside his throat, displaying his frustration on his face. He stood up sharply and spun on the man.

"Why in Lanser's name are you wasting my time? I gave you one job, Triliv, and you obviously are incapable of following directions. Remind me, why did I hire you in the first place?" he hissed at the tall man before him.

Triliv stood there, a look of resignation on his face. He failed to answer, which was probably better in this instance, anyway. Luden felt his anger starting to spiral out of control, the veins protruding out of his neck. He eyed Triliv, noticing how each of the man's arms was as thick as Luden's neck. His size didn't help his looks, for his eyes were beady and small, as was his nose. The only aspect of his face that seemed to match the size of his body was his mouth, which hung open most of the time.

Luden rolled his eyes and crossed his arms before him.

"Oh yes, you are impossibly large and practically unkillable."

Triliv smiled at the explanation, as if it pleased him to hear Luden saying the words. The man wasn't clever, but he sure could take a beating. In times when money and words would do you no good, brute force was often the only other way. Suddenly, the large man's pleased look melted away in an instant.

"Uhh, boss. There's a mite bit more yeh oughtta know," Triliv stated.

Taking in a deep breath, Luden steeled himself for the news. "What is it, then?" he snapped at the large oaf.

"Uhh, well. The woman killer, the assassin lady . . . uhh," the man paused.

"Triliv, will you get to the point, please?" Luden yelled.

The sound of Luden's raised voice made the man jump, but he spoke quickly.

"Th' gal, Janis, she became one of 'em—tha's what the informants 'ave said, a' leas'.

Energy sprang through Luden's whole body at hearing the news.

"Lanser's might, you can't be serious," Luden said.

Triliv just nodded. "Was a nasty one at tha', hurt lots a people."

Why in Lanser's name did the Seer not See that? Luden thought.

When the Seer had Seen Marric awakening, Luden immediately thought of hiring Janis to take him out. Normally, he and his men preferred to track down and kill Lightbearers on their own, but this one seemed different. The Seer had Seen relatively nothing about the awakening, and they were without a timeline for it. Consequently, Luden needed a discreet individual as opposed to a large group to protect his cover. Janis had seemed the obvious solution, with her minimal fee and surefire methods. There had also been the added benefit of her not knowing about Lightbearing or the risks associated with the job.

This time, though, hiring Janis hadn't been a risk worth taking. Luden offered her more than the normal bounty for the boy, but someone had intervened. His men were found dead after he sent them to Arivan to give her the job. By the time his operatives had gotten to Wurren, there were others already escorting the boy out of the town.

And one of them is a blasted Lightbearer, Luden thought, anger building inside.

He hated them all. If he could, he would eliminate them in one go. Unfortunately, he wasn't in a place to do that quite yet. He was getting closer, though. For now, he settled for little victories here and there. He'd tracked down and killed them for years, though with some effort. Meeting the Seer six months ago had changed that. Now his men could get to Lightbearers before they awakened, solving the problems before they started. In some cases, they were too late and the awakening had already happened. It complicated their elimination, but didn't make it impossible.

That is, if his men got there first. Luden knew that there were others gathering Lightbearers. They sometimes beat him to the awakenings, sweeping the targets away before his men could take them out. Working with a Seer made his success possible, but Luden had learned that Seers weren't always reliable. He assumed that, at least. It was the only explanation for why his men got to the target first sometimes, and other times they didn't.

Luden relaxed as best as he could into the chair before the fireplace. As he slumped down into the padded seat, he raised his hand in the air and wiggled his fingers. Just as expected, a servant woman appeared and bowed deeply.

"What can I git fer yeh, sir?" she said, her thick accent showing her lack of education.

"Please, the strongest thing you have."

Nodding, she turned and shuffled through the crowd of people.

A memory of his family struck a tone in his chest, sorrow building there until the woman appeared with a drink. Without too much of a pause, he grabbed it and held his other hand out, palm facing the woman, asking her to wait. He drank the contents in four swallows and put the empty flagon on the tray before asking for another.

The woman stared at him, shocked, but nodded and rushed away.

As he felt the effects of the spirits, Luden stared into the fire bitterly.

Dead—my whole family is dead, and for what? My sister's 'blessing' of Lightbearing?

The memory flashed in his mind of his sister doubled over in pain, his parents consoling her before they were blasted to pieces before his eyes. He'd lived for years in his grief, until he finally discovered the reality of Lightbearing and its plague on the world.

His throat burned from the strength of the drink. He could feel it in his stomach. It wasn't comfortable, but it wasn't painful, either.

"You called, sir?" a voice suddenly spoke behind him.

Luden's stomach clenched and he turned to see him—the Seer—standing behind the chair. Hair long and dark, he kept it tied back in a ponytail that stuck out straight from his head. Eyes green and brooding, they topped a slender nose and a tight, sharp mouth. One wouldn't know that he was a skilled fighter with practically any blade until they found it in their stomach. That, coupled with his Lightbearing power, was enough to keep Luden's anger in check.

"Ah yes, here he is, the man of the hour. Care for a drink?" Luden said, miming holding up a glass.

"You know I don't take drinks from anyone unless I've seen how they are prepared," the man said flatly. "You may be drunk, but you are not stupid—this I know. Why have you asked for me?"

Luden grunted at the man's brusqueness, but internally, he appreciated it.

"While your service has been helpful, *Seer*, you know I could kill you at any moment."

A pause.

"You know I'd See that long before it happened, and simply kill you first."

Luden's stomach twisted at the comment.

"You fogging *fool.* Was that a threat?" Luden shouted, standing up and facing the man.

"Threat—no. Reminder—yes. Now, what is it you wanted from me?"

"Have you Seen the boy? Have you Seen any awakenings? Ugglyn's backside, have you Seen anything at all?"

The Seer's face didn't change, other than a pointed stare and some exaggerated blinks.

"I cannot See Marric's location or where they are going. I *do* know that he's with a man named Avryn, and Janis, the assassin you wasted your funds on."

Luden's anger rose again, building like a wild sea in a hurricane. Still, he held it in reserve to avoid death from the man before him. He was faster than Luden, that was sure.

"Keep your opinions to yourself, Seer."

"I don't believe you hired me just to keep my opinions to myself. If I did keep my opinions in check, I imagine that you and your men would have been killed long before now."

The crackling of the fire behind Luden seemed to get louder as the anger continued to rise in him. As much as he hated to admit it, the man was right. When he'd first paid the Seer, he didn't have any idea how invaluable he would become. He was not only useful with his gifts, but with his intellect as well. Though the Seer didn't disclose much of his past, Luden knew that he had combat experience from his profession, though what it had been, Luden couldn't be sure. The Seer was unnervingly clever, and understood the general rules of engagement. Luden, against his better judgement, had taken the man's advice on numerous occasions, only to find that it was spot on.

Even so, Luden didn't have to like it. The fact that he employed any Lightbearers at all felt like a betrayal to his parents and his sister.

Pushing away the thoughts, he focused once more on the Seer.

"You may have been right in the past, but you are only here for one reason, and you seem to be failing at that right now."

The Seer smiled, clearly not threatened or concerned by Luden's tone.

"And *you* are well aware that I am only here for the substantial pay. If I found any other jobs as lucrative, I'd have left ages ago," the man said, a slight smile on face. He looked perfectly comfortable standing in front of the fuming Luden, which infuriated Luden even more.

"Let me remind you *again* that I cannot control when I See awakenings. I don't control when they happen. If I did, you wouldn't be wasting so much time fattening up your subordinates." As he said the words, he shoved his thumb over this shoulder. The party around them was unexpected, but

Luden couldn't have his men leaving and betraying him. If he treated them right, he was likely to keep them. Hiring greedy men and women was to his advantage, considering his unlimited access to money. Just then, one of his men laughed loudly and fell to his backside, where he giggled, half-conscious. It was clear that he had drunk far too much for even his own body weight. Cheeks red, he quickly fell into a drunken slumber.

Luden stared at him, unimpressed. A part of him thought to discipline the man for being so ridiculous and foolish, but he thought better of it. He *had* told them to have fun, to live it up and not worry about tomorrow. He couldn't take that back now, not without being loathed.

Some men got their power from their strength, some from fear, some from being smarter than those around them. Luden wasn't in a place to use any of those. His power came from something he was just born into: money.

Lanser help me if they realize I'm little more than that, Luden thought.

Luden looked back at the Seer and was about to say something when the man's eyes began to glow violent red, shining brightly, small beams shooting forward, spreading out and disappearing into the air.

Breathing heavily, Luden stood there, counting the seconds before the red glow softened and the man's eyes returned to normal.

"Well, wasn't that timing just right? There is an awakening right here in Stilten. I think we got lucky with this one—I don't See any interruptions from the others in the chase for this Lightbearer."

Luden bared his teeth, pleased at the news.

"Are you absolutely sure of this?" Luden asked.

The Seer looked at him, bored at the question.

"I can check again, if you like. I am sure, however, that I Saw enough before and after to know that this will be an easy target. The only thing we need to watch out for is that he'll be a Mover. Can't be too close to him when he awakens. That is, if we let him awaken at all. We could just kill him before he even gains his powers—"

Luden held up his hand, interrupting the Seer.

"No, I am very eager to try this new . . . serum of yours."

Pride showed on the Seer's face when he spoke.

"I am confident that it will work. The instructions were very clear when they were given to me."

Luden nodded.

"Yes, yes. I haven't had the chance to give it a try. Perhaps now is the right time?"

Pulling out a short dagger from his belt, Luden used it to pop the cork off a slightly glowing silvery poison. Oddly, it smelled of nothing. One would have thought the vial housed only water with such a lack of scent. The sight of it amended that impression quickly.

Taking care to not touch it, Luden stepped up to the man that had just fallen down. Crouching low, he tipped the vial into his mouth until a few drops fell in.

In his sleep, the man giggled at the feel of the liquid in his mouth and he gulped it down hungrily, likely expecting it to be more spirits. After a few beats, his eyes shot open and he screamed.

"The fog is 'appenin'?" he shouted, grasping desperately at the shirt over his stomach.

As the man pulled his shirt up, lines of silver streaked outward on his skin. They grew quickly, twisting around his back and down his legs.

The man tried to speak again but only gurgling came from his mouth. He bled from his mouth and nose, but only for a moment. The blood was consumed by the same silver liquid before turning to smoke as well. His eyes rolled back in his head and he collapsed, dead.

Luden stared at him, a bit nervous at the strength of what he'd just seen. Luden corked the vial immediately, afraid of any bits of the poison getting loose. Knowing that he needed to explain himself, he stood straight and announced loudly to the room, which had gone deathly quiet at the scene, "He was a traitor! I found him sharing secrets to our enemies! This is what happens to those who betray me."

It was a lie, of course, but Luden couldn't let them think he'd just killed a man for no reason. Money might not keep their loyalty through something like that.

A few people stared at the man's corpse, but most turned back to their tables and drinks, continuing as before.

By now his anger had faded, and instead he felt a joy that should have made him feel more self conscious, guilty even. Instead, he knew they had discovered something that could turn the tide against the blasted Lightbearers. For years, he'd tried to hunt them with little success, trying to best them one at a time. Unfortunately for him, fighting them without powers of his own proved too costly.

That is, until he'd met the Seer. He'd almost killed the man on sight, but when he had explained to Luden how he could help him, how they could get to Lightbearers *before* they got their powers . . . that had changed things.

And now we have something that will help us take them out even after they awaken.

The pleasure burned in his chest. Luden chuckled at the feeling.

"What of the boy's father? Have you found him?" Luden asked.

The Seer dipped his head in affirmation. "Yes, he's traveling north, though I am unsure where. It took me time to See him, but your description provided enough detail."

Luden smiled wickedly.

"I presume some other Seers, perhaps the boy himself, will soon locate the old man. Make sure our men know exactly when and where they can expect to run into the Lightbearers coming for him. I think a true test of this poison is in order," Luden said.

Lifting his hand, he looked at the vial and turned to the fire. He viewed the contents with the flickering light of the fire behind it. The liquid, almost black, but slightly silver and glowing, sloshed around the bit of empty space at the top as he moved it side to side.

It's time for me to eradicate every Lightbearer from Lindrad, Luden thought darkly.

Chapter 1

Janis sat in a stone chair, opening and closing her hand repeatedly. Her other hand held her favorite dagger, straight and slim, as long as her forearm. She wasn't looking at the dagger, however, but instead at the hand she was flexing. The stone walls around her were gray and made from the same material as the chair she sat in, which seemed comical to her as it caused the chairs and tables to blend into their background. She wondered if this was intended by Evenir or if it was a design oversight.

As she opened her hand again, Light flashed in her palm and a second dagger appeared there, this one made of blue Light. She squinted at the intensity of the burst of Light, but it was only a reflex. Despite the Light being piercing and bright, her eyes were unaffected by it. In fact, she could stare directly into it without any trouble at all. This only added to how unnatural it felt. As intended, it was an exact replica of the real steel dagger in her other hand.

Lightbearing is much more complex than I imagined, she thought to herself.

It had been two weeks since the incident at the hidden cave where she had nearly been killed—twice. She recalled bleeding profusely while Prost stood before her, ready to deliver the final blow. If Avryn had not shown up, she most certainly would have died right then and there, but he had. After Evenir operatives had come to help, the battle with Watchlight had turned for the better. Janis remembered engaging with Prost, his speed and battle prowess matching her own. Around them flashed blue and red Light repeatedly from the Lightbearing on both sides as they fought.

As if in rebellion to the thought, the Light-created dagger snuffed out, the blue Light disappearing into nothing. However, after only a moment, the Conjured dagger flashed back into existence in her hand.

Janis stared at her hand as she summoned and dismissed the blade a few more times before she gripped the blue-Light hilt of the dagger more tightly and raised both blades to compare them. She inspected the two different-but-same blades and found them to be virtually identical. There was a small nick in the metal blade of the real dagger. The same nick could be seen in the Light-made dagger, in exactly the same place.

In a rapid motion, Janis struck the two blades together and the familiar metal-on-metal clash rang through the cavern. The blade of Light held strong, as if it was made of the same material as the steel one. She placed the two blades together again and rubbed them, observing the sound that it made. It indeed was the sound of two metal daggers rubbing together, which still astounded her.

Her mind wandered back to the day of the battle. She remembered staring Prost down, bleeding from the new wound he'd given her after Evenir joined the battle. She wasn't panicked, she was merely taking her time to analyze the situation as she paused momentarily. Then it had happened.

Janis remembered the pain more than anything. It was by far the worst pain she had experienced at any moment in her life. That was saying a lot, considering her profession as an assassin. At any rate, the pain had started in her stomach, as if she'd eaten something bad and it was just getting to her. Unfortunately, it wasn't something that benign. Pain had rapidly spread through her chest, limbs, and even to her head. Her vision blacked out and she felt like she became a ball of pain, her mind losing access to all her other senses and thoughts.

Then she'd seen some pretty strange things; things that both made sense and not at all.

Janis shook her head slightly at that thought. She had analyzed and remembered what she'd seen multiple times, but didn't feel that now was the time to do so again. Instead, she thought about waking up on the bed of furs next to Marric, his youthful face full of concern for her. She had been relieved to see that he survived. What stood out more from that memory were his next words.

"Janis . . . you just awakened."

Her mind reeled at the words and she still could not believe them, even as she sat there now, holding a dagger made completely out of Light. She tightened her grip on the handle of the real dagger and felt her gut twist slightly. Lightbearing had always felt unfamiliar, and it *still* felt that way, even now. Janis felt tainted, though she couldn't describe why.

She let the Light dagger fall from her hand and it snuffed into nothingness.

Where is *Marric, anyway?* she thought.

Since the boy had Awakened, he'd been passionately training and learning about his new abilities. Janis could scarcely keep track of where he was at any moment, but it was clear that he was quite thrilled about his newfound powers. After all, he was somewhat of an anomaly, even for a Lightbearer. The people here at Evenir definitely treated him so as well. They called him *Iridar,* which to Janis meant absolutely nothing, since she didn't speak any of the old language. Avryn had said it meant thrice-powered.

Marric had awakened with three full powers of Lightbearing. Those who awakened normally only had one greater and one lesser power, thus making him an anomaly. Even more than regular combat skills, the people of Evenir gave the greatest weight to Lightbearing prowess. It was for this reason that Janis felt somewhat dismissed by Evenir at large, despite her considerable non-lightbearing abilities. Many simply saw her as "Iridar's scary companion," which showed their fear of her, but not their respect.

Janis had always appreciated being labeled as scary, but she didn't appreciate being underestimated. It was almost as if since she'd awakened, her poor Lightbearing had somewhat negated her other skills in the eyes of many in Evenir. Maybe they were right, to an extent. Something about being awakened had made her lose confidence.

She only stayed at Terris Green because she wasn't confident she'd be able to resume her assassin duties now that she had this plague of Lightbearing. An assassin thrived in the shadows, hiding either literally or figuratively from their mark, but more importantly from those that protected the quarry. What if she was in the shadows, about to eliminate the target, when a burst of Light exploded from her unintentionally?

Janis blanched at the thought. *So much for subtlety at that point.*

As much as she hated to admit it, Evenir knew about Lightbearing, and she knew absolutely nothing. It seemed in her best interest to stay for some time, to listen and learn. She *had* tried to train with some of their teachers, but she was no good. No one knew what to make of her. She had awakened, but to what, not a soul knew. As far as she could tell, she had minuscule abilities in each of the classes, each one so weak that it seemed as if she didn't have a class at all. They had tried her with all seven of the classes, but in each trial, she only displayed weak renditions of the powers. It was as if she had no real power whatsoever.

This only frustrated her more. She apparently had drawn the short end of the stick. When she'd first tried to come to terms with the fact that she had these powers, she thought she might at least be able to make use of them, but no. Instead, she had this inconvenient Light that just got in the way, and no added abilities to show for it.

That is, except for the strange things that happened every once in a while. It was actually because of one of these strange things that they'd given up on her. Yesterday, as she was failing to produce destroying orbs on command, she'd somehow exploded the whole cavern and caused the ceiling to come down, almost killing herself and the instructor. Fraltan, the Destroyer instructor, said it was one of the most impressive displays of Destroying he'd seen in a newly awakened Lightbearer. However, after the incident, she'd shown only weak Destroying abilities. Before that, she'd accidentally chopped down a supporting pillar with a summoned sword and the ceiling almost gave in. Before that, well . . . lots of unfortunate instances.

With each odd manifestation of extreme power, her Lightbearing had only been weak and unhelpful afterward, so many began to see her as some type of useless anomaly. She had heard the word 'broken' at one point. The speaker later found his belt cut by someone in the middle of the eating area, his pants sliding to his ankles.

Janis chuckled darkly. No one called her broken and got away with it.

With each incident, she'd spent time in the in-between, analyzing what happened to try to make sense of it. Not once had she gotten any answers. If anything, the in-between just made it all more confusing.

A shuffling sound to her left interrupted her thoughts. She stood to face the oncoming noise, stiffly gripping her real dagger. She relaxed slightly when she saw that it was just Avryn coming down the hall. He wasn't the quietest person when he walked, which surprised her, considering his fighting skill.

"What are you working on, here?" he asked, seeming genuinely curious.

"I'm merely reflecting on the irony of my situation," she said, looking past him to make sure there wasn't anything amiss.

He raised his eyebrow at the comment, clearly not understanding.

"I am not the least bit surprised that you don't understand, Avryn. You, who walk as loud as a donkey. Stealth used to be my main asset, but with my new *skills*—" the word dripped with sarcasm, "—well, I can kiss it goodbye."

Avryn just stared at her, opting to not say anything. Instead, his mouth turned up at the side.

Janis sighed in frustration and opened her empty hand. A flash of blue Light announced the arrival of the dagger, shining with brilliance. Taking the opportunity to not only prove her point, but get rid of some frustration, she shouted and jabbed the dagger into the wall, where it clanged off, not even putting a scratch there. She let it fall and disappear.

"Lightbearing is useless to me. I've managed to learn nothing in the past few weeks, and what I *have* learned about, my powers aren't capable of handling. At this point, Prost is more useful when up against Lightbearing."

The man's face looked thoughtful.

"Yes, being immune to Lightbearing has its advantages, save for the Fixing immunity."

Janis stared at him flatly, anger growing in her eyes and posture. Avryn's face flushed.

"But that doesn't help you. I'm sorry. I—"

"*What do you want?*" Janis said through gritted teeth.

"Hmm?" Avryn responded. It took a moment for him to realize that she didn't want to discuss the matter further. "Oh—yes, Magness would like to see us all in the war room."

Janis didn't feel in the mood to talk to that woman, or to anyone else for that matter, but it was better than sitting here wasting away and doing nothing. She stood and stalked down the hallway where Avryn had just come. Avryn followed without a word, which didn't bother her one bit.

Perhaps it isn't in my best interest to stay. I am getting nothing from these people, nor they from me, she thought.

But then there was Marric.

The boy had proven very adept at his powers since his awakening. Unlike herself, Marric clearly had a class. Well, *classes*. Before the incident at the safe house where she'd awakened, Marric had shown some skill with his Seeing powers. Though it unsettled her to no end, Seeing had proven very helpful. Considering the dangerous situations they were in while Marric used it, his Seeing had saved their lives a few times. Janis was impressed by Marric's quick development of his abilities, perhaps even proud. Though, she didn't relish the fact that he'd become the talk of Evenir while she'd become the liability.

Part of Janis was proud of his accomplishment, and part of her loathed him for it. The only thing that kept her going was knowing that she was still quite good at fighting and her speed was unmatched.

She and Avryn entered the last chamber before the war room, which was a type of library, just before the beautiful dark-wood doors with the carving of the tree. A man was sitting to their left, reading a book and starting to doze off. Each time he started to nod off, the hovering blue orbs Lighting the room would start to flicker and fade, causing him to wake up. For a moment, the two watched him, Avryn looking amused.

Avryn walked up to the desk where the man sat, and slammed his hand down loudly. The poor man threw himself backwards at the sound, his chair toppling over. As he fell, the Lights in the room flashed intensely, causing the other people in the room to grumble and cover their eyes. Janis knew that the effect had not only occurred here, but in the whole compound for the thousands of others in these caves.

"You need to stay awake, Ulig. We can't have this place going dark all of a sudden." There was a bit of sternness in Avryn's voice, but he smiled, clearly amused.

Ulig blushed and shuffled to his feet. He grabbed the book, which he'd thrown in his surprise, and positioned himself behind the desk.

"Uh . . . sorry, sir. Won' 'appen again, eh? Oi jus' ain't been able t'sleep, see?" the little man said sheepishly.

The short man was completely bald, and about a head shorter than Janis. His build was strong, clearly having worked physically hard in his life, yet his height made him seem like a child, much younger than his face actually showed him to be.

"Perhaps discuss the Lighting rotation with Narinda. See if you can't get time to capture some extra sleep."

"Aye, S'ren. Oi'll do jus' tha'. Sorry."

The little man sat back in his chair and resumed reading his book. Avryn, seeing this, walked over to one of the others in the room sitting on a couch, studying a book as well. He said something to the man, then gestured at Janis to follow him. This she did with curiosity, wondering what he said to the lounger. True to his nature, Avryn didn't wait a moment before telling her.

"I don't think that Ulig will be able to stay awake for much longer, so I asked Tralist to keep an eye on him and poke him awake if needed." Avryn was amused, that was clear.

How in Lanser's name does he remember all these people's names? Janis thought. She'd only met a few dozen whose names she could remember, but the fact that Avryn seemed to know everyone at Terris Green was fascinating.

Janis nodded at his assessment, but said nothing. Instead, she trained her eyes on the carving in the wood of the double doors just before them. It was an exquisite artwork, indeed. Each small branch of the winding tree had many smaller twigs breaking off into many different directions, and she wondered how long such a thing could have taken to make. Images appeared among the branches, most of them seeming random. Symbols here and there were carved and housed by circles to make them distinguishable. They were in the old language, so what they meant, Janis couldn't know. But they were quite fascinating, and somewhat familiar. Her eyes landed on one of the faces that was carved of a beautiful woman.

She really does look like Marric here.

Evenir's current leader, Magness, was sister to Talatha, the woman in the carving. Magness had intimated to Janis that Talatha was Marric's mother, who had since passed on. How she died hadn't been discussed, but Janis got the feeling it wasn't something that would be easy to get out of Magness.

It was obvious that the face was carved in a way to stand out, and it did that very well.

"It is quite a scene, isn't it?" Avryn followed her gaze. "The skill and time that had to have been required for this beautiful work of art is something that I can't fathom."

Janis grunted in response.

"Are you finished examining it, then? I didn't want to open it until you were done."

The assassin realized that they'd been standing just before the door for some time and hadn't moved to enter. Avryn apparently had seen her inspecting the door and didn't want to interrupt.

Janis tried to act casual about her interest.

"Fine artwork, however fine it may be, isn't worth an assassin's time unless it plays a part in their undercover role."

Then she unceremoniously pushed the doors open herself.

"I'll take that as a yes, you are done," Avryn said, raising his eyebrows at her statement.

Inside the room stood a medium-sized round table covered with an intricate map of Lindrad. Magness stood bent over the map, pointing at a spot that Janis couldn't see. With her were three others. One was a woman with long blonde hair down to her waist. Her features were sharp and petite, yet she was very tall, as tall as Magness herself. They both stood almost a handspan taller than Janis was. To her right stood a man of middle age with pure white hair. He wasn't balding in any place, so his hair seemed to stand out. He had a bushy white mustache which he twirled in his fingers, looking thoughtful. Finally, another woman, this one dark-skinned with deep black hair, sat brooding in one of the chairs that ringed the outside of the room. Her hair spun in tight ringlets, making her head appear much larger than it actually was.

A head popped out behind Magness and smiled broadly. Marric was almost fully covered by the leader's stature and height. He waved at Janis and Avryn and gestured for them to join the group.

"—we must not give up our search, it would really give us a tactical advantage over Watchlight if we could just locate their lair," Magness said.

"But General, we've 'ad no success findin' it," the mustached man said. "Even if'n we 'ad more people, which we don', Oi fear tha' we just don' 'ave wha' we need t'locate it. They 'ave Shielders prolly working overtoim, 'cause our Seers 'ave found no luck. Even Marric ain't Seen nuttin'."

Marric stiffened at the comment.

"I have been trying, ma'am, I hope you know that," Marric said, blushing deeply.

Magness merely waved her hand dismissively.

"You need not worry about that, Marric. I fear this has nothing to do with your newly developing powers. Our most skilled Seers are having trouble as well."

Janis noticed that when she said this, the tall blonde woman looked both embarrassed and offended.

"If there were some way to extract the information from Marric's subconscious, then we would have more success," Avryn said, causing the whole group to turn.

"Tha' is only a dream. Ain't nobody seen a thing such loike an' Oi don' think it be worth bringin' up again," the tall blonde woman said, apparently annoyed.

Avryn shrugged, unaffected by the tone of the woman.

"You know, I've said this before," Janis said, nonchalance lacing her words, "but I followed Prost when he abducted Marric at the falls. If I go there, I think that I could trace my steps back to where their lair is. I've done this hundreds of times, and I know I can find them."

"We've been over this, Janis," Magness said, "that place is not safe. Watchlight is inevitably there with an ambush. It's not safe for you or any of us to go there at this time."

The blonde woman scoffed loudly.

"Not t'mention tha' t'was dark when yeh followed 'em, no? Oi've Seen it. Can' see a Foggin' thing in yer past. No useful Seein' fer us at all."

"The darkness comes with the profession, which you'd know if you were more than a simpleton," Janis said condescendingly while giving the woman a simpering look.

The blonde woman's body stiffened at the comment, and she balled her fists at her side.

"For Lanser's sake, would you two please stop? We don't have time for this banter," Magness plowed ahead, "our scouting parties will continue to make their rounds. Based on what we've gathered from all of you, we feel that their lair is somewhere in this area."

She pointed to a spot on the table that Janis was still too far away to see. Even if she could, she wasn't confident she would know what it all meant. She could read maps to some degree, but only when there were major cities or landmarks; she hadn't learned to read coordinates yet. Then again, she'd never needed to.

"I could easily find my way there, this is a waste of time," Janis said under her breath.

Magness ignored her comment, continuing.

"It would be too risky for our soldiers to go back to the falls. Watchlight is most definitely watching the area, as *previously* mentioned."

Janis shrugged before doggedly arguing, "So we bring a bigger group than them. I could at least pick off a bunch before I went down, anyway. I see no other option."

Magness smiled, though not joyfully, more like she appreciated the sentiment.

"Though your commitment is refreshing, Janis, I do believe that isn't the best plan of action. At least, not yet."

The dark-skinned woman piped up suddenly at that.

"I agree with the assassin, we can't sit on this much longer. Each moment we wait is an opportunity for Watchlight to find Terris Green and ambush us. The faster we find them—" she paused, moving her hands toward the table where a few figurines suddenly glowed blue and were thrown off the table as if some invisible force and shoved them.

Janis tensed at the event and trained her eyes on the dark-skinned woman, reassessing.

Magness noticed Janis's reaction and looked at her curiously. The look lasted only a moment before Magness spoke.

"Oh—silly me, I failed to introduce you to my other generals, Janis."

Magness gestured to the dark-skinned woman first. "Alsry is a Mover, as you can tell, and she heads up companies six through ten. She also oversees the training of all Movers here at Evenir. As you have seen, she is quite skilled in the ability."

Alsry glanced again at Janis.

My kind of person, Janis thought, inclining her head in acknowledgement.

"Turrin, here," Magness said, pointing to the burly man with the mustache, "is a Conjurer, and heads up companies sixteen through twenty-one. Likewise, he trains and oversees all Conjurers here."

Turrin smiled brightly and walked over to them, extending his hand out.

"Pleased t'meet yeh, Janis. Heard a roit bunch about yeh an' 'ave been eager t'see yeh in person."

Janis looked at him, then down at his hand, then back at his face, not moving her own at all.

The burly man only chuckled and walked back to the table, shaking his head. Magness, observing the whole exchange, raised an eyebrow at Janis as if irritated by her reaction.

She shouldn't be surprised, Janis thought, *I'm not one for shaking hands unless I'm undercover.*

Clearing her throat, Magness continued on with the introductions.

"This is Rivelen," the Evenir leader said, gesturing to the unnaturally tall blonde woman. "She's our most accomplished Seer and leader of companies one through five."

Rivelen stood up a bit taller at the introduction and stuck her nose into the air as if she was the highest authority in the room. She did not, however, say anything else. Janis stared at her flatly, even more annoyed than before. It was clear by her comments that the woman had an ego, making Janis inclined to contradict everything that she said. Janis loved pushing audacious people to their limits.

"Could never afford an education, then?" Janis replied.

Rivelen's face turned red and she huffed out loud.

"Fog it, wench, 'ow dare yous attack me such loik? Oi ain't dun nuttin' t'ya, eh? T'ain't moi fault yous chose a roit man-loik job an' became a brute."

She was shaking her fist at Janis, much like an old crone would to a group of troublesome youngsters.

Janis smoothly whipped out her long dagger and held it aloft.

The blonde woman's eyes widened and she backed away, hands now in the air in surrender.

"Janis, stop that right now!" Magness said, stepping between the two.

Grunting, Janis put the dagger away and folded her arms.

"Sorry, it's just a habit when I see a towering urchin coming at me."

Rivelen's face seemed to take on a deeper shade of red, but she said nothing else.

"Are you two quite done with your spat?" Magness snapped at them both. "We don't have the luxury of time for any infighting. Either get over it, or get out."

That struck Janis. Technically, she could walk out at any time and move on with her life. Unfortunately, the blasted Light was preventing her from doing that, even if she wanted to. She had to learn some control over her powers.

Magness swept over to the table smoothly and resumed speaking.

"Of course, you've met Avryn, my second. With his unique abilities and excellent leadership, we are lucky to have him. With the rest of the generals and companies out scouring for the lair, we can't afford to let any more leave Terris Green. On the off-chance that Watchlight is able to track us down, we need to be prepared for an assault."

She gripped the table hard, her knuckles turning white as she did so. After a lengthy silence, she sighed.

"For now, the best we can do is pray to Lanser that the other companies find something," she paused and looked at Marric, "and continue training Marric. Perhaps there is something that he can glean from his past using his Seeing."

Everyone in the room looked at Marric and he blushed.

The boy turns red so easily, someone might think it's really his natural color, Janis thought.

As he always did, Avryn took the liberty to speak up and ease the tension of the conversation.

"And how is that training going then, Mar?"

The long-haired man had adopted Marric's nickname that he'd had since he was a boy. Janis thought it far too mushy and odd to use, so she continued calling him by his real name. Marric, however, appeared to like it—his expression lit up every time Avryn used it.

"It's going very well, as far I can tell," he said modestly.

"Why don't you show the generals your progress, Marric?" Magness asked kindly.

Making a show of it, Marric held out his hand and Conjured a bow, much like the one he'd carried on their journey from Wurren, seemingly ages ago. The bow was simple, but looked perfect for his size. In his other hand, an arrow of pure blue Light flashed into existence. Calmly, yet quickly, he nocked the arrow and drew it back in a clearly practiced fashion. With an exhale, he let the arrow fly. It zipped through the air with a swish and connected with the wall, a loud crack echoing in the stone room.

Janis narrowed her eyes as she saw that the arrow had pierced the stone wall easily, causing web-like cracks and chipping bits off here and there. The whole group nodded in approval. Marric smiled and let the arrow fall, causing it to disappear to nothing.

Turrin chuckled loudly.

"Well, Oi'll be. Oi fink Oi picked the roit person t'train yeh, din't Oi?" he said, putting both hands on his belly as he said it.

Rivelen spoke up then.

"What of yer Seeing? A class tha' needs o' bit o' concentration and *skill.*"

She gave a hard stare at Turrin as she said it, provocation in her eyes.

Marric nodded and breathed in, closing his eyes. Not a moment later, he opened them, eyes aglow with blue Light.

"What do yeh see?"

Janis's skin crawled slightly at the sight of his eyes, but mostly because he had said the same words back to Rivelen at the same time, with the same accent.

"I See us here."

As if it was rehearsed, Rivelen and Marric spoke the same words at the same time, in exactly the same way.

"Impressive. Oi'm 'appy t'see the old crone ain't killed yeh wif all the meditatin'."

Rivelen smiled, obviously pleased with the display. All along, Marric's eyes glowed blue and he looked off in the distance. Suddenly, he gasped and dove to the side, Janis crouching down and pulling out her dagger almost simultaneously. As soon as he jumped to the side, a glass mug flew through the air right where he'd been standing a moment before. Wreathed in blue Light, it flew with a force much stronger and faster than a normal throw would be. Rather than hitting the ground, however, it stopped and redirected toward Marric again. Eyes still aglow, he dodged the mug as it soared at his face a second time. Finally, his eyes dimmed and he cupped his hands as if gripping something. The chair to his side glowed an intense blue and he raised the chair in front of him as the mug flew at him once more. It hit the makeshift shield, shattering into pieces.

"Very impressive," Alsry said, lightly clapping her hands. "I see that your Moving has improved as well."

Marric sat down heavily, gasping loudly from the quick exchange. Janis stared at him, surprised at his quick reactions and how versatile his powers seemed to have become. How he'd made so much progress in such a short amount of time, she couldn't understand. His body wasn't up to the physical task yet, as she could see, but his reaction times and ability to not freeze up like before were impressive.

Janis felt a pang of jealousy, knowing that her Moving had proven useless in her own attempts at training.

"I appreciate the progress you've all made teaching Marric, but next time, can you show me without destroying the war room?"

Alsry put her fist to the palm of her other hand and bowed to Magness.

"I am sorry, mistress, but a Mover must be prepared at all times. He can't fully show you his progress without somewhat realistic threats."

The leader waved her hand dismissively, as she seemed to do frequently, and looked at Turrin. She pointed to the wall where the Light arrow had put a hole and a large set of cracks.

Turrin shrugged and put on an innocent looking face.

"Oi din' tell 'im to do tha'. 'E chose tha' 'imself."

Magness sighed, eyes rolling up with a slight shake of her head.

"And I'm sure that your training has *nothing* to do with it. As I recall, part of a Conjurer's training is increasing the strength and solidness of their Conjures. I know that you pay Fixers to clean up the messes in your training hall, you can't fool me."

The burly man grinned annoyingly and shrugged again. He reminded Janis a lot of Harmel.

Her mind shifted to the silly man, their jovial companion on their journey from Wurren. Inside, she felt annoyed as she thought of his antics, but at the same time she felt fondness for him that she couldn't describe. She hadn't seen him since she'd woken up, because he'd left Terris Green with one of the companies.

Harmel had taken a hard blow to the head from a rock wall that had exploded during the scuffle at the safe house, and Janis had thought him dead. It wasn't until she woke a few days later that she heard of him getting Fixed and going along his merry way.

"Avryn, if you don't mind."

The man smiled warmly and moved to the wall. Placing his hand there, a blue and intense Light glowed from his palm and a cracking sound occurred as the wall knit itself together again, pieces and dust from the floor moving swiftly back into their place.

"Thank you, friend."

“It’s my pleasure. I’m happy to make myself useful whenever I can.”

After Fixing the wall, he set to work on the mug, the table, and the chair that had been Moved by the exchange.

“As I said, I am pleased to see progress being made, Marric. Remember, however, to not wear yourself out. I fear that at any moment, Watchlight could appear on our terraces, ready to fight. We need all Lightbearers and warriors alike to be ready for that at any moment.”

Janis squeezed her daggers tightly at the comment. Part of her was itching for that to happen. She would be happy to dig her knife into Prost after their last exchange.

The door to the room suddenly burst open with a loud bang and Janis, clearly tightly wound from the conversation, crouched low and pulled her daggers into her hands aggressively.

Everyone in the room looked at her, a mixture of emotions on their faces from anger, to fear, to surprise.

The man who had entered stood there, frozen from seeing Janis move in such a combative way.

With a stern voice, Magness spoke loudly to the newcomer.

“What is it that would cause you to burst so suddenly into a war council, courier?”

He stood there shaking for a moment more, a bit of wetness on his trousers.

Janis noticed that his clothes reflected that he was a messenger. He was of medium height with long legs and of slender build. It was clear that he was not strong, but she had a suspicion that he was quite fast. Breathing loudly, he gasped for air again before turning to Janis and backing away as if she would jump out at him.

Without looking away from Janis, he spoke.

“Companies eleven and twelve have returned. They’ve taken a heavy hit from Watchlight.”

About the Author

Daniel grew up in the suburbs of Utah where he met his wife in the third grade. Reading fantasy has always been his favorite pastime, as he habitually maxed out the number of books allowed on a single library card. Writing his own fantasy books was merely a dream until he met a fellow fantasy author that challenged him to finally write his own stories down. The prologue of *Awakened* birthed the trilogy, The Lightbearer Chronicles. Daniel plans to keep writing and publishing as much as he can in the future, as writing is currently his favorite hobby.

Daniel attended Brigham Young University to study Linguistics and has a passion for foreign languages. Just after graduating with his bachelor degree, he began and completed an M.B.A. from Western Governors University within a year.

When he is not writing, which he'd happily do full-time, Daniel enjoys spending time with his wife and four children on their homestead in rural Utah, gallivanting with goats and chickens.

Find more at www.dankenner.com.

Loved it? Hated it? Please leave a review!

Also by Dan Kenner

Transformed: The Lightbearer Chronicles Book 2

Ascended: The Lightbearer Chronicles Book 3

Shielded: A Prequel to The Lightbearer Chronicles

Sunfire

Made in the USA
Middletown, DE
05 October 2023